Michele
McCarty

Deciding

BROWN-ROA

A Division of Harcourt Brace & Company

BROWN-ROA
A Division of Harcourt Brace & Company

O u r   M i s s i o n

The primary mission of BROWN-ROA is to provide the
Catholic and Christian educational markets with the
highest quality catechetical print and media resources.
The content of these resources reflects the best insights
of current theology, methodology, and pedagogical research.
The resources are practical and easy to use, designed to meet
expressed market needs, and written to reflect the
teachings of the Catholic Church.

Nihil Obstat
Very Rev. Jerome A. Carosella, Chancellor
Imprimatur
✠ John J. Nevins D.D.
  Bishop of Venice in Florida
  October 15, 1997

The Imprimatur is an official declaration that a book or pamphlet is free of doctrinal or moral error. No implication is contained therein that anyone who granted the Imprimatur agrees with the contents, opinions, or statements expressed.

Theological Consultant—Rev. Charles Angell SA
Rev. Charles Angell SA, STD, is a Franciscan Friar of the Atonement of Graymoor, Garrison, NY, where he is currently chaplain of St. Christopher's Inn, a shelter for homeless men. He is a former professor of ecumenical theology at the Pontifical University of St. Thomas Aquinas, Rome, where he also received his Doctorate of Sacred Theology in 1983.

The **Scripture** quotations contained herein are from the New Revised Standard Version Bible: Catholic Edition copyright © 1993 and 1989, by the Division of Christian Education of the National Council of the Churches of Christ in the U.S.A. Used by permission. All rights reserved.

Photo and art credits appear on page 344.

Printed in the United States of America

ISBN 0-15-950429-5

Contents

Chapter 9
Being Morally Responsible 222

Chapter 10
Developing Character 254

Chapter 11
Making Tough Decisions 294

Dedication

This book is dedicated in loving memory of my husband.

Lord, . . . we see life as through windows
that open on eternity.
We see that love abides, the soul abides,
as you, O God, abide forever.
We see that our years are more than grass that withers,
more than flowers that fade.
They weave a pattern of life that is timeless
and unite us with a world that is from end to end
the abode of your love and the vesture of your glory.
In life and in death we cannot go where you are not,
and where you are, all is well.
Sustained by this assurance, we praise your name,
O God of life. . . .
—from a Jewish prayer

*See, I have set before you today life and prosperity, death
and adversity. . . . Choose life so that you and your
descendants may live, loving the LORD your God, obeying
him, and holding fast to him; for that means life to you. . . .
Surely, this commandment that I am commanding you
today is not too hard for you, nor is it too far away. It is
not in heaven, that you should say, "Who will go up to
heaven for us, and get it for us so that we may hear it and
observe it?" . . . . No, the word is very near to you; it is in
your mouth and in your heart for you to observe.*

Deuteronomy 30:15, 19b–20a, 11–12, 14

Chapter 1

Why Be Good?

Overview questions

1. Why should you study morality?

2. What are some of the moral issues that confront you and the world today?

3. What is morality? What makes something right or wrong?

4. Why try to be a moral person? Why try to be good?

decisions
conclusions arrived at after consideration

morality
a sense of right and wrong

obedience
submission to the command of
another

Why study moral decision making?

How to make wise **decisions** in tough situations is one of the most important things you can learn in life, and one of the most practical. That is what this course and this text are all about—making wise decisions. When you were a very small child, **morality**—determining right from wrong—was simple for you in one sense. To find out what was okay or not okay to do, all you had to do was ask someone older—your mother, your father, or someone else you trusted. At that time in your life, they seemed always to know the answers.

Right and wrong were clearly spelled out. It was right to say "please" and "thank you" for favors, to eat all your peas at the dinner table, and to put your toys away. It was wrong to cross the street by yourself, accept candy from strangers, or pick on your brother, sister, or playmate. Figuring out the right or the wrong thing to do sure was much simpler way back then!

Probably the most difficult thing about making moral decisions when you were a child was whether or not to obey those who told you what was "right" or "wrong." Morality back then was mainly a matter of **obedience**—of "do as you're told," "do as I say," and "you know you're not suppose to . . . ."

While you live in your family home under the authority of a parent or adult guardian, this is probably still the case, at least to some extent. You are expected to abide by certain rules, and sometimes you probably find it hard to comply with them. At these moments, your decision remains whether to do "right" by obeying, or to do "wrong" by disobeying.

But you are also being given greater independence and more personal freedom than you had as a child. Your experiences and discoveries of the past few years have led you to look at other dimensions of right and wrong. You may have questions and doubts about the "rightness" or "wrongness" of certain things or about the necessity of obeying. You now realize that the almost godlike adult figures of your childhood are only human and can make mistakes.

As you've become more aware of the society around you, you have found that even the highest and mightiest can fall—that national leaders and the superstars you once viewed as heroes and heroines are sometimes far less than perfectly moral men and women. You've experienced how even trusted peers can sometimes let you down. You now realize that the world is filled with very human beings—people who don't know all the answers and who do make mistakes.

Although, as a teenager, you have a new set of do's and don'ts—"Mow the lawn," "Take out the garbage," "Help with the dishes"—some of the old ones remain: "Clean up your room," "Stop picking on . . . !" There are still some similarities between what was expected of you as a child and what is asked of you now. In fact, this might irritate you at times and lead you to resent still being "treated like a child."

Parents and legal guardians have a sacred duty as well as a legal right to expect their teenage sons and daughters to fulfill certain responsibilities. You undoubtedly realize that you owe obedience to the authority figures in your family as they legitimately exercise the obligation to look out for your welfare and that of your family.

Yet, as you grow into adulthood and confront new questions, you may find that some of the old answers don't always seem to fit the situation. The people you once relied on for answers no longer appear to have suitable answers for everything. More and more you may feel that **you** must solve your problems. In some ways this is a freeing thing. At times you might like to decide everything for yourself. Yet, like most people, you also wonder how you can do a better job of making decisions and finding solutions to your problems. This text will give you some help—some moral road signs that will help you find the right direction in your journey through life. First, though, it's a good idea to take a look at some of the ways you've changed over the years.

For discussion

1. *What were some of the "bad" things that, as a very young child, you were taught not to do?*

2. *What were some of the good things that you as a child were taught you should do?*

3. *What major moral decisions do you think confront most teenagers today? What are the main moral dilemmas you have faced thus far as a teenager?*

What is morality?

Morality, in general, is concerned about the rightness and wrongness, goodness and badness of human behavior. Whereas psychology and sociology are concerned mainly with how people **do** in fact behave, morality's concern is with how people **ought** to behave. When psychologists, sociologists, politicians, judges, parents, teachers, or students begin discussing how people **ought** to conduct themselves, they are entering the realm of morality.

A common mistake people make is to think that morality has to do only with religion, or should be confined to religion. Every major religion does have its moral guidelines or codes of conduct. But throughout history even people with no religious convictions have always had opinions about how people **ought** to act. In fact, it is difficult to think of any major decision that seriously involves or affects people that does not in some way involve moral questions, dilemmas, and principles.

People often confuse and misuse the following terms. It's important that you understand them.

- **Morality** generally refers to the broad area of deciding what is right or wrong, good or bad; specifically, morality refers to good behavior, virtue.

- **Moral** may likewise broadly refer to issues of right or wrong (as in "it's a moral dilemma"), or may more specifically refer to "that which is good" (as in describing someone as a **moral** person).

- **Immoral** generally refers to "that which is bad"—or to the way people ought **not** to act (as in "committing murder is **immoral**").

- **Amoral** refers to morally neutral actions—those which are neither good nor bad (for example, breathing). It can also be used to describe attitudes or behavior that show no sensitivity to the question of right and wrong, or to decisions made without any consideration of moral principles.

Thus, a **moral** issue is not always at stake in making a difficult decision. Morality

That is the issue that will continue in this country when these poor tongues of Judge Douglas and myself shall be silent. It is the eternal struggle between these two principles—right and wrong—throughout the world. They are the two principles that have stood face to face from the beginning of time, and will ever continue to struggle.
ABRAHAM LINCOLN

dilemma
a puzzle, something difficult to solve

guideline
policy or other indication for proper action

principle
fundamental law, rule, or code of conduct

moral
morality in general, that which is good in particular

immoral
that which is bad, how people ought not to act and behave

amoral
morally neutral (not good or bad) actions, people who act without reference to moral principles

is a consideration in making decisions when the results might be bad or good for someone.

Likewise, not all individuals, societies, or cultures evaluate *bad* or *good* in quite the same way. That raises this difficult question: **How it is possible to know for sure what truly is moral or immoral?** The rest of this book will address this basic question. For now, suffice it to say that the terms *moral, immoral,* and *amoral* commonly refer to a particular person's or society's ideas of morality—whatever those ideas may be.

So, according to their differing moral standards, one person or society might consider it immoral to drink alcoholic beverages in any quantity, others might deem it perfectly moral to do so, and a third may approve only of moderate use. Their views about behavior are based on different understandings of morality.

The following Scripture offers good advice about the task of moral decision making:

> *Be at peace among yourselves. And we urge you, beloved, to admonish the idlers, encourage the faint hearted, help the weak, be patient with all of them. See that none of you repays evil for evil, but always seek to do good to one another and to all. Rejoice always, pray without ceasing, give thanks in all circumstances; for this is the will of God in Christ Jesus for you. Do not quench the Spirit.*
>
> *1 Thessalonians 5:13–19*

Indeed, people learn a great deal about right living from the Bible. But, as you

Wet cement

Read the following true account and respond to the questions.

As nine-year-old Jeremy and a few of his younger friends were walking by a construction site, they saw a freshly laid cement sidewalk. One worker asked the boys if they would like to write their names in the wet cement after the workers had left for the day. The boys said that they would—and they did, also leaving their foot and hand prints.

Jeremy was arrested, strip-searched, and charged with the felony of maliciously destroying property. (His friends were deemed too young to be arrested.) Jeremy insists he had permission to write on the sidewalk. "The man said I could, so I did," he said.

A few weeks later, the sidewalk contractor contacted Jeremy's mother and told her she owed him the $11,000 it would cost to repair the sidewalk. When she refused to pay, saying she didn't have the money, and didn't respond to messages to contact the authorities, Jeremy was arrested.

Although the contractor later withdrew his demand for money, the judge set a date for Jeremy to go on trial. For adults, this offense could mean up to six years in prison and a $5,000 fine, but authorities thought it more likely that Jeremy, if convicted, would only be placed on probation.

People in their community were deeply divided about Jeremy's actions and his mother's responses and those of the authorities.

For discussion

1. Why does this incident have to do with morality?

2. What attitudes or behaviors described do you consider moral? Immoral? Amoral? Explain.

3. What moral issues were at stake in determining whether—and how—Jeremy and/or his mother should be punished?

4. Following the advice given in the Scripture passage from Thessalonians, quoted above, how do you think the situation should have been handled? Why?

5. If you were the judge, how would you decide Jeremy's case? Explain.

How can you learn to make wiser moral decisions?

Can anyone really tell you what is right or wrong for you? Students sometimes enter this course expecting to receive answers to all their questions about what is right or wrong, good or bad. They are bound to be frustrated and greatly disappointed. For no one can give up his or her responsibility to make good personal moral decisions in good **conscience**.

There are, however, principles and guidelines that people throughout the centuries have relied on in making moral decisions. Among these are certainly the Catholic Church's teachings about **personal integrity** and goodness, social justice and love of others, and our accountability to our loving Creator. A great many of the Church's beliefs and guidelines, by the way, helped form the foundation of our own society.

Leaders around the world and in our own country still consult religion's **wisdom** with regard to moral concerns. World leaders often meet and discuss these issues with the pope or other religious leaders. Hopefully, you will also accept the opportunity and responsibility of benefiting from this moral guidance.

A main source of moral wisdom is God's word in the Scriptures:

All scripture is inspired by God and is useful for teaching, for reproof, for correction, and for training in righteousness. . . .

2 Timothy 3:16

conscience

the human capacity to weigh and evaluate right and wrong

personal integrity

the quality of showing moral principles by knowing what is right or wrong and choosing to do the right thing

wisdom

insight, good judgment

know, the Bible can be misunderstood and its teachings misapplied—as when people quote passages out of context. An example is citing the phrase "an eye for an eye" in support of war, capital punishment, or vigilante revenge. This is why, in looking to Scripture for answers to life's problems, Catholics also need to really think about what this or that passage truly does and does not mean. They should properly understand the true message of certain passages in light of Church teaching and the Church's expert Scripture scholarship.

Likewise, we should consult and learn from each other's ideas, experiences, common sense, and sound advice.

Let the word of Christ dwell in you richly; teach and admonish one another in all wisdom. . . .

Colossians 3:16

We need to help one another sort things out. Yet we should also realize that, like ourselves, at times our friends can be mistaken. We must assume the responsibility for making our own decisions, rather than letting others make them for us.

Most regrettable decisions come not from bad intentions but from being mistaken about what's best. In short, when we do unwise and harmful things, it's usually from lack of good judgment. Our decision actually accomplishes the opposite of what we intended: it hurts instead of helps. This is often due to ignorance of the thought processes and guidelines (including those of the Church) which could help us decide wisely. Or maybe we are careless or apathetic about how we make our decision. If we had more skill and practice in making intelligent and proper decisions, we probably wouldn't end up so often saying "If only I had. . . ."

Learning to decide intelligently is a bit like learning to walk or bounce a ball. The first efforts are awkward, slow, and imperfect. But with determination and consistent practice, eventually the person runs, or dribbles the ball with ease. Wise decision making is likewise an acquired skill. Like physical skill, decision making becomes a habit, enabling one to proceed much more confidently, correctly, and, when necessary, quickly—as when having to maneuver suddenly out of harm's way.

So don't be surprised if some of the processes you are guided through during this course at first seem cumbersome. As you consider the moral dilemmas presented throughout the text, resist the urge to make instant decisions about complex issues. Many grave mistakes are made because people are too impatient to stop and think things through before they act.

When this course ends, you probably won't have the answers to all your questions about various moral problems. But you should be more insightful and adept at using your thought processes and religious beliefs to make better and wiser moral decisions. The major decisions you face now and in your future are important to your life and happiness, and to others. Take advantage of this opportunity to learn how to make these decisions more carefully, prayerfully, and wisely.

But as for you, continue in what you have learned and firmly believed. . . .

2 Timothy 3:14

Why be moral?

"Why bother trying to be good? It's a dog-eat-dog world—just look out for yourself. Do whatever works for you." People with this attitude think morality is for religious **fanatics** and goody-goodies, but not for the practical realist. They view morality as doing what one is "supposed" to do—as opposed to what one would like to do and what would really lead to happiness. They misunderstand morality entirely.

An eleven-year-old girl struggling with the "Why be good?" question couldn't think of any reasons why **she** should be good. But when asked why her older brother should be good and stop picking on her, she arrived at a rather wise answer: "Because he's a **person**, because I'm a **person** in this world!"

In so concluding, this girl touched on key reasons Catholic and other religious teaching also gives for striving toward the good and the right:

- Every person has God-given dignity and an immortal destiny.

- Created in God's image, we all share in God's own loving nature.

- Thus, we can find lasting happiness and harmony only by freely imitating God, and by walking in love and working together.

In the long run, therefore, exercising the freedom God has given us to do what's right is the only humanly good and fulfilling thing to do, the only choice that leads to life. Conversely, abusing our human freedom and failing to overcome evil with goodness leads only to destruction:

Those conflicts and disputes among you, where do they come from? Do they not come from your cravings that are at war within you?

James 4:1

It's funny, though, how many of us don't think about the negative **implications** of our own behavior until we have reason to complain about the wrong somebody is doing to **us!**

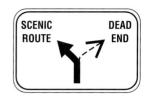
Activity
1. List the ten historical figures you most admire and tell why.
2. List the ten historical figures you think have done the most harm in human history and tell why.

Nobody likes a crook—nobody, including the crook who gets double-crossed by another crook! People generally avoid those who are corrupt or ruthless or unloving and uncaring; people generally admire those who are good—who live up to their ideals. In fact, the most consistently admired, emulated, and influential figures in history are not political or military leaders. They are those whose words and example have brought greater goodness into the world: Jesus, **Buddha**, **Moses**, the **prophets** of Israel, Mahatma Gandhi, Martin Luther King Jr. . . . In recent times, the person whom polls cited as most admired was not a rich or famous or powerful figure, but Mother Teresa, a humble nun who came to the notice of the world after she began to help the dying in the slums of Calcutta, India.

Buddha
the enlightened one, a representation of Gautama Buddha

Moses
Hebrew prophet who is associated with the escape from slavery in Egypt and the Law and covenant at Mt. Sinai

prophets
those who speak divinely inspired revelations

There's a big difference between having a moral halo and having moral integrity.

Research

Find five Scripture passages which you think provide helpful guidance concerning the process of moral decision making. Explain how each of them might help you.

But what's the difference between a "goody-goodie" and a good person? A goody-goodie does what is expected not out of conviction that it's the right thing, but because it's what is "supposed" to be done, or what will win others' praise and approval, or because she or he is afraid to do otherwise. Such persons can seem quite out of touch with how others view and face life's difficult decisions. And such persons may appear to look down on those who aren't always so sure at first which alternative seems right.

On the other hand, the truly good person **struggles** at times to understand why some things are right and others wrong, struggles to do the right thing. As a result, he or she is far more likely to understand human experience and to empathize with those who, in their honest search and struggle, sometimes fail and make mistakes.

For discussion

1. *What reasons, other than those mentioned above, might people have for choosing not to do what is right and good? What is your response to these reasons?*
2. *What reasons can you think of for being good or moral—for doing what is right? Which of these make the most sense to you? Why?*

The truly good person struggles to understand why some things are right and others wrong. As a result, he or she is far more likely to understand human experience and to empathize with those who sometimes fail and make mistakes.

The rabbit cover-up¹

Read the following humorous account about the ordinary type of moral temptations which occasionally confront us all. Then discuss the questions that follow.

The woman is helpful by nature, and when her neighbors asked her to watch their house for a few days while they were out of town, she was glad to do it.

"They wanted her to water the plants, pick up the newspapers, you know, the kind of thing neighbors do for each other," said the man who told me this story. "They also had a pool, and they told her she was welcome to use it whenever she wanted."

So the woman watched the house. She is a nurse at a hospital in the city, and after work, in the worst heat of the afternoon, she walked over to see that the place was all right.

She brought her bathing suit and her dog, and after she'd checked the plants and the windows, she got into the swimming pool to cool off. She closed her eyes, floating. The dog sat at the edge of the pool, watching her.

She had been in the water perhaps a quarter of an hour when she realized the animal was gone. She called him from the pool, but he didn't come. She got out and called again, and heard the reassuring sound of his collar jingling as he came around the corner.

As the dog cleared the corner, however, some of the woman's reassurance disappeared. The dog was, first of all, covered with dirt, nose to tail. He was, second of all, carrying a wet, dead rabbit in his

teeth, changing his hold on it every few seconds, tossing it around in his mouth so you couldn't miss the fact that he had something dead.

His head at this point, I am guessing, would have been high and proud. A dog never looks better in his own eyes than when he's carrying a dead rabbit.

Anyway, the woman was at first repulsed, and then, remembering that the family kept a pet rabbit in a cage on the other side of the house, she was horrified. And she ran to that side of the house, and saw the empty cage overturned on the lawn.

She pictured herself trying to explain to her neighbors what had happened to their rabbit, murdered while she floated a few yards away in the swimming pool. Every way she thought to say it was worse than the last. And so she did what many people do when their dog kills their neighbors' pet rabbit. She panicked.

From what I have been able to put together about this, she turned to the dog, who had followed her over, scolded him, and instructed him to drop the rabbit immediately.

You might as well tell a dog to hold its breath.

She pried open his teeth and removed the rabbit, wet and dead. She laid the animal on her towel, rolled it up like a wet bathing suit, and started home. The dog walked alongside, worrying over the bundle in her hands, stepping into her path. I am guessing that more than once the words "Bad dog" came into the course of the conversation.

At home, she took the rabbit to the bathroom sink and washed off the worst of the dirt. She drained the water, and shampooed the rabbit, which was getting heavier all the time. She rinsed off the shampoo.

She put the rabbit on a fresh towel and began to blow-dry its coat. Ears, tail, feet, everything. One side at a time. I have no idea at all how long it takes to blow-dry a rabbit, but I am sure it seemed longer than it was.

When she'd finished with the dryer, she carried the rabbit back to the house she had been asked to watch—I assume she again hid the rabbit in the towel, as there isn't really much difference, for purposes of evidence, between carrying a clean dead rabbit and a dirty one.

I am also assuming she did not bring the dog. Bad dog.

And so she took the rabbit back to his cage, laid him peacefully inside, and went home.

"Natural causes" . . . she didn't know a thing about it.

A day or two later, the neighbors returned.

Shortly after they pulled into their driveway, the woman's phone began to ring. She stared at it, knowing who was calling. She picked up the phone, and yes, it was her neighbor, who was hysterical.

The woman steeled herself for the lies she was prepared to tell, but never got the chance.

It was something the neighbor was screaming that stopped her, that a maniac was loose. That some pervert had dug up the neighbors' pet rabbit—who'd died the day before they'd left, by the way—removed the animal from its grave, and stuck it back in its cage.

How sick can you get, right?

I am only guessing here, but somehow I think the dog got in trouble all over again.

For discussion

1. *What was the woman's moral dilemma?*

2. *How did it involve choosing between things she valued? Between undesirable alternatives?*

3. *What kind of person is this woman? How can you tell?*

4. *What possible motives might she have had for deciding to conceal what she believed had happened to the rabbit? Which motive(s) do you think she probably did have? Explain.*

5. *To what lengths did the woman go to complete her cover-up? Why do you think she went to so much trouble?*

6. *To what extent do you think the woman's fears and feelings influenced her decision? Do you think her fears and feelings were reasonable under the circumstances, or somewhat exaggerated?*

7. *Was the dog really a "bad dog"? If the dog had killed the rabbit, who would have been responsible for its doing so?*

8. *For what, if anything, was the dog to blame? To what extent did the woman blame her own guilt on the dog? Whom did the neighbors blame?*

9. *Why do you think we often blame something or someone else for our moral weaknesses and failings?*

10. *What "moral" would you say this story illustrates about human nature? About morality?*

11. *How do you think you would have responded if you had been in this woman's situation? Why?*

12. *How was the cover-up's result worse than the consequences would have been if the woman had assumed responsibility from the beginning for what she believed had happened?*

13. *What mistakes and **judgment** errors are evidenced in this account? How could these have been avoided? How would avoiding them have changed what happened?*

14. *Describe a moral predicament you have faced, one in which you were tempted to cover up what happened rather than face the consequences.*

15. *Why, when confronted with unpleasant alternatives in everyday moral dilemmas, do people often fail to exercise the moral courage needed to do the right thing?*

16. *In what ways did this woman exercise poor judgment? What could she learn about making better moral decisions?*

judgment
decision, discernment

Addressing current moral issues

There are good personal reasons for learning better ways to solve moral problems, and there are also broader reasons for doing so—some of which concern our world's very future.

You have only to turn on the daily news to hear many important moral questions being widely discussed:

- Should there be a death penalty for certain crimes?

- Should the terminally ill be allowed to choose to die?

- Should abortion be legal?

- Should the use of marijuana or other illegal drugs be decriminalized?

- Should scientists be allowed to clone or genetically alter human beings?

- Is our personal privacy being invaded in our society?

- What moral standards should we require of politicians and public figures—and how should they be held accountable?

- What, if anything, should be censored—on television, in print, in the movies, on the Internet?

- When does exercising one's freedom violate another's rights?

- How can we curb the increasing violence in society?

- What can we do to eliminate racism, sexism, **homophobia**, and religious prejudice?

homophobia
prejudice against or fear of homo-sexual persons

These hotly debated questions are not just political or legal in nature. They are also important moral questions.

Furthermore, the world of tomorrow will be different from today's world. And your decisions will help to create and shape that world of tomorrow. Consider this fact: Humanity has attained more technological and scientific knowledge within the last thirty years than in its entire million-plus years of previous history. As the twentieth century began, not many people believed that a human being would really fly to the moon—much less walk on it, send televised pictures back, and then return safely home. Yet it happened. Scientific researchers predict that you will live to see equally amazing things accomplished within your lifetime in the twenty-first century.

People used to wonder if we would ever be able to talk to someone hundreds of miles away, fly to another continent in just hours, travel faster than sound. Today possible technological advances are viewed not in terms of **if** but in terms of **when**—when cures for diseases will be found or when we will be able to vacation in outer space. Due to the nature of scientific and technological possibilities, the world's major questions are now moral ones: **Should** we proceed down this or that techno-logical path? If so, with what guidelines and restrictions for human good?

- The question is not "Can we keep on sending satellites to Jupiter and beyond?"—but "Should we? Is this the right way to use our resources?"

- The question is not "Can nuclear power meet our increasing energy needs?"—but, given its very real hazards, "Should we take the risks?"

- The question is not "Can we launch all-out nuclear war?"—but "Should we? Does humanity ever have the right to use this power at all?"

A thorough education isn't just arithmetic; it's ethics and morality as well. Lawyers, no matter how smart they are, are not completely educated until they've studied ethics and morality and are proficient in them.
ATTORNEY MELVIN BELLI

moralists
those who weigh the good and bad, the right and wrong implications of various possible decisions

For discussion

1. *What do you think are the major moral problems facing society today?*
2. *What technological advances do you expect to see during your lifetime?*
3. *Which of these would you like to see occur? Why? Which ones would you not like to see? Why?*
4. *What moral issues are involved?*

Even if we can accomplish whatever we put our minds to—"Should we?" The most important questions facing our world from here on are, indeed, moral questions, questions of right and wrong.

Realizing this, international leaders have begun to call on expert **moralists** for help in weighing risks and benefits, right and wrong implications of decisions, and in deciding future directions and criteria for decision making. Some time ago scientists from around the world involved in researching the possible creation of new life forms agreed on a complete and international ban on further research in a certain area until the human hazards could be sufficiently minimized. They did this on moral grounds—not because they didn't have the know-how to proceed, but because their consciences would not let them. Once a technology exists, however, there is no guarantee that every scientist will abide by restrictions on its use. Given the possibilities of science and technology, there is great need for wisdom, careful deliberation, and moral decision making.

Alfred Nobel became one of the world's richest men by inventing many explosives that increased the terrible effect of weapons used in war. However, he tragically confronted the moral implications of his life's work when his younger brother was killed in an explosion caused by one of these inventions. Shortly before he died, Alfred himself wrote a will leaving all his money to establish the trust that, in accord with his stipulations, still presents the prestigious annual Nobel Peace Prize to those persons who, in the preceding year, have contributed the most to benefit humanity.

In studying moral decision making, you will find it easy to see how religion and moral principles spill over into all of life—and how your own moral principles affect your life and that of others. Throughout this course, you will be involved in one of the most crucial studies of our time. People around the world are now just an Internet link away, and many heatedly discussed chat-group topics have moral implications. You can have a voice in helping to influence how other people think and decide. This course can help you exercise this responsibility with intelligence and care.

Catholic teaching on science, technology, and human rights

- **Science and technology each have a moral aspect; there is a direct link between them and human rights, human dignity.**
- **True scientific and technological advances must reflect an active awareness of the value of each individual's rights, and of humanity's rights.**
- **This awareness must include the knowledge that every person has the right to the benefits that science and technology offer.**

For discussion

1. *Why do science and technology each have a moral aspect?*
2. *How does Catholic teaching define a true advance in science and technology?*
3. *Using that definition, how would you describe the difference between a technological development that is a true advance and one that expands human knowledge but is not a true advance? Give an example that illustrates this difference.*
4. *In Catholic teaching, what right does every person have with regard to scientific and technological development? Do you agree with this? Why?*
5. *Is it possible to really respect individual rights and still make full use of the benefits of science and technology? Explain.*

Amy's decision

Due to scientific advances in **genetics** and in the hope of one day finding better treatments or even cures, researchers are isolating many of the genetic defects that cause certain human illnesses. The discovery of these genetic flaws could make it possible for a simple blood test to reveal what debilitating or life-threatening illnesses we will experience in the future—perhaps long before a cure is available. Such a test might therefore tell us how we will die.

Read the following account about a college student for whom this scenario is already real, and respond to the questions. Then your instructor will tell you what Amy decided and her reasons for doing so.

*Amy's father was afflicted with a debilitating **hereditary** disease that inevitably leads to an early death. Amy, a college student, learned that a genetic test could tell her whether she carries the defective gene for this disease.*

Having this test done would tell Amy for sure whether she, too, will one day suffer from the same illness as her father. Positive test results would show that Amy does carry the defective gene. That would also tell her that she will most probably die at a relatively young age, perhaps in her thirties or forties.

Amy's friends at college have had differing views about what decision they would make in Amy's

situation. Amy's mother did not want her daughter to have the test done, but said she would support Amy in whatever she decided. It was Amy's decision.[2]

For discussion

1. If you were in Amy's situation, what reasons would you consider for and against being tested?

2. What choice do you think you would make in Amy's situation?

3. How would your beliefs about life and about death and dying affect your choice?

4. If the test results showed you did have the disease, would you plan to live your remaining years any differently than you hope to do now? Why or why not?

genetic
concerned with how certain characteristics pass by means of genes and chromosomes from parent to offspring

hereditary
can be transmitted genetically from parent to offspring

5. As more genetic tests like this become available, should everyone be allowed to have such testing done? If not all people, why not? If not all people, then who—and why them?

6. What guidelines do you think should be followed, or limits imposed on these tests? Explain.

7. What moral issues are involved here?

1. Why study moral decision making?

- Learning how to make decisions in tough situations is important and practical.
- Teenagers commonly struggle with obedience versus greater independence and freedom.

- Growing into adulthood involves learning to reach better decisions and solutions.

2. What is morality?

- Morality is concerned with how people ought to behave.
- The moral is that which is good.
- Immoral refers to that which is wrong—to how people ought not behave.

- Amoral refers to morally neutral actions, or to people who act without reference to moral principles.

3. How can you learn to make better moral decisions?

- Important moral decisions should be wisely, prayerfully, and carefully made.
- For Catholics, this includes prayer, understanding and applying Church teaching, and consulting Scripture and the wisdom of others.

- Making wise moral decisions involves skills and processes which can be learned through training and practice.

4. Why be moral?

- Created in God's image, every person has God-given dignity and an immortal destiny.
- Being moral is humanly fulfilling and leads to happiness, love, and harmony.

- Truly good persons understand the struggles involved in being good.

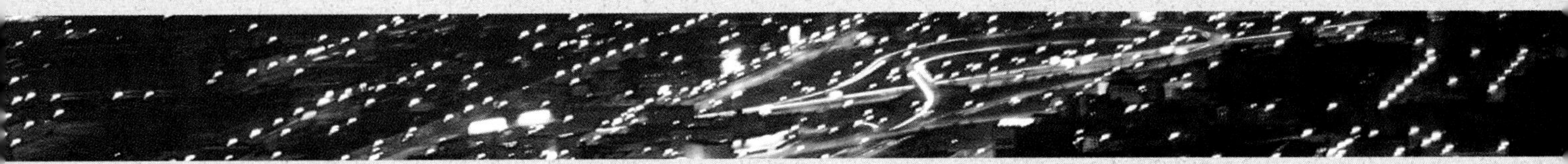

5. Addressing current moral issues

- Today's most important issues and questions have moral dimensions.
- Moralists are often called on to guide others in weighing moral matters and making moral decisions.

- Your religious and moral principles do affect your life and that of others.
- Morality is one of the most crucial studies today and for the future.

Key concepts

amoral

code of conduct

conscience

decision

dilemma

guideline

human dignity

immoral

intention

judgment

life-decision

moral

moralist

morality

obedience

personal integrity

principle

prophet

"... and you will know the truth,
and the truth will make you free."
John 8:32

Chapter 2

Feelings, Freedom, and Morality

Overview questions

1. What makes a decision right or wrong?

2. What role do feelings play in making moral decisions?

3. Why are some common approaches to making moral decisions inadequate?

4. What is human freedom? Why is it so important?

subjective reality
that which a person perceives to be so; a personal perception influenced by one's feelings or state of mind

logic
the science of reasoning correctly

objective reality
that which actually is so or exists, apart from whether or not a person thinks it is or does; that which actually exists as distinct from how people perceive it

The human struggle

Life's main drama is the basic struggle between good and evil. This moral struggle isn't a concern of religion only; it's a life concern. It is the theme—and the drama—of most of the comedies and tragedies you see on television and in the movies. For all of us, this struggle between good and evil involves the two main facets of moral decision making: (1) Figuring out the right thing to do, and (2) summoning up the courage to do the right thing.

This chapter will address the first of these.

Activity

Of the dramas or situation comedies you have seen on TV or in the movies recently, list five that dealt with one of the two facets of moral decision making. Describe how each drama or comedy involved the struggle between good and evil.

What makes it right?

"If I think it's right, does that make it right?" is one of the most common questions asked about morality. Many people are convinced that "right" and "what **I** think is right" are synonymous, but experience tells us that is **not** the case. Sometimes what we honestly thought was right turns out to have been one grand mistake! Two people who have contradictory views of what is right can't both be right. Simple logic tells us that. So what is the relationship between what **is** right and what I **think** is right?

It helps to look at this question from two different viewpoints: the **subjective** and the **objective**. **Subjective reality** is that which I perceive to be so. For example, if I think there is a puddle of water in the middle of the road, then to me there is a puddle of water in the middle of the road! I might arrive at the spot in the road where I "saw" a puddle, only to find that it was a mirage. The puddle represents how reality can be quite different from our **subjective** perception of it. A dog named Brandy learned this the hard way when she tried to run through a glass door that appeared to her to be open. A hard bump on the nose convinced the stunned dog otherwise.

People can perceive the same situation in completely opposite ways. If I say "There's a puddle there" and someone else says "No, there isn't," **logic** demands that the puddle is or is not there. Both of these things can't be true simultaneously, not in reality. One of us must be wrong, even though we both think we're right.

Objective reality is what actually is so or exists, apart from what I think about it. It might not make too much difference whether there really is a small puddle in the middle of the road. But, as with the dog, if I intend to go through a doorway, it can make a great deal of difference to my health and safety to double check that the door is open before I charge through it at full speed!

The same holds true with morality. Objectively speaking, in a given situation, there must be the possibility of an ideal, or good, decision. It is true that, when we make our decisions, we must ultimately rely on our subjective perception of what the right thing is. Therefore, we need to determine—especially if much is at stake— exactly what we think the right thing is, and why.

Catholic teaching helps us in our search for objective truth as we try to discover what is right and to make our decisions accordingly:

objective morality
judgment that corresponds to an action or attitude's goodness or badness in itself, without reference to how its moral quality is perceived

subjective morality
judgment concerning the perceived goodness or badness of an action or attitude, which may or may not correspond with its actual moral quality

responsibility
accountability, trustworthiness, reliability

- Using our ability to reason, we can tell the difference between what is objectively right and what is objectively wrong, and the difference between the various degrees of right and wrong.

- Answering these three questions can help us determine the moral rightness or wrongness of our actions:

  1. Is the object of my action truly good in the objective sense?

  2. Do I aim and intend to do the right and good thing?

  3. Are circumstances involved which may diminish or increase my **responsibility** for the action—even though these circumstances can't make good or right something that is wrong in itself?

- A good end does not justify using an evil means.

- Having morally wrong intentions can turn an otherwise good act into a bad one.

- Making moral decisions requires prayer, study, consulting with others, and, for Catholics, understanding and applying the pertinent Church teachings.

Discussion activity

A terrorist group threatens to destroy a city of a million people unless the government immediately executes a particular individual. This individual is innocent of any wrongdoing. If it were the only way to save all these lives, would it be morally justifiable for the government to take the innocent person's life?

Activity

Assess the rightness or wrongness of these person's actions:

1. Because he loves his mother, Julio wants to buy her a nice birthday present. Since he can't afford to buy a nice gift, he shoplifts one—a necklace—and gives it to her.
2. Cheryl was terribly upset when her boyfriend broke up with her. When she got home from school, she started an argument with her sister.
3. Robert made an insulting remark, intending to start a fight with Tony. Tony just laughed it off and walked away.

Activity

Poll ten teenagers about whether they think the end justifies the means—and why. Summarize your findings for the class, and, in view of class discussion about means and ends, talk about your own reaction to the poll findings.

As we make our moral decisions, we need to try to bring our subjective view of reality as close as possible to the objective reality. Otherwise, we can end up making a decision that we and/or others will truly regret.

Remember then: **Thinking** something is right doesn't necessarily mean that it **is** right. It may or may not be. But if you've tried your best to reasonably and objectively discover what is **in fact** right, the perception and conclusion you arrive at will be, indeed, right **for you**.

For discussion

1. *According to Catholic teaching, what things make an action right or wrong? Explain each.*
2. *Why do you think each is so important?*
3. *Why doesn't a good end justify using a bad or wrong means?*
4. *What would the world be like if everybody usually used bad or wrong means to achieve good ends? Give three examples that illustrate what would probably happen if teenagers did this all the time.*
5. *Do you agree that what a person might **think** is right might not be what actually is **in fact** the right or best possible thing to do? Explain and illustrate with examples from your own experience.*

A snake bit

Read the following true account and respond to the questions.

Not long ago, on his way to school, a young boy (who loved animals of all kinds) saw a small orangish and yellow snake. Wanting to show the unusual animal to his friends at school, he picked it up—gently—and put it in his backpack.

When he got to school and showed the snake to his teacher, she too was impressed, but for an entirely different reason than the boy had been! She immediately recognized the snake as the deadly coral snake—whose venomous bite can—within minutes—be fatal to a person. The teacher guided the boy to gently release the snake in the woods, out of harm's way. Then she gave the students a classroom lesson they'd never forget about why it's so important to know—before you get too close—if something can hurt you. She helped the students see how something that seems very pretty can sometimes also be very dangerous.

For discussion

1. What does this snake story illustrate about the difference between subjective and objective perceptions? About why it's important to seek objective truth?
2. What point might the story illustrate about the need to understand and apply Church teaching, and consult others' wisdom in forming and following our conscience?
3. How might this incident represent the way sin or strong desires can mislead us in moral matters?

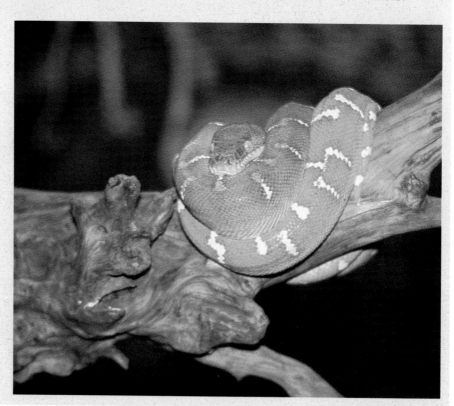

Feelings and morality

Feelings in themselves are not good or bad. But they can and do steer us toward or away from what is good or bad. As Chinese wisdom points out, you can't prevent birds from flying above your head, but you can keep them from building nests in your hair! We can't always control the fact that certain feelings arise in us, but we can control the extent to which we let them influence our decisions and actions.

Emotions, then, become good or bad only insofar as we encourage or discourage them within ourselves, or let our passions rule our reasoning. Feelings become good when they lead us to do what is right and good, and bad when they lead us to do what is wrong. All of us are certainly influenced by our feelings, and most often this is a very good thing. Feelings help give us the drive and courage we need to do good things in life for ourselves and for others.

One of the most confusing and difficult emotions to deal with is affection coupled with romantic attraction, because people often mistake this experience for real love. It may be—or it may be a cruel and crippling selfishness and possessiveness. Genuine love is the most noble of all human emotions. At the same time, it is also more than an emotion. It is an act of the **will** and desires only what is truly good for the one loved.

It is important to understand that feelings are not bad in themselves. Consider hatred and anger. Hatred of and anger toward injustice, evil, and intolerance have propelled human rights movements worldwide to achieve greater equality and respect for all persons. But when directed at people rather than at wrongdoing, and when turned into revenge rather than toward goodness, anger and hatred have destroyed millions of lives. Like rocket fuel, these emotions are extremely volatile. When we handle them carefully and direct them properly, they can help propel us to new and better futures. When we let them get out of control, they can cause explosive damage.

Hopefully, we manage our emotions sensibly, rather than **repress** them or unleash them indiscriminately. People who are truly unable to control their emotions suffer from a psychological or medical disorder for which they need professional help. Many other people have so much difficulty controlling their emotions that they too would benefit from such help. All of us at times experience feelings which are so strong or sudden that we need to take "time out" to be sure we respond properly to the situation. For we must use our head to direct our emotions toward what is truly, objectively good—and not let feelings carry us into doing things just because we "want to."

Scientists can't create the laws of physics by which the universe operates. They can only discover those laws and work within them. Morality isn't purely subjective either. We can't turn feelings and wishes into fact; feeling or wishing something were so doesn't make it so in reality. We can't make moral decisions based just on what we **feel** or on what we wish were so. We cannot make our own morality. We can only do our best to recognize the truth and reality of a situation and, based on that, try to determine what is objectively the right and best thing to do.

feelings, emotions
internal sensations and responses that are both mental and physical in nature and draw us toward or away from certain ideas, things, or persons perceived as good or bad

Journal entry
List the emotional "birds" that you find hardest to keep from "building nests in your hair," the feelings you find at times most bothersome and difficult to handle appropriately.

Journal entry
What feelings lead you to be the kind of person you want to be and to do the good you want to do?

will
the God-given ability to make rational, free, and intentional choices—especially between right and wrong, good and evil

repress
to hold back so as to keep from naturally expressing

RIGHT
TURN
ONLY

To love is to will the good of another.
St. Thomas Aquinas

What is right for you, therefore, is not merely what you may **feel** like doing or **wish** were right. What you honestly think **is** right, after you've carefully weighed and considered the matter, including the objective truth insofar as you can discover it— that is how you can know what is right for you.

> *The faith that you have, have as your own conviction before God. Blessed are those who have no reason to condemn themselves because of what they approve.*
>
> *Romans 14:22*

For discussion

1. *Explain why it's not feelings (emotions) themselves, but what you do with them that is good or bad.*

2. *When and why do feelings lead to something good or right? When do they lead to something bad or wrong? Illustrate with examples.*

3. *Why can affection, when coupled with romantic attraction, be such a confusing and difficult emotion to deal with? How often do you think teenagers confuse their **feelings** of attraction and affection for someone with **love**? Explain.*

4. *To what extent should people be able to control their emotions? Why? How is this different from not letting oneself feel or express emotion appropriately?*

5. *If everyone always did what they felt was right for them without first trying to discover the objective truth, what kind of world would we live in? Would you want to live in such a world? Why or why not?*

6. *What happens when people do behave that way? What impact does it have on society? On you?*

7. *What is meant by saying that we can't make our own morality? How would you answer this question: How can you tell what's right for you?*

society
an organized group working together to achieve a common end

Road rage

Read the following true accounts. Then respond to the questions.

The tailgater's tantrum

A station wagon driver, upset that a pickup truck was tailgating him, slammed on his brakes to stop the tailgater. The pickup driver then pulled alongside the station wagon, threatened to kill its driver, and aimed his truck at the station wagon. The station wagon driver had to keep swerving into oncoming traffic lanes to avoid a collision.

The pickup driver pulled in front of the station wagon and braked, trying to cause the station wagon driver to slam into the truck. The pickup driver then followed the other man home, where the two drivers argued over the incident.

Luckily, the pickup driver left before the incident escalated any further. Other drivers, however, have been killed—by women as well as by men—for driving too slowly, played their car stereo too loudly, or displayed an obscene gesture after being tailgated or cut off on the road.

The parking lot punch

Renee and her husband, Richard, were pulling out of a parking lot one evening when another young driver almost ran into them.

Scared and upset by the near-miss, Renee angrily yelled at the driver that he had almost hit her and her husband. Then she got out of her car and went over to the offending driver's car, waved her hand at the driver, and again yelled that he had almost hit their car.

Jai, the offending driver, slapped Renee's hand, whereupon she slapped him back. Richard then slapped Jai, and the two men began scuffling. By that time, a crowd had gathered. A few men tried to separate the drivers, but Jai still managed to deliver a fatal punch to Richard's head. Richard died in the parking lot. Jai was charged with second-degree murder for Richard's death. All of this happened because of anger over a close call in the parking lot.

For discussion

1. How did each of the individuals in these situations let his or her emotions get out of control? What harm resulted, or could have resulted?

2. Which of the individuals were in the right to begin with? Did that also give them the right to lose their tempers as they did? Explain.

3. Did any of these persons try, in a sense, to make his or her own morality? Explain.

4. Describe a situation in which you have been sorely tempted to lose your temper when someone wronged you. How did you respond? Why?

5. How do you think you would have responded in each of the road rage situations? Why? How should you respond? Explain.

Questionable approaches to morality

How does moral decision making differ from other approaches to decision making? Isn't it good enough just to try to be a good person? Isn't that the same as being "Christian"? Well, it all depends. Some ideas of what being a good person means agree with Christian principles, while others do not.

Let's look first at some of the faulty or questionable approaches people often take regarding **ethics** and morality. To help you understand, each faulty approach will be described in the extreme. In reality, manifestations of each approach are more subtle.

Keep in mind that we're all tempted at times to base our behavior on these faulty or questionable approaches to morality. Being honest with ourselves can help us avoid that and can help us shape our moral life around correct standards.

ethics
moral conduct; standards of moral judgment and behavior

"Anything goes"

"Morality is just a bunch of rules and regulations that religious people make up to keep other people in line." "Nobody can tell me what to do." "What's right for me is right for we." There are always people who think this way. They believe there is no fundamental **code of ethics** by which everyone should live.

Such persons usually have just one explanation for what they think or do: "Because that's what I think, that's why!" Their moral **philosophy** amounts to "It's everyone for themselves"; there are no constant standards, rules, or principles. Everything changes with every situation.

These "anything-goes" decision makers bend laws and regulations to suit themselves and their decisions. The one consistent thing is that their decision-making pattern centers around themselves and, indirectly, those they may like or love—at the moment. But when those close to them fall from favor, concern for their welfare quickly evaporates. The boy who tells a girl he loves her just to get her to have sex with him, or the girl who tells a boy she likes him just to get a date to the prom are examples of "anything goes" behavior.

Such persons **do** as they please to **get** what they want. They often **rationalize** and try to persuade themselves—and others—that what they're doing is right. They are great **manipulators**. But "right" to them is simply "what I want" or "what I feel like." It's almost impossible to predict what "anything goes" followers will decide next—except that it will be something which suits themselves.

code of ethics
a system of principles, rules or values by which to live

philosophy
the principles an individual chooses to live by

rationalize
positively: to bring into accord with reason; negatively: to provide plausible but untrue reasons for conduct

manipulator
one who directly or indirectly tries to control or take advantage of others

Reflection

1. When are you most tempted to rationalize that it's okay to do something, when you know deep down it's really not?
2. Do you ever bend the rules, use or manipulate people, or treat them selfishly in order to do or get what you want?

Journal entry

1. In what ways can you be more honest about your real reasons for doing things?
2. In what ways would you like to put caring for others above self-interests?

For discussion

1. *What is wrong with the "anything goes" approach to decision making?*
2. *What would happen if everyone in the world followed this approach to making moral decisions? What would the world be like?*
3. *Give other examples of this approach to life.*

"It's the law"

This approach to decision making centers on strictly abiding by the **laws**, rules, and regulations of society—civil or religious, family or friends, school or business. The "It's the law" person tries to learn and to abide by the "letter of the law," every detail of the law. Such people have little tolerance for ideas and moral codes other than their own.

"What are the rules?" is the law moralist's only concern. Why do this or that? Because you're **supposed** to in order to belong to the group. Only when no law or regulation covers the situation does the law moralist have to really think about what to do. Otherwise, decision making means simply following the rules, regardless. Circumstances and other influences that affect individuals facing moral decisions aren't considered important.

Lest you think only stuffy adults operate this way, reconsider. What about teenagers who feel inwardly (or outwardly) pressured to obey their peers' unwritten laws, codes, or pressures? What about those willing to do most anything to please authority figures? And, being honest, do you ever put being accepted and included above more important values?

Conformity is the hallmark of the person who above all needs to be accepted, to "fit in." Being an individual and standing on one's own, whatever anyone else thinks, just seems too hard. Conformists' primary law is whatever brings them acceptance in others' eyes.

> *. . . the letter [of the law] kills, but the Spirit gives life.*
> **2 CORINTHIANS 3:6**

law
binding custom or practice of a group; rule of conduct or action

conformity
agreement in behavior with that of another person or group

Journal entry

How can you increase your sense of self-confidence and self-worth so you don't feel pulled to do things just to be accepted?

Reflection

1. How important is being accepted to you?
2. When does your desire to be accepted or included most tempt you to override your better judgment?
3. When have you said or done something just to feel accepted or included—and then later wished you hadn't said or done it?

For discussion

1. *What are the problems with the "it's the law" approach to decisions?*
2. *What would happen if everyone followed this approach?*
3. *Give other examples of this approach to decision making—including those based on conformity.*
4. *Would you put organized teenage gangs in the conformist category? Explain.*

"It's only 'natural' "

The "doing what comes naturally" approach to decision making views right and wrong in terms of what feels or seems "natural." Followers of this approach may argue, for example, that "It's women's 'nature' to bear and raise children; women belong at home and not in the workplace." But the standard for these "naturalists" is purely subjective—**their** idea of what it is natural or unnatural to do.

Thus, one who holds this "If God wanted us to fly, we would have been born with wings" mentality generally has trouble defending what "natural" or "unnatural" is and explaining why. What some of these persons consider "natural" and therefore right, others might consider "unnatural" and wrong. (Do not confuse "doing what comes naturally" with belief in the natural law, which we will discuss later in this text.)

natural law
the God-given ability to distinguish right and wrong

Journal entry
Name one thing that would help you follow your better judgment rather than simply following the feelings that pressure you.

Reflection
1. When do you feel most tempted—or pressured by others—to do something just because it seems "natural" or feels good?
2. Which feelings exert the most pressure on you to behave in certain ways—for example, anger, romantic feelings, jealousy, or some other feeling?
3. When has following your feelings instead of your better judgment gotten you into trouble, hurt others, or otherwise made you regret your behavior?

This approach to morality is unfortunately a common one—among teenagers as well as adults. Consider, for instance, those who say that premarital sexual intercourse or marital infidelity is "only following your natural instincts and feelings." These individuals don't think first about meaning or consequences. They simply determine right from wrong by what they would like to believe is "natural" to do at the time. Practically speaking, this ends up being very similar to—and just as dangerous as—the "anything goes" approach.

infidelity
being unfaithful or untrue, not keeping one's solemn promise or commitment

instincts
inborn tendencies to act in certain ways

For discussion

1. *What is wrong with the "it's only natural" approach to making moral decisions?*
2. *What do you think would happen if everyone followed that approach in making decisions?*
3. *Give other examples of this type of thinking among teenagers and adults.*

Do you not know that . . . you are slaves of the one whom you obey, either of sin, which leads to death, or of obedience, which leads to righteousness?
ROMANS 6:16

Journal entry
In what situations are you most tempted to just follow your "natural inclinations" rather than thinking things through first?

The Spur Posse

Read the following true account. Then respond to the questions.

A group of high school buddies, most of whom were athletes, began calling themselves the "Spur Posse" and competing among themselves to see who could have sex with the most girls.

Many kids at school considered the boys "studs" and their female sexual conquests "trash." Some of their parents defended Posse members' behavior by saying "boys will be boys." Their girlfriends actually seemed proud that their boyfriends could score with so many other girls. Other students and parents, however, found it thoroughly disgusting.

When some of the "conquests" and their parents filed criminal complaints against the Spur Posse, Posse members gained national attention. On several nation-wide talk shows (some of which paid them for appearing), they explained how every girl they had sex with counted as a "point." They referred to these girls as "easy marks." One boy bragged of "scoring" over 60 points. Sex, for a member of the Spur Posse, was just another athletic contest.

The boys also boasted on television that they were better than everyone else and that girls were drawn to them because of their good looks, athletic ability, and popularity. They said if they considered the girl "easy," they just had sex with her quickly and then left. If a girl was considered "good" and "respectable," they would first "romance" her by taking her out to eat and doing what she wanted for the day or evening. The boys admitted that their friends' opinion of their conquests was as important to them as the "scoring" itself. They said they considered bragging about

it part of the "fun" and that their buddies look up to guys who can brag about their sexual conquests.

Several girls, however, told police that the boys had threatened, intimidated, and forced them into having sex—had raped them. The boys, of course, denied ever raping anyone. Police authorities said the Posse especially targeted younger girls who were in awe of the boys' popularity at school. One police sergeant called the boys a pack of wolves.

The female targets of the Posse's sexual game later said that they felt used and robbed of their dignity, self-respect, and self-esteem. Others regretfully admitted they had voluntarily had sex with a Spur Posse member because they had wanted to be valued—especially by someone popular. Later they described how stupid they felt for not realizing that they were just another "point."

The boys defended their behavior by saying society had "made" them that way by considering them more important than others because of their athletic abilities. One Posse member said all teenage boys want to have sex and will whenever they have the chance. He said the only difference in the Posse's behavior is that they talked about it openly and called their sexual conquests "points."

Other observers have called the boys' attitudes and behavior a sick effort to enhance their own self-esteem.

For discussion

1. What approach(es) to decision making were used by the Spur Posse members? By the girls who voluntarily had sex with them?

2. How does this case illustrate why it's important to have a personal code of ethics before getting into situations where one might be tempted to do something regrettable?

3. What do you think of the Spur Posse members' behavior and attitudes? Why?

4. What do you think of the fact that some TV talk shows were willing to pay the boys to appear on the show? Do you think they should have been invited to appear on any TV show—whether or not they were paid for it? Explain.

5. What do you think of the reactions of the boys' parents? Of their girlfriends? Explain.

6. How responsible do you think the female targets of the Spur Posse were for what happened to them? How do you think you might have felt in their situation? Explain.

7. What do you think of the things the boys and others said in defense of the Spur Posse's behavior? Why?

8. Which of the attitudes and behaviors illustrated by this case exist at your school, though perhaps in less exaggerated or obvious ways? Explain.

. . . freedom consists not in doing what we like, but in having the right to do what we ought.
POPE JOHN PAUL II

rational

able to reason, form judgments, and reach logical decisions

freedom

the ability to use our abilities of will and reasoning to make moral choices and act on them

Journal entry

1. What kinds of personal choices do you experience as uplifting or freeing?
2. Which of your choices have dragged you down or somewhat enslaved you?

For discussion

1. *What does it mean to be rational? To be free as a human being?*

2. *What is the goal of your freedom? How can you best achieve this goal?*

3. *Why is there no such thing as absolute freedom? Illustrate with examples.*

4. *Why is it enslaving to habitually do wrong? Why is it freeing to habitually do right? Give examples based on teenagers' experience.*

5. *Give examples of specific social conditions that you think keep people from fully exercising their freedom: in our society, in the world, in your school.*

6. *Why isn't personal freedom unlimited?*

7. *What would help you most to make moral decisions more freely and confidently?*

Morality and human freedom

What is freedom?

You are **rational**, and you are free. God gives you the **freedom** to choose, and the mental ability to choose wisely and correctly. Your freedom empowers both your decisions and your actions, enabling you to choose to love or hate, be just or unjust, become a good or a bad kind of person. How you use your freedom shapes your life, who you are, and who you become—and affects everyone your life touches.

The ultimate goal of human freedom is to choose, for all eternity, the Goodness which is God. The decisions we make in this life draw us toward or away from God as our final happiness. In choosing what is right and good, we choose to grow closer to God. In choosing wrong, we push ourselves away from God's love and from others. Christians believe that redemption by Christ has given us the freedom and power, grace, of God's Spirit to overcome being alienated from God and enslaved by evil.

Freedom and responsibility

There is no such thing as absolute freedom—freedom **from** or **for** everything. Choosing one thing is choosing to give up another. To choose against something is to choose in favor of something else. We can't have it both ways. Making a moral choice is always a decision to embrace one thing and to reject another. It is a commitment to something—to the goodness that lifts us up or to the evil that drags us down.

Constantly choosing what is wrong abuses human freedom and inwardly enslaves people. Often enough, it outwardly enslaves them as well—as any addict whose addiction started with one wrong choice at a time knows. Habitually choosing goodness, as Jesus did and showed us, is the only thing that can make us truly free.

Being free and being responsible for how we use our freedom are essential to being human and to our human dignity. Freedom and responsibility are what enable us to love God and others. No one can take away our right to exercise this freedom responsibly—especially in religious and moral matters. In fact, civil authorities have a duty to acknowledge and protect this basic human right, which not incidentally upholds public order and the common good.

Too often social conditions like poverty, intolerance, and injustice keep people from fully exercising their human freedom. We should all do our part to oppose whatever violates human freedom. For a threat to anyone's freedom is a threat to everyone's.

But people don't have the right to do or say whatever they please. **Personal freedom above all involves recognizing and respecting our relationship with God and others.** It includes exercising freedom in ways that respect others' rights.

The more you listen to God—in prayer and Scripture, in Church teaching, and in others' wisdom—the more free and confident you will feel to do the right thing, and the easier it will become to resist the things that pressure you to do what's wrong.

Now the Lord is the Spirit, and where the Spirit of the Lord is, there is freedom.

2 Corinthians 3:17

Cloning

Read the following, and then respond to the questions.

When Scottish scientists cloned the first mammal—an adult sheep named Dolly—the "freaky future" of science fiction became a startlingly real possibility. Since then, the issue of **cloning**—especially of cloning humans—has raised worldwide storms of concern and controversy.

Scientists who research animal cloning say they want to benefit humanity by helping to increase the world's food supply and by helping to conquer disease. They speak of breeding animals whose organs could be transplanted into humans

to save lives. Other scientists fear, however, that even applications of animal cloning such as this might unknowingly transmit to humans highly contagious and incurable diseases that could destroy much of the world's population.

One of the Scottish scientists who cloned Dolly told the U.S. Congress that "it would be quite inhumane" to try to clone humans. He says he hasn't heard of any possible reason that could morally justify cloning humans.

Most scientists, government officials, and religious leaders have strongly agreed with him, but some others have not. One U.S. senator is convinced that cloning humans will surely happen, says he's not afraid of it at all, and believes it could greatly benefit the search for medical cures. He says that limits should not be put on human knowledge and scientific progress, that it's "demeaning to human nature" to even try to impose such limits.

Both the pope and the World Health Organization have condemned the cloning of humans as "ethically unacceptable." Most scientists agree, believing that some things such as human cloning are simply off limits—that humans are not, and should not be, allowed to play God. Besides, the scientists point out, the risks are far too great.

For discussion

1. What is cloning? What issues does cloning raise about human dignity and what it means to be human?

2. Why is cloning an important moral concern for everyone? How does it illustrate the "Should we?" question discussed in this chapter?

3. Why must everyone—including you and I—participate in the debates and decision-making processes about cloning?

4. How do Catholic teaching about science, technology, and human rights apply to animal and human cloning?

5. What is your response to the idea of cloning humans? Why? What risks do you think there are?

6. Why do most scientific, government, and religious leaders strongly disagree with the senator who thinks "scientific progress" can't and shouldn't be stopped or even limited? What is your response to him? Why?

7. How does this senator's idea of "progress" compare with what Catholic teaching says about "true advances" in development?

8. What types of cloning research, if any, do you think should be allowed to proceed? What limitations would you place on cloning? Why?

Project

Search the Internet for what others have to say about the pros and cons of cloning humans. Write a paper giving your responses to their reasons in view of what Catholic teaching says about the topic.

cloning

producing a genetically identical copy of a living thing

Feelings, Freedom, and Morality

1. What makes it right?

- Being moral involves determining and then doing the right thing.
- Subjective reality is what is perceived as so, and objective reality is what actually is so.
- Objectively, there is always an ideally right or best possible decision.
- Using our reasoning, we can identify the nature and degrees of right and wrong.
- A good end never justifies using an evil means.

- An action's morality is determined by whether its object, goal, and intentions are right and good, and whether the circumstances diminish or increase a person's responsibility.
- Making moral decisions involves prayer, study, consulting others, and, for Catholics, understanding and applying Church teaching.
- To determine what is right for me, I must first reasonably try to discover the objective truth.
- Then, what is right for me is what I honestly think is right and in accordance with objective truth.

2. Feelings and morality

- Feelings themselves are not good or bad; they steer us toward or away from the good or bad.
- Our response to emotions may be good or bad. If we encourage the negative or discourage the positive within ourselves or let our passions rule our reasoning, our response will be bad.

- Love, the noblest emotion, is also an act of will that desires only good for the one loved.
- We should manage and express our emotions sensibly, rather than repress them or unleash them indiscriminately.
- We must direct our feelings toward what is objectively good.

3. Inadequate or questionable approaches to morality

- Some approaches to morality lead one astray.
- The "anything goes" approach lacks fundamental, unchanging standards of morality.
- The "it's the law" approach evaluates morality by laws only, without considering the people or circumstances involved.

- The "it's only natural" approach arbitrarily decides, based on feelings or ideas about what seems "natural," without considering meaning or consequences.

4. Morality and human freedom

- As persons, we are rational and free to choose.
- How we use our freedom shapes our life and draws us closer to or away from God, the ultimate goal of human freedom.
- No one has absolute freedom—moral choice is always a commitment to embrace one thing and reject another.
- Constantly choosing what is wrong is an abuse of freedom and enslaves people—only choosing goodness can make us truly free.
- Freedom and responsibility for how it is used are every person's right, and protecting freedom is civil authorities' duty.
- Personal freedom above all respects our relationships with God and others.

Key concepts

"anything goes" moral approach

code of ethics

conformity

end or object of an action

feelings, emotions

freedom

habitual choices

ideal right or good

inadequate approaches to morality

intention

"law" morality

managing emotions

means used to achieve a goal

moral philosophy

natural instincts

natural law

natural, unnatural

objective morality

objective reality

objective truth

one's better judgment

personal ethics

rational

rationalize

repressing emotion

responsibility

subjective morality

subjective reality

. . . whatever is true, whatever is honorable, whatever is just, whatever is pure, whatever is pleasing, whatever is commendable, if there is any excellence and if there is anything worthy of praise, think about these things. Keep on doing the things that you have learned and received and heard and seen in me, and the God of peace will be with you.

Philippians 4:8–9

PRIVATE
ROAD

Chapter 3

Conscience

Overview questions

1. What are some of the common theories about what conscience is?

2. What is the Catholic Christian understanding of conscience?

3. What is really meant by being free to follow your conscience?

4. What kinds of personal attitudes interfere with, or support, conscience?

5. What kinds of things influence your conscience?

6. How can you best search for the truth and make correct moral decisions?

Prayer

Spirit of Wisdom,

So many choices face us today, and so many things and people pull us in all directions.

Help me to not be a pushover, easily swayed.

Help me keep my conscience alive so it doesn't become dull to the pain and misery of others or to the great harm caused by doing wrong.

Guide me to use my head to make my decisions wisely.

Lead me in your direction.

What is conscience?

People are fond of saying "Let your conscience be your guide." But do we know what that means? What is conscience? Can your conscience ever be wrong? How can you tell what your conscience is telling you? These things confuse many people. So this chapter will discuss conscience—what it is, what influences it, and how we can make the right decisions by using our conscience. First, we need to identify our present ideas of conscience.

Conscience survey

1. What do you think conscience is?

_____

_____

2. When you speak of "following your conscience," what do you mean?

_____

_____

3. Do you think a person's conscience can ever be wrong? (Remember what you discussed about subjective and objective reality and morality.)

_____

_____

4. How can you tell whether your conscience is directing you toward what is right?

_____

_____

Common conscience theories

There are many theories about what conscience is. Here is your opportunity to evaluate critically for yourself some of the more common ones.

The "hunch"

When asked why they think a certain action or decision is the right or wrong one, many people simply respond, "I just **know** it is," or "Something just tells me it is," or "I'm **sure** it is," or "I just **feel** right (or wrong) about it." But when asked **why** they feel or think this way, they have trouble giving specific reasons. To them conscience is **intuition**—a built-in hunch about what is right or wrong.

intuition

a quick perception or understanding, without recourse to reasoning

"Doing what comes naturally"

Some people believe we're all born with moral instincts which automatically tell us the right or wrong thing to do in every situation. Most everyone respects things like honesty, sincerity, justice, kindness, and human dignity. Therefore, some people reason, if we all just "do what comes naturally"—instinctively, we will be doing the right thing. Simply by relying on our basic instincts, we can find specific answers even to complex moral dilemmas. This view is **not**, however, the same as belief in a **natural law** (which we will discuss in another chapter) by which we can distinguish **in general** between good and evil, right and wrong.

The "little voice"

Others view conscience as an interior voice that tells us exactly what to do—a higher force or power that inspires us with the specific answer in each moral situation. Perhaps an angel whispers the good choice in one ear, while in the other ear the devil tempts us to make the wrong choice ("The devil made me do it"). Or maybe it's God's voice that "speaks" to us. People who subscribe to the "little voice" theory can't seem to give specific **reasons** for their moral decisions. Often they simply say, "I just **know** that's what God wants," or "It's God's will," or "Something is **telling** me that's what is right (or wrong)." One's task, as they see it, is merely to obey the "voice" one hears.

"Follow the crowd"

Another common conscience theory holds that what society considers right and wrong should determine one's personal moral response. If enough people think something is right or wrong, then it must be: "Everybody else does it," "The majority can't be wrong," "Who am I to argue with everybody else?" In making moral decisions, persons who subscribe to this theory rely heavily on the opinion of others.

"Follow-up feelings"

Many people think conscience is how you feel **after** you decide or do something, or after you've actually done it. If you feel good after you've done something, then you know you've done the right thing. If you feel bad or guilty, then you know that what you did must have been wrong. To decide what's right or wrong, just anticipate beforehand how you will feel later about it. If you feel good about what you are considering doing, then the course of action is right. If you feel bad or guilty about your contemplated decision or action, then your conscience is telling you that the action is wrong and you shouldn't do it—or so these people believe.

The world has achieved brilliance without conscience. Ours is a world of nuclear giants and ethical infants.
OMAR N. BRADLEY

Following the crowd can be risky. When we rely on the opinion of others in making moral decisions, we are accepting their values.

The "no conscience" theory

Some think there is no such thing as conscience. Conscience, they figure, is just an idea religions have made up to keep us all in line by making us feel guilty about certain things. Those who believe there's no such thing as conscience believe people can be **legally** guilty of breaking laws, but that there's no such thing as moral guilt or violating one's conscience. Often they also believe we're all programmed by our upbringing, heredity, and/or environment to act in certain ways. So you're not free to make your own moral choices—you just can't help doing what you do.

For discussion

1. *Take each common conscience theory and project what would happen if everyone followed each theory in making moral decisions.*
2. *Take each common conscience theory and project what might happen if the president used that theory to decide whether or not to engage this country in a nuclear war.*
3. *Would you vote for someone who believes there is no such thing as conscience? Explain.*
4. *What do you think is the main problem with each of the "common conscience theories"? Explain.*

The Christian understanding of conscience

Whenever you've gotten angry that an injustice was done to you, or thought positively about something good you did for someone, you have been exercising your conscience (maybe without realizing it). For conscience enables you to discern and evaluate whether an action is good or evil. It's what tells you deep down inside: "That's outrageous—it's wrong!" "That's not fair!" or "That was a truly good and courageous thing to do." "This is what it means to have somebody really love you and care about what happens to you."

God has given us life and freedom with just one condition—that we must love. In practical terms, this means we are to do good and avoid what is evil. Genuine love (which is God's own nature) always seeks only what is good. To help us love, God has given us each a conscience and the obligation to follow it.

But what **is** conscience? Catholic belief holds that **conscience is the ability to reason to and distinguish truth and goodness from wrong or evil.** Using your conscience, then, is not a matter of relying on hunches, instincts, little voices, feelings alone, or what others do. **It is using your head to figure out what you prayerfully and honestly think is the best, most loving thing to do in a given situation.**

Our conscience, then, is what lights our way—shows us how we are to love God and others, and how to avoid what damages this love. Conscience is the most sacred, deepest heart of ourselves. There, alone with God, we confront who we really are. Listening to your conscience, then, requires listening to yourself. It means taking the time to look inward and examine whether you honestly are doing the right thing, or are just letting circumstances or others lead you into becoming a kind of person you don't really want to be.

Reflection

1. How often do you take some quiet time to reflect on the kind of person you are and would like to be?
2. Do you ever hesitate to do this for fear of what you might see?

DRIVE SAFELY SO WE CAN ALL ENJOY THE JOURNEY

Activity

For the next week, at the end of each day, take a minimum of five minutes alone in a quiet place to review the good and the wrongs you've done in the day. Consider how your decisions reflect on who you are as a person and how they affect you. Conclude by talking with God about it.

At the end of the week, write a statement in your journal summarizing what you've learned about yourself.

For discussion

1. How do you think the Christian understanding of conscience compares with the "common conscience theories" discussed previously? Explain.

2. What do you think would happen if everyone followed this understanding of conscience in making moral decisions? Why?

3. What would you think if the president made major national decisions based on this understanding of conscience? Why?

4. Can you think of any conscience theories besides those discussed? If so, explain.

5. Which understanding of conscience makes the most sense? The least? Why?

Freedom of conscience

We are each obliged to follow our conscience faithfully. To freely choose and act based on your properly formed and **informed conscience** is your privilege and your right as a human. The Catholic Church strongly believes that this is how we discover truth and draw closer in love to God. Thus the Catholic Church stresses that nobody should be forced to act against his or her conscience, or prevented from acting according to his or her conscience—especially in religious matters.

As we develop our ability to think, reflect, and exercise clearer and more objective judgments, our conscience matures. But in learning to make wise moral judgments, reasoning alone isn't enough. Our conscience must also be well-formed in other ways. The more we deliberately **do** the right thing, for instance, the more aware we become of the right thing **to do**. Finally, to develop our conscience correctly, we also need to

- pray for God's guidance as we try to discern right from wrong
- consult with others where warranted and listen to wise advice
- increase our ability to understand others, empathize with them, and feel compassion
- consider, as Christians, how Jesus' teachings and example should affect our life
- understand and apply, as Catholics, what the Church teaches about moral matters

Catholic teaching likewise cautions us to remember these rules that always apply in every moral situation:

The rules of conscience

1. Act toward others the way you would want them to behave toward you (the Golden Rule).
2. Respect others, and do nothing that would damage their conscience or cause them to do wrong.
3. You may never do evil in order to accomplish good.

For discussion

1. How important do you think conscience is? Why? Why do Catholics consider conscience so important?

2. What does the Catholic Church teach about the freedom to exercise one's conscience? How is this freedom generally respected? How is it commonly violated?

3. How does our conscience mature? Why and how must we develop our conscience?

4. In your own words, explain the "rules of conscience." Why do you think each is important? What additional rule would you recommend people follow? Why?

Journal entry

Describe your understanding of conscience and how conscience helps you make moral decisions.

informed conscience
decision-making ability which has the proper input; correct conscience

This above all: to thine own self be true, and it must follow, as the night the day, thou canst not then be false to anyone.
WILLIAM SHAKESPEARE, "HAMLET."

DON'T EVEN THINK ABOUT IT!

LOVE AND DO WHATEVER YOU WANT
— St. Augustine

Missile crisis

Discuss the following case and respond to the questions. The scenario is hypothetical, but is based on the kinds of crisis drills which do occur at top government levels in order to refine the decision-making process. Some of the facts presented are based on various officials' assessments of what might occur in such a situation.

As the U.S. Secretary of Defense, you have just been told that a missile has been launched against the United States from somewhere in Country X—a country known to harbor terrorists, to have nuclear weapons, and to have the ability to successfully launch nuclear weapons toward their intended intercontinental targets. You have also been informed that

- *The missile en route contains a nuclear warhead.*
- *It is targeted toward a densely populated U.S. city.*
- *An effort to shoot down the missile might not succeed and, if it doesn't, over two million people will die.*
- *If more nuclear missiles are launched from Country X, some will surely strike their targets.*
- *If the United States launches a first strike at Country X, then Country X will probably respond by firing more missiles at U.S. targets.*

Immediately after learning about the missile, you receive word that Country X has just sent the president an urgent message, saying that the missile launch has been a terrible mistake. The message attributes the launch to a group of radicals who somehow were able

to buy from the underground market the plutonium needed to build a single weapon. It says that Country X itself has no hostile intentions toward the United States and will cooperate fully in trying to catch and punish the rebels who are responsible.

Attempts have been made to reach Country X's leaders by telephone and satellite transmission, but communications appear jammed. Country X's diplomat in Washington says she knows nothing about the missile launch, but insists that it must be "a horrible mistake."

It is your job to brief the president on:

- *what is going on*
- *what the options are*
- *your recommended course(s) of action*

Your greatest enemy now is time. The president has less than thirty minutes to make a decision about how to respond. As one official tells you, "This is serious, sobering business."

For discussion

1. *What are the greatest dangers involved here?*

2. *What options do you think are available in this situation?*

3. *Which ones would you discard? Which ones would you consider most strongly?*

4. *What course(s) of action do you recommend the president take? Why?*

Ethics attitudes

You wouldn't want to make a decision about college or about whom to marry in the same carefree way you decided as a third-grader what brand of gum to chew. Complex, life-altering decisions require adult consideration. Likewise, making moral decisions now and as an adult requires a more mature ethical attitude than you had as a young child.

We all grow in moral sensitivity as we develop our sense of what is right and wrong. This growth differs with the individual, but most of us have similar early stages of moral growth. Unfortunately, though, what should be merely a transitional childhood phase of moral growth becomes for too many their permanent lifelong ethical attitude. So let's examine some of these "ethics attitudes" of childhood before we discuss the ones that should belong to adults.

transitional
passing from one thing or phase to another

Will *I* get caught—or rewarded?

When you were a small child, two of your first words were probably *yes* and *no*. You learned that yes meant something was okay to do—that, if you did it, you'd get hugged, kissed, patted on the head, smiled at, given a cookie, or otherwise rewarded. At least you learned you wouldn't get punished for it. You also learned that doing a "no-no" resulted in being uncomfortable—someone would be mad at you, you'd be talked to sternly and maybe punished. So, at that time, you saw good and bad in terms of earning rewards and avoiding punishments—and it was on that basis that you made your decisions.

Young children make decisions in response to reasons someone else dictates. It's not surprising that children's first moral decisions are made the same way. For example, out of fear of being caught and scolded, disappointing his or her parents, and being grounded, a child may choose to **do** the homework assignment instead of copying it from a friend.

Unfortunately, many teenagers and adults choose to avoid developing a more adult approach and continue operating with a childish moral attitude: Cheating is okay as long as I don't get caught, get an F for it, or have my folks called. It's okay not to report that I've accidentally hit someone's parked car if no one saw me and I can get away clean. It doesn't so much matter to these persons who else gets hurt or how unfair it is to others, as long as **they** themselves don't get hurt.

What's in it for *me?*

Like other children, as you grew a little older, your decisions probably became more self-centered—based more on what satisfied your internal personal needs than on external rewards or punishments—rather than parent or teacher centered. At that point, right was what made you feel good, gave *you* self-satisfaction or pleasure. Wrong was what made you feel bad, gave you pain, or caused *you* to be dissatisfied. You may have been nice to others mainly so that they'd be nice to you.

Regrettably, many individuals retain this self-centered attitude as teenagers and throughout adulthood: It's okay to break someone's heart, as long as mine isn't broken. Such persons operate by a strange Golden Rule: Do to others as you wish, but don't let others do as they wish to you.

Journal entry

What kinds of decisions do you still tend to base on reward and punishment?

Discuss

1. When you were a very small child, why did you do what you were told was right? Why did you avoid doing what you were told was wrong?

2. What would happen if everybody based their moral decisions on only what they'd be rewarded or punished for? Would you want such persons as your friends?

Journal entry

What kinds of decisions do you still tend to base on "What's in it for me?"

Discuss

To what extent do you think teenagers and adults base moral decisions on "What's in it for me?" Explain and give examples.

What does the law tell me to do?

Those who have the "it's the law" approach to morality—one of the faulty approaches discussed in the last chapter—often adopt a personal "law and order" attitude in which obedience is all-important. If a rule or law says a certain action is right, that action is deemed **morally right;** if there's **no** rule or law against a certain action, that action is considered **not morally wrong.** The rules or laws accepted blindly and unquestioningly as the moral **norms** may be those, for instance, of one's family, friends, employer, society, or religion. (But blind and unquestioning obedience is not the same as free, intelligent obedience to **legitimate** teaching or authority.)

Teenagers and adults who operate from a "What's my absolute duty?" basis of morality rely on authority figures (parents, teachers, employers, gang leaders, and so forth—some legitimate and others not) to hand them the moral solutions. These individuals have trouble making wise moral decisions on their own. They easily go astray in moral matters when those in authority fail to provide the proper moral direction.

Thus, a teenager whose dad has racist attitudes might consider it wrong to make friends with kids of another race. A teenage boy might think it all right to use an illegal drug because his parents do, or a teenage girl might think it okay to smoke or drink alcohol as long as her mom doesn't strongly and clearly object.

The problem here isn't in obeying the proper rules and laws of legitimate authority—which is a morally good thing for everyone to do. The danger lies in **blindly** letting rules and laws—or the lack of them—automatically steer one's moral behavior. Rather, we must use our conscience to assess the moral legitimacy and correctness of the rules and laws we follow. And, where there are no applicable rules or laws, we must carefully consider what is right and what is not right.

Ironically, members who give unquestioning allegiance to anti-government militia groups are just as stuck in this underdeveloped moral mentality as those who blindly follow their friends' or boss's or government's orders. Both are absolutely convinced they're acting quite independently. In fact, they are being easily led and manipulated. Thus the insecure "rebel" may seek independence from strict rules at home, yet unquestioningly obey the even stricter ones of a street gang. And a young person from a family which lacks a moral structure may follow the gang blindly in the search for a sense of structure.

"Law and order" mentality individuals may not be making moral decisions for purely self-centered reasons, but they still haven't achieved internal independence. They haven't learned to use their heads wisely, nor to assume personal responsibility in making their own moral decisions. When such persons unquestioningly follow good rules, laws, and leaders, there is a degree of order and stability in the family, at school, and in society. But when they blindly follow the charismatic lead of a Hitler, horrors like the **Holocaust** result. The law-and-order mentality is common, but is not the ideal on which to base one's moral decisions—at least not according to Jesus, as we will see later.

norms
standards or principles of right action

legitimate
established according to the proper principles, standards, or procedures

Holocaust
the Nazis' killing of over six million Jews before and during World War II in a systematic attempt to exterminate all Jews

For discussion

1. What would happen if everyone in the world made moral decisions based solely on pleasing others? Why?

2. To what extent do you think teenagers and adults make moral decisions based on duty and law? Why?

3. Some researchers think most adults make moral decisions based above all on pleasing others or on following orders. Do you agree? Do you think this is true of most adults or teenagers? Explain and give examples to support your opinion.

What will get others to like or accept me?

For those with this moral attitude, right or wrong depends on what pleases or displeases others. If somebody else approves of a decision or action, then it must be right. If they disapprove, that makes it wrong. Because the person's sense of self-worth isn't solid enough, being liked or accepted by others is all-important. Peer pressure rules.

In late childhood and the early teen years, relying on peer pressure becomes especially pronounced. (Does "everyone else does it" sound vaguely familiar to you?) Teenagers often want to go along with the crowd in order to win peer approval. Indeed, we are all in some way affected by others' opinions of us and of our actions.

Sadly, however, many individuals never reach a healthy adult **autonomy**. Instead of basing decisions on merit and taking an independent stand, they base decisions on gaining others' approval. So the politician votes according to what will boost him in the opinion polls. The teenager acts according to what will make him or her popular. The mother who thinks her constantly crying infant or disobedient toddler doesn't love her may respond abusively.

Doing things to please others isn't always bad. In fact, a sincere reading of the gospel message tells us it can be the right motive for our actions if done as a free act of love. But when one person lives to please another, perhaps out of fear, surrendering her or his own identity in the process, that aim-to-please-at-all-costs attitude is extremely damaging. A sense of right and wrong is replaced by a need to be accepted.

autonomy
state of being independent and self-reliant

Journal entry

1. In your school experience, how did peer pressure begin shaping the way you made decisions?

2. Being honest with yourself, consider to what extent peer pressure affects your thinking and decisions now. Explain.

3. In what types of situations do you most tend to make moral decisions based on pleasing others?

Discuss

1. How strongly do you think teenagers are influenced by peer pressure? Why?

2. Give other examples in our society of how people make moral decisions based on what will win others' approval.

3. To what extent do you think teenagers make decisions—especially moral decisions—based on what will win others' approval?

What are society's standards?

This moral-decision-making attitude goes beyond law and order and beyond seeking others' approval to the generally agreed-upon norms and rights behind the laws. In this approach, right is what society guarantees and upholds—what everybody agrees to as standards of common conduct. This approach favors obeying laws that support these standards. Laws deemed "unconstitutional" and laws that clearly violate society's standards are viewed as wrong. Laws are no longer seen as norms in themselves; they can be changed for the greater common purpose.

Some ethics researchers contend that most adults never get beyond themselves or beyond laws to reach a moral attitude of genuine concern for society's overall welfare. For example: Do teenagers obey school rules out of respect for others' rights, or because they're afraid they'll get caught and punished if they break the rules, or because "rules are to be obeyed," or in order to please rather than upset their parents and school officials?

It's the principle of the thing

A higher level of moral attitude is based on universal ethical principles. Principles are not as concrete as rules and laws, yet good laws and rules are based on worthy principles. Principles are ideal values that are good in themselves. Individuals are morally right who follow their conscience by trying to determine how best to apply the principles in which they believe. Going against one's principles and one's conscience is wrong.

These universal ethical principles go beyond what is merely good for oneself or even for society. They deal with how all others would like to be treated as, for example, in the Golden Rule. They deal with the equality that everyone would like to have, with the dignity and the rights that every person should have—regardless of his or her society or status in it.

Principled individuals with this ethical attitude can set aside self-interests for the sake of the rights and the greater good of others. This moral attitude is similar to what Jesus taught his followers—we're all obliged to do what we can to bring about the greatest good for others. The truly moral person believes every individual has a unique dignity and certain rights that should never be violated. All persons are loved by God and are therefore worthy of everyone else's concern.

Great truths are felt before they are expressed.
PIERRE TEILHARD DE CHARDIN

For discussion

1. *How does basing moral decisions on society's standards go beyond basing them purely on self-interests?*

2. *Why does that ethics attitude not go far enough—what possible problems might basing moral decisions solely on this attitude lead to?*

3. *What are principles? What is meant by universal ethical principles?*

4. *Why are universal ethical principles important, and how should individuals use them in making moral decisions? Why should a Christian take this approach?*

She's mine

Studies show that about one out of every three high school and college students has experienced some type of violence—sexual, physical, verbal, or emotional—in their dating relationships. Read the following situation and respond to the questions.

Jeremy tells Amy often that he loves her. He gets pretty mad at her if she talks to other guys at school, but then he's just as sweet and loving as before. He tells her she's "his" woman. That Jeremy feels so strongly about her—that he seems to care so much about her—makes Amy feel loved, wanted, and important.

Jeremy even takes an interest in how Amy dresses, telling her what to wear to please him (which, of course, she does). When they go out, it's usually Jeremy who decides what they will do for the evening. Amy likes the manly way Jeremy takes charge.

Inside, Amy doesn't know what she'd do without Jeremy. Amy also thinks she's good for Jeremy. She knows he has a hot temper—he'll sometimes yell names at or threaten others with violence. While this sometimes makes Amy uneasy, she knows that she's a good influence on Jeremy because he's almost always loving and charming when he's with her.

For discussion

1. Based on what you know, would you classify Amy and Jeremy's relationship as mostly healthy or unhealthy? Why?
2. Violence can take many forms, from verbal violence to emotional violence to physical violence. How would you define "dating violence"? Do you see any signs of it in Jeremy and Amy's relationship? Explain.
3. Young men and women often misinterpret possessiveness, jealousy, control exploitation, and even physical abuse as signs of love—instead of as signs of abuse. Why do you think this is? Do you see any signs of this happening in Amy and Jeremy's relationship?
4. How does society show that it values control and power? How do you think this rubs off on what individuals think is proper behavior in a relationship?
5. What negative ideas about male-female roles do you think encourage unhealthy or even violent attitudes between the sexes?
6. Which of the ethics attitudes discussed previously do you think Jeremy has? Which do you think Amy has? Why do you think Jeremy and Amy do not seem to exhibit the other moral attitudes? Explain.

Social influences on conscience

How often do you adjust your plans because of the weather? Does a dreary day outside affect your mood and attitude? Our physical environment does affect us, and can make us feel comfortable, uneasy, or miserable. The people and the ideas that surround us affect us even more.

People used to routinely live with their doors unlocked. No more. Instead, security and self-defense devices have become multi-million dollar businesses. But why? What's gone haywire? Why is there so much child abuse and other violence in our society (where 60 percent of rape victims are teenagers)? Why must some schools use metal detectors and hire armed guards to protect their students? Why are you afraid to go alone to certain places or to not padlock your locker or alarm your car?

Religious beliefs and moral upbringing certainly have an ongoing influence on our conscience. But other factors influence it as well—and not always in the best ways. Especially key are the ideas of our society and culture, and the example and opinions of people around us. When these ideas, opinions, and examples correspond to what is truly right and good, they sharpen our conscience and strengthen our will to follow it. When they promote what is wrong, they can weaken our moral sensitivity and resolve.

Journal entry

1. List the social influences you think influence you most in positive ways.
2. List those you think affect you most in negative ways.

I am a part of all that I have met. . . .
ALFRED LORD TENNYSON, ULYSSES.

desensitized
made less sensitive or responsive to, or less aware of

How much we are the woods we wander in.
FROM "CEREMONY" BY RICHARD WILBUR.

Desensitizing conscience

Any surgeon whose career started with cutting up a human cadaver in medical school can tell you: At first it makes you cringe or get sick to your stomach. But the more you get used to it, the less it bothers you, until eventually it's no big deal. Common sense, human experience, and research all tell us that this is also true of moral matters—but in a harmful rather than beneficial way.

Individuals constantly exposed to immoral influences eventually, and to varying degrees, become morally **desensitized**. What their conscience once clearly perceived to be good or bad gradually becomes morally confusing, until they just don't feel that what's wrong is so wrong, or what's right is so right anymore. If this seems like "no big deal" to you, consider how you might feel if you were raped, mugged, robbed, or otherwise ripped off. Or think about the last time you were lied to, gossiped about, offended by somebody's rude attitude, or deliberately hurt by someone who didn't seem to give a darn how their behavior affected you.

Police can catch and jails can hold only so many criminals—and that is only after the harm has been done. We must all help create a moral climate that will encourage everyone to want to do right and avoid wrong—and for the best reasons. We will be strong enough to do that, though, only if we protect and develop our own conscience.

Project

1. Write a "weather report" of your school's moral "climate" that includes the following:
   - Sunny areas (ways in which kindness, respect, and other positive qualities and responses are encouraged)
   - Cloudy areas (ways in which negative attitudes and behavior are encouraged)
   - Stormy areas (the types of attitudes and behavior at your school that most trouble you)
   - Specific ways you can improve the "forecast" by helping to improve your school's moral climate
2. Share your weather report with the class. Work together to develop a project that will make a positive difference in your school's moral climate.

For discussion

1. *What do you think has gone haywire in our society, morally speaking? Why do you think this has occurred?*
2. *What social influences do you think exert the strongest influences on teenagers' consciences?*
3. *How would you describe a desensitized conscience? Give examples of the kind of behavior to which this leads.*
4. *What social influences do you think play a major role in helping to desensitize people's consciences? Explain.*
5. *Why is it important that we create a moral climate? What do you think this **moral climate** should include? Should not include?*

The mass media

Among the most powerful secular influences on morality are the various **mass media**—television and movies, music (lyrics), electronic games, newspapers and magazines, and the Internet with its wide variety of options and opinions. Consider, then, what Catholic teaching has to say about the power and potential of the mass media, and sensible guidelines for the use of the media.

Catholic teaching on instruments of social communication[2]

The mass media can be instruments that bring us closer to God.

If used properly, they can refresh and enlighten us, help nourish our human spirit, and uplift humanity. If abused, these instruments can harm society.

Everyone who uses them must apply the correct moral standards in doing so, keeping in mind both the *subject matter* and the *circumstances* that may affect the moral quality of what is being communicated:
— What is the message and what audience will it reach?
— Why is this message being communicated, and why is it being communicated in this way?
— Where, when, and how is the communication to occur?

Pertinent, too, is the characteristic way in which a given instrument achieves its effect. Its power may be so compelling that people, especially if they are caught off guard, may scarcely be able to appreciate it, to moderate it, or, when necessary, to reject it.
"DECREE ON THE INSTRUMENTS OF SOCIAL COMMUNICATION," NUMBER 4.

We all like to believe we're independent thinkers, but (as researchers have often confirmed) the truth is that we are all influenced in some way by what we encounter often. The kinds of foods we put into our bodies all the time eventually can clog our arteries and kill us, or can keep us strong and healthy. The same is true of what we put into our minds. The key is to be aware enough, wise enough, and in control enough that we let ourselves be influenced only for good.

Since the various media so powerfully influence individuals, societies, and the world, it's critical that we examine carefully how we allow or should allow them to affect our own moral **integrity** and the social moral standards that surround and influence all of us.

Activity

List five of your favorite TV shows, songs, video games, recreational Internet sites, and/or magazines. The next time you access these media, record your evaluations by answering these questions:

1. What is the surface message? What are the underlying messages? Who are these aimed at?

2. What would the people I admire most do in the situation, or how would they respond to what is being portrayed here?

3. Is my exposure to this making me a better person in some way? Explain briefly.

4. Is there anything that bothers me—or that probably should bother me here? Explain briefly.

5. How is this medium trying to influence me? What is it trying to get me to do?

Share your findings with the class.

We often rationalize that frequent exposure to negative moral values in media "won't hurt me because I'm strong enough to handle it." This is false. In reality, a steady diet of those things that manipulate people, distort truth, and assault moral sensibilities will harm us morally. Thus, it is important to use our power of critical thinking to assess how various media are attempting to manipulate us. We must choose what will reinforce our moral values and actively guard against desensitization of our conscience.

Project

Following your instructor's directions, use the worksheet you are given to record specific instances of how the media you encounter

- reinforce your moral values
- offend your moral sensibilities
- enlighten or uplift your spirit
- attempt to manipulate you
- communicate the truth responsibly, intelligently, fairly
- distort the truth or don't fairly present both sides of a situation or issue

Journal entry

1. List five ways you influence the moral climate around you.
2. List one way you would like to do this more positively.

What youth needs is a sense of significant being, a sense of reverence for the society to which we all belong.
ABRAHAM JOSHUA HESCHEL

It is also important to understand the many ways you influence the moral climate around you. People often are unaware of how much their opinions and actions affect others. It used to be that the media's influence was mainly a one-way street: The media spoke and people merely listened. Yes, you could write a letter to a network, a sponsor, a movie studio, and so on. But it wasn't as convenient to do as it now is with electronic mail, and your single opinion couldn't have had as wide an audience as it can have now in the Internet era.

Now you can post a message that is read by thousands of people around the globe. Ordinary people are finally able to have a say—and be listened to. Sometimes their contributions are refreshing and profound. At other times, what they say (or how) isn't intelligent or responsible. Sometimes it's rude, trashy, unreasonable, and wrong.

As you participate in the international Internet dialogue, keep in mind the impact you can have. Realize the power you have when you buy—or buy into—the various media. When the adults in one community protested that a cigarette manufacturer's billboard was encouraging young children to begin smoking, they were ignored. But when the children from a local school voiced their opposition to it, the billboard ad was taken down immediately.

Though you may feel that your opinions matter little in an adult world, don't underestimate the impact only you can have, and right now, precisely because of your youth. Make your clout count. Use it to better humanity, rather than to drag the human spirit down. As you do so, consider these suggestions for maintaining your moral integrity and for helping to raise social moral standards as well—

- Be aware of the moral qualities of the media available to you—especially those you use or encounter most.
- Use media that are good—that uplift the human spirit.
- Reject media that are dishonest, degrading, or dangerous—and communicate to others why you disapprove.

• Realize how powerfully your choices do affect what becomes popular and available for everyone.

• Take time periodically to think seriously and honestly about how the various media you use affect your attitudes, how you think and act, and how you respond to others: Is a given medium helping you become the kind of person you should be and really would like to be?

• Ask yourself: Given what he taught us, what would Jesus think of my exposure to this type of media?

For discussion

1. *How much influence do you think mass media have on people's moral standards?*

2. *Which particular type(s) of media in our society do you think most influence the moral standards of children? Of teenagers? Of adults?*

3. *Describe in your words the Catholic Church's general guidelines regarding mass media. Explain how you think these guidelines should be applied to these media:*
   - *television programs*
   - *the things others place on Internet websites*
   - *video and computer games*
   - *the way you use or would like to use the Internet*

4. *Explain the Catholic Church's statement about the way a mass media instrument achieves its effect. What specific media would you place in this category? (Give examples of those you've encountered personally and state your reaction to them.)*

5. *In what ways do you think people need to more critically assess how the media may be manipulating them? In what way do you think you need to do this more?*

6. *In what ways do you and other teenagers uniquely influence society and public opinion? Give examples of both the positive and negative ways teenagers do this.*

Advertising ethics

By the time children begin first grade, media researchers estimate that they have seen about 250,000 advertisements. By the time young people reach 18 years of age, they have seen at least 100,000 beer commercials. None of us can see and hear that much of anything without somehow being influenced by it! Indeed, ads so effectively get people to believe they can achieve status and popularity by owning the product that some children and teenagers have robbed and murdered just to get a highly advertised pair of shoes or starter jacket or another article of clothing.

Advertising can be a wonderful tool, linking businesses and manufacturers with consumers who truly can benefit from the products. Hardly any business could be successful without advertising. What needs critical examining, however, are the not-so-ethical means used in advertising, and the ways and reasons we let ads manipulate us.

The preaching about morals that we're exposed to most often today doesn't come from the pulpit, the Bible, or a religion book. It blares and glares at us in the ads we hear and see, ads where moral judgment is too frequently twisted or suspended for the sake of sales. The true manipulation is not of our wallets, but of our moral sense. As the billions of advertising dollars confirm, if these strategies to redirect one's moral sense didn't work, if they didn't influence people so much, advertisers wouldn't use them. The question is: Why are we buying it? The following exercise will give you a chance to assess this for yourself.

Discuss

1. **What dishonest, degrading, or dangerous media have you encountered? Explain why you consider them such.**

2. **Give examples of five specific media presentations you think Jesus would wholeheartedly approve of and five you think he would disapprove of. For each example, explain why.**

Do you buy it?

Read about the various advertising tactics, and then respond to the questions.

What seems too good to be true—is

One of the oldest unethical advertising scams is the now-unlawful "bait and switch" trick: You see a too-good-to-be-true deal advertised on a used car. When you go immediately to the dealer, you're told the car (which never did exist) has "just been sold," or that it's "really a piece of junk." Then you're shown "a much better deal for you over here" (at a higher price, of course).

Deception

The ad says "More hospitals use Product X than any other pain reliever." What the ad doesn't tell consumers is the real reason more hospitals use this product—the pharmaceutical manufacturer steeply discounts the product for hospitals so that more of them will buy that brand than any other brand and the manufacturer then can advertise that as fact. For consumers, however, other pain reliever brands may be equally or more effective—and much cheaper.

Faulty logic and forced choices

The ads ask you to leap to the false conclusion that because "Doctors prescribe the medicines in Brand Y more than all others" (which may be true), doctors therefore prescribe Brand Y itself more than the others (which may be false). The "medicines" Brand Y contains might be something, for example, like aspirin. The truth is, it's the ingredients available in many pain reliever brands, and not Brand Y alone, that doctors prescribe most often. Yet the ad implies that if you want the most medically approved product, this is your only choice.

Beware the fine print

A common advertising tactic is to put appealing information in bold print and restrictions and exclusions in fine print. As one lawyer puts it, "The insurance agent who sells you the policy sells you the bold print, and the adjuster you meet when you wreck your car and have a claim sells you the fine print: 'The bold print giveth, and the fine print taketh away.'"

Selling morals cheap

More importantly, in addition to inducing us to buy products, many ads "sell" moral attitudes by cleverly and deliberately appealing to and then trying to manipulate our sense of right and wrong. Thus, individuals buy what is actively promoted as good for everyone without considering whether it's right or wrong for them: An avalanche of credit card ads hooks college students into spending irresponsibly and graduating neck-deep in debt. Beer commercials make drinking appear to be a proof of manliness. In the recent past, fashion magazines had models adopt a "heroin addict" look—until storms of public criticism caused them to revoke the ad campaign.

The sexual sell

Advertisers generally agree among themselves that "sex sells." Ads encouraging various kinds of sexual attitudes and expressions are widely used to promote products, as in alluring jeans or cologne ads that seem to encourage promiscuous behavior. Consumers are gradually led to believe (perhaps subconsciously) that sexually expressing oneself openly is good—without reference to personal dignity and self-respect, religious values, a loving relationship, or a permanent commitment. Ads that show seductive models tied up in a way that suggests rape or sexual bondage invite men to believe (absurdly) that women desire to be sexually abused. Presented as acceptable in a commercial is a woman jokingly using an offhand sexist remark toward a man. Thus, in addition to the manufacturers' products, ads promote sexual attitudes and expressions—whether or not the values presented are moral.

For discussion

1. How much and in what ways do you think advertising influences teenagers? How do the ads you see and hear influence you?

2. Three of the most common themes used in advertising are sex, death, and religion. Why do you think this is so? From ads you've seen or heard, give examples of how each of these themes is used to sell a product.

3. Have you ever been the victim of a "bait and switch" ploy or a "too-good-to-be-true" bargain that wasn't a bargain? Have you ever had "fine-print regrets"? Have you ever believed an ad, bought a product, and later regretted your purchase? Explain.

4. What kinds of ads hook you the most? (Be honest.) Why? Are these ads selling something besides the products?

5. What ads have you seen or heard that feature a wholesome, positive attitude toward sexuality? That use sex in a degrading or other negative way, or that encourage undesirable attitudes or behavior? Explain.

6. To what extent do you think advertising helps shape social moral values? Explain.

7. Why do you think people buy into the values—or the lack of proper values—that advertisers promote along with the products? When you see or hear an ad, do you think about the message it is communicating about moral values? Explain.

Project

1. Write a description of, or bring to class, two examples of ads that use each of these techniques
   - deception, faulty logic, and/or forced choices to induce consumers to buy a product
   - attitudes about sex, religion, or death (or riskily defying it) to sell a product
2. Critically evaluate each ad's moral content, explaining what moral attitude(s) or behavior(s) it appeals to and/or encourages and whether you think the attitudes and behaviors are morally good or not.

culture
the ideas, customs, and so on, that a group passes along to subsequent generations

human moral consciousness
people's awareness of what is right and wrong

Every person is the creature of the age in which he or she lives; very few are able to raise themselves above the ideas of the times.
VOLTAIRE

anthropologists
scientists who study human characteristics and practices from humanity's origins to the present

Discuss

1. Do you agree with Voltaire's statement? Do you think it's true today?
2. Which persons do you think have elevated humanity's moral consciousness the most in recent times?

Culture and conscience

"Why isn't something that is considered all right in another **culture**," students often ask, "also considered right here? For example, some cultures don't frown on having sex outside of marriage, so why does ours? If no clothes are required at public beaches in some cultures, then why is ours so uptight about what people wear—or don't wear?" It's interesting, however, that, if other cultures have allowed head-hunting, cannibalism, and the stoning of those who engage in premarital sex, nobody usually asks why we don't!

Human moral consciousness has been developing over thousands of years. We might compare it to the individual's growth in moral consciousness from infancy to adulthood. In the first years of life, the child is concerned with basic physical needs—being fed, having diapers changed, and being physically comfortable. These physical needs are primary in infants' and toddlers' awareness. If they could express themselves in words and moral concepts, infants would say that right is having these needs met and wrong is not having them met—and they would be correct. In fact, it is wrong to neglect anyone's need for food, clothing, shelter, and basic physical comfort.

As the young child grows a bit older, he or she also grows aware of other needs—to be praised, accepted, and loved, for example. Right or wrong begins now to include how the child's own emotional needs are met. With age and experience, the child grows in sensitivity toward others, and begins to realize that unnecessarily hurting others is bad and helping others is good.

So it is with humanity as a whole. Early humans were concerned mainly with meeting basic physical needs. A simple criteria arose—it was right to provide food for one's clan and wrong to have it stolen by others. As human consciousness grew more sensitive to personal growth and relationships, humanity began to consider things like human rights in a moral context. This is, however, a relatively recent development in human history—and one not yet fully realized in our own society!

Even today, not all groups and cultures are at the same stage of moral awareness and sensitivity regarding human dignity, equality, and rights. Thus cultures have differing ideas of right and wrong. Lest we smugly consider ourselves advanced, a glance at the daily news (and some of our own less-than-noble tendencies) should tell us that we have quite a way to go. In fact, **anthropologists** tell us we actually are behind some "less civilized" cultures in certain areas of moral behavior. For instance, some "underdeveloped" cultures show greater respect and support for the elderly than does our youth- and productivity-oriented society.

The growth process involved in becoming morally sensitive can be difficult because we sometimes learn the hard way. But with an increased understanding of the wrongs to be avoided comes an increased awareness of what constitutes happiness and human fulfillment. For example, until recent times, women were considered the property of their fathers and then of their husbands. That lack of moral understanding kept many people from experiencing the fulfilling joys of loving family and spousal relationships. Once they have experienced freedom and meaningful relationships, some college students studying away from their home country refuse to return home for an arranged marriage.

An action that is meaningful in one culture can be meaningless in another culture. Harmless words and gestures in one society may be offensive in another. For example, if a friend bowed to you when coming into your home, you might think it strange. But, in some instances in Japan, to omit such a greeting is rude.

Most cultural differences are merely social, but some do involve views of what is or isn't morally acceptable behavior. While the fundamental moral norms underlying the Ten Commandments are generally shared throughout the world, other rules and guidelines can and do differ from one culture to another. Two examples: In some African cultures, having more than one wife is considered acceptable. Singapore punishes the recreational use of illegal drugs with death!

One of morality's main roles is to help society evaluate its flaws and limits in moral consciousness and continually reach beyond these. Morality, then, must help society criticize itself and better itself. It is by helping humanity become more fully human, as Jesus taught, that God's desire for all of us ultimately will be realized. Your role is to participate in this task intelligently and responsibly. Hopefully, what you are studying during this course will help you do that more courageously and wisely.

For discussion

1. *Why do certain cultures evaluate the rightness or wrongness of some actions differently?*

2. *Explain the development of human moral consciousness. How is this reflected in individuals' and cultures' differing moral perceptions?*

3. *What other factors influence why different cultures evaluate some actions differently?*

4. *What benefits does increased moral consciousness bring for individuals and societies?*

5. *Would you like to see morality play a more important role in our society's moral consciousness? Explain.*

Activity

Read one of the passages from Israel's prophets in which the prophet criticizes the society of his time. Then respond to these questions:

1. What was being criticized as wrong and/or held up as a better way here?

2. Whom do you think this prophet's message is addressing today?

Portraying "reality"

Read the following and respond to the questions.

Societies worldwide are concerned about the desensitizing effects the amount of gratuitous violence and sex portrayed in the media have on crime and unwanted pregnancy rates. People's attitudes and behavior are affected by what they see constantly. Exposure to too much violence and sexual promiscuity dulls moral perceptions of these problems, helping them appear attractive or at least acceptable, rather than wrong.

So it then seems okay to slap one's girlfriend around, punch one's boyfriend, or sleep around—because that's the way the daytime dramas portray "reality." There seems to be no risk in sex outside of a faithful marriage relationship. People get punched and kicked brutally and repeatedly—and then, unfazed, bounce back for more, when the real reality is that one blow or fall often maims or kills.

Those who are psychologically vulnerable and/or morally weak (and a great many people are) tend to transfer the misguided lessons they learn about morality from the media to their own lives. That, in turn, results in ruined futures, messed-up relationships, and even murder. (Whether justifiable or not, lawyers now claim "The media made me do it" as a defense for certain crimes.)

In recent surveys, most teenagers said they think there is too much violence on television. While some say the violence bothers them, others say it's only entertaining. Interestingly, most think there should be some kind of advisories notifying parents that a show has violent content. Teenagers add that they think toy and video-game manufacturers, along with movie and TV producers, are the least likely to want to remove violence.

Producers themselves have various views about the violence in the media. One said: "Make no mistake about it. Film companies are out to make money. And if it takes something gory, horrific, or shocking to make money, they don't care about morality." One of Hollywood's most famous movie directors thinks that merely suggesting violence is more effective than showing it close up. He says he prefers to suggest it, and then focus on someone's reaction to it. A young boy, however, responds, "It's not as interesting as when somebody gets shot and there's blood all over the place."

And there certainly is blood all over the place. Researchers find that the average child in our society watches thousands of murders and over 100,000 violent acts on television. About half of the television episodes that contain violence show no real harm or pain. In most instances, the violence appears to go unpunished, while in relatively few cases are long-term—or, in fact, any—negative consequences portrayed. One pay TV channel has even begun featuring "ultimate fighting" where two men fight no-holds-barred inside a cage. Although this program has been banned in many places, satellite transmissions make it possible for viewers to watch it anyway.

For discussion

1. Explain what is meant by media portrayals of violence and sex that are gratuitous. That are justifiable.

2. What is the difference between (1) violence and sexual promiscuity in reality and (2) how you've seen them portrayed on television?

3. How much influence do you think media portrayals of violence and sexuality have on people's consciences and behavior in our society? On teenagers' attitudes and behavior? Give examples.

4. Do you think there's too much violence and sex portrayed in the media? Give examples to support your opinion.

5. The chairwoman of a TV network popular with teenagers has said that network executives have the attitude that "you program only to boys because girls will watch anything." How do you react to her comment? Why?

6. What TV shows have you seen that portrayed violence or sexuality non-gratuitously and responsibly? That have contained violence without consequences or sex without responsibility?

7. How would the Catholic guidelines for sensibly using the media apply to this issue?

gratuitous
unnecessary, not called for, not justified

Using your head to make right decisions

[Jesus asked,] "And why do you not judge for yourselves what is right?"
— LUKE 12:57

Jesus taught us the importance of being responsible for our decisions. For Christians, this means that the role of conscience in moral decision making isn't a matter of intuition, hunches, or listening to little voices. While feelings are important to being human and should be considered, by themselves they are not an accurate guide in making moral decisions. Nor is the majority always right—what "everybody else" says or does is not always good.

The Catholic understanding of conscience is much more realistic: **Using our conscience means using our head**—using our ability to reason. It means considering the alternatives in light of the correct values and priorities—especially those Jesus taught, so that we are able to assess moral matters the way God judges them. Finally, it involves trying to do the most loving and least harmful thing in the situation.

Making conscientious judgments

No one else can or should make your moral decisions for you. You must make them freely according to **your own** conscience. But we must not use our freedom of conscience as an excuse or cover-up for just doing whatever we please. We're not free just to do our own thing. Our conscience must be well-informed. We must try to find out what is the best thing.

This means that you must reason to make what you think is the best judgment—**only after you have done all you can to determine carefully what is objectively the best decision in the situation.**

You wouldn't want to be operated on by a surgeon who wasn't well-trained in medicine, or who didn't know enough about your particular case. You wouldn't want to fly on a plane if the pilot didn't know how to operate that particular aircraft. Likewise, making correct moral decisions requires preparation and information.

The more important the matter involved, the more you need to take enough time beforehand to think, study, pray, and consult with others about the decision. For Catholics, this includes considering how we think Jesus would decide here, and understanding and applying the relevant Church teachings. If you make your decisions that way, then you act in good faith whenever you follow your conscience. As Catholic teaching tells us:

- When we act according to our conscience, we are living in good faith.

- We must form our conscience correctly, and then follow it.

- Catholics must base decisions of conscience on prayer, study, consultation, and an understanding of Church teachings.[3]

> "Clearly, then, it is necessary to do everything possible to see to it that judgments of conscience are informed and in accord with the moral order of which God is the creator. Common sense requires that conscientious people be open and humble, ready to learn from the experience and insights of others, willing to acknowledge prejudices and even change their judgments in light of better instruction. Above and beyond this, followers of Jesus will have a realistic approach to conscience which leads them to accept what He taught and judge things as He judges them."
> **NATIONAL CATECHECTICAL DIRECTORY, NUMBER 103.**

DANGER
PROCEED
WITH
CAUTION

Reflection
Do you think you are usually conscientious enough about making moral decisions?

Journal entry
How might you do an even better, more conscientious job of making moral decisions?

conscientious

thorough and careful about doing what is right

Catholic teaching tells us that to be a person of conscience, we must be **conscientious**. Rather than being closed-minded, we should learn from the insights and experiences of others. We should be honest enough to admit and change our mind when new information shows us we're on the wrong track. We should be willing to grow as God's Spirit of wisdom and love leads us.

Once we've conscientiously determined what we think is the best decision, we must act accordingly. To do this is to follow our well-informed and caring conscience—not merely a hunch, a feeling, an instinct, what everybody else might think, or some little voice inside. We must follow the truth as we see it, even if others disagree with us.

For discussion

1. How would you describe the Catholic understanding of conscience? Does this understanding of conscience make sense to you? Explain.

2. What things does making moral decisions in good faith require of everyone? For Catholics in particular?

3. What is the difference between (1) following your well-informed conscience freely and (2) using freedom of conscience as an excuse or cover-up for doing whatever you please?

4. What happens when people don't sufficiently inform their conscience before making major moral decisions? Give examples.

5. Is it ever wrong for a person to follow his or her conscience? Explain.

6. How would you want someone to prepare for making a major moral decision that directly and significantly affects you? Why?

7. What do you think it means to make conscientious judgments of conscience?

Conscience and religious freedom

Perhaps the most important of all our freedoms is religious freedom. Recognizing this, people have made extraordinary sacrifices—and continue to do so—just to be able to practice their religious beliefs freely. Some people mistakenly think, however, that belonging to an **organized religion** means your decisions are all determined in advance by religious laws. They misunderstand the nature of religion and the crucial difference between an organized religion and a cult.

Cults employ techniques that require blind, unthinking obedience from their members. They usually require that members cut off or strictly limit their contact with their families and former friends, warning that these people endanger their "salvation." A bland diet, sleep deprivation, extremely routine tasks, and an overwhelming bombardment of "loving" attention by group members adds to the numbing of a recruit's judgment. **Most** religions, on the other hand, recognize and support religious belief as a relationship with God to which one must **assent** freely. It must be admitted, however, that religious freedom has not always been a priority with religions and Churches. The Catholic Church today does urge religious freedom, as do most mainstream Christian Churches.

organized religion

a generally recognized Church group

cult

broadly, a religious group or sect; more narrowly, an extremist or fanatical religious group that seeks to control members' thoughts and behavior

In 1997, a small group in California came to the attention of the media; it had the usual hallmarks of a cult. Members of Heaven's Gate, who called themselves Christians, believed that it was better not to "trust in your own judgment" or to "use your own mind." Group leaders apparently enforced this prohibition with rules and techniques designed to eliminate members' feelings of autonomy. The cult's teachings, practices, and interpretations of Scripture did not truly support religious freedom. Its core beliefs also contradicted many things Catholics and most other mainstream Christian Churches believe about Jesus and his teachings.

Heaven's Gate members surrendered their freedom so completely to their earthly leader that they blindly and tragically chose to die with him. They remained convinced to the end that they were following the leader's dictates of their own free will. When their leader told them that the appearance of the Hale-Bopp comet was a supernatural sign, thirty-nine members of the cult believed him. They packed their bags and then, along with their leader, committed suicide. They anticipated that, as their leader had told them, after "shedding their earthly containers," they would be rescued and taken aboard a UFO.

It is not uncommon for naïve, vulnerable, and lonely people to be targeted by cults. These groups may be led by a sincere but perhaps psychologically unstable leader, or they may be deliberate frauds. Even within recognized religious groups, there may be small cults or cult-like groups. And some members of recognized Churches and religions expect their religious leaders to provide all life's answers for them; they create a cult-like situation for themselves.

Genuine religion, on the other hand, ought to promote and allow for religious freedom—the freedom to believe or to not believe, to follow or to not follow. Anything else violates the dignity God has given us as human beings who are to freely choose our relationship with God and our eternal destiny. You must never give up your sacred responsibility and freedom to decide—especially in religious matters. A genuine religious group will never ask that of you.

> *Foolish persons fail to learn from their mistakes. Smart individuals learn from their own mistakes. Wise persons learn from the mistakes of others!*
> **OLD SAYING**

For discussion

1. *What is a cult? How does it differ from a religion?*
2. *What does the Catholic Church teach concerning religious freedom?*
3. *How did Heaven's Gate approach religious freedom? Why do you think so many of its members went along with the suicide plan?*
4. *Why do you think cults are considered by most people to be dangerous?*
5. *Why do you think people become involved with a cult in the first place?*

Discuss

Cults use the Internet, as well as personal contacts, as recruiting tools.

1. **Have you ever come across a website or been approached by a person you think might be involved with a cult? How would you know if you had?**
2. **How do you think you would respond if you did encounter a cult on-line or elsewhere? Explain.**

Searching for truth

Being less than perfect, our conscience can be mistaken. We can be so strongly pulled toward what is wrong that we try to convince ourselves and others that it's right. Those accustomed to giving in to the pull toward what's wrong are even more likely to be misled in judgment. Our **biases** and prejudices can easily pull us in the wrong direction. We need to confront and correct these biases in ourselves so that we're not swayed or blinded by them. We also must not let other people interfere with our search for truth.

Catholic guidelines on searching for the truth[4]

We are to freely seek the truth.

- **How we do this should respect our dignity and interrelationships as human persons.**

- **We should use helpful teaching and talk matters over with others.**

- **We should help each other search for truth by explaining to one another the truth we think we've found.**

- **It should be by personal consent that we agree to and follow the truth we find.**

For discussion

1. How important do you think searching for the truth is—especially in moral matters? Why?

2. What kinds of things can lead people astray in their search for moral truth? Which of these do you think is most common? Explain and give examples.

3. Why do you think each of the Catholic guidelines for searching for the truth is important? Do these guidelines make sense to you?

4. Which of these guidelines do you usually follow? Which one(s) do you think you should probably follow more often than you do?

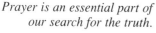

Prayer is an essential part of our search for the truth.

What if we make the wrong decision?

What if we make a decision based on our conscience and it turns out that we were mistaken? We are capable of human error. We have the responsibility to search out and understand the truth. **Catholics take seriously** our obligation to be guided in this search by the Church's teaching and by open communication with the Church's teachers. Certainly we all need to pray over our decisions as we make them.

Catholic teaching on the dignity of conscience[5]

- When we are faithful to our conscience, we join the rest of humanity in searching for the truth and for the best way to solve individual and social problems.

- The more correct our conscience is, the more we will reject choosing ignorantly and the more we will try to follow objective moral norms.

- Our judgments can be mistaken, especially when sin or strong desires keep us from seeing things clearly or lead us in the wrong direction.

- Despite the mistakes people make out of ignorance, conscience keeps its dignity.

- Individuals, however, violate their dignity by not caring about what is true and good, or by doing wrong so constantly that their conscience becomes almost blind.

objective moral norms
basic moral standards which exist apart from whether people perceive them or not

Even if we've tried our best to do the right thing, we might be **intellectually** wrong at times. What **we think** is best might not turn out, **objectively** speaking, to **be** the correct decision or the best one. But **subjectively** we will have made the right moral decision. If we follow our well-informed conscience, we will know that we have done what was for us, at the time and under the circumstances, the right thing to do.

For discussion

1. *What does the Catholic Church believe about the dignity of conscience and how to safeguard it? What does this teaching mean to you personally?*

2. *Without mentioning names, have you ever met (or been the victim of) someone whose conscience seemed almost blind? Explain.*

3. *In following your conscience, should you be willing to risk making mistakes? Explain.*

4. *Is following your conscience always the right thing to do? Can you ever go wrong by following your conscience? Explain.*

Be careful then how you live, not as unwise people but as wise. . . .
EPHESIANS 5:15

The moral decision-making process

Only, live your life in a manner worthy of the gospel of Christ. . . .

PHILIPPIANS 1:27

Making wise decisions, especially moral ones, is a process and skill that can be learned. As with most complex things, it is not learned all at once, but step by step. Certain important steps in the decision-making process are commonly used in one form or another by persons in government, medicine, law, and other businesses and professions. (In fact, they sometimes pay a lot of money just to be instructed in decision making.) Throughout the rest of this text, you will learn how you can apply these steps to help you make wise moral choices (and better decisions in general).

Beloved, do not believe every spirit, but test the spirits to see whether they are from God; for many false prophets have gone out into the world.

1 John: 4:1

Movement by movement, the best athletes analyze slow-motion replays of themselves practicing. They watch how well or poorly their efforts correspond to the ideals they admire and the goals they've set for themselves. This tells them what skills they need to focus on, reinforce, and improve. They also work diligently on the kinds of mental attitudes and thought processes which can help or hinder them from reaching their goals.

This is the same sort of thing you will be doing with decision making as you discuss the cases from here on in this text. Understand that learning how to solve problems and make decisions wisely is like the athlete's slow-motion analysis of a practice session—a process in which you focus on developing one skill at a time. Thus, each chapter will emphasize one or more of the decision-making steps. As you practice the steps in discussing the moral dilemma cases, resist the temptation to think you're spending too much time analyzing details. Your in-depth analyses will sharpen your conscience to help you make wiser, more correct moral judgments.

Here is an overview of the questions you will focus on in developing your moral decision making skills.

Steps to moral decision making

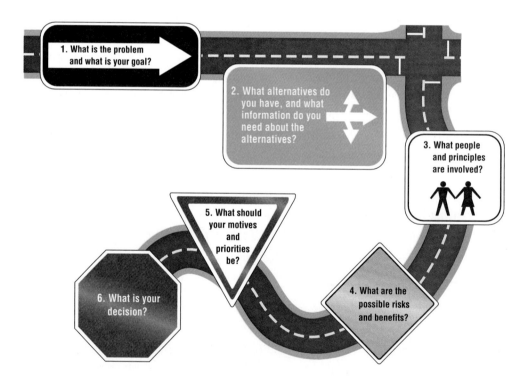

Step 1A: What's the real problem?

The first thing to do when you're faced with a major dilemma—especially a moral one—is to determine exactly what the problem is and what type of decision is called for. Sometimes this will be clearly spelled out; at other times, it won't be so simple.

It's amazing how people can jump to the (usually wrong) conclusion before they even know the problem! What is first thought to be the problem, is often only a symptom of a deeper, more complicated problem. When this happens, a business manager may mistake a temporary fix for a solution, only to be dismayed later that she hasn't solved the problem at all. Likewise, constant arguments about trivial matters can signal deeper problems with a personal relationship. It's no wonder people keep finding themselves right back where they started!

Surface solutions often only cover up major problems, which worsen until they become difficult or impossible to resolve satisfactorily. If a doctor hastily prescribes aspirin for a painful arm, the immediate problem—the pain—might temporarily ease. But if the pain is caused by serious injury or illness, the underlying problem may only get worse.

Whenever you're confronted with a moral or other serious dilemma, stop and think about what the **real** problem is. For instance, it might not be someone's mouth that always gets him or her into trouble. It might be the person's lack of self-discipline and self-control, or lack of self-esteem. Things aren't always what they first appear. But you can't solve a problem successfully if you can't even identify it correctly!

Even in your daily relationship difficulties, think more about what is really going on, rather than just reacting hastily. When your mom seems out of sorts for no reason, instead of just snapping back at her for her bad mood, you might ask her kindly if she's had a hard day at work. In fact, whenever you start to overreact or to quickly react emotionally, step back mentally and consider what's really eating you inside. Then address that issue head on, instead of taking it out on innocent bystanders.

You see, moral issues aren't just the life-threatening kind. Most of us constantly make much smaller moral decisions, decisions that nevertheless affect us and others for good or for ill. If you practice identifying the real problem in these instances, you'll also become much better at making wiser decisions when confronted with the big questions.

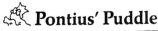 **Pontius' Puddle**

Faith healing and religious freedom

Our courts go to great lengths to protect our religious freedom. Thus they may permit certain activities otherwise considered improper or hateful. Sometimes individuals take advantage of this outlandishly, as when prison inmates file lawsuits saying their religion requires them to eat steak and beer dinners! In other cases, the behavior of certain individuals conflicts with civil laws when they sincerely follow their conscience and their religious beliefs. Then the issue of what to allow in the name of religious freedom becomes much stickier. Read the following true account and respond to the questions.

Sixteen-year-old Shannon, like her parents, believed in faith healing rather than in doctors. So when Shannon started feeling tired and thirsty, her parents didn't take her to the doctor to treat her diabetes. Instead they took their daughter to her grandfather, pastor of a church affiliated with a Christian sect that believes in healing with prayer and faith rather than medicine.

Shannon died three days later of a heart attack caused by her untreated diabetic condition. Authorities charged her parents with involuntary manslaughter and child endangerment. During the trial, the prosecutor told jurors how, "Even at the point of coma, this illness was treatable." A police officer testified how Shannon's grandfather, following the advice of the Bible verse, James 5:14–15, had anointed her with oil when she began feeling ill.

According to state law, parents must protect their children until the age of eighteen. The prosecutor said Shannon's parents were negligent for not providing her with medical treatment. He pointed out that Shannon had been to a dentist before and had seen a doctor in order to get her driver's license.

The parents' attorney, however, said they had tried to help their daughter as best they could without violating their religious beliefs. He said, if she had wanted to, Shannon was old enough to have gotten medical help herself.

Several years before, Shannon's eight-year-old brother had died from an ear infection that had gone medically untreated. In that instance, the parents had pled no contest *to manslaughter charges and been sentenced to probation and volunteer service at a hospital. The judge had hoped they would learn about the need for and effectiveness of medicine. Unfortunately, no hospital would accept their community service. There are now eight other children in Shannon's family.*

For discussion

1. In deciding whether to prosecute Shannon's parents for her death, what was the district attorney's surface problem? What were the underlying problems? The main problem?

2. For what, if anything, regarding Shannon, do you think the parents should have been prosecuted? Regarding her younger brother?

3. At the time, would you have agreed with the sentence given the parents in the younger brother's death? Do you think it turned out to be the best one?

4. What issues of subjective and objective morality are present in this case?

5. Legally speaking, should Shannon's parents have sought medical treatment for her? Morally speaking, from your religious viewpoint, should they have done so? From their religious viewpoint?

6. Do you think prosecuting Shannon's parents for her death violates her parents' religious freedom? Why or why not?

7. If you had been on the jury, what verdict would you have rendered in this case? Why? As the judge, what sentence would you have given the parents this time if they were convicted? Why?

Chapter 3 summary
Conscience

1. What is conscience?

- There are many different theories of conscience.
- The "hunch" theory is based on intuition.
- The "doing what comes naturally" theory is based on the belief that people will naturally do what is right.
- The "little voice" theory assumes that a higher (though difficult to define) force or power guides people's decisions.
- The "follow the crowd" theory believes moral decisions should be determined by majority opinions.
- The "follow-up feelings" theory is based on one's emotional reaction to a possible decision.
- The "no conscience" theory denies the existence of conscience and moral guilt.

2. The Christian understanding of conscience

- Catholic belief holds that conscience is the ability to reason to, and distinguish, truth and goodness from wrong or evil.
- Using your conscience is using your head to prayerfully determine the most loving thing to do.
- Conscience enlightens us and is the deepest, most sacred heart of ourselves.
- We are obliged to faithfully follow our properly formed and informed conscience.
- Catholic teaching upholds freedom of conscience—especially in religious matters.
- To develop our conscience correctly we must ask God's guidance, seek wise advice, increase our understanding and compassion, and reflect on Jesus and his teaching. Catholics must also understand and apply Church teaching.
- The rules of conscience tell us: Treat others as you'd want to be treated; respect and never damage another's conscience; never do evil to achieve good.

3. Ethics attitudes

- Some people view right and wrong in terms of earning rewards and avoiding punishments.

- The "me first" attitude results in decisions based on what feels good or bad to me.

- For those with the "it's the law" attitude, duty and law determine what is right.

- The "aim-to-please" attitude sees what is right as that which pleases others and wrong as that which displeases others.

- The "social standards" attitude determines right and wrong according to commonly accepted social standards.

- The "it's the principle of the thing" attitude is an understanding of right and wrong in terms of universal ethical principles such as the Golden Rule and, for Christians, other principles Jesus taught.

- Since God loves us all, we should believe in and protect every person's rights and dignity.

4. Social influences on conscience

- Social and cultural ideas affect individuals' consciences negatively or positively.

- Constant exposure to immoral influences can eventually desensitize one's conscience.

- To help create the proper moral climate in society, we must protect and develop our own conscience.

- The mass media exert a powerful and often damaging influence on people's moral sense.

- Catholic teaching urges us to use the media properly in order to uplift rather than harm the human spirit.

- We must assess honestly how our exposure to various media helps or harms us morally.

- We should do our part to positively influence the moral climate around us.

- We should do what we can to make sure that media tools such as advertising benefit rather than harm society.

- Human moral consciousness has developed, and continues to develop—leading to greater moral sensitivity and human fulfillment.

- Beyond the basic commandments, different cultures may evaluate differently the morality of certain actions.

- Morality should help society criticize and better itself in order to become more fully human as Jesus taught us.

5. Using your head to make right decisions

- Conscience means using our reasoning ability to try to assess moral matters as God judges them.

- Catholic belief obliges us to follow our properly informed conscience.

- Freedom of conscience is no excuse for doing whatever one pleases.

- The correct moral decision is the best judgment we can make, while attempting to be objectively right.

- Before making major moral decisions, we should think, pray, and consult with others. Catholics should also understand and apply Jesus' teachings and those of the Catholic Church.

- To live in good faith, we must form our conscience conscientiously and correctly and then act according to it.

- The Catholic Church, as do most religions, believes in religious freedom, the free assent to one's religious beliefs and relationship with God.

- Cults violate religious freedom by damaging individuals' ability to make moral decisions of their own free will.

- We should be allowed to seek the truth freely and prayerfully, in a way that respects human dignity and avoids desires and biases that can lead us astray.

- The more correct our conscience is, the more it will accurately perceive and follow objective moral norms.

- Even if our judgment is mistaken, our conscience keeps its dignity if we've sincerely tried our best to correctly form, inform, and follow it.

- Moral decision making is a process and learned skill whose first step is accurately assessing the real moral problem.

Key concepts

advertising ethics
autonomy
Christian understanding of conscience
common conscience theories
conscience, conscientious judgments
cults
culture and conscience
desensitized conscience
dignity of conscience

ethics attitudes
freedom of conscience
genuine religion
Golden Rule
growth in moral sensitivity
human moral consciousness
identifying the moral problem
informed conscience
integrity
intuition
mass media's influences on conscience

moral decision making process
norms
objective moral norms
peer pressure's influence on conscience
principles
rules of conscience
searching for truth
social influences on conscience

Blessed is anyone who endures temptation.
Such a one has stood the test and will receive the
crown of life that the Lord has promised
to those who love him.
James 1:12

"You shall love the Lord your God with
all your heart, and with all your soul, and
with all your strength, and with all your mind;
and your neighbor as yourself. . . . do this,
and you will live."
Luke 10:27–28

Chapter 4

Moral Convictions

Overview questions

1. What kind of morality did Jesus teach?
2. What guidelines did Jesus give for being happy?
3. Why is it important to know your goal before making moral decisions?
4. What does it really mean to be Christian?
5. What is fundamental in Catholic moral belief?

Prayer

God of our conscience and of creation,

There is too much coldness in the world: give us the heart to show more concern for others.

There is too much indifference to what is wrong: give us the nerve to get involved and help make it right.

There is so much damaging of our environment: give us the willingness to better care for our world.

There are so many assaults on the truth: give us the strength to defend what is true.

Give us the courage to act according to our moral convictions.

marginalized

on the edges of a society, out of the mainstream

Journal entry

Describe one way you can help "outsiders" at your school feel—and be—more included.

Jesus' approach

"I give you a new commandment, that you love one another. Just as I have loved you, you also should love one another."

JOHN 13:34

Active concern for others

Active concern for others is the morality Jesus preached and practiced. In our acts and decisions, according to Jesus, we must look out for each other. God cares about all of us. So we should also care about one other. In particular, Jesus preached that we should have special concern for the "underdogs"—the outcasts, the marginalized, those with special needs.

"Those who are well have no need of a physician, but those who are sick; I have come to call not the righteous but sinners."

Mark 2:17

Scripture activity

Read Mark 2:13–17, the full context of this Scripture passage.

1. To whom do you think these words are especially addressed today? Explain.
2. If Jesus were to say these things today, to what groups in our society do you think he would be speaking? To what groups in your school? Explain.

Reflection

1. Have you ever been judged unfairly at school, judged on the basis of those with whom you associate?
2. Have you ever judged others unfairly, on the basis of those with whom they associate?

Religion isn't just a matter of what we believe about God and how we worship God. It must also involve being a good person, and helping others—especially those in greatest need, as the apostle James wrote:

Religion that is pure and undefiled before God, the Father, is this: to care for orphans and widows in their distress, and to keep oneself unstained by the world.

James 1:27

Scripture insight

Read James 2:26.

1. What was the apostle saying here?
2. How does it apply to how we practice our religion today?

Activity

Develop a bumper sticker or T-shirt slogan that expresses your attitude about what it really means—and/or doesn't mean—to practice one's religion.

Right from the start, Jesus' ministry certainly involved this concern for those in need. In fact, according to Luke's Gospel, Jesus begins his ministry reading from the prophet Isaiah (Isaiah 61:1–22):

> *"The Spirit of the Lord is upon me,*
>   *because he has anointed me*
>   *to bring good news to the poor.*
> *He has sent me to proclaim release to the captives*
>   *and recovery of sight to the blind,*
>   *to let the oppressed go free,*
>   *to proclaim the year of the Lord's favor."*
> *Luke 4:18–19*

Discuss

1. How does this passage that Jesus quotes from Isaiah sum up why Jesus came and what he did during his earthly life?

2. How does it sum up what Jesus and his teaching are to mean for our lives today?

Jesus' message was far different from an arbitrary "anything goes" selfishness—which often hurts most of all those whom Jesus said we should help the most. Throughout the Gospels, Jesus lets us know that inner faith and convictions by themselves aren't enough. If we're really to call ourselves Christian, we must also be willing to walk in Jesus' footsteps.

For discussion

1. Explain in your words how the apostle James defines religion. How would you define it? Why?

2. What groups do you think are the most in need and the most marginalized in our society? At your school? Explain.

3. Why do you think some teenagers criticize one another for associating with those who are less popular or outside their circle of friends? Have you ever been criticized among your peers for this? What would Jesus have said about it? Explain.

4. How was Jesus' message different from the "anything goes" approach to morality?

5. What do you find hardest about practicing the kind of active concern for others that Jesus lived and preached? What do you find most meaningful? Explain.

. . . whoever says, "I abide in him," ought to walk just as he walked.
1 JOHN 2:6

Jesus' guidelines

The Beatitudes

We all want to be happy. This desire for happiness isn't just our bright idea. It comes from God and attracts us closer to God. This desire cannot be satisfied by money or fame or earthly accomplishments, which are temporary. This desire can be satisfied only by God, who is our eternal joy. Only God can completely satisfy our hearts.

To realize the ultimate joy God calls us to and freely promises to give us in communion with all those we love, we need to learn how to see and seek God in this life. We do this first of all, Jesus tells us, by changing our attitudes. For our happiness in life doesn't depend on what **happens** to us, but on how we **respond** to what happens to us.

> ### Discuss
> 1. When you wish to be happier, do you usually recognize this as God inviting you to draw closer?
> 2. Why can only God satisfy our heart's desire for happiness?

Many of Jesus' guidelines about right living are found in his Sermon on the Mount, his Last Supper discourse (see John's Gospel), his parables, and his reflections on his own moral choices. What we refer to as the "Sermon on the Mount" is a collection of Jesus' sayings about how to live a life that goes beyond the letter of the law. The discourse begins with the **Beatitudes** (Matthew 5:3–10).

The Beatitudes present the types of loving attitudes and actions Jesus says will give you hope in the middle of your troubles and bless you with true happiness—not only in the next life, but also in this one. As you study them, think about how this can be true for you.

"Blessed are the poor in spirit, for theirs is the kingdom of heaven." If you clear your life of attitudes and material possessions that keep you from hearing and living by God's word, then you will realize God's everlasting kingdom. That can be the only true fulfillment of your desire for happiness in life.

"Blessed are those who mourn, for they will be comforted." As you mourn, don't despair that you've lost someone forever. Find comfort in Jesus' promise that you will meet again in God's kingdom. Then, comforted, reach out your comforting hands, as Jesus reached out, to those who still suffer.

"Blessed are the meek, for they will inherit the earth." Don't seek power and fame, but rather seek to do good with your life. In a humble, gentle way, treat all persons and things with respect and care. Then, rather than dominating the earth, you will inherit it.

"I am the way, and the truth, and the life."
JOHN 14:6

. . . in seeking you, my God, I seek a happy life. . . .
ST. AUGUSTINE, CONFESSIONS.

Activity

Find two examples in the media which suggest to teenagers that wealth or fame is good in itself, is the most important thing in life, or is the criterion for measuring success and respect. Present and explain your examples to the class, evaluating their truth and impact in view of Jesus' Beatitudes.

"Blessed are those who hunger and thirst for righteousness, for they will be filled." To help right the world's wrongs, work for truth and justice; this must begin with individual efforts. Realize, though, that life's not always fair. When you're dealt an unfair outcome despite your best efforts, don't give up on trying in the future. Jesus didn't promise you'd be rewarded for achieving justice, but for desiring and doing your best to bring it about.

"Blessed are the merciful, for they will receive mercy." Show others mercy and forgiveness—without limit. Challenge your social groups and society itself to show mercy. Then you will be shown mercy.

"Blessed are the pure in heart, for they will see God." Respond to God in every person and situation. Don't prejudge and misjudge others. Give them the benefit of the doubt wherever reasonable, rather than automatically presuming the worst about them. Look for goodness in the people and ordinary events of your life. There you will encounter God.

"Blessed are the peacemakers, for they will be called children of God." Be the peacemaker and the problem-solver, rather than the one who stirs up the trouble. Seek to overcome what divides people, rather than creating or widening gulfs between them. Actively and firmly stand for peace—between individuals, among Churches, between nations. Consider it noble to be known for your efforts to bring people together, for we are all God's children.

"Blessed are those who are persecuted for righteousness' sake, for theirs is the kingdom of heaven." Jesus never sugar-coated his message. Instead of being honored for it, at times you will be looked down on, excluded, ridiculed, or insulted for doing what is right. But yours will be the self-respect, honest pride, and ultimate reward Jesus promised.

righteousness
longing for and working for truth and justice

justice
the principle, ideal, or virtue of just dealing or right action; giving God and others their due

Scripture activity
Look up Jesus' last discourse, John 14–17. What guidelines for living do you discover there?

To love another person is to see the face of God.
FROM THE DRAMA
LES MISERABLES.

Scripture activity
Read Luke 6:22–23 in which this Beatitude is further explained.
1. When do you think teenagers are most put down for doing the right thing?
2. What do you think is the best way to respond when you're in this situation?

For discussion

1. *What attitude does each Beatitude call for? How can each of these attitudes change the happiness we find in life now?*

2. *Which Beatitude is the most meaningful to you? Which one do you find the most difficult or challenging to live by? Explain.*

3. *How do Jesus' guidelines differ from following self-centered approaches like "anything goes" and "it's only natural"?*

4. *What do you think the world would be like if everyone actually followed the Beatitudes' guidelines?*

5. *What did Jesus promise us if we live by his moral guidelines?*

Step 1B: What is your goal?

> **1. What is the problem and what is your goal?**

Our ultimate goal as persons is the one Jesus highlighted in the Beatitudes: being united in love with God—and, in God, with others—forever and ever. It is the only goal that will bring us the completely fulfilling, lasting happiness we seek. In addition, knowing your goal is the first important step in resolving moral problems.

goal
aim, purpose, end

When facing a moral dilemma, along with assessing the real problem, you must focus on what your **main goal** should be. Businesses establish goals because they realize that you can't **get** where you want to go if you don't first **know** where you want to go! (You certainly can appreciate this if you've ever witnessed an annoying "**I** don't care, where do you want to go?" "**I** don't know, what do **you** want to do?" dialogue between two people who can't make up their minds.)

It's similarly important to know your main goal **before** you make a major decision—especially in moral matters. Sometimes, in complex situations, you might want to attain more than one goal. To avoid confusion, at least try to focus on one major goal at a time, and focus first on your most important goal.

objective
purpose, direction, aim

It also helps to list the intermediate steps that will lead you to a goal. Businesses often use "management by objectives" to help realize their goals. They identify a single, overall long-term goal, and then the more specific immediate objectives that will help them reach the goal. The key is that the short-term objectives must all be directed toward helping achieve the long-range goal. Otherwise the business will flounder.

Hospitals, for example, find that patients get well faster when nurses have both overall goals for the patients and clearly defined objectives for helping them achieve those overall goals. An overall goal might be that "Felipe Martinez will leave the hospital by Thursday well enough to continue healing on his own." On the patient's daily chart, however, Tuesday's objective might be much more detailed and specific: "We will bring Felipe Martinez's fever down to normal and relieve his gastric distress with a 20mg dose of medication X every four hours."

Clearly specifying the goal and objectives lets nurses know exactly how to help Felipe Martinez today. It also enables the nurses on different shifts to work together as a team. That makes the patient's treatment consistent and effective, so that the longer-term goal of discharging him from the hospital on Thursday is achieved.

If you've ever felt class time was wasted because a teacher kept wandering off the subject, you can readily understand why having teaching objectives or outcomes (as your teacher does for this class, by the way) is important. The more specific your teacher's objectives or outcomes, the more likely you are to learn the class material—and the less likely you are to think the class irrelevant and boring!

Be careful, though, because here's where shortsightedness can be a problem. If you concentrate on **only** immediate objectives, you can lose sight of your more important, though more distant, goals. Reaching for something desirable at hand can keep you from achieving your future goals. It's forgetting about the future when making a decision now that often causes people to bemoan later: "If only I had thought . . ." or "If only I had done. . . ," "If only I could go back and change things. . . ," "If only. . . ."

The emotions of the moment can blind us to important future considerations. So don't underestimate or brush aside this step in your problem solving and decision making. Identify and never lose sight of your primary goal. Then shape your immediate objectives accordingly. Otherwise, you might choose a short-term objective that seems desirable at first, but which, on further prayerful consideration of Christian principles and long-term consequences, is inconsistent with your real goals. So identify and keep your goal(s) in mind when solving any major problem.

St. Paul followed and advocated this advice in his own life, as his letters tell us. He always kept in mind his long-term goal of reaching the everlasting life and happiness Jesus promised his faithful followers. And Paul made it his daily objective to act in such a way that he would one day reach that goal:

I do it all for the sake of the gospel, so that I may share in its blessings.

1 Corinthians 9:23

I have fought the good fight, I have finished the race, I have kept the faith. From now on there is reserved for me the crown of righteousness, which the Lord, the righteous judge, will give me on that day, and not only to me but also to all who have longed for his appearing.

2 Timothy 4:7–8

They are to do good, to be rich in good works, generous, and ready to share, thus storing up for themselves the treasure of a good foundation for the future, so that they may take hold of the life that really is life.

1 Timothy 6:18–19

To achieve your ultimate goal in life, make it your daily objective to do good and to reject what is opposed to goodness. In whatever moral decisions you make, keep your eyes on the prize of "the life that really is life," and run so as to win it.

For discussion

1. *Why is establishing your goal important and one of the first things that you need to do in resolving moral dilemmas?*

2. *As discussed in this section, what is the difference—in decision making—between your goal and your objectives? Why must your goals and your objectives work together?*

3. *Why is it important to not concentrate on only immediate objectives?*

4. *What was Paul's long-term goal in life? What daily objective helped Paul reach that goal? What should be every Christian's long-term goal in life?*

> *Do you not know that in a race the runners all compete, but only one receives the prize? Run in such a way that you may win it.*
> **1 Corinthians 9:24**

Reflection
What is your ultimate goal in life?

Journal entry
Write down today's objective(s) that will help you reach your main goal in life.

"What if we're in love . . . ?"

Read the following case and respond to the questions.

Jeff and Kristin have been dating only each other for the past five months. Feeling very much in love, they've begun talking about getting married in the future. On their dates, they spend more and more time "making out" and many times have felt like "going all the way," but up to now they haven't. They don't talk to each other about it, but the desire to make love is constantly uppermost in their minds. Neither has ever had sexual intercourse with anyone before.

Kristin is very confused. She knows Jeff really loves her and hopes he will marry her someday. She's been taught to wait until she gets married to have sex—one of the most special experiences two people can share. Her parents, her Church, and her school say sexual intercourse properly belongs in the loving, committed, lifelong relationship of marriage. Kristin agrees about the specialness of marriage, but she has never felt this deeply about anyone before. "Why is it wrong to make love if two people love each other as much as Jeff and I do?" she sometimes wonders.

Kristin thinks having sex would be beautiful, but the idea also scares her. How would she feel if she broke up with Jeff after having had sex with him? If that happened, how would she feel about him and about herself? If her future husband is someone else, how will he feel about her if she's already had sex before—with Jeff?

A friend of Kristin's was terribly hurt after breaking up with a guy she'd been intimate with. Kristin doesn't want that kind of hurt. She knows it will be hard enough if she and Jeff ever break up; having sex would only make it worse. The hurt would be mixed with guilt and regret.

Sometimes Kristin feels left out when another young woman hints around about how fantastic an experience it was for her. Kristin feels like she may be missing out on an experience of being a complete woman. Besides, some young men and women think it's no big deal—that it's only natural, especially for two people in love. It seems so acceptable in movies and on television for unmarried adults to have sex. "Why isn't it for teenagers?" Kristin wonders.

Meanwhile, Jeff is going through a similar experience. Sex with Kristin is very much on his mind, but he also is scared.

He hasn't had sex before—what if he'd be clumsy and awkward or unable to please Kristin? A few of his friends say they've had sex, though some may have just made up stories to impress or fit in with the other guys. Whenever they ask about him and Kristin, he makes a joke or a knowing remark—insinuating that they have had sex, without actually saying so.

Jeff realizes some people presume that because he and Kristin are so close and have been going together for so long, they have had sex. But he is more preoccupied with the fact that they haven't had sex than he is about what other people think. He wonders what the experience would be like and sometimes feels he isn't as much of a man as some of the other guys.

At times Jeff feels guilty about wanting to make love to Kristin, since she is a virgin—at least she's told him she is, and he's pretty sure he can believe her. Part of him wants to wait, as the Church teaches, until he marries. But his body, some of his friends, and (it seems) the rest of society keep telling him it's only natural to have sex—especially for guys, especially when they're in love. So Jeff presumes it will be only a matter of time, and if Kristin wants to make love, as he senses she does, he figures he can hardly refuse.

For discussion

1. What is Jeff and Kristin's primary problem? What do you think Kristin's main goal should be in making her decision? What do you think Jeff's should be? Explain. ➡

2. What expectations do Jeff and Kristin have? What do you think the odds are they will marry?

3. Why are they afraid to talk to each other about their fears and concerns? What does this tell you about their relationship?

4. If a couple breaks up after having had sex, how do you think the young woman feels? Why? How do you think the young man feels? Why? Do you think most young men feel the same as most young women in this situation? Why?

5. Kristin is concerned about how someone she might marry or consider marrying will react if he finds out she has had sex with someone else. How do you think another young man would feel and react? How do you think a young woman would feel and react in the same situation? Why?

6. Why do parents, teachers, and others tell teenagers to avoid premarital sex? Why does the Church oppose it?

7. Is Kristin's concern about feeling left out and not a complete woman common among teenage girls who haven't had sex? **Should** they feel this way? Explain.

8. Is there a double standard in society regarding teenagers having sex vs. unmarried adults having sex? Explain.

9. Is having sex a proof of one's love? Explain.

10. Kristin feels she might lose Jeff if he asks her to make love and she refuses. Would someone break up with the person he or she truly loves because that person refuses to have sex before marriage? Would you? Explain.

11. Who do you think tends more to cover up their lack of sexual experience and/or exaggerate their sexual conquests—teenage men or teenage women? Explain.

12. What social factors seem to be influencing Kristin and Jeff?

13. Is Jeff's feeling of not being manly common among young men? Does a teenager's sexual experience make him more of a man? Explain.

14. What decision would Kristin and Jeff make according to each of these perceptions of conscience? Why?
    - Basing decisions on "hunches"
    - Doing what's "only natural"
    - Listening to a "little voice"
    - "Following the crowd"
    - Acting according to "follow-up feelings"
    - Believing that there is "no conscience"
    - Using one's head to follow a well-formed and sufficiently-informed conscience based on Christian principles

15. If prayer and reflecting on Jesus' ideals and teachings were a part of Kristin and Jeff's decision-making process, what things would this help them consider more wisely and carefully? What decisions do you think it would help each of them reach? Why?

16. Which decision would best help Kristin reach her main goal? Which decision would best help Jeff to achieve his main goal? How would the alternative decision(s) not help them do this? Explain.

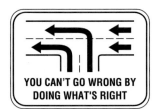

YOU CAN'T GO WRONG BY DOING WHAT'S RIGHT

Being Christian

"What's the difference between being Christian, and just being a good person?" students often ask. If you want to know the real hallmark of the Christian approach to morality, here it is: Following Jesus' example, make the extra effort to be kind—not just to those you like, but to those who've hurt you and those you don't like at all. It's usually a lot easier to be kind to and want to help those who are nice to us. As Jesus taught and showed us, however, those who need our love and assistance most are those who seem unloving and unable to love.

"[God] makes his sun rise on the evil and on the good, and sends rain on the righteous and on the unrighteous. . . . Be perfect, therefore, as your heavenly Father is perfect."

Matthew 5:45, 48

Jesus didn't ask his followers to sign a contract based on legal do's and don'ts. He invited them, as he invites us, to be his **disciples**. In doing so, he offers us a challenge that calls for our wholehearted response. He has assured us that the sacrifice this entails won't go unrewarded. Jesus asks of us our best—and promises us life!

disciples
those who are willing to learn

Following Jesus' example can take us out of the security of our comfortable environment when we respond to the needs of others.

Scripture insights

Read these Scripture passages, and explain what each says about being Jesus' disciple. Apply each passage to what being Christian means today.

- Matthew 19:16–21
- Mark 10:28–31
- Mark 10:42–45
- John 8:31–32
- Mark 8:34
- John 13:34–35

"Do not be afraid, little flock,
*   for it is your Father's good pleasure to give you the kingdom.*
Sell your possessions, and give alms.
Make purses for yourselves that do not wear out, an unfailing treasure in heaven,
*   where no thief comes near and no moth destroys.*
For where your treasure is, there your heart will be also."

Luke 12:32–34

Jesus' parable **of the good Samaritan** is perhaps the story that best sums up Jesus' teaching. In his day, the priests and Levites were the established religious authorities who prepared and conducted ritual worship. For Jesus' listeners, the priests and Levites stood for the exact and faithful observance of religious laws. This, to them, was the way to holiness. Jesus' parable, however, presented a new way to look at what God wants of us. As it did for people then, the story challenges us today to re-think our attitudes, values, and actions.

parable
a short, simple story which teaches a moral lesson

The parable of the good Samaritan

Just then a lawyer stood up to test Jesus. "Teacher," he said, "what must I do to inherit eternal life?" He said to him, "What is written in the law? What do you read there?" He answered, "You shall love the Lord your God with all your heart, and with all your soul, and with all your strength, and with all your mind; and your neighbor as yourself." And he said to him, "You have given the right answer; do this, and you will live."

But wanting to justify himself, he asked Jesus, "And who is my neighbor?" Jesus replied, "A man was going down from Jerusalem to Jericho, and fell into the hands of robbers, who stripped him, beat him, and went away, leaving him half dead. Now by chance a priest was going down that road; and when he saw him, he passed by on the other side. So likewise a Levite, when he came to the place and saw him, passed by on the other side.

"But a Samaritan while traveling came near him; and when he saw him, he was moved with pity. He went to him and bandaged his wounds, having poured oil and wine on them. Then he put him on his own animal, brought him to an inn, and took care of him. The next day he took out two denarii, gave them to the innkeeper, and said, 'Take care of him; and when I come back, I will repay you whatever more you spend.' Which of these three, do you think, was a neighbor to the man who fell into the hands of the robbers?" He said, "The one who showed him mercy." Jesus said to him, "Go and do likewise."

Luke 10:25–37

Scripture activity

1. Find and read in the Christian Scriptures two instances where Jesus went out of his way to help someone.
2. In each case, what did Jesus' example show us about how we are to help others today?

Journal entry

1. What aspect of Jesus' moral teaching do you find the hardest or most challenging to follow? Why?
2. In what caring ways would you like to reach out more to others?

Reflection

1. When you've felt among the lowest and least, how have others been good Samaritans to you?
2. How do you feel when someone you don't like sincerely tries to help you?
3. How often do you go out of your way to help someone you don't like?

> *"Truly I tell you, just as you did it to one of the least of these who are members of my family, you did it to me."*
> MATTHEW 25:40

People often think a "good Samaritan" is simply someone who helps another. There's more to Jesus' story, however. In Jesus' day, the Samaritans were despised by most Jews because of intermarriage with non-Jews and for complex religious and political reasons. So if Jesus had made the injured man in the story a Samaritan, it would have been startling enough if someone had stopped to help him. But to say that a Samaritan was the one who stopped to help—and after a priest and a Levite had passed by—must have been really hard for Jesus' audience to swallow. Even more amazing, beyond just getting emergency help for the injured stranger, Jesus said that the Samaritan continued to look after the man's care.

In this good Samaritan story, Jesus leads us step by step into new realms for making decisions and being real disciples. His message to us is simple, clear, and challenging: **"Go and do likewise."**

Reflection

1. Who would be considered the "least" of Jesus' family members in our society?
2. If you were in the situation of the least ones, how would you want someone to be a good Samaritan to you?
3. How can you be a good Samaritan to these persons?

Project good Samaritan

1. Without naming names, identify the groups at your school or in your local community who are considered among the "least," seem the most left out, or who otherwise need a helping hand.
2. Draw up a plan for one practical way you can be a good Samaritan for these persons.
3. Carry out your plan, and report back to the class on your efforts.

For discussion

1. *How would you explain what a disciple is? What do you think it means to be a disciple of Jesus today?*
2. *In the good Samaritan parable, why do you think Jesus chose to say both a priest and a Levite passed by without helping the injured man? What message does this have for us?*
3. *Why do you think Jesus chose the Samaritan as the one who went out of his way to help? What does that say to you about being a good Samaritan?*
4. *Who do you think are the passersby and the true good Samaritans in our society? In your school?*
5. *What other examples of Jesus' approach to morality stand out most in your mind and memory?*

Wayne's way

Read the following true account and respond to the questions.

Wayne was a fun-loving, practical joke-player—until his close friend suddenly died. Wayne found himself at a loss to try to make sense of what had happened. He began to think about his own life, and about what really matters. He turned to his Christian faith for answers and found a new direction in life. As Wayne's wife told friends, he then began to live each day as if it were his last.

From that point on, Wayne became more loving and caring. He decided that he would try to help people in whatever ways he could. He focused especially on donating his money, time, and skills to assist people who were helpless and poor. For example, he donated carpeting to local churches and hired unemployed skilled workers to lay it. If a poor family needed something, Wayne would figure out a way to get it for them. And, according to his friends, Wayne's help was always "unconditional, with no strings attached."

While driving in a rainstorm one day, Wayne noticed two young women stranded by car trouble along the roadside. He stopped to help. As he was working on the car, Wayne was struck and killed by a lightning bolt.

As the minister at Wayne's church described it, instead of looking for the pot of gold at the end of the rainbow, Wayne had seen life itself as the rainbow of God's promise that touched people's lives everyday. So the following week on Wayne's birthday, when his family gathered, they celebrated his life and the motto by which Wayne had tried to live: "You can't outgive God."

For discussion

1. How did Wayne become a true disciple of Jesus?
2. Would you describe Wayne as the kind of good Samaritan Jesus talked about? Explain.
3. What do you think Wayne's goal in life was? What did his motto in life mean?
4. Where did Wayne find his real wealth? What treasures did he leave behind?
5. What do you think Wayne found at the end of his life's rainbow? What do you hope to find at the end of yours? Explain.
6. What incident challenged Wayne to re-think his attitudes, values, and actions? What incidents have caused you to re-think yours?
7. Have you ever thought about living each day as if it were your last? How might this affect how you live and relate to people?

Reflection

If you had known beforehand that yesterday would be the last day of your earthly life—
1. Would you have changed anything?
2. Without changing what you did, what would you have changed about *how* you did things?

Journal entry

Write one way you will try to live the rest of this day better, keeping in mind your ultimate goal in life.

Bear one another's burdens, and in this way you will fulfill the law of Christ.
GALATIANS 6:2

compassion
"feeling strongly with"; concern for others and sensitivity and understanding toward them in their difficulties

Getting involved

It's understandable that we sometimes feel overwhelmed by all the world's problems. It's tempting to get tired of trying and to give in to what some call "**compassion** fatigue"—to just give up, shrug our shoulders and say, "It's no use." Instead, Jesus' good Samaritan parable tells us we've got to get involved and stay involved. For the only possible way things can change for the better is if enough individuals speak out and do something.

As an old woman was walking along the beach collecting seashells, she spotted in the distance a young man jogging in her direction. Every so often, she noticed, he would stop, pick up something from the shore, and throw it back into the surf.

When the young man approached near enough, the woman called to him, "What are you tossing into the water?"

"Starfish," he called back, somewhat out of breath.

"Why?" she queried as he jogged nearer.

"Otherwise they'll die," he replied.

"But why bother?" the woman asked cynically as the young man stopped to bend down and pick up a stranded starfish lying near her feet. "You can't save 'em all. Besides what difference does it make? There are millions more starfish in the sea," she said as he tossed the one in his hand back into the water.

"It made a difference to that one," the young man said, smiling, and then jogged on.

Businessman Oskar Schindler certainly made a difference. When he realized that Hitler's Nazis were systematically exterminating Jews and certain other groups in his homeland, Schindler could have reacted like many others and done nothing. He could have concluded that, no matter what he did, the killings would continue. Instead, his conscience wouldn't let him just ignore the situation. So he used his business to employ—and thus to keep alive—over a thousand people who otherwise would have perished in concentration camps.

On the other hand, when two passengers noticed cracks on the airplane they were boarding, they said nothing. While in flight, the jetliner's fuselage ripped open because of those same cracks, and two other passengers were killed. Sometimes speaking up requires nothing more than alerting others to what is going on, and then letting them take it from there. (Certainly that plane's pilots and flight attendants wouldn't have allowed the plane to fly if they had known about the cracked fuselage!) At other times, speaking out can be costly. Whistleblowers have been reprimanded, demoted, or fired for bringing to light situations and practices that can harm people.

One government official said she grew accustomed to rationalizing or looking the other way at safety violations and hazards that were occurring in airlines overseen by her agency. Then one day she suffered a life-threatening medical emergency while at her desk. That caused her to reassess her priorities, to think about what really matters most in life, and to begin doing the right thing. Since then she has been using her knowledge and expertise to point out serious airline safety problems to government leaders and the public. As a result, changes are continuing to be made that make flying safer for all of us.

> *To sin by silence when one should protest makes cowards of people.*
> **ABRAHAM LINCOLN, ADAPTED.**

> *I am only one. But still, I am one. I cannot do everything, but I can still do something. And because I cannot do everything, I will not refuse to do the something that I can do.*
> **EDWARD EVERETT HALE**

Activity

Search the daily news for examples of individuals whose actions made a positive difference for good, and/or whose failure to act resulted in harm. Analyze why you think they acted or didn't act, and present your assessment to the class.

Why do we keep quiet when we really should speak up? There are many reasons We may lack self-confidence and may fear being embarrassed. We might be in a hurry and not want to take the time. We may presume nobody will listen, or that our contribution won't matter and nothing will change anyway: "It won't make any difference."

Well, it **does** make a difference—to God, to our own personal integrity, and to those we help or inspire to lean toward goodness by having the care and courage to do the right thing. Making a positive difference, however small—that is also part of what being Christian means. We might not be able to solve an entire problem single-handedly, but even individually we can always make some kind of a difference for the better. And if we join with others who feel as we do, together we can have an even greater impact for good.

Activity

Write a poem or song about the "power of one" in making a positive difference.

For discussion

1. *Do you ever feel "compassion fatigue"—a sense of being overwhelmed by all the world's problems? Explain.*

2. *What meaning do the starfish, Schindler, and airplane stories have for you?*

3. *Why do you think some people speak up about something that seems wrong? Why do you think others keep quiet?*

4. *There is a saying in Jewish wisdom that the world is kept from being destroyed because of the goodness of thirty-six people—who don't know who they are. What insight about morality do you find here?*

The hazing of Michael

Read the following true account and respond to the questions. When you have finished, your instructor will tell you the case outcome.

Michael, a college student, was invited by a fraternity to enter its pledge-week program in order to become a full member of the fraternity. Fraternity members conducted the initiation activities.

During the week's initiation, according to court documents, fraternity members subjected Michael and the other four pledges to "repeated physical abuse, including repeated, open-hand strikes to the back of the neck, the chest, and the back, caning of the bare soles of the feet and buttocks, blows to the back with a heavy book and a cookie sheet while on hands and knees, various kicks and punches to the body and 'body slamming,' an activity in which an active member of the fraternity lifted a pledge in the air and dropped him to the ground."

Two of the pledges dropped out of the initiation program during the week's hazing, but Michael remained in it. While being put through a "seven-station circle of physical abuse," Michael passed out and remained unconscious. One of the fraternity members directed some of the others to put Michael to bed and to check on him all during that night. Throughout the night, this member kept calling them to see if Michael was all right. He later said that he would have taken Michael to the hospital if he had thought the situation was that serious.

Michael never regained consciousness and died the next afternoon. The autopsy showed that he had suffered "broken ribs, a lacerated kidney, a lacerated liver, and bruises over his upper body," and had died from an injury to the brain—possibly due to the body-slamming activity.

Afterward, the fraternity members involved explained that no one meant to hurt Michael. They just didn't think anything bad would happen. One of them admitted that everybody involved knew the hazing activities were wrong—that's why they did them secretly. He maintained that Michael wouldn't have had to pledge in order to belong to the fraternity and that it was Michael's own choice to do so.

The county prosecutor filed charges against several of the fraternity members, those who had conducted the hazing and carried out the physical abuse. In general, the young men didn't challenge the details of what had happened, but just repeated that they hadn't meant to harm anyone. But "once that happens, you can't turn back the clock," one of the attorneys for Michael's family remarked. Michael's mother says she wishes somebody would teach kids in high school how dangerous this kind of activity is.

For discussion

1. What do you think of the activities in the pledge-week hazing? What do the activities say about the students involved? About their respect for themselves and for others?

2. Why do you think the pledges and fraternity members were so willing to become involved in the initiation?

3. Why do you think nobody got help for Michael? What would you have probably done in the same situation?

4. Why do you think fraternity members participated in the hazing activities, even though they knew it was wrong?

5. What do you think the members' ethical attitudes were in this case? Why?

6. Do you think criminal charges should have been filed against the fraternity members involved, even though they didn't mean for anyone to get hurt?

7. Have you ever learned the hard way that you "can't turn back the clock"? Explain.

8. What activities do teenagers you know participate in that you think are risky and dangerous?

9. What lessons have you learned from the hazing of Michael?

10. Do you think the fraternity members should reassess their goal and objectives regarding the welcoming of new members? What would you suggest?

➡

Pulling together

Just before they risked their lives by signing the Declaration of Independence, Benjamin Franklin remarked to John Hancock: "We must indeed all hang together, or, most assuredly, we shall all hang separately." That statement still accurately describes the human condition. If we don't all learn to pull together in human solidarity, we will lose our beautiful world—to pollution, violence, biological or nuclear war or accidents, or other forms of human selfishness, greed, and intolerance.

It's so easy to get lost in the crowd, in a sea of people where no one seems to care. As Catholic teaching tells us, it's up to us to be the good Samaritans:

Being good Samaritans[1]

- We are to be everyone's neighbor.
- We should actively help everyone we meet who is in need—an elderly person who is lonely, a stranger who feels out of place, a foreigner who feels lost, those who are poor and hungry...
- Human solidarity is the way to peace and human development.
- We have to depend on, instead of trying to dominate, one another socially, economically, politically, or militarily.
- Instead of distrusting each other, we must try to work together.
- If we achieve justice, solidarity, and human unity, we will eliminate violence and bring peace among us.
- As Christians, we must learn to give, forgive, and reconcile totally. We must respect others' rights and equality, and view everyone as a living image of God, worthy of our love and sacrifice.

Society is **us.** So when we get upset at news about the awful things people do to one another, we should look in the mirror. We need to examine how we contribute in small ways to the problems that become socially significant when everyone thinks and behaves similarly. We should especially assess how our failing to speak up against things that are wrong helps allow those things to continue.

For discussion

1. *Describe the kind of neighbor you would like next door. Describe an unneighborly neighbor. Which kinds of neighbors have you and your family experienced?*

2. *What does it mean to you to say that you're to be everyone's neighbor? What is your response to this?*

3. *What is human solidarity? Why is it so important today? What dimensions does Christian solidarity add?*

4. *What evidence of increasing divisions do you see today among nations, in our society, and at your school? Of increasing togetherness in each instance?*

5. *What do you think are the main obstacles to togetherness in the world? In our society? At your school?*

6. *How is it more possible today than ever before for us to be everyone's neighbor? What special obligations does this create on our part?*

7. *In order to achieve solidarity, what sacrifices should people be willing to make in this country? In your local community? In your school? Explain.*

Project

At some high schools, younger students are subjected to initiation activities that range from positive, helpful, and fun to fearful, abusive, and dangerous.

Draw up a plan which includes the main goal and objectives you think older students at your school should have in welcoming new students. Be able to defend the values and ethical attitudes your plan reflects.

solidarity
unity with a group, usually based on common interests, objectives, and standards

The only thing necessary for the triumph of evil is for good people to do nothing.
EDMUND BURKE, ADAPTED.

Project pulling together

1. List the main sources and causes of tension and division among the students at your school.
2. List the main obstacles to achieving greater solidarity at your school.
3. Draft a plan that includes two practical ways to lessen the tensions and divisions and help students pull together.
4. Carry out your plan, and report back to the class on its success.

The stealing spree nobody stopped

Shoplifting costs businesses millions of dollars a year. It's not the stores that pay for the crime, however; it's the consumer. Stores build into their prices the cost of theft, and it's the customer who pays the higher price at the checkout counter. Either consumers don't realize this, or they don't mind getting ripped off—as the following true account seems to indicate. Read it and then respond to the questions.

For three hours, a trio of teenagers stuffed their jacket pockets full of several hundred dollars worth of candy, perfume, and other merchandise at a local store, while about fifty customers watched and did nothing about it. When their pockets were full, the teenagers went out and emptied them, and then came back in for more.

Chris, Scott, and Gayle continued their "stealing spree" in full view of other customers, but no one reported them to store personnel. One customer gave them a dirty look, but the other bystanders either walked away or looked in the other direction—even those who were standing right next to one of the teenagers said and did nothing.

The teenagers, one of whom worked part-time at the store, later told their teacher they were astounded at people's lack of willingness to get involved. Their shoplifting spree had been a class experiment, conducted with the permission of the teacher and the store manager.

For discussion

1. Whom do shoplifters really steal from? Are you willing to pay higher prices so that they can do this? Explain.

2. Why do you think most people would just stand by and do nothing if they witness someone shoplifting?

3. Do you think a similar experiment would produce the same response in your local area? Explain.

4. What would you do or not do about it—and why—
   • If you saw someone shoplifting at a local store?
   • If you saw an adult you knew shoplifting at a local store?
   • If you saw a student from your school shoplifting?
   • If you saw a friend shoplifting?
   • If you saw a student stealing from another student's purse, locker, or unlocked car?

5. What kind of environment does the failure of people to get involved help create for you? Why?

6. If others saw someone stealing something that belonged to you, what would you want them to do about it? Why?

7. What underlying problems or causes do you think lead individuals to shoplift? Explain.

8. What things do you think teenagers most often steal from others? Why do they do so? With what "ethics attitude" do you think they do this?

Project

1. Assess the main problem involving stealing at your school or by students at your school.

2. Develop a campaign around the goal of helping to change students' attitudes to view this behavior as wrong.

Caring for our world

When viewed from outer space, our Earth is incredibly beautiful, yet so small amid the cosmos. How very fragile and vulnerable it seems! As our population on "Spaceship Earth" grows, we are using up more and more of the natural resources that support us. We are increasingly jeopardizing our Earth's environment.

Our wildlife is becoming extinct—we lose another animal species every twenty minutes. Our **biosphere**'s air is polluted, and the rain forests essential to our atmosphere are disappearing. Soil nutrients are being depleted. Drinkable water and places to safely dump our garbage are running short. Although humanity has been exploring outer space for only a short time, we've already cluttered it with debris that might endanger future space missions—not to mention space itself!

God has created Earth's resources for all humanity—including the generations that will follow us. We don't own the earth or the universe; we are simply the caretakers of God's creation. Thus we have a moral responsibility, as Catholic teaching reminds us, to use our resources in ways that benefit and sustain everyone fairly and enable us to pass these resources on to future generations.

biosphere
the essential life-supporting atmosphere surrounding Earth

Scripture activity

Read the Genesis creation accounts (Genesis 1:1–2:4 and Genesis 2:5–23) and 1 Corinthians 4:2. What do these passages tell you about the kind of caretakers we are to be of the world God has given us?

Project

On the Internet and/or in your library, find information about one or more of the following and present it to the class:

• Reasons why animal species are becoming extinct
• Practical ways to conserve water and energy
• Practical ways to stop air pollution
• How to minimize and properly dispose of waste products
• Practical ways you can recycle the things you use

Spirit is the power of all of us pulling together.

Journal Entry

Describe your personal ecological ethic.

Being caretakers "calls us to use the gifts of God's creation for the benefit of all and raises basic questions of equity, fairness, and justice."²

ecological

having to do with the relationship between living beings and their environment

adhered

held fast, observed loyally

Science can do a lot to help resolve some of the **ecological** problems that threaten Earth's future; however, unless each of us does our part, what science does won't be enough. We must develop an *ecological ethic*. We have to insist to our government officials that strict anti-pollution laws be passed—and **adhered** to. We need to pressure companies to stop wasteful packaging that is much larger than needed for the product. We must also cooperate individually—for instance, by not wasting water or tossing soda cans out the car window, by not buying products from manufacturers who dump hazardous chemicals into the environment, by disposing of our own household and automotive garbage properly, and by recycling whatever we can.

Reflection

For which natural resources are you the most grateful to God?

Activity

1. Describe the kind of ecological ethic you think should be adopted today.
2. Explain what putting your new ecological ethic into practice would involve—including the attitudes that would have to change.

Project

1. Develop five main points you think our society's ecological ethic should include.
2. In order to put your new ecological ethic into practice, briefly describe
   • what moral decisions would be necessary
   • what moral attitudes people would have to change
   • what moral actions would have to be taken

Journal entry

1. How do you most often help in caring for our Earth and its environment?
2. In what two ways do you most often fail to do this?
3. What one thing are you willing to do to become a better caretaker of our environment?

For discussion

1. *What moral problems does caring for the environment involve? What questions of fairness and justice does it raise?*
2. *Why should you and your generation care about what happens to future ones?*
3. *What's the difference between saying we own our world's natural resources, and believing we are caretakers who hold them in trust? How does each attitude affect individuals' behavior regarding the environment?*
4. *What kind of ecological ethic is exhibited by persons who have each of the faulty moral approaches discussed in the last chapter? What are the negative results?*
5. *What was humanity's ecological ethic in the past? Why is a new ecological ethic needed?*
6. *In what ways do you think teenagers most often fail to take good care of our Earth and the environment? Most often help in this effort?*
7. *What does caring for God's gift of creation mean to you? Give practical examples.*

The graffiti proposal

Read the following true account and respond to the questions.

It costs over $10 million a year to clean up the graffiti in this country, most of which is created by teenagers or young adults. In an effort to help decrease graffiti, officials in one state have proposed an anti-graffiti law. If passed, the law would take away the driving privilege for one year of anyone convicted of defacing public property. Those not old enough to obtain a driver's license would have their right to drive postponed a year.

Some attorneys have argued that this solution is unsuitable. They say it would be purely punitive, rather than helping to teach these young people greater responsibility for their environment. Officials, however, think the law would be a good deterrent. They say they can't sentence the offenders to clean up the graffiti because of hazards related to the chemicals that would have to be used.

For discussion

1. What is the main problem facing society here?

2. What do you think the main goal should be in solving this problem? Why?

3. How might the proposed graffiti law help achieve this goal? Why might it not help accomplish this?

4. What other possible ways can you think of that might solve the problem and achieve the desired goal?

5. Why do you think individuals deface others' property with graffiti?

6. If someone were caught defacing something that belonged to you, how would you feel about it? What would you want done about it? Explain.

7. What do you think would be the best way to solve the problem in a way that accomplishes good and meets the desired goal here? Explain.

Being a Catholic Christian

"When it comes to morality, what difference, if any, does being a Catholic Christian make?" students ask. Catholics believe that we each are and must be free to make moral decisions according to our own conscience. As we have seen already, Catholic teaching emphasizes that belief. But as pointed out in the last chapter (and as we will discuss more later), this does **not** amount to "anything goes" or doing "whatever I **feel** is right." Catholic teaching holds that some moral norms and values are absolute—they must never be ignored or violated. This understanding of moral norms and values is also held by many other people today.

Realistically, though, we must often make decisions in fuzzier areas that absolutes don't cover. Yet the moral rules we follow must apply to these real-life situations. That's why Jesus also gave us ideals to strive for, and **principles** and **guidelines** to use in our moral decision making. Jesus did reaffirm the need to observe the Ten Commandments, and on several occasions he summed up all moral laws this way:

"'You shall love the Lord your God with all your heart, and with all your soul, and with all your mind.'
This is the greatest and first commandment.
And a second is like it: 'You shall love your neighbor as yourself.'
On these two commandments hang all the law and the prophets."
Matthew 22:37–40

Unfortunately, some people distort what Jesus taught. Irresponsible televangelists, for instance, have been known to take advantage of people's vulnerabilities in order to obtain money from them, and fraudulent "faith healers" have promised easy miracles. It's important that you have confidence in your religion and its moral teaching. For Christians, this means belonging to a Church whose teaching is in keeping with what Jesus taught. Our confidence is strengthened by scholarly research and historical records which show how carefully and faithfully the Church community has tried to preserve and pass down Jesus' teaching through the centuries.

Admittedly, Catholics haven't always understood or fully followed Jesus' teaching. There will always be—as in the Church of the apostles' day—heated discussions over how best to interpret and apply what Jesus taught for our time. That is often how God's Spirit helps us grow spiritually as individuals and as a Church community. But we can certainly trace the Church's fundamental, unchanging moral teaching back to Jesus, and that is crucial. For it is **his** religious and moral principles which are to guide our decisions and actions.

absolute
definite, not conditional

ideal
standard, ultimate aim

Responding to the truth

Regarding the truths of our Christian faith, we have a most serious **obligation** to

- understand, proclaim faithfully, and defend actively the truth we have received from Jesus

- never do this in ways that are not **compatible** with the spirit of Jesus' gospel message[3]

obligation
duty, responsibility, commitment

compatible
agreeing or in accord with, harmonious

For discussion

1. *How would you describe a Christian approach to morality?*

2. *What do you find most valuable in this approach?*

3. *Do you think most people correctly understand Catholic belief about morality and moral decision making? Do you think all Catholics understand and follow it? Explain.*

4. *Why is it important that you can trust and believe in your religious faith and its moral teaching?*

5. *What must be the touchstone for all Christian (and Christians') moral views and behavior? What obligations do Christians have regarding how we respond to the truths Jesus taught?*

6. *What moral matters have you heard Catholics disagree about? Does it bother you to hear heated discussions among Catholics over how best to interpret and apply Jesus' teaching for our time? Why?*

7. *What do you like most about Jesus' moral teaching? What aspects of it do you find hardest to practice? Explain.*

touchstone
the standard, test, or reference point by which to measure or judge something's true nature or quality

Moral Convictions

1. Jesus' approach

- Jesus preached and practiced active concern for others, especially for the marginalized and the less fortunate.
- In addition to interior faith and worship, religion must involve being a good person and helping others.
- Jesus challenged and challenges his followers to be disciples by living as he lived.

2. Jesus' guidelines

- Jesus gave us principles, guidelines, and ideals for decision making.
- The Beatitudes contain Jesus' guidelines on the loving attitudes and actions that will help us achieve our ultimate happiness—union with God and, in God, with others.
- Identifying your main goal and the intermediate objectives consistent with reaching that goal are important steps in resolving moral problems.
- To achieve our ultimate goal in life, we must daily do good and reject evil.

3. Being Christian

- The hallmark of Christian morality is loving everyone, as Jesus did—including persons we may dislike or who have hurt us.
- Jesus' invitation to be his disciples is both challenging and rewarding.
- Jesus' parable of the good Samaritan illustrates what it really means to love our neighbor.

4. Getting involved

- Rather than letting problems overwhelm us, we must get involved and do something about them.
- Sometimes we choose to not get involved when we should—for many reasons; thus we allow harm to occur or continue.
- We can make a positive difference, especially when we join with others in human solidarity to solve problems, and this is part of what being Christian means.
- We need to examine how we contribute to our society's problems when we don't speak out and when we don't work to solve the problems.
- Caring for the world God has given us and seeing that its resources are properly shared and preserved is also our moral responsibility.

5. Being a Catholic Christian

- Catholic Christian morality recognizes the importance of freedom and of moral values and norms such as the Ten Commandments.
- It also realizes that we must rely on Jesus' ideals, principles, and guidelines in moral dilemma situations not covered by moral absolutes.
- Christian teaching must always be in keeping with what Jesus taught.

- Catholics trace our Church's fundamental, unchanging moral teaching back to Jesus, whose principles must guide our decisions and actions.
- We have a most serious obligation to proclaim faithfully and defend actively the truth we have received from Jesus in ways that are compatible with the gospel's spirit.

Key concepts

absolute moral norms and values
active concern for others
Beatitudes
being caretakers of God's creation
being Christian
disciple
ecological ethic
establishing objectives
getting involved
goal setting
Jesus' ideals, principles, guidelines
justice

loving one's neighbor,
making a positive difference
marginalized
parable of the good Samaritan
peacemakers
poor in spirit
pure in heart
responding to the truth
righteousness
Sermon on the Mount
solidarity

"'You shall love the Lord your God with all
your heart, and with all your soul,
and with all your mind.'
This is the greatest and first commandment.
And a second is like it:
'You shall love your neighbor as yourself.'
On these two commandments hang all
the law and the prophets."
Matthew 22:37–40

"I am giving you these commands so that you
may love one another."
John 15:17

Chapter 5

The Path to Love and Freedom

Overview questions

1. What is the natural law? How does it affect moral decision making?

2. What is the meaning of the Ten Commandments historically and for us today?

3. What further dimensions did Jesus add to guide human conduct?

Prayer

*Loving God,
    May our love be genuine.*

*May we hate what is evil,
    and hold on tight to
    what is good.*

*Help us love and respect
    one another.*

*Boost our spirits so we
    don't grow lazy about
    trying to do good.*

*Make our hearts happy,
    but help us endure
    suffering patiently.*

*Help us not give up in
    trying to draw close
    to you.*

*May we be generous in
    tending to others' needs
    and being kind to
    strangers.*

*Expand our hearts to bless
    and not curse those who
    would wish us harm.*

*Give us the empathy to
    share others' joy, and the
    compassion to feel their
    sorrow.*

*Give us an understanding
    heart.*

*Help us to be humble, not
    arrogant or snobbish.*

*May we not act like we're
    better than we are.*

*Teach us how to live in
    true harmony with one
    another.*

BASED ON ROMANS 12:9–16.

God's law of love in our hearts

. . . I will put my laws in their minds,
    and write them on their hearts,
and I will be their God,
    and they shall be my people.

HEBREWS 8:10

What tells our conscience right from wrong?

What do you do in a situation when you get the feeling that something just isn't right—especially when somebody is trying to convince you that it is? We've already seen that our feelings aren't always an accurate guide to what's right or wrong. And we know that outside influences might not be correct either. So how **do** you sort things out when you're confused about whether to do something or not? How can your conscience figure out what's right or wrong in **that** situation?

Conscience relies on God's law written in our heart, leading us to love good and avoid evil. We find our human dignity in obeying this built-in natural moral law, our God-given ability to understand right from wrong. As mentioned before in the discussion of conscience, most people recognize (even if they don't always practice it) that being honest, just, and kind is desirable and good. Even if no one had ever told us, hopefully we'd understand that murdering, stealing, and being unkind and unfair are wrong.

It's this natural moral law which draws us toward God by enabling us to recognize instinctively that goodness is a good thing and evil is a bad thing. Natural law is the understanding God has given us to distinguish **in general** between good and evil, to know right from wrong.

Belief in the natural moral law, as pointed out previously, is **not** the same as believing in instincts that automatically tell us the specific right or wrong thing to do in every situation. Natural law doesn't give us a roadmap to the right decisions in complex dilemmas. But it is our compass. It shows us the way. It helps us know in general whether we're at least headed in the right moral direction. It's what signals our conscience that something does or doesn't seem right.

Clarify

1. What is the natural moral law and what does it enable you to do?
2. What is the difference between the natural moral law and acting according to instinct, hunches, following one's feelings, or just "doing what comes naturally"?

In fact, this universal and unchanging natural moral law and its basic principles actually form the basis for all other human rules of conduct, whether in schools, families, businesses, or our civil laws. The U.S. Declaration of Independence, for instance, clearly acknowledges this when it says "We hold these truths to be self-evident"— that all persons are "endowed by their Creator with certain **unalienable** rights."

unalienable, inalienable

may not be taken away or given away

Thus, civil authority recognizes this fundamental law in our hearts which comes from God, and further recognizes that, precisely **because** it comes from God, people or government can never take it away. **The natural moral law applies to everyone, everywhere, always.** As Catholic teaching points out and history confirms, even when oppressive societies try to suppress this natural moral law, it can't be removed from the human heart. It will always rise again.

Because this natural moral law is universal, it provides us all with the basis for building human community. From there, we must use our heads to figure out how to best do this in practice. When we become close to someone, we both just know the unwritten rules of friendship without being told. We know we should be able to trust each other. But one person might have to tell the other that a particular personal matter isn't to be shared with others.

Athletes know that they should not try to poke their opponent's eye out. But because less obvious maneuvers can cause injurious accidents, players must learn that these maneuvers constitute fouls and will be penalized.

Not everybody perceives the natural moral law's principles clearly or right away. This is especially true when feelings, hunches, direct pressure from others, or other social and cultural influences try to out-shout conscience's voice of reason. It is also true that recognizing the natural moral law's principles in general can be much easier than applying them in specific circumstances. It's usually a lot easier to say "I believe in human dignity and equality" than it is to decide whether voting for a particular law or school policy is a good way to support these principles.

Think it over first

So what do you do in a situation when you feel like something just isn't right, but somebody is pressuring you to think that it is? **Stop and think.** Take the time to use your head, your conscience, to reason things out. The rest of this course will show you sound ways to do this—and give you plenty of real-life situations with which to practice!

Whether in business, personal, or other matters—especially serious ones, don't make hasty decisions. If necessary, tell others, "I need more time to think things over first." You don't have to be apologetic about it or think up a good excuse. It's not only your duty as a human being to think before you act, it's your right to have a reasonable amount of time to inform your conscience before deciding.

When you absolutely must make an immediate decision, quickly ask God's help. Focus inwardly for an instant on what reason tells you makes sense and is the right thing to do. Then you'll be a lot more likely to make the correct decision, and a lot less likely to make a big mistake.

For discussion

1. *In what types of situations do you think teenagers feel pressured to do something that just doesn't seem right?*

2. *What do you usually do when you feel that something might not be morally right? Do you usually stop and think things over enough before you act? Explain.*

3. *Why do you think teenagers sometimes pressure each other into doing morally questionable things? In what situations is this most common?*

> *The natural law is nothing other than the light of understanding placed in us by God; through it we know what we must do and what we must avoid. God has given this light or law at the creation.*
> **THOMAS AQUINAS**

Clarify

1. How is natural moral law related to civil laws?
2. Why does this law help form the basis of human community?

Think before you act.

> *Do not fear,*
> *for I have*
> *redeemed you;*
> *I have called you by*
> *name, you are mine.*
> *When you pass*
> *through the waters,*
> *I will be with you;*
> *and through the rivers,*
> *they shall not*
> *overwhelm you;*
> *when you walk through*
> *fire you shall not*
> *be burned,*
> *and the flame shall not*
> *consume you.*
> *For I am the LORD*
> *your God,*
> *the Holy One of*
> *Israel, your*
> *Savior.*
> *ISAIAH 43:1–3*

Ten Commandments

a list of ten basic moral laws found in the Hebrew Scriptures of the Bible

4. *Why do you think people so often don't think things through enough before they act? What harm might be prevented if people did think things through? If teenagers in particular did this?*

5. *What's the best way to let someone know you need more time to make a decision? Do you think teenagers are too apologetic about doing this? Are you? Explain.*

God's law of love in Scripture

We believe that God is Truth. Therefore, if we know any aspect of the truth, we know more of God. Particularly important to our lives are the truths God has shown us through *divine revelation*—

- **the Bible** (especially Jesus' life and teaching) and

- **Tradition** (the teachings of the early apostles who were chosen to transmit Jesus' message to the world)

Thus, out of faith, we as Catholics are first of all to fully entrust our entire selves to God, submit our intellect and will to God and the truths God has revealed, and obey God freely by living according to these truths.[1]

If you obey the commandments of the LORD your God . . . by loving the LORD your God, walking in his ways, and observing his commandments . . . then you shall live. . . , and the LORD your God will bless you. . . .

Deuteronomy 30:16

Even after several thousand years, humanity still acknowledges as valid the moral norms spelled out in the **Ten Commandments**. Nevertheless, students ask: "Are the Ten Commandments still relevant? Maybe these laws were good for people back then, but aren't they outmoded now?" Others misapply the commandments' meaning by quoting the Bible out of context. They arbitrarily turn biblical passages into arguments for or against certain stances on moral issues. So let's look at the environment in which these moral norms developed, what they meant for people then, and how and why they apply to us today.

The **Hebrew Scriptures** record God's word to us through the early ethical and religious development of the Jewish people in the period up to Jesus' time. (The Old Testament in the Christian Bible contains the Hebrew Scriptures and a few other books.) The Bible's first book, Genesis, relates that as the human population increased, "the earth was filled with violence" (see Genesis 6:11). Genesis tells, probably pretty accurately, how people carried things way too far in attempting to seek justice for crimes against themselves. With no police force—historians tell us—vengeance was common and brutal back then. A person who gave someone a black eye might have his ear cut off, for instance. That wasn't just **retaliation**, it was all-out **revenge**—going beyond "getting even."

Hebrew Scriptures
the Bible of the Jewish people; most of the books that comprise the Old Testament of the Christian Bible

retaliation
returning like for like, that is, causing the same kind of injury that was inflicted on oneself

revenge
damaging, injuring, or punishing the offender in return for an injury done to oneself

Discuss

How would you compare justice in ancient times to that of the "wild West" days in our history? To our society's approaches to justice today? Explain.

Israelite law addressed this problem of no-holds-barred revenge by saying, for example, that you were not to hang someone for calling you names or spraining your wrist: "Anyone who maims another shall suffer the same injury in return: fracture for fracture, eye for eye, tooth for tooth; the injury inflicted is the injury to be suffered." (Leviticus 24:19–20) In those ancient days, "eye for an eye" retaliation—and no more—certainly was a moral step forward!

Discuss

1. Why was retaliatory justice a step forward in ancient times?
2. How common do you think retaliation and revenge seeking are among teenagers today? Why? Have you ever seen someone start a fight after being called a name?
3. Do you think people today are getting so fed up with crime that we are inching backward toward retaliation? Explain.
4. What law enforcement attitudes and practices in our society do you think are more advanced than "eye for an eye" retaliation? Less advanced? Explain.
5. Have you ever been in a discussion with someone who quoted Bible passages out of context—especially from the Old Testament—and used these to support their opinions about a contemporary moral issue? Give examples and explain.

Scripture insight

Read Genesis 21:22–27 for a better sense of what this law meant in its original context. Summarize the incident and explain its significance.

The ancient writers told us why some laws became necessary, but left unmentioned the actual reasons for others, such as dietary regulations. The ancient **Hebrews** simply said the laws came from God—a customary way of saying that these restrictions were right and good.

Common sense tells us, though, that dietary regulations like those in the Book of Numbers probably originated to protect people's health at the time. Pork, for instance, was likely taboo because it spoiled quickly in the desert heat and caused sickness even when fresh (undercooked pork carried bacteria). It was just safer to ban all eating of pork. Animals that had fallen dead on their own were not to be eaten because they were probably diseased. Many Jews still eat no pork and observe more or less strict dietary laws.

Hebrews
the Jewish people's early ancestors, who later became known as the *Israelites*

Let's look next at the Ten Commandments and how people understood them at the time they originated (probably about 1250 years B.C.E.). Then we'll consider some reasons why the Ten Commandments are still meaningful and relevant.

The Ten Commandments

The Commandments can be divided into two groups—those that deal with our relationship with God and those that deal with our relationships with one another. Together the two groups form a whole, since truly loving God means we must love others, and in loving others we love and honor God. So violating any single commandment will influence our relationship with both God and others.

While the Bible calls other regulations "the law of Moses," it attributes the Ten Commandments directly and uniquely to God—the real point of the account described in the Book of Exodus. Perhaps, as Scripture scholars suggest, the formulating of these commandments resulted from the Israelites' developing moral consciousness under Moses' leadership and God's guidance. In any case, the Israelites realized that, unlike their social and dietary restrictions, these commandments were fundamental norms for all human conduct.

Isn't it rather odd that we need over 50,000 laws just to try to enforce the Ten Commandments?

The Israelites concluded correctly that these laws must have originated, not with people, but with God. It was after the Israelites' escape to freedom from Egyptian slavery that they came to understand these commandments as the path to God-given freedom in their new life. On their own, and free to develop whatever kind of society they wanted, they came to realize that the only way they could stay truly free was to establish right relationships with God and with one another.

The Israelites recognized that God, loving us first, gave us freedom and invited us to a special **covenant** relationship by which we are to love God and one another, as God's children. Every just law can be traced back to one or more of the principles represented in the Ten Commandments. So, when you're outraged at a social or personal injustice and you say, "There ought to be a law . . . !" or "How can she or he do that to me?" you are really saying that people should practice and uphold these commandments more. In the Israelites' new life of freedom, the Ten Commandments were to be the foundation of their relationships with God and others (see Deuteronomy 5:6–21). They are still the backbone of moral and social life.

covenant
an agreement of loving support and fidelity, as the one God initiated with humanity through the Jewish people's ancestors

Putting God first

"You shall love the LORD your God with all your heart, and with all your soul, and with all your strength, and with all your mind. . . ."

LUKE 10:27

1. I am the LORD your God . . . you shall have no other gods before me.

The original Hebrews were probably not **monotheists**. Probably, they were **polytheists**, believing in a number of gods. This first commandment told their descendants, the Israelites, that there was one God above all gods, the God whose name we know as **Yahweh**.

Today this commandment tells us to be true to our deepest beliefs about what life means. For most of humanity, these beliefs are specifically religious in nature. To betray our most basic beliefs is to betray ourselves. Thus, this commandment has meaning for everyone—even atheists, and certainly for Christians. It tells us we should safeguard, strengthen, and witness to our religious faith by how we live. We should have hope that God will bless us and fear only what we might do to separate ourselves from God's love.

We should never despair that God doesn't love us or won't show us mercy. And we should never presume that we don't need God and can achieve fulfillment in life on our own. We should respond to God or sacred things reverently; we should not respond **superstitiously**, nor should we respond **sacrilegiously**.

We are called to love and worship God our Creator and Savior, who is infinite Love and merciful Goodness itself, who gives us life and freedom and who is the Source of all the good things we have in life. We should likewise praise and thank God, and ask God's help for ourselves and others.

Loving God keeps us from the unhappy dead-ends of making ourselves or material things the be-all and end-all. We are commanded to not do anything that will keep us from loving God. Why **would** we do such things? How could we **not** love God?

2. You shall not make wrongful use of the name of the LORD your God . . . .

Like most ancient peoples, the Israelites believed that invoking a god's name invoked divine power for cursing their enemies or blessing their friends. Using "the Lord's name" was believed to have powerful effects. With this commandment, they were cautioned not to use this power without a good cause. (They still thought it perfectly all right to pile all sorts of curses on **legitimate** enemies! It just wasn't right to do so without good reason.) The great Hindu leader, **Mahatma Gandhi,** once advised Christians: "I suggest that you learn to practice your religion without calling it down." We should be true to our religious convictions, but not use them to threaten other people.

Today people understand that this commandment tells us we must take our religious beliefs seriously, and not take them for granted. We should also speak respectfully of God, and never swear an oath in God's name casually or for a reason that opposes human dignity or our religious beliefs. As the ritual name-giving in the Rite of Baptism represents, a person's name is and should be respected as sacred because it represents the person. Shouldn't that go for God's name, too?

monotheists
those who believe only one God exists

polytheists
those who believe in many gods

Yahweh
the Gentile pronunciation of the Hebrew name for God, the sacred tetragram YHWH, which was not to be said

Discuss
What did this commandment originally mean to people? What does it mean to you today?

superstitious
believing that merely performing certain acts makes them effective, apart from what God wills and one's own internal state of mind and heart

sacrilegious
violating or disrespecting persons, places, things, or ideas which are considered sacred

legitimate
proper, justified, lawful

Mahatma Gandhi
leader in India who spoke for nonviolent resistance to colonialism and all forms of oppression and who led the people to independence from Britain

liturgy

worship; a religious rite or ceremony

3. Observe the Sabbath day and keep it holy. . . .

Even in ancient times, this was another way of saying "practice what you preach." If one believes in God above all, then the very least one can do is set aside time to contemplate and celebrate God. The Sabbath—Shabbat—extended then, as it does for Jews now, from sundown on Friday to sundown on Saturday.

This commandment means much the same for humanity today: Take the time to reflect seriously on why we are here, what our lives mean, and how we should live. Sunday is the usual time Christians set aside to do this. Sunday, the first day of the week, recalls creation's first day; it is also the day we celebrate Jesus' resurrection from the dead and, thus, our own hope of everlasting life.

In many places, instead of on Sunday, Catholics may gather for worship on Saturday afternoon or evening, which is in keeping with the traditional Sabbath day. It is also an opportunity for those who must work on Sunday to gather with the community for worship. For Christians and Jews, the Sabbath recalls the completion of the first creation by God, the Israelites' freedom from Egyptian slavery, and God's permanent covenant with all of us. For Christians, Sunday **liturgy** celebrations recall the beginning of God's new creation in Jesus and Jesus' resurrection to a glorious new life.

What is most important is taking the time to think about, pray about, and celebrate together in worship the relationship with God and others that gives our life its real meaning. This is why employers in our society have traditionally given workers Sundays off as a day of worship and rest from work, and why Catholics are to participate in the Eucharistic liturgy each Sunday and on other special days of religious celebration during the year.

Leisure is also an important aspect of celebrating Sundays. While some people must work on Sundays, we should all find enough time each week to relax and renew ourselves, and allow others a chance to do the same. We should also support efforts to ensure that employees are given a reasonable amount of time for worship and leisure. Life is demanding enough. We all need—and need to give each other—a weekly break!

What does putting God first mean to you?

Read the following descriptions of various individuals' attitudes and behavior regarding God and religion. Answer these questions about each one:

1. *Which commandment is involved, and how do you think living its moral principles better might benefit the person(s)?*
2. *Do you think the action or attitude described is morally right or wrong? If wrong, how does it hurt the person(s) involved? If right, how is it beneficial?*
3. *How serious a moral matter do you think is presented in this situation?*

1. *Nicole has a lot of questions about her religious faith. Sometimes she wonders if God really exists, but then she feels guilty for wondering.*

2. *Dean is Catholic. One of his friends belongs to a Satanic cult. Dean thinks it would be cool to see what Satanists believe and do. His friend is urging him to come to a meeting and see what it's all about.*

3. *Lynn's every other word, or so her mother says, is "God" this and "God" that. Her mother is always telling her to stop throwing God's name around. But Lynn doesn't see the harm in it—"everybody does it," she says.*

4. *Ernesto figures he's young and strong and doesn't need God in his life right now. Someday, when he's old, he guesses, he'll probably turn to religion. But he just doesn't think it's necessary right now.*

5. *All her life Alison's mother has told Alison she's no good, that she'll never amount to anything or match up to her older sister. Alison has begun to agree with her mother. Lots of times she feels like she's not important to anybody, not even to God.*

6. *Keith just doesn't care about religion. He's too interested in cars, girls, and sports to think about God.*

7. *Vanessa has trouble praying. She never seems to get what she asks for—like a date with a certain guy or a good grade (on a test for which she really hasn't studied enough).*

8. *When Drew gets mad about something, he explodes to God. Sometimes he even gets mad at God when he doesn't understand why bad things happen to him and the people he loves. When he jokingly mentions that he tells God off sometimes, his grandmother furrows her brow and tells him that's a sin.*

9. *Amy is always stressed out because she never takes enough time just to relax and enjoy herself.*

10. *Kimberly makes promises to God all the time—when she really wants something. She's serious about it when she makes the promises, but most of the time she doesn't keep them.*

11. *Ramon, a Catholic, attends a Catholic school. But he says being required to attend religion classes violates his religious freedom. Ramon's friend, Dan, a Lutheran who attends the same school, doesn't see a problem with learning more about what Catholics like his friend Ramon believe. In fact, he says he's surprised Catholics and Lutherans have so many beliefs in common.*

12. *Dawn and a group of her friends are spending the weekend at Dawn's house. While watching a late-night TV show, they see an ad for a "psychic network" urging them to call and talk to a "master psychic." Dawn's friend, Toni, says she believes that psychics are for real, like the ads say. She says her sister talked to one who told her she'd meet somebody interesting, and the next day she met her current boyfriend. She and the other girls want Dawn to call the hotline just for fun—especially since the first call is free. Dawn believes "psychics" are fake, but thinks it might be fun to call just to see what it's like.*

13. *Marty just has to wear his "lucky" four-leaf clover medallion around his neck whenever he plays a baseball game. It boosts his confidence and gets him in a winning mindset.*

14. *Richelle swears a lot—an awful lot. She has a habit of saying "I swear to God" in order to emphasize a point or to get someone to believe her—even when she's telling a lie.*

15. Carlos's elderly grandmother doesn't want to miss going to Mass on Sundays. Her doctor, however, tells her that because of her poor health, she shouldn't go out in cold weather. She tells Carlos she feels like she's sinning if she doesn't go to Mass and asks him to take her despite doctor's orders.

16. When Alicia appears before the judge in traffic court because of a speeding ticket, she "fibs" under oath about how fast she was going. She rationalizes to herself that it's no big deal, and that, for all she knows, her speedometer might be wrong anyway.

17. Vu, a gang member noted for being tough and picking fights, wears a medal of Mary around his neck. He figures the medal will protect him against getting hurt.

18. When her mother carried eight-month-old Kristin up to Communion with her, Kristin grabbed the Eucharistic Bread out of the priest's hand and then dropped it. Kristin's grandmother worries that what Kristin did was a sacrilege and says dropping the Blessed Sacrament is bad luck.

19. Mark is arrested for drunken driving. It's the first time he's ever been in trouble with the law. In the squad car on the way to the police station, he prays to God, "If you really exist, you'll get me out of this jam without my folks finding out."

20. Taryn tends to judge people by the kind of clothes they wear and the money they have. Marrying somebody rich seems to be an important goal in her life. Her boyfriend, Vic, sells drugs so he can afford to drive an expensive car and buy the things he wants for himself and for Taryn.

21. The neighborhood gang Luke is trying to join wants him to take an oath before God to be loyal to the gang.

22. Mariya prays to a statue of Jesus because she feels like it has a sort of spiritual power that answers her prayers. It's worked for her so far, she says.

23. John makes the sign of the cross for luck before every free-throw shot. Since his average for making the shots is pretty good, he figures it must be working.

24. Robyn always reads her daily horoscope in the paper and tries to heed the advice it gives. She also tries to match her girlfriends up with guys according to their respective astrology signs. A friend read Robyn's palm the other day and told her she had a long lifeline. Robyn's brother, Tony, tells her he thinks all that stuff is a bunch of bunk.

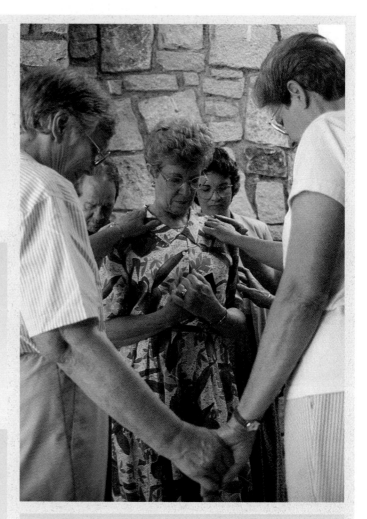

25. Yutaka's sister, a single parent, hasn't been to church since her baby was born. Her baby's health is somewhat fragile, and Yutaka doesn't think she should leave her in someone else's care just yet. But she's afraid that because she hasn't been to Mass in recent Sundays, the parish priest will refuse to baptize her daughter.

26. Natalie, a Catholic, notes that a famous "faith healer" she's seen on television is coming to town. Her boyfriend, David, says it's all a fake, a money-making scheme, but he thinks it would be fun to see what all the fuss is about and wants Natalie to come with him.

27. Manuel wants to go with a group of his friends to see a world-famous magician's show while it's in town. His grandfather says such magicians are evil and that Manuel shouldn't go.

28. Jake and Sherri are planning to marry, but haven't much money. Jake, who is not a Catholic, tells Sherri he's afraid they won't be able to afford to get married in a Catholic Church ceremony because it will cost too much. He favors eloping.

"You shall love . . . your neighbor as yourself."

LUKE 10:27

Respecting the human community

4. Honor your father and your mother. . . .

At first, Israelite society wasn't divided into cities or states. The Israelites were nomads whose desert home was wherever they traveled. Their society—with its system of administering justice—was built around tribes and clans, at the heart of which was the family. So this commandment didn't merely reinforce personal family relationships; it also promoted law and order among and within the tribes. To maintain civilization, some form of authority must be recognized, established, and respected. Those who disobeyed this law at that time could be stoned to death!

Children certainly need guidance and discipline. But today we further recognize that while the word *honor* may have originally meant mere obedience, it also includes mutual respect, affection, gratitude, and growth in love within the family. Thus, our increased moral understanding of this commandment includes parents' responsibilities as well as children's responsibilities. This commandment involves caring for family members—especially those who are young, elderly, ill, disabled, or poor. This commandment likewise addresses society's responsibility to support and protect marriage and family life. The family, not the government, is the foundational unit of society.

Somewhat rebellious adolescents can find this commandment one of the hardest, but also one of the most supportive. A common—useful—reason given to one's peers for not doing something one considers wrong is "My folks will ground me if they find out, and I'm not taking any chances!"

You and your friends may eventually go your separate ways. However, you might find your family members your most solid support system throughout life, with its joys and hardships. Family members should always lovingly give each other positive feedback, honest advice, and wise cautions, while respecting each other's individual privacy and adult freedom. We should help see each other through sickness, loneliness, and troubles. So as you prepare to seek your adult independence, don't neglect to strengthen your family bonds now as much as you can.

Although you'll always owe some type of respect to those who have raised you, you won't be legally bound to obey them forever—only until you're legally free of their authority and living on your own. Remember that. Unfortunately, some adults continue letting their parents control their lives in psychologically unhealthy ways. The respect and honor you owe your parents must always take into account your self-respect and their responsibility to respect your right to make your own decisions as an adult.

The fourth commandment also encompasses the obedience we owe other legitimate authorities, and their duty to look out for our good. For we acknowledge that legitimate authority is right and that obeying its reasonable laws and directives is necessary. Our nations, cities, and families couldn't exist without obedience to just laws. And, if the ancient Israelite's punishment seems too harsh, consider that some modern societies still accept capital punishment for disobeying certain laws.

Discuss

1. Why was respect for parental authority especially important in ancient times? What did it mean back then?

2. What does this commandment include today about family relationships and about obeying authority?

3. What are the usual ways teenagers are disrespectful or disobedient to their parents today? What are the typical punishments?

What does respecting the human community involve?

Read the following descriptions of attitudes and behavior that pertain to the fourth commandment. Answer these questions about each case:

1. *Do you think the action or attitude described is morally right or wrong? How is it harmful or beneficial?*
2. *How do you think living the fourth commandment better might benefit the person(s) involved?*
3. *How serious a moral matter do you think is involved here?*

1. Cody's father wants his son to be a courier for illegal drugs the father is selling.

2. Linda, who is twenty-four, wants to move across the country to take a new job and live in a climate she likes much better. Her mother, who is fifty, commands Linda not to move and makes her feel guilty by telling her that she has an obligation to stay here and look after her mother (who is in excellent health).

3. Moses' mother hardly hears from her son who is away at college—unless Moses needs more money.

4. Stephanie is always picking on and putting down her eight-year-old sister, calling her "a little twerp" (and much worse).

5. Shawna wants to go into computer science. Her father is pressuring her to become a lawyer so that she can one day take over the family practice.

6. Steven wants to stay single for a while longer, but his mother is always nagging him to marry his long-time girlfriend, Deanna. Steven's mother is anxious for her son to start a family so that she can have grandchildren to enjoy before she's much older.

7. María is twenty-one and unmarried. She has a job and wants to move into an apartment with a young woman she has been friends with since high school. Her father insists María must live at home until she marries. María doesn't want to marry for several more years.

8. Derek, who is working to get money to go back to college, fudges on his taxes, not reporting all of his tip income. He figures that the government should just collect more from the idle rich and stop "milking" hard-working people who are struggling financially—like him.

9. Carrie's not voting in this next election because she doesn't like any of the candidates. She sums up what she thinks of them by calling it a choice between Ms. Corrupt and Mr. Dumb.

10. Consuello has just moved into this country legally, hoping to make enough money to send back to her family who are living in poverty. Since moving here, she has received lots of warm welcomes from citizens and offers to help her get settled in her new home, and a few snide remarks from strangers, insinuating that she should "go back where she belongs."

11. Just to make a sale, Brian's boss tells him to lie to a customer about when an order will be ready.

12. Paul and his gang members feel it's okay to protest police brutality by letting the air out of the tires on police cars at every opportunity.

13. Laura wants to study political science in college and maybe have a career in politics. Her father insists politics is a "dirty, immoral profession full of liars and cheats—and definitely no place for a woman."

Respecting human life

5. You shall not kill (murder).

The Israelites interpreted this commandment much the same as we do today in some respects. In their Hebrew language, the prohibition referred not to all acts of homicide, but to what we term unjustifiable homicide, or murder. It was considered all right to kill in war or self-defense, but not because one just didn't like someone.

Today people agree that human life is precious—a sacred gift of God, the author of life. We must respect life as the sacred gift of God alone, since only God can create life. That is why human life is not to be harmed or taken away without just cause. This is why society and the Church both take so seriously those major moral issues which involve human life and welfare—self-defense, war, abortion, suicide, euthanasia, murder, scandals, major health concerns, proper respect for the dead, suicide, organ transplant guidelines, and crimes like murder, kidnapping, hostage taking, and terrorism. Nevertheless, there are often heated disagreements about the best ways to protect human life in specific circumstances (as we will see in discussing some of the tough cases in the rest of this text).

This commandment has further positive implications:

* to help ensure human life's **quality** by working to alleviate human pain and suffering

* to bring peace between people and among nations

Human life is sacred and to be safeguarded from its beginning through its end.

> *. . . you are precious in my sight, and honored, and I love you. . . .*
> ISAIAH 43:4

Discuss

1. How does this commandment's meaning for people today compare with what it meant in ancient times?

2. What do you think are the greatest threats to human life today?

What does respecting human life mean in practice?

Read the following descriptions of attitudes and behavior pertaining to the fifth commandment. Answer these questions about each case:

 1. *Do you think the action or attitude described is morally right or wrong? How does it harm or benefit the person(s) involved?*
 2. *How do you think living the fifth commandment's moral principles better might benefit the person(s) involved?*
 3. *How serious a moral matter do you think this situation involves?*

1. Salvador thinks it's okay to murder a member of another gang who has been infringing on his gang's turf.

2. Marcie has had to push away guys she's dated when they've wanted to have sex with her and had trouble taking "no" for an answer. She wonders how far she should fight back if the guy doesn't back off.

3. When Officer McDonald asked Shane to move along instead of loitering in front of the store, Shane immediately started to comply. Officer McDonald nevertheless gave Shane a hard shove to "help" him move along.

4. On investigating a noise that woke him up in the middle of the night, Aaron catches a burglar escaping out a back window. He shoots the burglar in the back.

5. Concert-goers get carried away and begin fighting and tearing apart the outdoor stage. Fearing that the situation will escalate until someone is severely hurt or killed, the police use tear gas to disperse the crowd. The concert-goers, all of whom were unhurt, later complain that they were the victims of "police brutality."

6. After Rod gets a speeding ticket for driving fifteen miles an hour over the limit, his father suspends his driving privileges for a month.

7. Jaime thinks kids who vandalize school property should be jailed. Roberto thinks that, as punishment, they should make restitution to the school and be required to do community service.

8. Jeff says he doesn't see any big deal about telling a pregnant girlfriend to have an abortion. His friend Dan vehemently disagrees.

9. Dr. Martin believes abortion is wrong, but performs abortions anyway to make extra money. He says it's the woman, not him, who has to make the moral decision about abortion.

10. Lisa confides to her friend Jackie that she's thinking seriously of committing suicide. Jackie wonders what, if anything, she should do to help her friend.

11. Grady encourages his little brother to try smoking marijuana. He thinks it would be funny to see how his brother behaves when he's high.

12. Bezarah enjoys drag racing down the street against cars he challenges at stoplights.

13. Shawn wants more than anything to get into college on a football scholarship, so he uses illegal methods of bulking up.

14. A major pharmaceutical company likes to use college students for its experiments on the possible side-effects of new drugs. College students are often eager to sign up because they always need money.

15. Marcelino likes to arm-twist his little brother into telling him what he wants to know.

16. Mr. and Mrs. Hill are elderly Catholics who want to make advance funeral arrangements. They don't have much money and have discovered that cremation is less expensive and about all they can afford. Somebody tells them that cremation is against the Catholic faith.

17. Debra is furious and out to get Krista for "stealing" Debra's boyfriend. She's decided to do whatever she can to give Krista a hard time about it.

18. Jarilyne says she hates Aurelio for breaking up with her, and hopes that he's in a car accident and dies.

Respecting persons and relationships

6. Neither shall you commit adultery.

At the time the Ten Commandments were promulgated, the Israelites didn't necessarily see this commandment as a protection for the mutual trust, personal commitment, and special love relationship of marriage. To them it was a matter of justice and applied mainly to married women, who were viewed as property just like any other property their husbands owned. When a wife committed adultery, her husband's sense of justice was offended because the act violated his property rights. Unmarried women were considered their father's property until they married. So if a man had sexual intercourse with an unmarried woman, he was obliged to pay her father money for having violated the father's property—or, if the man were unmarried, to marry the girl and make her **his** property! The woman had no rights.

If a married man had sexual intercourse with an unmarried woman, this wasn't considered adultery. However, if a married woman had sexual intercourse with an unmarried man, this was adultery. There was indeed a double standard for men and for women regarding this commandment!

Today we realize the much deeper meanings of this commandment: Male and female persons are equal in human dignity, and love is every person's basic vocation. We must cherish God's gift of human sexuality by expressing affection appropriately for our state of life, whether single or married. We should never express our sexuality in ways which demean or harm ourselves or another.

A man and a woman's loving commitment in marriage is sacred, faithful, and lifelong. Catholic belief and ideals in this regard reflect the personal hopes of most people. "Trial marriages," **extramarital** affairs, and **adultery** (by **either** spouse!) are wrong because they violate this love and commitment which require a complete gift of each person to the other.

Having children is one of God's most wonderful gifts and one of the main purposes of marriage. That is why marital intercourse should be open to the transmission of life and the procreation of children. Participating in the creating of life is as grave a responsibility as taking a life, and should require serious and deliberate reflection beforehand! Every child has a right to be wanted, loved, cared for, and educated properly. Any form of child abuse—sexual or otherwise—is morally detestable because it violates those who are among the most innocent, vulnerable, and defenseless.

We must try to change the social attitudes that condone sexually irresponsible, selfish, and abusive behavior. Rape, sexual abuse, and sexual harassment should be more widely recognized as crimes against human dignity. We should also oppose the prudish view that sexuality itself is bad or dirty. But changing human behavior involves first changing human minds and hearts. So where we can, we should take a stand for the sacred dignity of human sexuality and voice our disgust at whatever demeans it.

Scripture insights

Read the New Testament story of Jesus and the woman about to be stoned to death for being "caught in the act" of committing adultery. See what consequences were mentioned for her male partner.

extramarital
outside marriage

adultery
sexual intercourse with someone other than one's spouse, or sexual intercourse with a married person

Discuss

1. What is the main difference in how this sixth commandment is understood today and what it meant originally?

2. What was the double standard back then regarding this commandment? What double standards do you think still exist regarding sexual behavior?

3. Why is child abuse so detestable?

4. What attitudes regarding sexuality do you think need to be changed in our society? How do you think this can best be accomplished?

What does respecting persons and relationships involve?

Read the following descriptions of attitudes and behavior that pertain to the sixth commandment. Answer these questions about each case:

1. *Do you think the action or attitude described is morally right or wrong? How does it harm or benefit the person(s) involved?*
2. *How do you think living the sixth commandment's moral principles better might benefit the person(s)?*
3. *How serious a moral matter do you think this situation involves?*

1. *Lucas wants to have sex with his girlfriend, Andrea. She says she wants to wait until marriage. Lucas tells Andrea that it's unhealthy for a guy not to have sex when he gets turned on.*

2. *Rob doesn't see anything wrong with taking out a girl just to have sex with her. He's an advocate of sex solely for pleasure—no relationship, no commitment attached.*

3. *Anthony likes to read pornographic magazines and check out the graphic sex sites on the Internet. His sister, Kim, tells him he's getting perverted ideas of sex from this, and she keeps threatening to tell their mom.*

4. *Columbo's friend Ted says that, for Columbo's birthday, the guys want to buy him a session with a prostitute.*

5. *Angela's mother is a cocaine addict who spends much of the little money the family has on drugs. Angela works hard at after-school and weekend jobs to help support herself, her mom, and her little brother. But when bills are due and money is short, she sells her body to help pay for rent and groceries.*

6. *When Samuel gets sexually aroused after making out with a girl, he'll force her to have sex. Even though the girl protests that she doesn't want to have sex, Samuel is convinced she does—or at least that the girl owes it to him. He reasons that, after he's spent money taking her out, and she gets him all turned on, it's not fair for her to suddenly turn into an ice cube.*

7. *When Denise was about nine, her older brother used to force her to have sex with him every once in awhile— usually when he came home drunk after an evening out with his high school buddies. Denise still feels like what happened was her fault—that she was wrong for never telling her mom, even though her brother used to say he'd beat her bloody if she did.*

8. *Sometimes to their face and sometimes behind their back, Mike and his friends make fun of and put down the kids at school whom they suspect of being gay.*

9. *Cindy likes to dress in a sexually provocative way that leaves very little to the imagination. She enjoys being noticed and attracting guys that way. She figures, "If you've got it, flaunt it."*

10. *Todd and Renee are about to get married. They both hope their marriage will last, but figure they can always get a divorce if it doesn't.*

11. *Ramon and Lucia have been married just a few months. Ramon says he's ready to start a family—that he wants to have a huge family just like the one he comes from. Lucia says they can't afford to start a family just yet.*

12. *Ms. Cadence, a social worker, gets very upset at all the childhood poverty she sees as the result of teenage pregnancies. She favors a law that would put all adolescent girls on birth control until they reach adulthood.*

13. *After trying unsuccessfully for three years to have a child, Jennifer and her husband John just found out that he is sterile—from repeated cases of venereal disease he had contracted before he met Jennifer. Jenny, a Catholic, wants so much to have a baby that is "part of her" that she's considering being impregnated by a donor's sperm at a fertility clinic. John would rather adopt a child who needs a loving home.*

14. *Heather's husband, Victor, is an alcoholic. As a Catholic, Heather doesn't believe in divorce, but she's afraid that Victor (who has a hot temper—especially when drunk) is one day going to hurt or kill her and their small children.*

15. *Tim and Rhonda are thinking of maybe marrying after graduation from college. For now, they want to live together first to find out how compatible they are. They figure that will help increase their odds of success if they do decide to marry.*

Respecting others' rights

7. Neither shall you steal.

9. Neither shall you covet your neighbor's wife.

10. Neither shall you desire . . . anything that belongs to your neighbor.

These three commandments will be discussed together here, though out of their usual order, because they all treat the same general idea—desiring or taking what doesn't belong to us.

In ancient times "You shall not steal" referred to kidnapping, to stealing people. While in our society, this rarely occurs, in some places in the world, children are still stolen and put into slavery. The commandment to not desire "anything that belongs to your neighbor" means to not steal another's property (**other** than persons).

Today the commandment to not steal refers to respecting and protecting people's right to private property, and thus to not taking another's possessions unjustly. People must abide by this universally accepted basic rule in order to live together peacefully. Those who cheat, steal, or damage another's property have an obligation to compensate the victim for the harm done.

In the positive sense, this seventh commandment addresses giving others what is justly due them. It means, in whatever ways are morally just, keeping our promises, paying our bills and our taxes, giving a fair day's work for a fair wage, and honoring our contracts. It means being good and respectful caretakers of the animals, plants, and land God has given humanity for our sustenance, survival, and enjoyment. It means recognizing the dignity of human work, working to see that the earth's wealth is shared more fairly, helping people find jobs and giving them equal opportunity for employment, and working to eliminate hunger and poverty and to achieve justice, equal rights, and human freedom everywhere.

There's nothing wrong with wanting enjoyable things we don't have, as long as our desires are within reason and don't involve infringing unjustly on others' rights. The commandment to not desire your neighbor's goods refers to the greedy ("whoever dies with the most toys wins") attitudes that put money and material things above all else in life. It also refers to jealously bemoaning another's good fortune. Like greed, that can also destroy harmonious living.

One of these days when we die, we're going to have to leave all our material possessions behind, for it's true that you can't take them with you. Ironically, what we can take with us is what we've already given away throughout our lives—the love we've given God and others. So while enjoying material things, we should, as Jesus told us, become poor in spirit—setting our hearts, our faith, and our hopes on the only lasting treasure in life: love.

If you can do that, you will go through life much happier and freer. You won't be bound up in knots inside by the "How might I lose what I've got?" worries that haunt so many people. You won't spend so much time trying to accumulate wealth that you have little time to really enjoy living.

Those conflicts and disputes among you, where do they come from? Do they not come from your cravings that are at war within you? You want something and do not have it; so you commit murder. And you covet something and cannot obtain it; so you engage in disputes and conflicts.
JAMES 4:1–2

> *". . . out of the abundance of the heart the mouth speaks. The good person brings good things out of a good treasure, and the evil person brings evil things out of an evil treasure."*
> **MATTHEW 12:34–35**

moral personality
the distinctive characteristics of moral goodness or badness a person expresses

It is from our hearts that our actions arise.

To not "covet your neighbor's wife" meant for the ancient Israelites that no man was to actively try to possess another man's wife—again, as a matter of justice and property rights rather than of sexual morality. Today this commandment tells us not to harm or jeopardize a married love relationship. It commands us to have a proper respect and reserve for human sexuality. It rejects the kind of moral permissiveness that says "anything goes," sexual or otherwise, in the name of freedom.

This commandment also speaks more to the root of our **moral personality**—to the overall inner attitude of being pure of heart that Jesus taught us. It means seeing that our intentions and desires are good and not evil. For it is from our hearts that our actions arise.

Clarify

Compare how the seventh, ninth, and tenth commandments were understood in ancient times with their meaning for us today.

Journal entry

Personality deals with the unique ways we express what is inside of us.
1. List and briefly describe the three main positive and the three main negative traits of your inner and your outer moral personality.
2. Explain how you think others would describe your moral personality.

Reflection

1. Which aspects of your attitudes, intentions, and desires are generally morally positive, seeking what is true and good?
2. Which aspects of your inner self tend to be more morally negative?

How are we to respect others' rights?

Read the following descriptions of attitudes and behavior that pertain to the seventh, ninth, and tenth commandments. Answer these questions about each case:

1. *Do you think the action or attitude described is morally right or wrong? How is it harmful or beneficial?*
2. *How do you think living the seventh, ninth, and tenth commandments' moral principles better might benefit the person(s)?*
3. *How serious a moral matter do you think is involved in this situation?*

1. Matt has a habit of borrowing things and not returning them. Sometimes he deliberately keeps the stuff he's borrowed, not intending to return it unless the owner asks for it back.

2. Darlene operates by the "finders keepers" premise that if she finds something that's been lost, she's entitled to keep it. It upsets her, of course, if she loses something of hers and nobody returns it.

3. Although he's pretty deep in debt, Gene likes to play the lottery every week. He and his wife fight about the money he spends gambling, but Gene has big dreams of how he'll pay off all his bills when he wins.

4. Marlin sells high-interest loans to high-debt customers. He knows his company especially targets and takes advantage of desperate people.

5. Katie's cat has recently had another litter. Katie just never seems to get around to having the cat neutered.

6. Dwight, a vegetarian, thinks killing animals for food is morally wrong. He likes wearing stylish leather belts and jackets, though.

7. Yuko, a construction worker, hopes for tornado or flood damage to homes every year so business will pick up and he'll make more money.

8. When the hurricane threatens, Anne, who franchises a small food market, doubles the prices on canned goods and other essentials people will stock up on.

9. The Alenta Cosmetic Company experiments on animals to test the safety for humans of their new lipstick ingredients. Some of the experiments are painful for the animals. Dilondal Pharmaceuticals uses the same kind of experiments to test the safety of life-saving drugs for humans.

10. Gregory is always bringing home materials from work for his own personal use. He doesn't see anything wrong with it ("Others do it, too"). But he makes sure no one sees him do it.

11. Melissa is always undressing guys with her eyes. She likes giving them the "come hither" stares of the commercial models. A key topic of conversation with her is guys' sexy physical attributes.

12. Getting rich is Russ's ultimate goal in life. Even if he has to "step on a few toes" to do it, he's determined to be a millionaire by age thirty.

13. Orlando marks things—autos, lockers, library books, desks, bathroom stalls—with the tip of his car keys. He's done it for so long that half the time he doesn't even realize he's doing it.

Respecting truth, privacy, and personal freedom

8. Neither shall you bear false witness against your neighbor.

In ancient times, this commandment referred to testifying falsely against someone in court. It was so crucial to the Israelites' legal system, where two persons' **testimony** was enough to convict someone, that disobeying it in any way was punishable by death. Without modern scientific aids in establishing guilt or innocence, human lives generally depended solely upon witnesses' honesty in court. Their testimony was often a life or death matter for both witnesses and defendant.

Our legal system still deals out stiff penalties for perjury—lying under **oath** in legal proceedings. In fact, where the death penalty is allowed for crimes, a witness whose perjury results in executing an innocent person can also be charged with murder and executed.

Most people understand that the eighth commandment goes beyond testifying in court; it also refers to upholding truth in general. God is Truth, and, created in God's image, we are to live lives of sincerity and truthfulness. This means standing up for what is true. When it comes to religious matters, the holy **martyrs** have done this to the utmost. This commandment tells us to be honest. For without belief in upholding truth and basic honesty, our civilization and all our personal relationships would quickly crumble.

Living the eighth commandment likewise involves respecting others' reputations and not defaming, ridiculing, or otherwise cutting them down. It means not encouraging or participating in the wrong conduct of others. Even our legal system acknowledges that being an accomplice to a crime is also a crime! Whenever we cause harm, we should try to make **reparation** for it.

Finally, this commandment upholds our legitimate right to privacy and personal freedom, and requires that we respect others' rights in these areas. In addition, it supports those artistic expressions which reflect truth and beauty in the world, thereby mirroring some aspect of who God is.

testimony
solemn declaration, sometimes under oath

oath
a solemn swearing which calls on God to witness to the truth of what one says

martyrs
faithful witnesses who die for their religious beliefs

reparation
the act of repairing some of the damage caused by our wrongdoing

People could not live with one another without the mutual confidence that they were being truthful to one another.
THOMAS AQUINAS

Reflection
Which of Jesus' ideals or examples do you especially try to follow in your actions and decisions?

Discuss
1. Compare how the eighth commandment is understood today with how it was understood in ancient times.
2. What do you think are the main ways today that people personally violate truth? Violate personal privacy? Violate personal freedom?
3. On the broader societal level today, what do you think are the main threats to truth? To personal privacy? To personal freedom? Explain.

". . . by your words you will be justified, and by your words you will be condemned."
MATTHEW 12:37

What does respecting truth, privacy, and personal freedom involve?

Read the following descriptions of attitudes and behavior that pertain to the eighth commandment. Answer these questions about each case:

1. *Do you think the action or attitude described is morally right or wrong? How is it harmful or beneficial?*
2. *How do you think living the eighth commandment's moral principles better might benefit the person?*
3. *How serious a moral matter do you think this situation involves?*

1. *Wishing Dean were her boyfriend instead of Pamela's, Lupe starts a vicious rumor that Pamela has been cheating on Dean. Lupe hopes Dean will believe the rumor and dump Pamela for her.*

2. *Melinda is quick to presume the worst about others. Without checking out the facts, she usually believes the negative gossip she hears about somebody.*

3. *José is always boasting that he's the strongest, the bravest, the best, and bragging that he can outdo someone.*

4. *Monette savors juicy gossip and loves to pass it along. If she discovers a fault about someone, she can hardly wait to hit the phone in the evening to tell her friends.*

5. *Ricardo tells lies about others, lies that will put him in a better light.*

6. *Toshiyasu draws editorial cartoons for the school newspaper. He's especially good at caricatures—one of which pokes fun at the outlandish ties his math teacher likes to wear "to keep the students awake." Another ridicules the appearance of Tamara, a quiet girl the other kids consider homely.*

7. *Romero tells Toshiyasu his caricatures are terrific—especially the one of Tamara.*

8. *Mariana stays home from school on Tuesday to spend the day with her boyfriend from another school who has no classes that day. On Wednesday, she writes a phony excuse for her teachers and signs her mother's name.*

9. *Sumiko overhears Kareem telling Brad that he's going to break up with Karen. Karen has no idea that Kareem is about to break off their relationship, and will be extremely hurt by it. But Sumiko can hardly wait to tell the rest of the kids the news first.*

10. *Dan overhears one of his teachers talking about a personal problem another student has at home that is affecting the student's attendance. The student's mother has asked the teacher to communicate this information to the other teachers, but Dan communicates it to some of the other kids.*

11. *Placida tearfully confides to her close friend, Carmen, that she's contracted a sexually transmitted disease from her boyfriend, Alex. Carmen, in turn, confides the information to her other very close friend, Dominic, who confides it to his other close friend. . . .*

The Christian dimension

Studying the Ten Commandments' historical interpretations and context is interesting. But it's perhaps more interesting that people still consider these moral norms basic, binding, and meaningful. Though minor interpretations may differ, people essentially agree on the meaning and significance of these ten simple commandments. These commandments, though, are merely the basics—the beginning. They certainly weren't intended to spell out all aspects of the concern we're to have for one another.

Jesus spoke about these other aspects of morality and provided further guidelines for increasing humanity's moral consciousness. The next few chapters will discuss in greater depth the dimensions Jesus added. He didn't "come to abolish . . . but to fulfill" the law (see Matthew 5:17)—not to do away with the Ten Commandments, but to show us what further meanings they have for improving human life.

Christians view the Law of Moses, which is summed up in the Ten Commandments, as preparation for the Law of Jesus which is based on love. Jesus' message showed us new dimensions of God's law which can make our lives and relationships richer than humanity had ever realized possible. Jesus placed all the commandments within the commandment "to love." Paul, in his letter to the Christians in Rome, put it quite concisely:

> The commandments, "You shall not commit adultery; You shall not murder; You shall not steal; You shall not covet"; and any other commandment, are summed up in this, "Love your neighbor as yourself."
>
> *Romans 13:9*

For discussion

1. Which commandments are most relevant in today's world? The most violated? Why?
2. Which of the commandments are most important in your own personal social life right now? Explain with examples.
3. How do the Ten Commandments fit in with the Christian view of morality?
4. How is a person's view of the Ten Commandments influenced by his or her understanding of their historical context? Give examples of what you mean.
5. What importance should the Ten Commandments have for Christians? For our society and the world today? For your own life?

Rules to live by[2]

A young man in his twenties once drew up his list of beliefs about "how to live." When he read it again later in life, he thought it sounded way too pretentious. He realized that, even as an adult, he still tried to live according to the values behind many of the simple rules he had learned as a very young child. So he rewrote his rules to live by in the words of a kindergartener. Like the Ten Commandments, if not just interpreted literally, these rules can also apply to a wide variety of behavior on the part of individuals, societies, and nations. Read these rules, and then respond to the questions below.

Rule 1: *Share everything.*
Rule 2: *Play fair.*
Rule 3: *Don't hit people.*
Rule 4: *Put things back where you found them.*
Rule 5: *Clean up your own mess.*
Rule 6: *Don't take things that aren't yours.*
Rule 7: *Say you're sorry when you hurt somebody.*
Rule 8: *Live a balanced life—learn some and think some and draw and paint and sing and dance and play [and pray] and work every day some.*
Rule 9: *When you go out into the world, watch out for traffic, hold hands, and stick together.*
Rule 10: *Be aware of wonder.*

For discussion

1. What values underlie each of the above rules?
2. Explain how each rule can be more broadly understood and applied to the moral conduct of
   - teenagers
   - parents and their children
   - students and teachers
   - people in general
   - employers and employees
   - societies
   - nations
3. Which of these ten rules did you learn as a small child? Which other rules were you taught as a young child?
4. Which of the rules you were taught as a child do you still try to live by today? Which ones do you no longer consider relevant, or only in a practical sense and without a moral application? Explain.
5. Compare the values these rules support with those upheld in the Ten Commandments. On which commandment(s) are some of these rules based?

Chapter 5 summary
The Path to Love and Freedom

1. God's law of love in our hearts

- Conscience relies on the God-given natural moral law to lead us to love good and avoid evil.

- The natural moral law is an interior understanding placed in us by God through which we can distinguish between good and evil, right and wrong.

- The natural moral law doesn't give us specific answers, but points us in the right moral direction.

- The natural moral law's principles are universal and unchanging, and form the basis for all other human rules of conduct.

- The natural moral law applies to everyone, everywhere, always, and is the basis for building human community.

- Stop and think before you act—especially when you feel like something isn't right.

2. God's law of love in Scripture

- The Ten Commandments are still basic norms for moral conduct.

- The Ten Commandments have taken on further levels of meaning since their beginning.

- The Ten Commandments are still meaningful, basic, and binding.

- The Ten Commandments are the **beginning** of moral living.

- Jesus added further dimensions to guide human conduct.

Key concepts

adultery	Law of Moses	rape
covenant	martyr	reparation
coveting another's property	monotheists	retaliation
coveting another's spouse	moral personality	sacrilegious
envy	murder	superstitious
extramarital affairs	natural moral law	Ten Commandments
inalienable rights	oath	testimony
Jesus' New Law	perjury	unjustifiable homicide

Owe no one anything, except to love one another; for the one who loves another has fulfilled the law. . . . Love does no wrong to a neighbor; therefore, love is the fulfilling of the law.
Romans 13:8 and 10

Chapter 6

Following Your Conscience

Overview questions

1. When is authority legitimate and to be obeyed?
2. What if laws or commands conflict with a person's conscience?
3. What role should the Church play in politics and lawmaking?
4. What role does human freedom have in moral decision making?
5. What is the role of Catholic teaching in moral decision making?
6. What's the best way to inform our conscience and find workable solutions to moral problems?

legitimate authority
the God-given right and responsibility to make rules or regulations which others are expected to obey

Conscience and authority

Without obedience to **legitimate authority**, civilization couldn't survive. There would be anarchy and chaos. All legitimate authority ultimately comes from God. We therefore have a duty to respect those with legitimate authority who are responsible for our welfare. All authority, however—from the family to the state—is to be exercised as a **service, not** as a power seeking to control others.

Scripture insight

1. Read Matthew 22:15–22.
2. What point was Jesus making here about obeying civil authority?

Authority and responsibility

To serve people's welfare, those in authority must exercise that authority in a reasonable way and in keeping with the natural moral law and human dignity. Those in authority must have a proper sense of priorities, recognizing which values are more important than others. Whenever human beings are given responsibility over others, however, there is always the danger that they will try to grab more power than they were given, or otherwise misuse their authority. History's tyrants and revolutions, abusive parents, and unfair employers attest to that.

People shouldn't exercise any more control over others than they really need to. This applies to all authority—from personal and business relationships, married life and families, or groups of friends, to the broader arena of government. Keep this principle in mind whenever you're in charge of a project or otherwise given authority over others.

Activity

Managers sometimes keep a plaque on their desk or a poster on their wall stating the management principles by which they try to live. Based on what you've discussed in this section, create a poster that sums up your own management principles. Present and explain your principles to the class as you would if presenting them to those over whom you exercise authority at work or at school.

View any leadership position you may have as an opportunity to serve, rather than to boss others around. Instead of trying to micro-manage everything—or trying to do it all yourself, give those you work with access to the information and support they need to perform their tasks well. They'll consider you a good leader and will probably accomplish their tasks better and more enthusiastically because you've generated such a positive, cooperative spirit.

> *". . . whoever wishes to be great among you must be your servant. . . ."*
> **MATTHEW 20:26**

For discussion

1. *What happens when people exercise their authority in a way that is not reasonable? That does not reflect a proper sense of priorities? Give examples you've encountered.*

2. *Without mentioning names, have you ever dealt with other students or siblings who try to exercise more authority than they have or should? How does this affect their effectiveness as a leader? Your and others' relationship with them?*

3. *Give three additional examples which illustrate why people shouldn't exercise more control over others than they really need to in*

   - *marriage*
   - *other personal relationships*
   - *families*
   - *business relationships*
   - *friendships*
   - *government*

4. *In your experience, why is it so important that managers and other leaders and authority figures*

   - *"practice what they teach"*
   - *not try to micro-manage everything*
   - *not try to do it all themselves*

5. *Describe someone in authority whose leadership qualities you admire. Explain why you admire the person.*

6. *Describe your best and worst leadership qualities. How do you think others would describe your best and worst leadership qualities?*

Civil authority

We owe a great debt of gratitude to our good and honest civil leaders, and should pray with Pope St. Clement that all leaders exercise their authority with "devotion, peace, and gentleness." Civil authorities must respect basic human rights—especially those of families and the disadvantaged. Civil leaders must put the community's welfare before their own self-interests. In reality, however, there is widespread debate about the proper limits and scope of civil authority.

- In order to protect the few, when is it fair to restrict the many or to increase the price of goods and services for everyone?

- When would—and wouldn't—it be fair to be grounded at home for something you've done or failed to do at school?

- Should civil authorities have the right to pass a law forbidding parents to spank their children?

As you discuss such issues, consider Catholic teaching on the principle of **subsidiarity**: **Always keeping in mind the common good, a community with greater authority should not interfere in the internal affairs of a community with lesser authority. Rather, the greater should assist the lesser and help blend its activities with the rest of society's.** God delegates to each creature whatever functions it is able to do, rather than accomplishing everything through the power of direct divine intervention! So must we!

> "... therefore, do whatever they teach you and follow it; but do not do as they do, for they do not practice what they teach. They tie up heavy burdens, hard to bear, and lay them on the shoulders of others; but they themselves are unwilling to lift a finger to move them."
> MATTHEW 23:3–4

Projects (choose one)

1. Search the Internet or your local newspaper for three examples each that you think illustrate
   - the proper exercise of authority
   - the improper exercise of authority

2. Draw up and conduct a poll at your school of students' ideas, criticisms, commendations, and recommendations with regard to student government.

Present and explain your findings to the class.

END OF SCHOOL ZONE

RESUME NORMAL SPEED

subsidiarity
giving auxiliary support to, or being subordinate or secondary to

Pay to all what is due them—taxes to whom taxes are due, revenue to whom revenue is due, respect to whom respect is due, honor to whom honor is due.
ROMANS 13:7

justifiable
able to be sufficiently explained, supported, and defended as right, reasonable, or correct

proportionate
in keeping with the size, degree, or extent of something else

Scripture insight

Read Romans 13:1–7. What does this passage say about the responsibilities of citizens and the reasons for these responsibilities?

The duty of government officials in exercising their authority is to look out for the common welfare. Because the state wields enormous power, citizens should be vigilant. Governments should never be allowed to own everything, do everything, or overly regulate citizens' lives. This is why it's a good idea to have a balance of power in the government so that power is excercised within proper moral and legal limits.

Rather than being expected to march in unison to others' dictates, people should be allowed as much freedom and autonomy as the common good will permit. As Catholic teaching points out, the state should not intervene excessively or to the point that personal initiative and freedom are jeopardized. Before civil authority can take away a citizen's rights or freedoms, it must have a morally **justifiable** reason for doing so and must see to it that the punishment is **proportionate** to the situation—neither excessive nor too lenient.

As citizens we have duties as well as rights. We must respect and submit to legitimate authority by obeying just laws and helping to defend our country for just cause.

We have an obligation to vote—first informing ourselves about the candidates and their positions on the issues. In a free society, we citizens are ultimately responsible for the kinds of leaders we get. If we don't like the political choices we're offered, then we need to change these choices. To do this, we must become more politically aware and involved. Society is composed of individuals. Ultimately, it is only by changing each person's attitudes to what is good and just that society can change.

As a nation, we must also be good Samaritans—aiding those who are suffering and disadvantaged in our communities and around the world, and welcoming and assisting those who come here to escape oppression, hunger, and poverty.

Project (choose one)

1. Choose a student regulation at your school that you think is too restrictive. Identify the problem(s) it addresses and its desired goal. Based on Catholic teaching's criteria presented in this section, assess the regulation's moral merits and propose a better alternative.
2. Identify a problem that affects students at your school and the goal you would like to achieve in solving it. Draw up a regulation or other solution for the problem that meets the criteria of Catholic teaching presented in this section.

Present a formal proposal of your solution to your student government representative(s).

For discussion

1. How well do you think civil authorities are respected in our society? Who seems to be respected the most, and who the least? Explain.
2. How would you respond to the three questions posed at the beginning of the section on civil authority? Give reasons for your responses.
3. Why does Catholic teaching emphasize the principle of subsidiarity? Why is this principle important? How do you think the principle of subsidiarity should be applied to student government in your school?
4. Why is it a good idea to delegate authority? To have a balance of power?
5. How does Catholic teaching about personal freedom and initiative apply to relationships within the family? At school? Explain.

6. *Why is it important that punishments be justifiable and proportionate to the crime?*
   Give an example from your own experience to illustrate your point.

7. *Why is voting an important moral obligation? Why is it important to vote even*
   when there is a poor choice of candidates?

8. *What types of aid is, and is not, this country morally obligated to give to*

   • *citizens who are poor*

   • *citizens who are elderly*

   • *citizens who are homeless*

   • *citizens who have mental and physical disabilities*

   • *citizens who are the victims of natural disasters in this country*

   • *non-citizens living in this country legally*

   • *non-citizens living in this country illegally*

   • *victims of war in other countries*

   • *those fighting for human rights in other countries*

   • *people who are poor and homeless elsewhere in the world*

What's fair?

Read about the following laws which have been enacted or proposed. Then respond to the questions.

Truancy laws

In one city, students are fined for skipping school and assigned community service. Since the policy went into effect, school attendance has increased more than 5 percent and daytime crime has dropped more than 10 percent.

Teen curfews

In one large shopping mall, some teenagers have been creating a major security problem. The teenagers engage in fights and threaten children and other shoppers with weapons. Several injuries have resulted already from the teens' behavior.

To eliminate the problem, the mall has decided to not allow anyone under sixteen in the mall after one under sixteen in the mall after dark on weekend nights without an adult escort. The mall's representatives defend the regulation by saying that without it there is the potential for even more trouble and more serious injuries. They say the mall has a responsibility to provide a safe environment for its shoppers. If enough security guards are hired to control the problem without the time restriction, the cost will have to be passed on to customers—something they and mall officials don't consider fair.

Some teenagers admit they're afraid of being accosted by the other teenagers at the mall on weekend nights. But others feel the regulation discriminates against peaceful kids. They point out that only 1 to 2 percent of the kids who frequent the mall cause all the problems. They favor cracking down on those kids instead.

For discussion

1. *What is the main problem each law addresses? Is there an underlying problem involved in each case?* ➡

2. *What do you think the goal(s) should be in trying to solve each problem?* ➡

3. *Do you consider each of these laws—the truancy law and the mall law—to be*

   • *just*

   • *reasonable*

   • *legitimate*

   • *moral, immoral, or amoral*

   • *a good law*

4. *Would you favor or oppose each of these laws as a good solution to the problem? Can you think of a better solution in each case? Explain.*

Politics and morality

Citizens should be able to freely choose their rulers, political parties, and styles of government. The state and its political leaders are to promote, serve, and defend the common good. Authority is legitimate only when it uses morally allowable means to do this.

To the extent that governments or political leaders work against basic moral principles and oppose human rights and the common good, however, they lose their moral legitimacy. People have no obligation to follow oppressive dictators. Government itself should be a moral force based on freedom and responsibility.

What role, if any, should the Church play in politics and government? Unfortunately, when Church leaders speak out on political issues, this is sometimes misunderstood as a threat to the healthy diversity of viewpoints that makes democracy work. The Church supports democracy and affirms the importance of the political process. And the Church has a right to be heard—especially on public policy regarding religious freedom or other issues of moral consequence. It's up to the Christian communities in each country to determine how best to voice these concerns.

The Church isn't out to take over governments. Far from it! In fact, based on the wisdom gained from historical experience, the Church today realizes there should be a healthy separation between church and state authority. In fact, for example, it is the Church's policy that Catholic clergy should not assume leadership roles in civil government.

> *By preaching the truth of the gospel and shedding light on all areas of human activity through her teaching and the example of the faithful, [the Church] shows respect for the political freedom and responsibility of citizens and fosters these values.*
> "Pastoral Constitution on the Church in the Modern World," number 76.

Rather than helping to run the political process, the Church helps assess—according to gospel values—the religious and moral dimensions of public policy issues. Church leaders couldn't do this objectively and effectively if they were also responsible for making the policy. There would be a conflict of interest between running the government and providing moral guidance about its public policy.

In addition, history confirms that **theocracies** simply don't work. They usually become intolerant and oppressive. It's much better that the Church lend its wisdom and voice to the public debate—especially on issues of social justice, human rights, and religion's role in society. Then citizens and government leaders will be better informed and can more wisely establish public policy. Changes in social policy begin internally anyway—by changing the mind and heart of one person at a time.

theocracies
governments ruled by God or by those claiming to rule in God's name and with divine authority

Project

1. List some of the major political issues the Church is presently addressing. Describe what values and/or courses of action the Church is promoting in each instance. Tell how that value/action relates to the role of the Church in politics.
2. Analyze the moral problems inherent in a theocracy by considering a current or historical example of a theocracy.

For discussion

1. *What should and shouldn't be the role of the Church in the political process? Why do people sometimes misunderstand this role?*
2. *How might a religious group pose a threat to the political and democratic process? To a healthy cultural, ethnic, social, religious, and/or political freedom and diversity within society? Do you think any religious groups pose such a threat today? Explain.*
3. *Respond to someone who says: "The Church should stay out of politics and stick to religion where it belongs."*
4. *In what sense do both politicians and Church leaders deal with morality? In what sense do they do this in different but complementary ways?*
5. *Unlike in previous centuries, Catholic clergy today are not allowed to hold political office. How does this policy affirm political diversity? How does it protect the Church's integrity and rightful role in the political process?*

Those who say that religion has nothing to do with politics do not know what religion means.
MAHATMA GANDHI

Conscience and the common good

Rather than being limited to "just me" concerns, persons with a well-formed conscience respect others' rights and seek the common welfare. In determining the morality of our actions, we should always consider how our decisions will affect others. Civil authority is to be based on the common good. What, then, is the common good?

The common good is all that is good "in common"—that is, what is good for everyone. **The common good is all the social factors that help people become humanly fulfilled.** It is based on respect for persons and basic human rights. These rights include the right to privacy and to personal freedom (especially in religious matters) and to act in morally sound ways according to one's conscience.

Justice doesn't mean "just us."

Clarify

1. What is meant by the common good?
2. What kinds of things does the common good include?

vigilantism
enforcing the law oneself instead of reasonably relying on lawful authorities to do so

criminal mischief (in common law)
willfully destroying personal property out of ill will or resentment toward the person who owns it

The common good requires working for human development so that every person has access to the food, clothing, housing, health care, education, employment, and other things needed for a reasonable quality of life. People also have the right to live in safety. Children shouldn't have to be afraid of being assaulted at school or have to sleep on the floor out of fear of being shot by a bullet coming through the window. Society has the duty to establish peace and security, and to do so through morally acceptable means.

Global communication, economic interdependence, and pressing ecological concerns are increasingly uniting humanity. More than ever before, these factors give nations and individuals the opportunity to work together for the universal common good. And the need to do this is perhaps greater than ever. For something is horribly wrong when people in one part of the world must grind wood into porridge just to have something to eat, while other nations pay farmers to **not** grow food. Something is wrong when millions of people still die of starvation each year—or when one person does. We've got to figure out fairer ways to share our resources.

But our society and our nation are us. Things will change for the better for all humanity only if each of us freely and actively works to improve the human condition.

Discuss

1. Do you think humanity is drawing closer together or pulling farther apart? Explain.
2. In what areas do you think our society does the best job of looking after the common good? The poorest job? Explain.
3. What is meant by saying that "justice is not 'just us'"?

The crack house crime

Read the following account and respond to the questions.

Sam burned down a one-room shack that served as a crack house. Some believe Sam was justified because he helped rid the neighborhood of drug dealers and the violent crime they brought with them. Others say his action constituted vigilantism and they can't condone it. Sam was arrested and put on trial for arson, trespass, and criminal mischief.

For discussion

1. As a member of the jury in Sam's case, what would your goal be in rendering a verdict? What, if any, problem would you have? ➡

2. In what way does the legal definition of criminal mischief closely mirror the seventh commandment?

3. Why is vigilantism morally wrong? What is the difference between exacting vigilante "justice" and helping to enforce the law by reporting a crime or making a citizen's arrest?

4. Under which circumstances would you find that what Sam did was morally right but legally wrong? Both morally and legally wrong? Both morally and legally right?

5. Are there any conditions under which you would refuse to find Sam guilty of a crime? Explain.

6. If Sam were found guilty of all charges—arson, trespass, and criminal mischief—what sentence would you give him? Why?

"Good Samaritan" laws

Read the following, and then discuss your answers to the questions.

Several years ago, Kitty Genovese was stabbed to death outside her apartment. Neighbors heard her scream and saw the crime taking place, but did not call police or otherwise intervene. When several men raped a woman in a bar, bystanders applauded and encouraged her assaulters. A teenager was raped by two youths in a public park while adult passers-by watched. A child who also witnessed the teenager's rape in the park rode his bike to get the police.

When two perceptive pedestrians noticed a confused and apprehensive blind man at a busy downtown intersection, they immediately offered him assistance. And in many other situations, good Samaritan bystanders have immediately stepped in to help—sometimes risking their lives to do so.

Situations like these obviously involve religious principles and moral decisions. Some people certainly have a special legal duty to help: parents, their children; doctors, their own patients; and public servants, the citizens they serve. There is usually no legal obligation for someone else to step in and give aid or call for assistance. Many think the civil law should require people to help those in serious jeopardy, that those who could help but don't should be considered legally—as well as morally—guilty.

Others believe that, because lawsuits are so common, reluctance to step in and help is under-

standable. Many people are afraid that, despite their best intentions and efforts, they might later be sued. These fears may be well-founded. While the law generally protects those who offer necessary help in a reasonable manner, it doesn't always do so forcefully enough. Doctors or other "good Samaritans" have been successfully sued for compounding injuries—even though they responded reasonably considering their background and qualifications.

*To address the public fear and indifference about helping others, some areas have enacted "good Samaritan laws" to protect individuals from being sued after providing reasonable help. Under one such law, individuals can even be fined if they **don't** help in an urgent situation.*

People's reactions to good Samaritan laws vary. Some people believe these laws are a good idea, and point out that most civil laws already enforce moral obligations that have social dimensions. They believe good Samaritan laws prevent injuries and death and therefore are needed and justified.

Others feel good Samaritan laws aren't necessary. They say indifferent-bystander incidents get lots of publicity, but are too rare to justify laws requiring that people help. A few states' good Samaritan laws have been contested all the way to the Supreme Court. One such law required lawyers to donate a certain portion of their time to defend people who are poor or indigent. Another required

doctors to help anyone they came across who was in urgent need of care.

Those opposing such laws say that "be a good Samaritan or else" laws infringe on individuals' freedom to not get involved. It's all right to pass laws against harming others, they say, but it's overstepping the law's bounds to legally oblige people to go out of their way to do good. Being a good Samaritan, they argue, should generally continue to be a moral but not a legal obligation.

For discussion

1. How do good Samaritans exemplify Jesus' teaching?
2. How do emergencies requiring help involve religious principles and moral decisions?
3. Were you aware that, if you are in serious jeopardy, those nearby probably aren't legally obliged to help you? What is your reaction to this? Why?
4. Who are generally legally obliged to help someone in an emergency? How is this legal obligation also a moral obligation?
5. What are "good Samaritan laws"? What different kinds of good Samaritan laws are there?
6. Which arguments favoring good Samaritan laws do you think have the most merit? The least merit? Why?
7. Which kinds of good Samaritan laws do you favor or oppose? Explain.

The Church and the individual conscience

When John F. Kennedy became the first Catholic president of the United States, many people feared that the pope would run the country and tell the president what to do or not to do. Nothing could have been further from the truth. The function of the pope and other Church leaders is primarily to guide Catholics in understanding and applying Jesus' message in religious and moral matters. It is **not**, however, their function or even within the scope of their authority to make moral decisions **for** others.

Catholic teaching clearly points out that **every person has an obligation and thus a right to seek religious truth. Thus, by using all the means appropriate, we may make prudent judgments of conscience that are correct and true.** Because of our human dignity, we have a moral duty to freely search for truth. **God has given us free will and the ability to use it by reasoning to and acting according to the truth. By so doing, we assume personal responsibility for our decisions.**[1]

Catholic teaching and morality

Church leaders are obligated to study God's word prayerfully, communicate Jesus' saving truths about faith and morals, and guide us in living according to moral principles. If they did not make judgments about matters that safeguard basic human rights and eternal salvation for those in their care, they would be failing in their duty. In fact, the wisdom contained in Church statements about moral matters is taken seriously by individuals and government leaders of all faiths throughout the world.

Catholics believe that, through the Church, Jesus has given the pope and the bishops in union with the pope the authority to teach the religious truths we are to believe and live by in order to fulfill our ultimate destiny in God. The pope and bishops do this as teachers of the faith—usually through religious instruction and preaching—and with the help of theologians and spiritual writers.

Creed
statements of Christian belief which date back to the early Church and the apostles' teaching

Catholic moral teaching is based on the **Creed**, the Lord's Prayer, the law of love, and the Ten Commandments. This teaching includes the specific moral norms of the natural moral law. The Church's moral teaching has been handed on by Catholics who live their faith and by Church guidelines, rules, and precepts.

Catholic teaching doesn't automatically provide specific answers for all of life's moral questions. (Even popes, bishops, and clergy sometimes disagree on how best to approach specific moral issues.) However, there are many ways in which the Church proclaims who we truly are and reminds us of what God calls us to be.

We worship God not just in church, but also by how we live. Catholics celebrate God's love—the source and pinnacle of our moral life—in the liturgy and the sacraments, especially the Eucharist. Through the Church community, we come to understand better Jesus' teaching and God's will for us as proclaimed in Scripture, clarified and strengthened through prayer, and exemplified in our experiences and in history.

doctrine
official Church teaching

For this reason, "In the formation of their consciences, the Christian faithful ought carefully to attend to the sacred and certain **doctrine** of the Church."[2] We have a duty to observe, in addition to the official teachings of the Church, the constitutions and decrees of those who have legitimate authority in the Church. As far as possible, in good conscience, we must not choose anything opposed to the natural moral law, the moral law revealed in Scripture, and the Church's authoritative moral teaching.

Church authorities aren't the only ones charged with teaching religious truth. Through Baptism, all Christians have an obligation to teach and witness to the faith. Through our Christ-like convictions and moral living, we help build up the Church and contribute to God's reign of love, justice, and peace.

In fact, God's Spirit sometimes inspires even the most unassuming persons to enlighten Church authorities and the rest of the Church. A good example of this is Mother Teresa of Calcutta—the humble nun whose dedicated service to the poor and dying enlightened and inspired the world.

For discussion

1. *What does Catholic teaching say about forming one's conscience? About personal responsibility for decisions?*

2. *Respond to someone who says: "It's too bad Catholics don't have freedom of conscience. Their Church always tells them what to do and makes their moral decisions for them."*

3. *From where do Catholics believe the pope and bishops' authority to teach comes? Why would Church leaders be failing in their duty if they didn't guide Catholics on moral matters?*

4. *On what is the tradition behind Catholic moral teaching based? How has this been handed on?*

5. *What **doesn't** Catholic moral teaching provide for Catholics?*

6. *How does the Church help Catholics clarify and strengthen their moral convictions?*

7. *When forming their consciences, what obligation do Catholics have in relation to Church doctrine and authority?*

8. *In what sense are all Christians teachers of the faith and of its moral teaching?*

> *Conscience is the perfect interpreter of life.*
> **KARL BARTH**

Mother Teresa died in 1997 after a life of service to others. India honored her with a state funeral.

Infallibility and individual conscience

Jesus promised that God's Spirit will always be with Jesus' followers to guide us in living according to his teaching. Catholics believe that God will not let us, as an entire Catholic Church community, be mistaken in our shared beliefs about what is essential for salvation. Thus Catholics' belief in the ability of Church authorities to teach infallibly under certain conditions is based first on our belief in the infallibility of the whole Church. It is also based on the belief that Jesus gave his apostles, and the pope and other bishops as their successors, the authority to guard and authentically interpret the gospel and the moral law for the Church.

Some people believe incorrectly, however, that every time the pope or a Church council makes any kind of statement related to matters of faith or morality, every Catholic must accept the statement as absolute truth. Such persons misunderstand the doctrine of infallibility, which is limited in its nature, scope, and implications.

Infallibility applies to matters of *faith* or *morals* which have been revealed by God as necessary for salvation. *Faith* here refers to beliefs. *Morals* refers to what Catholics do to ritually celebrate and/or otherwise live the Christian faith.

The Church's highest teaching authority, called the magisterium, may exercise its infallible authority to defend, authentically explain, or preserve beliefs or practices necessary for salvation.[3] In fact, not just the Church's leaders, but all Catholics are obliged to understand, proclaim, and defend the truth Jesus has taught.[4]

The infallibility of a teaching pertains only to what that teaching means, and does not apply to the way it is expressed. The way an infallible teaching is phrased or communicated may change in the future to reflect the Church's fuller understanding, or to make the teaching clearer or more meaningful for a new generation.

The pope and the bishops also commonly teach without doing so infallibly. The pope and the other bishops of the Church exercise this non-infallible, although authoritative, teaching, for instance, when, as Christ's representatives in the Church community, they teach as individual or groups of bishops (or the pope as spiritual leader of the entire Church) about matters of faith and Christian life.

People all over the world often rely on and expect Church authorities to offer wise religious and moral guidance. For Catholics, the teaching of the Church's ordinary magisterium is far more than just another important opinion. It is the "constant teaching of moral norms in the light of faith."[5] Catholics have a serious moral obligation to carefully listen to and attempt to agree with and follow this authentic Church teaching, even though it has not been formally declared to be infallible. Thus Catholics should consider with a positive attitude the reasons for the Church's teachings, and honestly try to make the Church's viewpoint their own:

The Church is, by the will of Christ, the teacher of the truth. It is her duty to give utterance to, and authoritatively to teach, that Truth which is Christ Himself, and also to declare and confirm by her authority those principles of the moral order which have their origin in human nature itself.

"Declaration on Religious Freedom," number 14.

infallibly
without error

magisterium
the Catholic Church's highest teaching authority, the pope and the bishops in union with him

The Church's leaders have an obligation to speak out about how the natural moral law and Jesus' teaching apply to particular issues today. Catholics must look to the gospel and the teaching of the Church for guidance in forming our consciences and evaluating particular moral problems. We are also to reflect on the insights and wisdom of our own and others' experiences as we look for the truth in resolving moral dilemmas.

The Church recognizes that today's moral dilemmas are often complicated, and understands that future issues may be even more complicated. While some specific answers to particular moral questions are not always readily available, decisions must always be carefully thought out.

Neither we nor the pope can make our own moral laws. Through our properly formed and informed conscience, we **discover** what is true and good. Catholic teaching helps us do this. In addition to guidelines, values, and moral principles, the Church gives us binding norms, or standards, for many situations. In these situations, Catholics must base decisions on these norms, not because they express the judgment of people in authority, but because their source is God's revelation to us (Scripture and tradition).

Blind or forced obedience is not expected. Such "obedience" would contradict the Church's teaching on human freedom and the sanctity of conscience. Personal decisions must be free of undue pressure or coercion. Our human dignity demands that we "act according to a knowing and free choice. Such a choice is personally motivated and prompted from within. It does not result from blind internal impulse nor from mere external pressure" ("Pastoral Constitution on the Church in the Modern World," number 17).

In essentials, unity; in doubtful matters, liberty; in all things, charity.
POPE JOHN XXIII, "AD PETRI CATHEDRAM."

> *In the use of all freedoms, the moral principle of personal and social responsibility is to be observed.*
> "DECLARATION ON RELIGIOUS FREEDOM," NUMBER 7.

Infallibility doesn't rob Catholics of personal freedom or the right and responsibility to prudently make moral decisions based on conscience. If you understand this, you can help correct the common misconception that, as Catholics, we follow the pope **instead** of following our conscience!

God could have created each of us incapable of making a moral mistake or committing a moral wrong. Instead, God created us free. We are to love God of our own free will, not because we're pressured or forced into it. We must always do our best to discover, understand, and live by the truth. We must form our consciences so that we judge according to truth. Above all, we should rely on God's help to use our freedom of conscience well to choose what is good.

For discussion

1. *What do Catholics believe about infallibility? On what is this belief based? How is it limited?*

2. *In what sense might an infallible Church teaching change? How may it not change?*

3. *Until now, what has been your understanding of Church law and pronouncements by the pope?*

4. *What obligation do Catholics have regarding Church teaching?*

5. *What misunderstandings about authoritative teaching in the Catholic Church community do each of the following reflect? Explain how you would respond to someone who says to you:*

   - *"The entire Catholic faith depends on the pope's being infallible. If the pope weren't infallible, Catholics couldn't be sure that their religious beliefs are true."*

   - *"Catholics have no right to question anything the pope and bishops say, because they are teaching with the infallible authority of God."*

   - *"Catholics really need to believe in and follow only the infallible Church doctrines—other Church teachings are just the pope and bishops' opinions."*

   - *"Catholics don't have the freedom to follow their conscience, because the Church makes their moral decisions for them."*

6. *What is the relationship between Church teaching and following one's conscience? Why is blind or forced obedience not required?*

7. *Where are Catholics to look for moral standards in order to apply them to real-life situations?*

> *No one is an island,*
> *entire of itself; every person is a piece*
> *of the continent, a part of the main . . .*
> *any person's death diminishes me, because I am involved in humanity;*
> *and therefore never send to know for whom*
> *the bell tolls; it tolls for thee.*
> ADAPTED FROM JOHN DONNE.

Society and the individual conscience

We need one another, and the right to associate and assemble freely with others is guaranteed in our constitution. Societies are necessary for physical survival and in order for humans to carry the best knowledge, wisdom, and experience through time. All social groups are organized around a unifying principle. Thus, the whole of a social community is more than the sum of its parts.

Essential social groups include the family and the state. But other social groups are also important, because together we can achieve things we could never do alone. We owe certain loyalties and responsibilities to the human communities to which we belong. But what happens when being loyal and obedient to laws or rules conflicts with what your conscience tells you is right? When are you justified in breaking the law or violating the rules? To answer this, you must first understand the nature and purpose of laws, and the difference between good laws or rules and bad ones.

Law and morality

Jesus' message was quite different from the mentality that puts rules, regulations, and **laws** above people. He preached a higher law than any civil or social code—to love one another as God loves us. In fact, Jesus harshly criticized those who made the observance of religious rituals their moral priority.

Scripture insights

1. Read the full context of these Scripture passages in Matthew 15:1–20 and Luke 11:37–46.
2. What attitudes and behavior was Jesus addressing in each? What did he say about these?
3. If Jesus were to say the same types of things today, to whom would he say them?
4. Read Mark 2:27 and 12:17, and Matthew 12:9–15. What points was Jesus making here about laws and obeying them?

At the same time, Jesus also tells us that **legitimate laws** are to be obeyed—so long as concern for others remains primary and overriding. In fact, **the purpose of all good laws is to promote the common good and protect people's basic rights.**

Following the same principle that applies to authority in general, there shouldn't be more laws than are necessary to achieve this end. When there are too many laws, people tend to disregard them. Then there is no law. On the other hand, if we didn't live by the rule of law, we would all become the subjects—or the victims—of one another's whims. (Remember the pitfalls of "doing what comes naturally"?)

To warrant our obedience, laws must be just. **A law is just only to the extent that it is both reasonable and in accord with God's law.** Thus morality and human-made laws are not necessarily the same. God's law of love—as expressed in the heart's natural moral law and God's revealed law in Scripture—is superior to every other kind of law. Unlike civil law, God's law is always and everywhere binding for everyone.

What is morally right or wrong in relation to God's law therefore may or may not correspond to what civil law says is right or wrong. Yet people sometimes erroneously presume that something is morally wrong just because there's a law against it—or that it's morally right just because there's no law against it. As St. Thomas Aquinas defined it: **A good law is "a rule of reason for the common good, made by [one] who has care of the community."**

"But woe to you. . . . For you . . . neglect justice and the love of God; it is these you ought to have practiced, without neglecting the others. . . . For you load people with burdens hard to bear, and you yourselves do not lift a finger to ease them."
LUKE 11:42 AND 46

laws
binding customs or practices of a group; rules of conduct or action

legitimate laws
rules of conduct enacted by a rightful authority to promote and safeguard the common good

"But what comes out of the mouth proceeds from the heart, and this is what defiles. For out of the heart come evil intentions, murder, adultery, fornication, theft, false witness, slander. These are what defile a person, but to eat with unwashed hands does not defile."
MATTHEW 15:18–20

[The human person], considered as a creature, must necessarily be subject to the laws of our Creator. . . . This law of nature . . . dictated by God . . . is of course superior in obligation to any other. It is binding over all the globe, in all countries, and at all times: no human laws are of any validity, if contrary to this; and such of them as are valid derive all their force, and all their authority . . . from this original. . . .
SIR WILLIAM BLACKSTONE, 1765, *COMMENTARIES ON THE LAWS OF ENGLAND.*

Good laws foster the common good and the welfare of people. To the extent that a law does so, it agrees with the objective purpose of morality: achieving human good and fulfillment in relationship with God and others. If a law doesn't affect the welfare of people one way or another, it is *amoral*—without moral implications. To the extent that a law is contrary to God's law and the common good, it is *immoral*—morally wrong.

Immoral laws have, for example, upheld slavery—sometimes even while the lawmakers maintained a belief in human freedom and individual rights! **A**moral laws may include outdated laws that remain in legal codes only because no one's bothered to remove them. In Pennsylvania, Virginia, and Ohio, taking a bath was once banned or highly restricted. One city's law still says you mustn't tie up your horse on Main Street between 2:00 A.M. and 3:00 P.M. on Sundays. One major city made it illegal for women to wear shoes with skinny heels. The city didn't really intend that women not wear these shoes; it just wanted to protect itself from being sued for negligence when women caught their high heels in sidewalk cracks!

While a law may correspond with objective moral norms, the way that law is interpreted and enforced may run contrary to those norms. It is a universally accepted moral principle, for instance, that it's wrong to kill people "without just cause." World cultures and legal codes **subjectively** agree on this basic moral perception of what is **objectively** wrong. What constitutes "just cause" for killing someone, however, differs from one place or court case to another. Interpreting what "justifiable homicide" means requires further refinement.

Punishments for the same crime often differ according to the subjective moral perceptions of those who make the laws. Some Middle Eastern cultures believe it right to stone an adulteress to death. Our society generally believes marital infidelity is a personal moral concern and not a civil crime. In some places, it is still legitimate punishment for stealing to cut off the thief's hand or finger! In our culture, however, mutilation is prohibited as "cruel and unusual punishment." Yet even here the same crime might have different punishments in different places.

Laws, and their punishments, are "only as good as the people who make them." Laws and punishments are based on the lawmakers' idea of right and wrong, and on society's understanding of what is fair and just. As we have seen, these perceptions may or may not accurately reflect what is morally right or wrong.

It's not possible—or even desirable—to keep morality out of politics and laws. By definition, laws and social policy must serve the common good, That's precisely morality's main concern—what is good or bad for people. So it's impossible to keep from "legislating morality."

Morality goes beyond the law, but it should at least provide norms for making laws and punishing violators. The question is: On whose ideas of good and bad, moral and immoral, is society to base its social policies and laws? Objective morality—seeking the objective truth, not just blindly accepting opinions—is the standard for judging whether laws, social policy, and personal behavior are right or wrong, good or bad, just or unjust.

For discussion

1. What did Jesus say about laws and obeying laws? About putting obedience to laws before people's welfare?
2. Why is it bad to have too many laws? Do you think we have too many laws in our society, or not enough? Explain.
3. When is a law just? What is a good law? What is the difference between morality and law?
4. What is the difference between moral, immoral, and amoral laws? Give examples of each.
5. Why do punishments for breaking the same law often differ?
6. Agree or disagree with this statement and explain your position: "When it comes to making laws, people shouldn't try to impose their morality on others."

> *Law is those wise restraints that make people free.*
> **JUDGE STEPHEN BREYER, U.S. SUPREME COURT JUSTICE, ADAPTED.**

Robot rules

Technologies are developing so rapidly that, if public policy makers don't keep up with them, grave and unstoppable harm will occur. Consider, for instance, the implications of robotics.

Increasingly, artificially intelligent robots will perform many routine tasks previously done by humans. Cars can already "drive" themselves, having been programmed to make "decisions" about maneuvering under various road conditions. As artificial intelligence technology is refined, robots will function and "make decisions" more and more on their own.

Experts say we must start seriously deliberating now about what kind of laws and moral rules our robots should be programmed to abide by. It is vital that you participate intelligently and actively in helping to steer our society—and our robots—in right directions.

Consider these three "robot laws" attributed to science-fiction writer Isaac Asimov, and then respond to the questions.

1. Robots must never injure a human.
2. Robots must obey humans—except when doing so would violate law number 1.
3. Robots may protect their own existence—except if doing so goes against laws 1 and 2.

For discussion

1. Explain the difference between a human being and a robot that might think and act like a human.
2. As robots look and function more like humans, what dangers and moral problems do you foresee?
3. What goal(s) should regulate how robots may be programmed and used? ➡
4. In view of what you discussed about law in this chapter:
   • Do you think the above "robot rules" would be morally good ones to program into artificially intelligent robots?
   • In what ways do you think these rules don't go far enough?
   • What laws would you add or substitute?
5. Why is it important that citizens like yourself and religious groups participate in formulating "robot laws"?
6. In what ways do you think the reliance on personal robots will eventually change people for the better? For the worse?

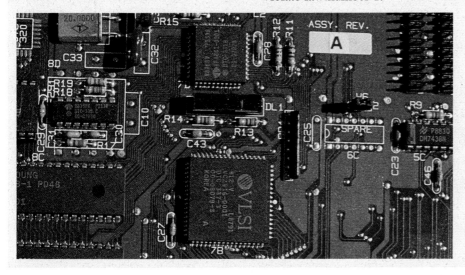

> *The best use of good laws is to teach people to trample bad laws under their feet.*
> WENDELL PHILLIPS, ADAPTED.

Conscientious disobedience

In following your conscience, you will sometimes disagree with others' moral judgments. Your conscience may conflict with the opinions of your friends or your boss, or with the rules, regulations, or practices of a group to which you belong. You might disagree in conscience with the laws or policies of a segment of society, or with having to obey a law in a particular circumstance. What should you do if you are faced with that type of conflict? When would it be right for you to deliberately disobey a legitimate law or command?

Any laws or rules should be moral. When a law is morally good, breaking it is generally both legally **and** morally wrong. Without the laws that protect our safety on the streets and highways, for instance, people would mow each other down much more often than they do now. Running a red light is legally wrong because it breaks a civil law. It's also morally wrong because it endangers others' lives.

Remember, the purpose of all good laws is to promote the common good and protect people's basic rights and freedoms. If following the letter of the law contradicts the law's spirit and obstructs its purpose, you need to reconsider whether you should obey the law. **Out of respect for legitimate authority, you may still have a moral duty to obey a poor or unfair law. But at the same time, you should work to change it.** It is Christians' responsibility to work to change laws that do not adequately protect basic human rights and promote the common good.

Laws are only as good as the lawmakers (and the citizens who elect them) are wise and responsible. Lawmakers can and do make honest mistakes when trying to subjectively determine what is **objectively** best or right. Sometimes they're just not smart enough to make good laws. Sometimes they put their own interests above the common good. Or they lack the courage to pass the right kind of law. Or they may let other influences corrupt them into passing a bad law. That is why as citizens we must hold our lawmakers accountable.

To the extent that a law is not reasonable or in accord with God's law, it is unjust, oppressive, and abusive. People don't have an obligation to obey it. Unjust laws—those that have no legitimate authority behind them or that harm the common good—are not binding in conscience. We have a right and a moral duty to try to change immoral, unjust laws. Remember that there is a difference between an unjust law (which we don't have to obey) and a legitimate, reasonable, and moral, but imperfect law (which we usually should obey).

Projects (choose one)

1. Write a letter or e-mail message to a public official or the newspaper urging a change in a law you consider inadequate or unjust, or asking for a new law to correct inequalities or injustices. Explain your position.
2. Interview students, teachers, and administrators to determine what rules are most often violated at your school and to explore the reasons. Write a paper on your findings and your response in light of what you've learned about law and obedience.

Times when conscientious disobedience is called for

Some countries call for forced sterilization or abortion after a couple has two children. Sometimes people are drafted to fight an unjust war or taxed to pay for it. Some discriminatory laws still exist—laws that protect and promote racism, sexism, homophobia, and discrimination on the basis of religion. People are not morally bound to obey such unjust and immoral laws. In fact, if the injustice is serious enough, we're morally bound to **resist** the law as well as try to change it.

Just because a country considers itself civilized doesn't mean its every law—or its law enforcement—is good and right. For example, consider the fact that people with enough money to hire excellent legal experts can almost always avoid the death penalty for capital crimes in the United States—apparently one reason criminals on death row are disproportionately poor. Enforcing laws unjustly is wrong, and a truly just society has an obligation to correct the injustice. Thus there is no excuse, for example, for police brutality—for applying more force than necessary to restrain and arrest someone.

There may be times when you have to disobey a human-made law, rule, or directive in order to do the morally right thing. A woman carefully and safely made an illegal left turn to make way for an approaching ambulance. She did the morally right thing—even though she got a ticket and the traffic court judge didn't believe her story and found her guilty. After waiting five minutes for a red light to turn green at 3:00 A.M. on a seemingly deserted road, a man proceeded because he reasonably thought the light was stuck. He wasn't morally wrong, even though the patrol officer who had been observing out of sight pulled him over and ticketed him.

In both instances, the individuals were legally wrong but morally right. After assessing the situation carefully, they took a safe and reasonable course of action. Both violated the law deliberately, but neither did so lightly. Once convinced of the right course of action, they made responsible and moral decisions—even though civil authorities deemed the decision illegal. On the other hand, a driver who goes the speed limit on a rain-slick highway, or one who carelessly drives ten miles below the limit on a clear day, could be morally responsible for endangering lives—even though neither exceeds the maximum speed the law allows. (In fact, most jurisdictions now stipulate that the driver must always drive at a safe speed for the circumstances.)

Sometimes individuals find it necessary in conscience to actively oppose a government policy they believe is immoral. There have been many **conscientious objectors** in history. When the early American settlers dumped the tea in Boston Harbor to oppose unjust taxation, they were practicing conscientious disobedience.

When the civil rights movement began in the 1960s, by law Blacks were forced to use separate public restrooms and drinking fountains, and ride in the back of public buses. They were denied access to public beaches and were not allowed to vote or run for local government office. When African Americans refused to sit in the back of the bus or chose to sit at a "white" lunch counter, they were practicing conscientious disobedience. And the freedom riders who refused to obey the racial segregation laws on interstate buses and in bus terminals were conscientious objectors.

Injustice anywhere is a threat to justice everywhere. We are caught in an inescapable network of mutuality, tied in a single garment of destiny. Whatever affects one directly, affects all indirectly.
MARTIN LUTHER KING JR.,
LETTER FROM A BIRMINGHAM JAIL.

No laws are binding on the human subject which assault the body or violate the conscience.
SIR WILLIAM BLACKSTONE, 1765, *COMMENTARIES ON THE LAWS OF ENGLAND.*

conscientious objectors
those who, for carefully deliberated reasons of conscience, actively and responsibly oppose civil laws they consider unjust

integrated
blended, intermixed, connected

At that time, an all-white jury took only twenty minutes to acquit a bus driver who had shot and killed a young black soldier just because the soldier wouldn't move to the back of the bus. Proponents of segregation were attempting to burn racially **integrated** busloads of children. So when a team of white students crossed town to play basketball secretly with the team from an all-black school, they were all breaking the law and risking expulsion from school. When a racially integrated group of Catholic high school students sat wherever they wanted to on the bus going to a retreat, they were risking their lives.

The civil rights movement succeeded in overturning racial segregation laws because the movement's participants resisted those laws and did so courageously, consistently, and nonviolently—and because racist laws and practices thus became, at least to some extent, economically untenable. Throughout the struggle for civil rights, African and Native Americans remained steadfast in respecting human rights, as they were urging others to do. Their example began changing a nation's conscience far more quickly and effectively than could any kind of armed aggression. The civil rights movement's organized conscientious objection to racial segregation has made an enormous positive difference (although we still have a long way to go in eliminating racial intolerance and **discrimination**).

discrimination
acting in ways unjustly partial toward or biased against certain persons or groups

Research project (choose one)

1. Read Dr. Martin Luther King Jr.'s *Letter from a Birmingham Jail.* Briefly explain what you think are his best points about opposing injustice.

2. Read about how the system of apartheid in South Africa was successfully overthrown. Write a brief report on why you think this was finally achieved.

3. Read about Mahatma Gandhi's nonviolent campaign to free India from British rule. Write a brief report on the nonviolent methods he espoused, why they proved so effective, and how they affected this country's civil rights movement.

4. Write a report on the beliefs and methods of Christian pacifists in opposing immoral civil policies.

Choosing conscientious objection

All civil laws must be weighed against the moral law's higher norms. We must determine in conscience whether, according to the higher moral law, we should obey or disobey a civil law. As citizens, we have a duty in conscience to **not** obey civil laws or commands which contradict the moral order or violate basic human rights or gospel teachings. But when we defend our rights or those of others, we must do so in ways that are in keeping with the gospel and the natural moral law. At the same time, we must continue to obey just aspects of the law and do what the common good demands.

The same principles that apply to obeying civil laws also apply to obeying the commands of other authorities—such as one's parents, teachers, or employer. As long as you are living at home in your parents' or guardians' custody, you are responsible for obeying them when what is asked is for your own good or that of your family. You must also obey your employer's and teachers' reasonable directives. (Yes, this includes doing your homework and not disrupting class!)

If you are convinced in conscience, however, that it would be morally wrong for you to obey a specific command of your parent, guardian, teacher, boss, or other person in authority, you must not obey it. Your attitude in disobeying it, though, mustn't be defiant. Rather you should be courageous in doing what is right, while regretting that it's necessary for you to disobey.

For discussion

1. *When is it morally right to break a civil law? Why? List your criteria for determining this.*

2. *What is the difference between a poor or unfair law and one that is unjust and must be disobeyed?*

3. *When do you have a moral duty to obey a poor or unfair law? Explain why.*

4. *Give five examples of how enforcing laws unjustly is wrong.*

5. *Have you ever broken a civil law, believing you were morally right, or do you know of someone else who has? Explain.*

6. *Explain in your own words what a conscientious objector is. Looking back at history, which conscientious objectors' struggles would you probably have joined at the time?*

7. *Why do you think nonviolent conscientious objectors have often been more successful than armed aggressors at changing people's hearts and behavior?*

8. *Which laws, commands, or rules do you have a duty in conscience to resist? If you must disobey an unjust law, morally speaking **how** are you to do it? Give examples.*

> *Values are measured in terms of what a person is willing to pay for them.*
> YESHAYAHU LEIBOWITZ

Campus rebellion

Read the following true account. Then respond to the questions.

When residents began complaining that drinking among the local college students was getting out of hand, police started cracking down on underage student drinking. Some of the students likewise have become fed up with the campus drunkenness. They say they're sick and tired of the noisy dorms, having to clean up after vomiting roommates who've been on drinking binges, seeing their friends hurt through sexually demeaning behavior while drunk, watching helplessly as good friends become alcoholics and drop out of school, and fearing personal assaults by drunken students. Many of them have applied to live in alcohol-free dorms for the following year.

Some other students, however, have opposed as "harassment" the police department's efforts to curb the underage student drinking. They've said they feel drinking is part of "the college experience." They decided to hold a block party where alcohol was served, and hundreds of students became drunk and rowdy.

When police arrived, things got completely out of control, and drunken students began pelting the police with rocks, bottles, and bricks. One officer was knocked unconscious by a thrown brick. Twelve police officers and about twenty other persons were injured in the free-for-all.

Some of the students set dumpsters on fire, rolling one downhill at the police. Others looted stores, smashed and stole cash from parking meters, or threw rocks through windows. Even the students who had helped host the party became frightened and barricaded themselves in locked rooms when drunken party-goers started beating them and destroying their furnishings.

Student government leaders say police have been treating students as "a nuisance rather than valued members of the community." Other students defend student conduct by saying students are just protesting police harassment over drinking. Some admit that they just got caught up in "the party atmosphere." A teenage girl who helped host the party said students had become so "sick of the stuff going on" with the police crack-down on student drinking that they decided just to do what they wanted.

Some students point out that only a small minority of the students feel and act that way, and that this small group gives all the students and the school a bad name. Many students organized to help clean up the damage caused in the campus rebellion.

For discussion

1. What moral problems (including the underlying ones) are involved in this situation? ➡
2. What goal would you have in addressing each of these? ➡
3. How would you assess the morality of the student rebels' actions?
4. What better ways do you think should have been tried to solve the problems?

Armed aggression, disarmament, and peace

Although war is a terrible scourge, too often we don't see it as such. Often we see it in terms of weapons, soldiers, and strategies. Or we see it as history. You've probably read in your history classes about ferocious "barbarians" like Attila the Hun, who was nicknamed "Scourge of God." Yet 160 million people have been killed by war and conflict **in this past century**—the bloodiest in human history. It's modern warfare that is the real scourge.

According to the United Nations, in the past ten years two million children (more children than soldiers) have died in war, over four million more children have been injured in war, and over ten million children have been left homeless from war. The question then is: When soldiers are sent off to fight the enemy, who is the enemy? Whom are they fighting? Who is really being sentenced to suffer and die? Evidently, it's the innocent.

Let us have faith that right makes might; and in that faith let us to the end dare to do our duty as we understand it.
ABRAHAM LINCOLN

Clarify

How and why must our understanding of war today differ from that of previous generations? Statistically, who are usually the victims of war?

Might does **not** make right. In fact, as Abraham Lincoln points out, the reverse is true. Societies have the right to use morally acceptable means to defend themselves legitimately in order to ensure a just peace and security for their members. In Catholic teaching, the idea of a "just war" means that when war is unavoidable and all efforts to achieve peace have failed, a society has the legitimate right to defend itself by military force under certain strict conditions which must **all exist at the same time.**[6]

1. The violation of basic human rights by an aggressor is certain, gravely serious, and prolonged.

2. Every other means of relieving the oppressive conditions has been tried and has failed.

3. Armed resistance won't give rise to even worse evils or wrongs.

4. There is well-founded hope and serious possibility of succeeding.

5. Better ways of solving the problem can't reasonably be foreseen.

In the past it was possible to destroy a village, a town, a region, even a country. Now it is the whole planet that has come under threat.
POPE JOHN PAUL II

Even during war there are moral limits—as the world's nations recognize in prohibiting certain war crimes and requiring humane treatment for non-combatants, prisoners of war, and the wounded. **Genocide** and the indiscriminate destruction of entire regions or cities of people are terrible moral wrongs, and individuals have a moral duty to oppose commands to participate in such activities.

genocide
the attempt to exterminate a people, nation, or ethnic group

Clarify

Why must there be moral limits, even in war? What are some of these limits?

It is our clear duty, then, to strain every muscle as we work for the time when all war can be completely outlawed by international consent. . . . Peace must be born of mutual trust between nations rather than imposed on them through fear of one another's weapons.
"PASTORAL CONSTITUTION ON THE CHURCH IN THE MODERN WORLD," NUMBER 82.

disarmament
the reduction, elimination, or rendering harmless of destructive weapons

Project (choose one)

1. Find out more about the Holocaust, in which over six million Jews and millions of others were killed in a genocidal effort by the Nazis. (Tip: Check out the Holocaust Museum's Internet site.) Write a brief report on why you think so many ordinary citizens did not or could not live up to their Christian moral principles, and why others courageously helped to rescue Jews and others during the Holocaust.

2. Find out what additional crimes against humanity are not allowed even in war. (Tip: Check the United Nations' and Amnesty International's Internet sites.) Write a brief report on why these crimes are both morally and legally wrong.

Nuclear, biological, and chemical warfare's potential for global destruction raises perhaps the most profoundly troubling moral concerns. A single missile unleashing just one pound of the deadly disease Anthrax could kill everyone in a large city. No nuclear, biological, or chemical war could ever be justified. Such a war would undo God's earthly creation and wipe out thousands of years of human achievement. We all know such weapons should never be used. Yet even one mistake, such as a leak-causing accident at a biological containment facility, or one deliberate wartime or terrorist act could unleash mass destruction.

When societies over-arm, the danger of armed conflict and catastrophic accidents increases. We must all support efforts to finally end all arms races and achieve complete nuclear, biological, and chemical **disarmament** in a way supported by genuine, workable safeguards. Nations must find better ways together to ensure humanity's security and the earth's continuance. All of us should support leaders' efforts to do away with the unspeakable weapons and other horrors of war.

Realistically, there is no way to "win"—or very likely even survive—a nuclear war. There's no way to limit the all-out destruction of certain types of biological or chemical warfare. Our only hope lies in preventing these terrors. While the Bible doesn't give specific answers to the moral questions humanity faces about war and peace, the teaching of Jesus does make one thing very clear: **Peace should always be our goal.**

Clarify

1. What is the essence of the modern problem of war, especially regarding the maintaining of nuclear, biological, and chemical arsenals?

2. Why is nuclear war or biological or chemical warfare a no-win prospect?

Jesus showed us that humanity can live harmoniously together by applying the principles he taught. By being peacemakers in the world, we respond to the gift God has given us in the risen Christ. His resurrection gives us the confidence that we, too, can live and pass on peace each day and experience peace forever with God.

"Peace I leave with you; my peace I give to you."
JOHN 14:27

Clarify

Some Christians claim the Bible foretells a nuclear destruction that will one day end the world. According to Catholic belief, how does God's gift of peace in Jesus contradict that interpretation?

In your own life, try to be at peace with yourself and with others. Constantly fighting yourself can only make your life an uphill struggle, and can create tension and conflict between you and others. When you are stressed, take time to calm and quiet yourself. Ask God's help to put things in perspective so that you don't react inappropriately to situations and end up harming yourself or others. We can't expect that the world will ever achieve peace if each of us can't even find it in our own heart and soul.

If it is possible, so far as it depends on you, live peaceably with all.
ROMANS 12:18

For discussion

1. *What is wrong and dangerous about the "might makes right" philosophy of aggression? Do you know teenagers with that attitude? Why is the reverse true?*

2. *If you were drafted to participate in a military action in another country where people were resisting political oppression, what criteria would you use in deciding if your participation would be moral?*

3. *If this country entered a war, considering Catholic teaching's "just war" theory, what conditions would have to be present for you to consider the war just? Under what conditions would you actively oppose the war as immoral?*

4. *If this government ever (God forbid) began to exterminate a segment of the population on the basis of religion, race, or gender identity, would you have the courage to risk your life to help these individuals escape death? Explain.*

5. *Some think the greatest danger of catastrophic war today lies in the part-computer, part-human chain of control and command wherein one mistake might lead a country to believe it's being attacked, and thus to retaliate. What do you think is the greatest danger today? Why?*

6. *Considering the available options for war, what do you think must be done to change the precariousness of humanity's situation? How would this involve a moral change of heart on the part of individuals and societies?*

7. *Why must world peace begin with individuals like us? What can you do to contribute to world peace?*

8. *What do you think the Church can and should do to promote peace and discourage war?*

Peace plan activity

1. Assess the main sources of tension or aggression among the teenagers you know.

2. List ten practical ways of addressing these problems and achieving a greater peace among the students at your school.

Agree with God, and be at peace; in this way good will come to you.
JOB 22:21

The uNclear option

One of the statespersons involved years ago in the Cuban missile crisis between the United States and the Soviet Union later said that "nuclear catastrophe was hanging by a thread. And we weren't days away, or even hours, but minutes." He said both countries' presidents had considered it "insane" that two individuals could lead the whole world so close to nuclear war. Keeping that in mind, read the following story and respond to the questions.

The Final Four, as they later came to be called, were chosen and presented at a special secret meeting of the United Nations Commission on the Inspection of Nuclear Arms. . . . As a team, they would personally visit every missile site, where they would inspect and confirm the number and types of missiles, the exact number (and megatonnage) of warheads atop each missile, and the actual computer programs that had been designed to guide each warhead to its pre-programmed destination.

Every three months the group would repeat its inspection, and then . . . hand-deliver reports to the heads of the superpowers. . . . Disarmament talks continued in Geneva, but each side continued to reject the "build-down" proposals of the other. Session after session ended in a stalemate, for each government had come to rely upon the strength of its own deterrence for the avoidance of Armageddon.

The whole world, in fact, was growing accustomed to this reliance. Speeches were received with increasing enthusiasm in which the speaker would praise the balance of power as the chief cornerstone for the building of peace. . . .

ON THE TWENTY-FIFTH of March . . . a courier appeared in [each superpower's capital with this message for its president]. . .

Dear Ms./Mr. President:
We have listened with genuine interest to your recent address . . . in which you declared, and we quote, "Nuclear war is suicide." . . . Nuclear war is indeed suicide. . . . In the event of a nuclear attack, it will matter little who launches which missile first, and it will matter not at all whose missiles reach whose targets. The Final Four Team of Inspectors has designed and put into place a plan which has rendered this precarious balance of terror ineffective and entirely obsolete.

The purpose of this letter is to inform you that a certain percentage of your own nuclear missiles has been reprogrammed, and, if launched, will strike at [your own country's] targets; and that a certain percentage of [the other superpowers'] missiles has been reprogrammed to strike at [those countries]. . . . any attempt to access the missiles . . . even for the purpose of decoding their programs, will result in the immediate and permanent disarming of that individual weapon. . . .

Though we were unable to remove your option to launch, we did what we could: we rendered that option unclear. This is our contribution to the survival of the planet. . . .
Sincerely. . . .
The Final Four Inspection Team [7]

For discussion

1. Why do you think countries usually find it hard to agree on reducing and eliminating weapons of mass destruction? Given what's at stake, what do you think of these reasons?

2. Look up the scriptural reference to Armageddon in the Book of Revelation. What does this reference mean here?

3. In the story, what had become the chief cornerstone of peace and the way to avoid nuclear war? Do you think this mirrors reality today?

4. How would you define or describe genuine world peace? Is your idea compatible with the existence of weapons of mass destruction? Explain.

5. Why are nuclear, biological, and chemical warfare considered "suicide"?

6. What did the Final Four's plan accomplish, and how? How was it made "fail-safe" and irreversible? How did it shift the incentive to avoid nuclear war from one kind of fear to another?

7. How did the Final Four's actions constitute civil disobedience? Do you think they were morally justified in what they did? Would you do the same thing if you had the opportunity? Would you reward or punish the Final Four? Explain.

8. Can you conceive of a situation in which it would ever be morally right to initiate a nuclear holocaust? Explain.

9. What points does this story make about harboring and using weapons of mass destruction?

Step 2: What alternatives do you have?

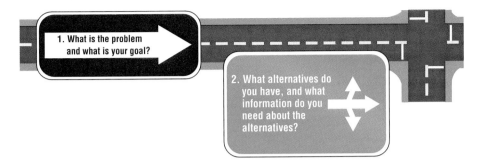

Step 2 in moral decision making: Determine and assess your alternatives

Once you've identified the moral problem and established your goal, your second step in moral decision making is to inform your conscience—to figure out your workable alternatives. (A solution isn't a solution if it won't work!) This step involves very careful thought—and often a lot more ingenuity and creativity than people bother to use. It was just such imaginative yet practical thinking, however, that saved the crew of a space mission years ago.

When vital systems aboard the Apollo 13 space shuttle malfunctioned in outer space, it became evident that the crew might not be able to make it home. The ideal high-tech solutions that would have been available on the ground weren't available to the astronauts in space. Engineers at the ground-control center therefore had to find a solution the Apollo's crew could implement using only materials they had on board. So the technicians dumped these odds and ends items on a table and together devised an imaginative but workable solution which they then communicated to the astronauts.

As was the case for the Apollo crew, solutions which seem ideal in theory aren't always possible in reality. Just as your real problem might be an underlying rather than apparent one, so too the usual, obvious, or ideal solutions might not be your best ones in the particular situation. You might need to create a better alternative than what initially pops into your head. Sometimes a compromise combines alternatives to successfully solve the problem for everyone involved. That is why it's always wise to give yourself **three** alternatives from which to choose.

. . . the Spirit of truth . . . will guide you into all the truth. . . .
JOHN 16:13

When situations seem impossible, try brainstorming as well as praying. List every idea or alternative you can think of—however wacky. Notions that at first seem crazy can inspire a unique practical alternative you otherwise might not have thought of.

This worked successfully for some sailors during wartime when their ship was blocked from its destination by mines set to explode on impact. If the sailors deliberately blew up the mines, they would give away their position and lose the element of surprise. While those in charge seemed stymied, one sailor joked that they should just spray the mines away with the hoses used for cleaning the ship's deck. This wisecrack provided the solution. By directing the hoses' spray near the floating mine, the crew created a tidal motion that carried each mine far enough away to allow the ship safe passage through the mined waters!

> *Beloved,*
> *do not believe every*
> *spirit, but test the spirits*
> *to see whether they are*
> *from God. . . .*
> 1 JOHN 4:1

> *Do not quench*
> *the Spirit. Do not*
> *despise the words of*
> *prophets, but test*
> *everything; hold fast to*
> *what is good. . . .*
> 1 THESSALONIANS 5:19–21

Reflection

1. Do you tend to want instant answers to problems, or do you usually think a problem through carefully?

2. How open-minded are you in listening to and considering all the facts about an issue or problem?

The point here isn't to encourage you to dream up weird solutions to problems! It's to convince you to not rule out imaginative problem-solving approaches that may spark highly reasonable solutions. Especially when the situation seems hopeless, don't view any alternative solution as too dumb to consider. Be resourceful! Open your mind to all alternatives, not just those obvious from the start. Then see which ones you can make work. This creative problem-solving process, which many businesses use, can result in constructive, productive, and wise moral decisions.

Prayer is a vital part of the decision-making process. Communicating with God through prayer and reflecting on Jesus' ideals and teachings are important ways for Christians to form their consciences. God always desires to help and inspire each of us—but we've got to make the effort to listen. Being open to new possibilities can be one way of listening to God's Spirit. Another way is to give your mind time for calm, quiet reflection and prayer about your dilemma. That may be how God's Spirit will inspire you to best resolve a problem.

Don't be superstitious about this, though. Just because a solution pops into your head while you're praying, that doesn't necessarily mean it's from God! Before deciding to act on it, use your God-given common sense and reasoning to test the idea for its practical and moral soundness.

Inform your conscience

People tend to want instant answers even when situations call for careful thought and deliberation. Instead, we must take the time to consider the facts and circumstances involved in the situation. Recalling lessons learned from previous experiences certainly can be beneficial, but we can't assume that the best solution is the one that worked last time. While using the wisdom we've gained from prior experience, we must consider each moral situation on its own merits.

This involves organizing and assessing the data you have—what you already know about the problem. Then you must determine what else you should find out about the situation before you can make a fair and wise decision. Therefore, it's an excellent idea to first ask relevant questions before trying to come up with decisions and conclusions. What you don't know but should find out might change your options and your mind, resulting in an entirely different decision than you otherwise would have made.

At this stage of the decision-making process, Catholics should consider how understanding Church teaching can enlighten us by showing us how to apply Jesus' principles in our situation. This guidance can be an essential part of our making decisions in good conscience.

Realistically, you'll probably never know everything you'd like to know before making major decisions. Sometimes that just isn't possible. But the information you **don't** have at the outset can be crucial. So at least try to inform your conscience as much as possible. Remember, having an "I've already made up my mind—don't confuse me with the facts" attitude does not lead to wise decisions!

Journal entry

Write down one thing you could do that would help you do a better job of considering the alternatives in resolving a moral issue or problem.

For discussion

1. What is involved in determining your alternatives in moral-dilemma situations?

2. Why aren't ideal solutions always the best ones to problems? Why are brainstorming, praying, and resourcefulness important?

3. What should you think about in trying to find possible alternative solutions to moral problems? How can understanding Church teaching help?

Consider other viewpoints

To make wise moral decisions, it's crucial to consider all relevant information and possibilities. Sometimes it's our own prejudices and pre-judgments that keep us from listening to a different point of view. People often don't want to listen to a side they're strongly opposed to. They may think it's a waste of time or will only confuse them further. If we adhere to our principles while becoming well-informed on the various viewpoints involved, however, we're far less likely to make poor decisions. In fact, we must do that in order to seek the truth.

When we initially **feel** comfortable with only one side of an issue, we may not readily see the validity of other viewpoints. One-sided feelings can block our ability to be objective. We shouldn't base important decisions simply on feelings. Yet we mustn't ignore the wisdom that can come from our heart's ability to **empathize**. Following the *Golden Rule* for morality, we need to put ourselves in others' situations—to imagine what **they** face, how **they** feel, what **their** strengths and weaknesses are. Then we can better understand their point of view. Rejecting others' input just because they disagree with us is foolish, and it isn't the loving, caring attitude we must have for **all** concerned when resolving moral dilemmas.

empathize
feel with another

When we consult others, we often see factors we had failed to consider when we first looked at the problem.

If others seem closed-minded or unreasonable, then it's even more important that we keep a level head and assess the situation objectively. When someone is being difficult to reason with, we need to be the understanding one. Maybe the person is still reacting negatively, for instance, to some past experience. If we understand **why** someone is being unreasonable, we're more likely to break through the barriers that block mutual understanding and our search for truth. Keep in mind, too, that we're all imperfect and at times can be a little biased and unreasonable.

Remember, **you must first understand a viewpoint before you can either embrace or disagree with it intelligently and responsibly!** So, intelligently and with empathy, try to understand all relevant viewpoints—including those you might be tempted to reject because of others' attitudes. Avoid giving a quick, thoughtless answer to any difficult question. Instead, ask more questions and seek more information. Then you'll know you've done your best under the circumstances to inform your conscience and discover the morally right thing.

When you have a well-formed and well-informed conscience, you can go ahead and act according to the truth as you see it, but be willing to accept responsibility for the consequences of your actions.

For discussion

1. *Why is empathizing with others an important part of resolving moral dilemmas?*
2. *How do you usually react when, in trying to solve a problem, others seem closed-minded or unreasonable? How could you handle this better?*
3. *Why is understanding all relevant viewpoints important in moral decision making? What usually keeps you from considering all the relevant information and possibilities when making a decision?*
4. *What does it mean to follow your conscience in making moral decisions?*

Stella and the teenage shoplifters

Read the following true account and discuss the questions. When you have finished, your instructor will tell you the outcome.

When film from the local grocery store's security camera was reviewed, it was clear that Stella had shoplifted about ten dollars worth of items from the store. Store officials notified police that they wanted Stella arrested for stealing from the store. Police were dispatched to Stella's home to assess whether or not there were sufficient grounds for charging her with a crime.

For discussion

1. *What should the police officers' main goal be in investigating this situation?* ➡
2. *If you were the officers, what information would you try to gather in order to determine whether or not to arrest Stella?* ■
3. *Can you think of any circumstances in which Stella might have been morally justified in breaking the law and shoplifting?* ■
4. *Even if convinced that Stella was legally guilty of shoplifting, under what circumstances, if any, would you decide not to arrest her, based on your moral convictions?* ■
5. *If you did conclude that Stella was legally and morally wrong for having shoplifted, what punishment would you give her if you were the judge? Explain why.*

Passing the test

Read the following true account and respond to the questions.

Many teenagers now have extra reason to worry about their breath before school dances. Schools and school boards throughout the country are discussing whether high school students should be given a breathalyzer test to detect alcohol before they're allowed into the prom or other school dances.

Adults who favor the idea (which has been adopted in many places) say the practice curbs drinking and rowdiness. Students generally favor the idea when they think the drinking at their school functions has gotten out of hand.

Opponents say requiring the breath test is overreacting and violates the students' right to privacy. Students opposed to the breath test claim it's not necessary, and that those planning to drink will do so anyway, after the dance.

Punishments for flunking the breathalyzer test range from not being allowed to attend the prom, to being excluded from school events and extra-curricular activities for the rest of the year, to being suspended, to not being allowed to participate in the graduation ceremony, to being expelled.

For discussion

1. *What are the main moral problems involved in using breathalyzer tests before student dances?* ➡

2. *If you were on the school board considering whether or not to use the breathalyzer as a way to address a drinking problem at your school, what would your main goal(s) be?* ➡

3. *Under what circumstances, if any, would you favor this policy as a morally good solution to the problem? When would you oppose it? Explain.*

4. *What punishment do you believe is fair for students caught drinking alcohol at school functions? Explain.*

5. *How widespread is alcohol use among the students at your school? What are the main problems associated with this, and how serious are these problems for the students themselves and for others?*

6. *What is morally wrong about drinking irresponsibly? What would you say constitutes drinking irresponsibly for an adult? For a teenager?*

7. *What alternatives would you recommend for curbing the drinking problem among teenagers you know? How might you best help a teenager you know who has a serious drinking problem?* ■

Following Your Conscience

1. Conscience and authority

- Legitimate authority must serve others' welfare reasonably and properly and abide by subsidiarity. It must allow people the freedom and autonomy that the common good permits.

- Citizens must respect legitimate authority, obey just laws, defend their country for just cause, be informed voters, and choose their manner of government freely.

- Nations must aid those who are suffering, disadvantaged, and oppressed, and must work for human development.

- We must disobey what opposes basic moral principles, human rights, or the common good.

- The Church must help assess the morality of public policy according to gospel values.

- We should consider how our actions affect others and the common good.

2. The Church and the individual conscience

- We must seek and act according to truth and accept personal responsibility.

- The Church helps us interpret, believe, and practice Jesus' moral teachings.

- The liturgy and sacraments support moral life; we also worship God by living morally.

- Catholics should understand and apply the natural and revealed moral law, and the Church's authoritative moral teaching when making moral decisions.

- Catholic belief holds that the Church has infallible authority from Jesus to guard and authentically interpret essential matters of the gospel and moral law.

- Most commonly, Christ's representatives teach with non-infallible truth and authority.

- Catholics must listen to, and try to agree with and follow, authentic Church teaching. We must rely on God's help in using our freedom of conscience in following the good.

3. Society and the individual conscience

- We should be loyal and responsible to the communities to which we belong.
- We must put God's law of love first, and we must generally obey all good and just human laws.
- Morality and politics each serve the common good, but in different ways.
- We must disobey immoral laws, but we may be obliged to obey imperfect ones.
- Conscientious objectors may actively and responsibly oppose unjust civil demands.
- Peace should be our goal, but armed aggression or just war may be morally acceptable as a last resort and under certain conditions.

4. Using your conscience to solve moral dilemmas

- The second step in moral decision making is to inform our conscience by determining workable alternatives and gathering and assessing the necessary data.
- Prayer, creative problem solving, and understanding Church teaching and other viewpoints can enlighten us in this process.

Key concepts

armed aggression

the common good

conscientious disobedience

conscientious objectors

creative problem solving

disarmament

empathizing

genocide

Holocaust

infallibility

informed conscience

just war

justifiable

laws—legitimate, good, just, moral, amoral, unfair, immoral, unjust

magisterium

morality and the political process

morally acceptable defense

peace

personal responsibility

proportionate

public policy

subsidiarity

theocracies

vigilantism

war crimes

*Love is patient; love is kind;
love is not envious or boastful
or arrogant or rude.
It does not insist on its own way;
it is not irritable or resentful;
it does not rejoice in wrongdoing,
but rejoices in the truth.
It bears all things, believes all things,
hopes all things,
endures all things.
Love never ends.*

1 Corinthians 13:4–8

Chapter 7

Person-centered Morality

Overview questions

1. Why are people the main concern of morality?

2. In what sense are we to love everyone? Whose needs should get priority?

3. What is personal sin? What are its effects?

4. What are the worst types of wrongdoing?

5. What are social justice and social sin? How are they manifested in our society?

People come first

When right and wrong are mentioned, do you cringe as if moral responsibility were a burden? Do you still see moral responsibility mainly in terms of following rules and feeling forced to do something you don't want to do or don't feel like doing? Do you obey grudgingly—or rebelliously disobey—because you don't like being told what to do? Is morality, to you, mainly obeying rules and commandments you wish you didn't have to follow? If so, you may identify with this person's feelings:

I hate the rules[1]

Why do I feel so sick inside, so mad at myself?
And why do I want to take out my feelings on someone or something?
Why am I so confused about what is right and what is wrong? . . .
God, if my parents ever knew some of the things that go on in my head,
I think they'd disown me!
They taught me the rules!
Don't steal! Don't swear! . . . Don't answer back!
Don't be rude!
And every time I break the rules I sin, they say!
I am guilty!
I am wrong!
I am bad! . . .
But sometimes I'm not so sure about the rules or my parents
or the church, . . .
or being born,
or me!

I hate the rules because,
well, because they are just rules.
They are like squares on the floor,
like the circles of a target at the rifle range,
like the lines running down the highway!
That's it! They're like the lines on the highway,
double yellow danger lines
and very hazy dotted lines
that vanish in the rain.

And so I've begun to wonder about the rules
and the lines
and the rings.
What if those targets were really faces?
And what if those lines were really lives?
And what if those rules were really people?
Then sin would be breaking people
instead of breaking rules.
Sin would mean breaking up with God
instead of breaking [God's] laws.
Sin would be personal
and cruel
and wrong. . . .

If you ever "hate the rules," you're not alone. Yet you too may be confused about morality. This chapter will help clarify why we should **want** to be morally good rather than feeling forced into it.

Where the rules don't seem to fit or when they're confused about what's right, people sometimes dump morality overboard. They may conclude it's just laws and regulations, which can't answer tough, real-life moral problems. These people, too, misunderstand morality.

Morality is person-centered. Christian morality is first of all centered on the person and example of Jesus, who taught us to love one another as he first loved us: "Just as I have loved you, you also should love one another" (John 13:34). Morality is therefore also centered in the persons of our neighbors—everybody whose lives our decisions and behavior affect, especially those in greatest need.

Finally, morality pertains also to our own well-being, for we're to love our neighbor as we love ourselves (see Leviticus 19:18 and Matthew 22:39). Morality's main practical concern, then, is **people**—both ourselves and others.

> *"'Truly I tell you, just as you did it to one of the least of these who are members of my family, you did it to me.'"*
> **MATTHEW 25:40**

For discussion

1. How do you usually respond when you hear about what's morally right or wrong to do? Why do you respond this way?

2. Have you ever felt like the first part of the "I hate the rules" poem? Explain.

3. What does "morality is person-centered" mean? Does this make sense to you? Explain.

Step 3A: Who is involved?

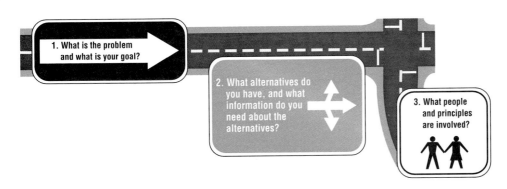

How will your choices affect **people?** Which **principles** are at stake that uphold people's dignity and welfare? Answering these questions is your third step in wise and responsible decision making. (The next chapter will discuss the principles question involved in step three.)

People and principles are the primary considerations for the Christian making moral decisions. It's common sense to consider people and principles in **any** kind of decision making. As Catholic teaching points out, God wills that the standard for all human activity should be how it harmonizes with what is genuinely good and how it helps people pursue and fulfill their purpose in life.[2]

People must come first in moral decision making. If you don't give enough thought to who is involved, you may end up harming yourself and others. You must also be fair about it. Be sure you adequately consider the people involved on **both** or **all** sides of a situation, especially where interests conflict. Lack of concern hurts people, including oneself.

So always think seriously about **who** your decisions will affect, and **how**. Try not to look at morality negatively, that is, only in terms of breaking rules: "What will I feel guilty about?" or "What do I **have** to do?" View it positively, in terms of people: "How can I be more considerate, more loving, more giving to others?" In fact, your goodness and happiness in life depend greatly on your attitude about this.

If athletes only tried to not break rules, they'd never enjoy their sport or be outstanding at it. Rules are certainly essential, as are the penalties for violating the rules. But those with a "faster, higher, stronger" positive attitude play by the rules so that they can transcend the boundaries. They break the records, not the rules!

Morality is more a concern for people expressed in action than mere obedience to rules or regulations. **Wanting** to be considerate, loving, and giving makes an enormous difference in how free and happy you feel about yourself and your life.

Journal entry
1. In what ways is your attitude about morality too negative? How could it be more positive?
2. How would a more positive attitude about morality affect you and your life?

"By this everyone will know that you are my disciples, if you have love for one another."
JOHN 13:35

Jesus' basic command wasn't "obey the rules," but "love one another, as I have loved you" (John 15:12). As you saw in the last two chapters, commandments and laws must have people's welfare at heart. **Figuring out the right thing to do is discovering the most loving thing to do in the situation.** Doing wrong is the opposite—failing to love, deliberately choosing to hurt or risk hurting ourselves or someone else unnecessarily.

That is why St. Augustine could say, "Love, and do whatever you want." If you really love and care about others, the last thing you will **want** to do is hurt them. **People should never be used as a means to an end.** Remember, real love wills another's good. Love can never, would never, willfully harm anyone—not even to accomplish something good.

Love does no wrong to a neighbor; therefore, love is the fulfilling of the law.
ROMANS 13:10

Activity (choose one)
1. For one day, try to be as aware as possible of the loving and unloving actions and attitudes around you (and on your part). Without mentioning names, write a paper on your findings and conclusions.
2. List five human-interest stories (those about specific individuals) from one day's news. Summarize each story's content, ranking the behavior from most to least loving, and briefly explaining your ranking.

For discussion

1. What is the "people standard" for all human activity? How does it relate to the third step in moral decision making—determining how your decision(s) will affect people?

2. What usually happens when you don't think enough beforehand about who might get hurt as a result of what you say or do?

3. What's involved in making a fair decision for all concerned?

4. Describe how an unfair decision affected you negatively. Do you always make decisions fairly yourself? Explain.

5. What difference do you think one's attitude about morality makes? Would you say your attitude is mostly positive or mostly negative? Explain.

6. What was Jesus' basic command? How does this command relate to the decisions you make about the right or wrong thing to do?

7. What do you think St. Augustine's statement, "Love, and do what you will" means in terms of morality? What doesn't it mean?

Isn't loving everyone unrealistic?

Love of God can't be separated from love of neighbor. We're even to love our enemies as we love ourselves—and as God loves us.

I give you a new commandment, that you love one another. Just as I have loved you, you also should love one another.

John 13:34

What's "new" about Jesus' command? It gives us new insights into love by unselfishly including absolutely everybody. It tells us that one way God loves us is through others' love, and that one way God loves others is through our love for them. Thus it gives our love the power of God's own love.

In case you wonder, "How can I 'love everyone' when there are some individuals I just can't stand?"—Jesus didn't say we had to "like" everyone. He certainly didn't say we had to "fall in love with" everybody. The Greek word used here in the Scriptures for *love* didn't refer to either of these special love relationships.

> *God is love, and those who abide in love abide in God, and God abides in them. . . . Those who say, "I love God," and hate their brothers or sisters, are liars; for those who do not love a brother or sister whom they have seen, cannot love God whom they have not seen. The commandment we have from him is this: those who love God must love their brothers and sisters also.*
> **1 JOHN 4:16, 20–21**

While our language uses one word for many different types of love, the ancient Greeks used different words to describe specific kinds of love. Their word *agape* didn't refer to liking or feeling fond of. It meant "to wish well"—to desire another's good or well-being.

We can love someone genuinely, then, without liking the person. We don't have an obligation to **feel** positive emotions toward somebody, but we do have the responsibility to not harm anyone. Even beyond that, we're obliged to do what we can for others' good. Christian love isn't an emotion. It's an attitude with which we want to help everyone as Jesus did—even the worst and most despised (who are among those who need help the most). Christian love considers the well-being of everyone, not just of those we like, love, or feel like helping:

"Do to others as you would have them do to you.

> *Love is the only force capable of transforming an enemy into a friend.*
> MARTIN LUTHER KING JR.

"If you love those who love you, what credit is that to you? For even sinners love those who love them. If you do good to those who do good to you, what credit is that to you? For even sinners do the same. If you lend to those from whom you hope to receive, what credit is that to you? Even sinners lend to sinners, to receive as much again. But love your enemies, do good, and lend, expecting nothing in return. Your reward will be great, and you will be children of the Most High; for he is kind to the ungrateful and the wicked. Be merciful, just as your Father is merciful."

Luke 6:31–36

Suppose that, for her own good, yours, and everybody else's, you need to confront a friend about her faults, although you don't **want** to do it. To prevent harm in the future, you explain to her that she has a habit of hurting you and others. By telling her this, you're doing what you believe is best for all concerned, and you're doing the right thing.

On the other hand, suppose someone wrongfully made you so mad that you just **feel** like telling him off. Expressing some anger might help him realize the seriousness of his action and the damage it did. But hurting him more than necessary would be just as wrong as what he did. So even though you **feel** like leveling him with a piece of your mind, you restrain your temper and avoid saying hurtful things needlessly.

A mother isn't justified in disciplining her child just because she's angry and **feels** like it. (Much child abuse occurs for just this reason.) The mother should discipline for the child's well-being, for example, to protect the child from harm.

A person in love won't want to risk hurting the loved one unnecessarily. If the love is genuine, in the *agape* sense, both persons will want only what is good for the other. Neither will pressure the other into violating his or her beliefs or conscience.

Being a moral person, then, is being a loving person who really cares about people and what happens to them. Without this loving concern, all emotional kinds of love are meaningless. If you care, you won't want to harm others. You won't directly intend to hurt them. You won't knowingly do something that results in their being hurt unless it's necessary either to prevent greater harm or to accomplish a proportionately greater good. If you care, you'll want only to help.

Ideally, morality is that simple. In reality, it's not always easy to love perfectly in the unselfish, *agape* sense. But unselfish love is what all other kinds of love are based on and what makes them genuine and worthwhile. Loving unselfishly, with everyone's well-being at heart, is the only kind of love that leads to inner peace and true happiness.

For discussion

1. What does loving in the agape *sense mean? Why is* agape *the basis for all genuine kinds of love?*

2. What was new about Jesus' command to love? What does loving in the Christian sense involve?

3. What is involved in really caring about someone? What does being a moral person mean to you?

4. Why is love false and meaningless without genuine concern for the other's welfare? Why is not wanting to harm someone absolutely essential to love?

5. Would you rather base your personal morality on caring unselfishly about people's welfare or obeying rules? Why?

Stand by me?

Read the following and respond to the questions.

Jay and Kim, twelfth-grade students, have been going together for about a year. Jay keeps pressuring Kim to have sex, but, so far, Kim has stalled him with one excuse or another—she's having her period, she doesn't feel well, she's got to get home, they don't have enough privacy, she wants to wait for a better time and place.

But Kim has thought about it a lot. What if she got pregnant? If she did, she doesn't know what she'd do. She's sure Jay would stand by her and probably marry her. But she knows her parents would be terribly upset, and she doesn't know what they might want to do to Jay! She knows she can't just keep putting Jay off with excuses. She's got to make a decision soon—one way or the other.

Jay hasn't really thought about the possible consequences for Kim. He figures that if Kim did get pregnant, she'd probably have an abortion so no one would find out and so she wouldn't have to deal with a baby. He supposes that's what most girls do. Personally, he doesn't think abortion is right, but he thinks it's the girl's problem and decision. He feels he loves Kim, but he knows he's not ready to get married.

For discussion

1. What is Kim's moral dilemma? What do you think her goal should be? Why? ➡

2. What alternatives does Kim have? What are all the things Kim needs to consider before making her decision? ▩

3. Are Kim's fears realistic? How realistic is she in thinking Jay will want to marry her if she gets pregnant? That he'll stand by her? Do you think most girls in this situation feel the same way? Explain.

4. What people are involved in this situation? Who could benefit or be harmed by what Kim decides? Explain how and how seriously. 👫

5. Do you think Jay's love for Kim is genuine? Explain.

6. Evaluate the morality of Jay's thinking about how he'd react if Kim becomes pregnant. How common do you think this attitude is on a young man's part when his girlfriend becomes pregnant? Explain.

Who should get top priority?

Jesus' teaching clearly emphasizes that the "neighbors" we're to look out for first are the persons who need our help most—especially those who suffer, or who are vulnerable, helpless, powerless, or poor. As individuals and as a country, we're to make what Catholic teaching calls "a fundamental option for the poor and powerless." We're to put the basic needs of the most vulnerable persons before the nonessentials that involve the rest of us.

To love our neighbor as ourselves, we must try to put ourselves in our neighbor's place. We tend to take so much for granted—until it's us facing the problem. Bounding up steps is easy when you're not disabled, but have you ever had to navigate them on crutches? Many people criticize unemployed workers as lazy—until they're the ones laid off by "corporate downsizing" and find it hard to get a new job and pay the bills.

Personal catastrophes and natural disasters can leave anyone dependent on others. What if something like that happens to me? What would I do? What would I want and need? Thinking that way can help us see how difficult it is for those who must cope with such situations. Mentally trading places can help us understand why we must put persons who are suffering, poor, and powerless first in our social and economic policies, and first in our personal contributions to society.

Yet our society is still too indifferent to citizens' special needs. Somebody who's not disabled zips into the "handicapped parking" space, leaving no room for someone who needs closer, quicker access. Meanwhile, someone with a sprained ankle who pulls into a disabled spot without a permit is angrily told to move—although obviously unable to hobble a longer distance into the pharmacy for crutches and medicine to relieve the pain. Even beneficial laws can be unwisely enforced.

Denying individuals' rights, or wrongly leaving certain people out of participating or having a voice, threatens all of us. When it is discovered that an innocent person was convicted because he or she merely resembled the perpetrator and was in the wrong place at the wrong time, we should shiver and say, "That could be me!" Justice for all must be justice for absolutely everyone.

Instead of viewing people with special needs as burdens, we have a duty to help improve their living conditions. In one sense, we are these people. When we realize that we could experience similar hardship, we understand how closely connected we are—God's children who must care for one another. Everyone has the right to life and to basic human opportunities. People must not be valued mostly for what they can produce, but should be valued first of all for the fact that they're persons and capable of reflecting God's absolute love and goodness.

Everybody in society should be able to contribute actively to the common good. People of different social classes shouldn't view each other as foes, but as partners.[3] We're a human family. When one member of your family is ill and helpless, everybody in your household is affected. When one person in society is deprived and powerless, all of us are wounded. As has often been said, the true measure of a society's greatness is how it cares for its most needy and suffering members.

Discuss

1. How does it affect those in your household when a family member is ill or needs much help?
2. How does the marginalization of some students affect your school's spirit and sense of community?

"Then they also will answer, 'Lord, when was it that we saw you hungry or thirsty or a stranger or naked or sick or in prison, and did not take care of you?' Then he will answer them, 'Truly I tell you, just as you did not do it to one of the least of these, you did not do it to me.'"
MATTHEW 25:44–45

Indeed, the body does not consist of one member but of many. . . . If the whole body were an eye, where would the hearing be? . . . . If all were a single member, where would the body be? As it is, there are many members, yet one body. The eye cannot say to the hand, "I have no need of you," nor again the head to the feet, "I have no need of you." On the contrary, the members of the body that seem to be weaker are indispensable. . . . God has so arranged the body. . . that there may be no dissension within the body, but the members may have the same care for one another. If one member suffers, all suffer together with it; if one member is honored, all rejoice together with it. Now you are the body of Christ and individually members of it.
1 CORINTHIANS 12:14, 17, 19–22, 24–27

Activity

Rewrite St. Paul's analogy from 1 Corinthians, applying it to your school's student body.

For discussion

1. *Explain who you think should be our top moral priority. Why? What does Catholic teaching say concerning which individuals and countries must receive a preferential option? Why should they?*
2. *What have you experienced that helped you better understand others' hardships?*
3. *Who do you think are most often denied their rights in this country? Why does an injustice to anyone threaten everyone? Give examples.*
4. *How does the fact that so many people in our midst are poor, homeless, or neglected wound our whole society?*
5. *If a country's true wealth and worth depends on how it cares for its most needy and suffering members, how wealthy and worthy would you say this country is? Explain.*

Project

Find out which persons are among the most vulnerable, helpless, powerless, or neglected in your local community and find out whose needs aren't being sufficiently met. Become involved in a project or service designed to help one such person or group. Report to the class on what you learn from your experience.

economics

science that deals with how wealth and material resources are produced, distributed, and consumed (including finances, taxes, employment issues)

capital

wealth, financial assets, resources that can be converted into cash or exchanged for goods or services

"For where your treasure is, there your heart will be also."
MATTHEW 6:21

People before profits

The world's main problems used to center on one country's military intentions against another. Today they center on **economics** and **capital**—on which countries have the most financial resources and power, on who's got the most wealth, and on how it should and shouldn't be used.

This is the root moral question here: Is money more important than you are as a human being? No! **People's welfare must always come before things.** People are more important than profits! In a just economy, people's right to work and their right to decent conditions and fair wages must have priority over accumulating and manipulating capital.

Employees are too often treated impersonally, as if they count only for what they contribute to the "bottom line," to making profits. Catholic teaching's *priority of labor principle,* however, holds that this is wrong—that human beings and the work we do have priority over capital, machines, and technology. People are not tools or machines for making money. Companies and countries that put profits and technologies above workers' dignity and welfare violate the true meaning of human labor.

People are the very purpose for having any economy at all. As the classic King Midas children's tale points out, there's no point just sitting around counting your money and bragging about how much you've got. Money's only value is in the good it does for **people.** When the systems that produce the money become the end in themselves, rather than a legitimate means for accomplishing good for people, then they become our enemy.[4]

For discussion

1. *In a just economy, why are people (labor) given priority over money (capital) or machines (technology)?*

2. *Would you want to work for a company that gave capital and technology priority over people and their work?*

3. *In what ways are people being treated impersonally in our society? Explain.*

4. *What's the difference between a business that respects and serves basic human needs, and one that is just interested in profits or advancing technology?*

5. *At school or at your job, how do you feel valued as a person? Do you ever feel you're important only for how you fit into the larger "system"?*

6. *When are technology and the accumulation of wealth the ally of people? Their enemy?*

Failing to love

Personal wrongs

Our biggest roadblock to achieving true happiness isn't the troubles and tragedies we endure, but our own failure to love. **Personal sin** is the inward rejection of God's commands to love and is usually also expressed in outward actions that go against God's law.[5] We can fail in loving either by knowingly **committing** wrong actions, actions that unnecessarily hurt others, or by **omitting**—by knowingly not doing things we should do to help others or to prevent them from being harmed.

Sin isn't just breaking a moral or religious law. That notion equates moral wrong only with violating rules or regulations. The command to love God by loving others always stands, whether or not a specific law covers the situation. **Doing right is essentially a matter of seeking people's welfare. Doing wrong—*sin*—is failing to love people, and therefore God, as we should.** It is because we are free that we can love or that we can fail to love by sinning.

The results of doing wrong

Through our personal moral wrongdoing, we knowingly and intentionally harm or unnecessarily risk harming ourselves or someone else. All personal sin fits this description. While it offends reason, truth, conscience, and God's goodness, sin doesn't "hurt" God. **Sin harms people.**

The effects of sin, what happens when people hurt people, are evident everywhere. Sin isn't just something religious leaders thought up long ago to keep us all in line. Sin is a sad reality that affects everybody everywhere—in unloving marriages, abusive relationships, dishonest business practices and campaign promises, social policies and structures that burden the weak, scams that take advantage of people who are vulnerable, racial tensions and religious bigotry, widening gulfs between social classes, allowing people to suffer from deprivation of necessities and die of starvation while selfishly wasting precious goods and resources that should be shared. Sin is indeed a cruel reality.

> ### Scripture activity
> Read one of the Gospel accounts of Jesus' Passion, including his confrontation with Pilate. Make a list of all the ways it demonstrates the effects of sin.

Our personal wrongdoing isolates us. When we selfishly fail to love, especially when we neglect to help meet the basic needs of others, we construct a barrier between ourselves and them. Sin distances us from God and our ultimate happiness with God and others by turning our hearts away from God's love. Jesus' account of the last judgment makes this clear:

> ". . . for I was hungry and you gave me no food, I was thirsty and you gave me nothing to drink, I was a stranger and you did not welcome me, naked and you did not give me clothing, sick and in prison and you did not visit me."
> *Matthew 25:42–43*

So speak and so act as those who are to be judged by the law of liberty.
JAMES 2:12

Clarify

1. What is personal sin?
2. What are the two ways we can fail to love? What is the root of this failure?
3. What is meant by *doing right*? By *doing wrong*?

For whoever keeps the whole law but fails in one point has become accountable for all of it. For the one who said, "You shall not commit adultery," also said, "You shall not murder." Now if you do not commit adultery but if you murder, you have become a transgressor of the law.
JAMES 2:10–11

By doing wrong—no matter what the crime or who the victim—every criminal creates some degree of mistrust and fear between himself or herself and the rest of us in society. Likewise, wronging any one person—including oneself—creates spiritual, emotional, psychological, and social obstacles between oneself and others. Even private sin, in addition to hurting the one who sins, also distances that person from others.

Something is wrong morally, then, not because it's been declared sinful and not because there's a rule, regulation, or law against it. It's morally wrong because it damages or breaks the relationship between the person and God and the relationships between the person and everyone else. Sin offends against but doesn't hurt God. Sin hurts **us.** The natural law and the Ten Commandments, and all the civil laws based on them, are standards of right and wrong which are intended to help **us,** to keep **us** from being broken.

> *"Resist not evil" means "Do not resist the evil person," which means "Do no violence to another," which means "Commit no act that is contrary to love."*
> LEO TOLSTOY, ADAPTED.

For discussion

1. *As a small child, what ideas did you have about sin? How do those ideas compare with the way you now think of right and wrong?*

2. *What makes something morally wrong or sinful? Describe what **you** think personal sin is.*

3. *How does sin affect God—or does it? Explain.*

4. *What are the main ways individual moral wrongdoing (personal sin) affects people? Give examples of each way.*

5. *Give one example each of how*
   - *wronging one other person creates spiritual, emotional, psychological, and social obstacles between oneself and everyone*
   - *wronging oneself creates obstacles between oneself and others*
   - *every private sin distances one from others*

It's possible to contribute to social sin by passing by.

Intending wrong

Personal moral wrongdoing is different from honest mistakes, which are the result of being limited. It's different from an accident we just can't avoid. **Sin is deliberate.** Personal sin is willfully violating and rejecting, partly or completely, the bond we as God's children have with humanity. It is also rejecting the goodness which is the best part of ourselves and which shares in God's own goodness. That is why **it is never right to intend wrong.**

Not every wrong you intentionally do is morally wrong, even if it hurts or harms someone. **It's wrong to directly intend or cause unjustifiable harm. It's wrong to knowingly risk causing unjustifiable harm.** Sometimes it's necessary to risk hurting feelings or to cause physical pain in order to achieve a proportionately greater good or to justifiably prevent a greater harm. But you're intending the good, not the harm.

For example, getting a shot of medicine to cure an infection can hurt or cause pain. But to not give or receive the shot could result in greater harm. You certainly risk life and limb whenever you get on the highway to drive home from a party. But the risk is generally morally acceptable because of the increased quality of life such mobility allows you and the relatively low risk of harm (that is, if you drive safely).

But if you take a risk or cause a harm that is significantly greater than the good you intended or desired, then that risk or harm is not justifiable. It is wrong. So it would generally be wrong to give an antibiotic shot to someone highly allergic to it. It would be wrong to let a drunk friend drive you home from the party.

Some acts are always evil in and of themselves. For instance, murder—maliciously killing another person—is always wrong. Personal sin, however, (and generally civil crime) has more to do with the intention and motive than with the act itself. Justifiable homicide—such as killing with the reasonable intention of protecting oneself—can be morally and civilly defended as right. It is not murder.

Project

Bring to class examples from the daily news of how and why sin

- hurts people
- affects people everywhere
- damages, breaks, or creates obstacles in relationships
- is deliberate and different from mistakes and accidents
- unnecessarily harms or risks harm
- is different from causing necessary hurt or justifiable harm

Clarify

1. How is personal sin different from accidents and honest mistakes?
2. Why is it never right to intend wrong?
3. When is it wrong to hurt someone intentionally? When can it be right to do so? Explain.
4. When is and isn't it justifiable to take a risk that might result in harming yourself or someone else? Give examples.
5. Why is murder considered always morally wrong, while justifiable homicide isn't?

So morality isn't just a matter of **doing** wrong. It's even more a matter of **intending** wrong. As Jesus said, "Listen to me, all of you, and understand: there is nothing outside a person that by going in can defile, but the things that come out are what defile" (Mark 7:14–15). With an example, Jesus further pointed out how **intending** something that's morally wrong is morally wrong, whether or not the intention is actually carried out: "But I say to you that everyone who looks at a woman with lust has already committed adultery with her in his heart" (Matthew 5:28).

Being ignorant of a civil law is generally no excuse for breaking it. If you don't realize you're exceeding a speed limit and thus doing something illegal, you'll still get ticketed for violating the law. Being unintentionally ignorant of what's harmful may lessen or eliminate moral guilt (although it is assumed that everyone has some knowledge of basic moral principles). If you reasonably and sincerely believe something will achieve only good, but it ends up causing harm, you're not guilty of sin. **To commit a moral wrong, a sin, one must intend to do so.**

That does **not**, however, excuse us from the responsibility to determine the best course of action. Good intentions aren't enough when they're a substitute for finding out what's truly, objectively right. "I didn't mean to" or "I meant well" is a cop-out when we don't first try to consider what is right or wrong about an act and to foresee the consequences.

We can't escape moral responsibility just by claiming, "I didn't know" or "I never realized." Empty words are no substitute for meaningful effort. But as long as we've tried our best to make the wisest choice, we're not morally guilty for our honest mistakes—even the most stupid, hurtful ones. In fact, it's the opposite that's morally wrong—to do the correct thing but with an immoral motive.

For discussion

1. *Why do you think personal sin is more truly found in the intention and motive than in the act?*

2. *Do you agree or disagree with the quotation about doing the right thing for the wrong reason? Explain.*

3. *Give and explain three new examples that illustrate when it may be morally justifiable to*
   - *Risk harming someone*
   - *Do something you know will cause others harm*

4. *For a proportionately greater good, or to justifiably prevent a greater harm, have you ever had to risk causing harm or do something you knew would harm someone? Explain.*

5. *When aren't good intentions enough when considering whether an action is right or wrong?*

6. *Do any concepts in this section confuse or bother you? Are there any you think you don't agree with? Explain.*

The last temptation is the greatest treason: To do the right deed for the wrong reason.
T.S. ELIOT, *MURDER IN THE CATHEDRAL.*

Pontius' Puddle

Pain, suffering, and the right to die with dignity

People do have a right not to suffer pain needlessly and to be helped to die with dignity, but **euthanasia** isn't the only way or the right way to achieve that. Euthanasia is an act or deliberate failure to act which directly causes or is intended to cause death in order to end or prevent suffering for a person who is disabled, ill, or dying. Euthanasia, then, involves a person's intention and the means used to cause death. There are three circumstances in which people are sometimes tempted to consider euthanasia:

- A person is faced with being severely and permanently disabled and dependent on others
- A person is in chronically intolerable pain
- A person is facing grave illness or is dying.

Our society promotes youth, health, and activity as absolute virtues; thus aging and disabling illness are feared as burdensome fates worse than death. Christopher Reeve, the Superman star who became paralyzed from the neck down after a fall from his horse, and many individuals like him have shown that being physically disabled needn't mean losing one's personal dignity or meaningful quality of life. With proper treatment, support, and love, disabled persons can be helped to live a happy, rewarding, and fully satisfying life. If, after an understandably difficult initial period of psychological adjustment, the disabled person doesn't understand that, perhaps it's because the rest of society doesn't.

People with disabilities are often shunned and ridiculed, rather than welcomed and appreciated as persons. Their special needs aren't sufficiently considered, and so the practical aspects of life remain an unnecessary obstacle course.

The problems of pain and physical or mental suffering haven't been addressed adequately by our society as a whole, our laws, or our medical professions. As a result, many people now live and die in unbearable pain, often hooked up to high-tech medical devices that only prolong and worsen their agony.

As a result, many people fear dying more than death. The projected increase in our elderly population makes it especially urgent that we all address now the issues surrounding pain, disabilities, aging, and dying with dignity.

Doctors themselves admit they're often poorly trained in **palliative** medicine and do an inadequate job of treating pain. Pain is invisible—it can't be seen or surgically dissected, and each person's response to pain and pain medications is different. It's easier to understand and treat the visible physical disorder, like the tumor or the broken bone than the pain that accompanies it. So, instead of empathizing with their patients' pain and persisting in finding a medication regimen that works, most doctors, by their own admission, distance themselves from their patients' suffering.

euthanasia
literally, *good death*—to die with ease and not in severe suffering; mercy killing

Clarify

1. What is euthanasia and what does it involve?
2. Under what circumstances are people most tempted to consider euthanasia?

palliative
that which eases or alleviates pain or discomfort, making it easier to bear

Be the living expression of God's kindness.
MOTHER TERESA

Patient welfare and relief from pain should come first. But, for fear the patient will become addicted, needed pain medicines aren't prescribed—even though the other option is chronic, unbearable pain. When a patient is terminally ill, pain medication should be given. Fear of addiction shouldn't be a consideration. Unfortunately, many doctors fear that regulatory agencies may revoke their licenses for over-prescribing pain medicines. Hospital patients sometimes remain in agonizing pain for hours because "it's not time" for another dose of pain reliever. Patients should not live or die in intolerable pain! Yet some doctors (with good reason) fear being sued or arrested if the patient becomes addicted or dies sooner as a result of pain-relieving medicine, even though the addiction or death was unintended, indirect, and secondary.

Many doctors and nurses risk their medical careers by administering the needed pain medications anyway. But as you read this, many other patients are suffering needlessly and, in many instances, horribly. Some have turned to morally unacceptable solutions like suicide or asking a doctor to end their life. Catholic teaching makes it clear, however, that euthanasia isn't the answer. There are morally acceptable alternatives. New medications and ways to treat pain are being developed every year; this research should continue.

Catholic teaching firmly prohibits directly killing or intending to kill any innocent person at any stage of life, no matter what the circumstances. It is also wrong to ask for or consent to this—whether expressly or by implication, either for oneself or for another. No one has the authority to suggest or permit euthanasia. A person who suffers for a long time with great pain may come to think that it's all right to ask to die. Such a person's conscience is incorrect and the act of killing is still wrong. None of us, however, is to pass judgment on these persons, who may be acting in good faith and be guilty of a lesser moral wrong or of none at all.

It can, however, be morally justifiable to discontinue medical procedures that are dangerous, out of the ordinary, too much of a burden, or disproportionately unlikely to benefit the patient. People don't have to submit to or continue treatments under those circumstances. In this case, it's not that one wills death to occur, but rather that one accepts the fact that death can't be prevented. In certain circumstances, ordinary treatments may become extraordinary, morally speaking (even though the law might still consider them ordinary).

Decisions regarding treatment should be made by the patient, if capable, or by those who can legally decide and act for the patient. These others should always respect the patient's reasonable wishes and legitimate welfare. Laws now generally support a patient's right to refuse treatment initially. But they often make it legally difficult or impossible to discontinue certain medical procedures, even when these procedures become extremely burdensome.

People do have a right to die with dignity and to know that their loving presence is precious until the end. When gravely ill persons ask to die, it shouldn't be presumed that that is what they truly want. The request to die may be an appeal for help and love from family, friends, and caregivers. Often it's a plea for relief from pain or other physical discomfort—or from the feeling of being a burden. Loving reassurance can help them understand how much they are cherished.

"Death has been swallowed up in victory."
"Where, O death, is your victory? Where, O death, is your sting?"
1 CORINTHIANS 15:54–55

Those who are dying must be given ordinary care, the practical care and loving support provided by loved ones, medical personnel, and the many dedicated **hospice** workers and other volunteers. It is morally acceptable—and often a moral duty—to give painkilling medication to a dying person, even if there is a risk that the medication may shortening the person's life. Of course, the intent must be to relieve pain and not to hasten or cause death. Giving palliative care is actually a special way of loving unselfishly as Jesus taught us.[6]

Some people are working for laws that make euthanasia acceptable. It would be far better morally to push for changes in awareness, attitudes, laws, care levels, and medical practices that will make euthanasia seem the undesirable and unnecessary alternative that it is.

hospice
a service which provides care and support for terminally ill patients in their homes or in a homelike facility at little or no charge to the patient or family

Clarify

What stand does Catholic teaching take, and why, regarding

1. **euthanasia**
2. **suffering persons who ask to die**
3. **discontinuing medical procedures**
4. **dying with dignity**
5. **giving painkilling medication to a dying person—even if it risks further shortening the person's life**
6. **giving palliative care**

For discussion

1. How do you think you would respond to the above reading if you were severely disabled? How do you think we, as a society, could better respond to persons with disabilities and their needs?

2. Why is pain so often not adequately understood or treated? What is your response to this and why? Have you found it true in your own experience? Explain.

3. What do you think are morally acceptable alternatives to euthanasia? What is your response to this moral issue? Why?

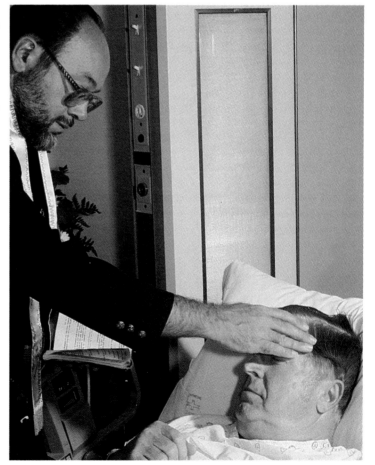

When faced with death, everyone is entitled to physical and spiritual comfort.

Murder one—or compassionate care?

Read the following account based on news reports and court transcripts. Then, by responding to the questions, determine how you would decide if you were a juror.

Thirty-six-year-old Dr. Ernesto Pinzon has been charged with first-degree murder for lethally injecting a 70-year-old terminally ill cancer patient with a combination of drugs—morphine, a potent painkiller; Valium, a muscle relaxant; and potassium chloride, used also in some places for executing criminals. The patient, Rosario Gurrieri, died within an hour of receiving the injection. If found guilty, Dr. Pinzon could be sentenced to life in prison—or to die in the electric chair.

Gurrieri had recently been diagnosed with cancer and told he had only weeks to live. A few weeks later, he was rushed to the hospital in excruciating pain and respiratory failure. Over and over he begged his family and the nurses to relieve his distress. Dr. Pinzon, who was on call, ordered by phone that Gurrieri be given a potent dose of morphine. When the nurse on duty refused to give it, Dr. Pinzon went to the hospital and administered the drugs himself, with Gurrieri's family gathered around the bedside. Gurrieri died within the hour. Neither Gurrieri nor his family had asked Pinzon to hasten his death.

A hospital nursing supervisor told the grand jury that, when she asked Dr. Pinzon why he had given Gurrieri the potassium chloride, Pinzon replied that it was to make Mr. Gurrieri's heart stop. It is common when a patient in Gurrieri's condition is dying for the heart to race, sometimes causing respiratory distress. But grieving relatives said they had asked Dr. Pinzon to relieve Mr. Gurrieri's pain, not to kill him or cause him to die sooner.

When the nursing supervisor lodged a complaint that there was no clinical reason to give Gurrieri the potassium chloride, hospital administrators notified police who charged Pinzon with "willful, premeditated and unjustified murder." A few weeks later, the state medical board suspended his license. Pinzon pleaded innocent, saying he had no intention of killing Gurrieri, but injected the potassium chloride to slow down Gurrieri's heart and breathing and relieve his pain to make his last moments easier.

Doctors and the many medical personnel and others who support Pinzon maintain he used only a small dose of potassium chloride—one designed not to kill his patient, but to possibly make the morphine more effective in relieving Mr. Gurrieri's pain. One of Pinzon's attorneys says his client is a young doctor just starting out, a doctor who wants to cure people.

Dr. Pinzon's partner, Gurrieri's primary physician, calls Pinzon's actions "compassionate" and "medically sound." He says that if he had been on call and had been told Gurrieri was dying and in extreme pain, he would have chosen to let it happen without doing anything to intervene. But Pinzon, he says, had the compassion to go to the hospital and help the dying man. Others who know Pinzon concur that he is a compassionate person who cares about his patients as well as his career.

Those opposed to what Dr. Pinzon did maintain that doctors should learn how to relieve pain without hastening death. Otherwise, they say, helpless patients may be pressured or pushed into receiving treatments intended to end their lives sooner. They say Pinzon is just trying to justify murder and medical incompetence in the name of compassion. Gurrieri's widow contends that Pinzon's actions deprived her of the final precious hours she might have had with her husband.

For discussion

1. As a juror, what is the main problem in this case? What would your main goal be? ➡

2. What alternatives did Dr. Pinzon have? Which ones were morally acceptable? Which were not morally acceptable? Explain. ▪

3. As a juror, what alternatives do you have? What are the most important facts of the case? Is there any further information you need to make a decision?

4. Whose welfare was under consideration in this situation? How was it considered? Who stood to be helped by whatever Dr. Pinzon did or didn't do? Who stood to be harmed? 🚹🚹

5. Whose rights were involved here? Whose rights did Dr. Pinzon have an obligation to place first? Explain.

6. Which aspects of this case bother you most? Why?

7. How would Catholic teaching on euthanasia apply here?

8. Based on your consideration of that teaching, would you find Dr. Pinzon legally guilty or innocent? If you had made the same decision, would you be morally guilty or innocent?

Evil extremes

The two extremes of moral evil against persons are deliberate acts of cruelty, and indifference.

Terrorism

Terrorism now rivals nuclear war as humanity's most dangerous threat. In the past, only governments could afford to construct weapons of mass destruction. The threat of widespread destruction is now vastly multiplied. With a homemade bomb made from easily obtained materials and Internet information, one person can destroy a building containing hundreds or thousands of innocent people. With one of the mobile missiles increasingly available on underground world markets, one person can shoot down a passenger plane. One toxic virus added to the water supply could threaten an entire city—or perhaps all humanity.

Is terrorism ever justifiable?[7]

Terrorism is the intention to kill people and destroy property *indiscriminately* and to create a climate of terror and insecurity, often including the taking of hostages. With obviously good reason, Catholic teaching takes a strong moral stand against the "painful wound" of terrorism:[8]

- *No political or religious beliefs can ever warrant such inhuman conduct.*
- *No propaganda motive of benefiting a cause can excuse kidnapping or massacring totally innocent people.*
- ***Hateful means may never be used to achieve good ends.***
- ***Terrorist acts are never justifiable.***
- *Governments must work together energetically to oppose terrorist threats to public safety and innocent lives.*

indiscriminately
randomly, not carefully selected

For discussion

1. *What is terrorism? How is it different from war?*

2. *In the world today, how dangerous a threat do you think terrorism is? In our country?*

3. *Why is terrorism "inhuman conduct"? Why are terrorist acts never justifiable?*

4. *Terrorists often claim to be revolutionaries fighting for a just cause. What's the difference between terrorism and justifiable revolutionary attempts to overthrow unjust oppression?*

5. *What occurrences of terrorism have you heard of? Which kinds of terrorism do you think pose the greatest threat in this country?*

6. *What specific measures should be taken to combat terrorism? (Be able to defend your solutions as morally justifiable.)*

7. *In what ways does terrorism affect everybody?*

"What Christianity forbids is to seek solutions . . . by the ways of hatred, by the murdering of defenseless people, by the methods of terrorism." . . . It is still worse when they are an end in themselves, so that murder is committed merely for the sake of killing.
POPE JOHN PAUL II, *ON SOCIAL CONCERN*, NUMBER **24**.

torture

intentional infliction of severe pain in order to coerce, punish, or retaliate against someone

Torture

Authorities routinely used to **torture** criminals to "make them talk." Centuries ago, humanity saw the need to somewhat limit warfare's brutalities. Finally, in the 1929 Geneva Convention, many (but not all) nations agreed to ban the torturing of prisoners, even in wartime. The 1987 Convention on Torture determined that torture couldn't be justified even to foil a terrorist attack. Torture designed to inflict maximum pain on a human being is certainly at the worst extreme of moral evils. But is it wrong to torture one's enemy for a good cause?

Is torture ever justifiable?

1. The standard principle applies here: **Hateful means may NEVER be used to achieve good ends.**

2. The "do not do unto others" ban on torturing enemies also protects us from being tortured. (One reason this country signed a treaty that forbids using the moon for military purposes was so that we wouldn't get shot at from outer space!) Despite the agreements banning it, torture is still too common—especially in war.

3. Torturing another person fundamentally violates one's own goodness and human dignity by turning one's intentions directly toward evil. (Remember, morality is rooted in our intentions, which give rise to our actions.)

4. One becomes guilty of the same kind of morally reprehensible action that one opposes in others. Morally speaking, torturing makes one as inhumane, cruel, and wrong as one's enemy, and often even more so.

What is the difference between torture and, say, the agonizing pain a physical therapist puts a patient through to help the person regain mobility? As a patient, you may freely consent to or refuse the treatment. You're not an unwilling victim. The painful therapy is necessary for your welfare, and it directly benefits you, the one being "tortured," by aiding your recovery. Torture, however, is forced, and causes severe pain without directly benefiting the victim. Whether by arm twisting or more barbaric methods, torture is never morally justifiable.

For discussion

1. *What is especially horrible about torture? About torturing children and other people who are innocent or helpless? Animals? Insects? What moral principles does torture violate in each case?*

2. *Would you consider certain types of torture "worse than death"?*

3. *Why is torture considered never morally justifiable? What's the difference between torture and justifiably causing severe pain?*

4. *Criminal laws generally don't punish torture very severely, as they do murder. Do you think they should? Explain.*

5. *What does torture usually say about the torturers? Why?*

The caning of Michael

Read the following true account. Then respond to the questions.

While staying in Singapore, Mike, an American teenager, was accused of spray-painting cars and charged with vandalism and malicious mischief. Mike maintained that the police had no evidence that he had committed these crimes, except his confession—which Mike maintains was coerced from him by torture. He says authorities hit and stripped him and then put him in a cold room, pouring water over him to chill him.

Mike was found guilty and sentenced to be caned—beaten across his buttocks, in a manner which often causes "considerable bleeding" and leaves permanent scars. The U.S. president voiced his opposition on the grounds that caning is a cruel and inhumane punishment.*

Streets are considered safe in Singapore, where punishment for crimes is often harsh. Nevertheless, vandalism continues to occur. Meanwhile, to curb the high crime rate here, many people are beginning to favor some type of physical punishment for crimes or public shaming to deter criminals and humiliate offenders into not committing the crimes again. In one area, citizens have seriously considered imposing spanking (fully clothed) as a punishment for "tagging" public and private property with graffiti. Other places publicize the names of parents behind in child-support payments, rapists, and those who solicit prostitutes.

For discussion

1. Do you think caning constitutes a form of torture?

2. What punishment do you think would be appropriate for the crime of which Mike was found guilty? Explain.

3. Why do you think the fear of being caned hasn't stopped all vandalism in Singapore?

4. Would you favor any type of physical punishment or public humiliation for offenders in our society? Could it be justified morally?

5. Which types of physical punishment or public shaming would you oppose on moral grounds? Why?

Moral indifference

Hatred isn't the worst moral attitude. Hatred at least acknowledges that someone's important enough to hate. It seems that the worst moral attitude according to Jesus is indifference—not even bothering: "I was hungry and you gave me no food. . . ."And recall how, in the good Samaritan story, the priest and the Levite crossed to the other side of the road rather than deal with the injured man. Ignoring someone completely, as in absolute solitary confinement, can be a form of torture many deem worse than death.

We are responsible for caring—and thus, for being *care-full* in our decision making. The care we're to take for people's welfare obviously extends to ourselves. We're responsible for protecting our own welfare and for not unnecessarily risking harm. Jesus said: "Love your neighbor **as yourself**" (Matthew 22:39).

We should have the same concern for ourselves as for others. This is **not** being selfish—too concerned about ourselves and not enough about others. Loving ourselves, as Jesus implies we must do, means recognizing that our fundamental happiness, dignity, and rights as a person are important.

Loving ourselves properly doesn't contradict the noble generosity Jesus calls us to practice by putting others' welfare before our own and loving them as he has loved us. In fact, there is nothing that can truly benefit oneself more now and eternally than freely and unselfishly helping others. There is no greater love than to sacrifice one's life for another, as Jesus laid down his life for us.

ROAD CLOSED

The worst sin toward others is not to hate them, but to be indifferent to them: that's the essence of inhumanity.
George Bernard Shaw, **adapted.**

For discussion

1. *What do you think is the worst moral attitude? Why? Where do you think deliberate indifference ranks?*

2. *If you had to, which would you choose—solitary confinement for life or execution? Explain.*

3. *What does loving your neighbor as yourself mean? Why isn't that being selfish or conceited? Why doesn't it rule out unselfishly putting others first?*

4. *Which do you think is more true: (1) People don't help each other because they don't care, or (2) People do care but are afraid to help? Explain.*

5. *When you see somebody who needs help, but you don't stop to help, what usually are your reasons? Which can you defend as morally justifiable? When do you usually stop to help, and why?*

Will somebody please help me!

Read the following, which is based on true accounts, and respond to the questions. Your instructor will then tell you what seems the best way to get bystanders to help you in such a situation.

It's Sunday afternoon, broad daylight, in a busy mall parking lot. You are being attacked by someone crazed on cocaine. The person's physical strength is easily overpowering you. Afraid for your life, you yell and scream for help.

Although about thirty teenage and adult shoppers have gathered and are watching the attack on you, no one responds to your cries for help. No one jumps in to aid you. No one goes to get mall security or call the police. They just stand there watching you get beaten bloody. Even the bystander carrying a mobile phone doesn't call for help. Finally, a young boy passing by on his bike sees you getting attacked and rides to get help.

For discussion

1. *What are your real problem and goal here?* ➡

2. *What alternatives do you seem to have?* ▬

3. *In determining how to achieve your goal, what factors do you need to consider about the people involved?* 🚹🚹

4. *Why do you think teenage and adult bystanders might do nothing to help you? Why do you think a child goes for help?*

5. *In a similar situation that did happen to a woman, do you think the bystanders were probably callously indifferent?*

Why else wouldn't people try to help?

6. *One experiment found college students, if alone, more likely to help somebody in trouble than if they were with others who didn't respond. Why do you think this is so?*

7. *Have you ever been in a situation in which someone needed immediate help and you or others responded promptly? A situation in which you or others hesitated to respond or didn't respond? Explain.*

Social justice and social sin

The social dimension of justice

Whenever you want to scream "It's not fair!"—your sense of justice is feeling violated. **Justice is the sense of what rightfully belongs to people and of what they rightfully owe others.** Justice concerns the practical obligations human beings have toward one another by right. Justice deals with fairness, though it's important to realize that life itself isn't always fair.

As God's children, we're all equal in value and dignity. This is always true and should never be forgotten. It is also true that, while we are equal in value and dignity, we are not equal in ability and opportunity. God could have seen that talents and luck were dished out equally. Instead God created us to need each other. Why? Because life's whole point is sharing, being loving and kind. How could we develop these qualities essential to our happiness and fulfillment if we didn't need one another? Thus it's a privilege to be able to help others and a blessing to be helped.

There are four main types of justice:

- **Commutative justice** concerns what one person rightfully owes another person. It forms the basis for the other forms of justice.

- **Legal justice** concerns what citizens in fairness owe their society.

- **Distributive justice** concerns what society owes its members in proportion to their needs and contributions.

- **Social justice** refers to how the broader issues of justice are handled within societies, especially those involving large numbers of disadvantaged people. It encompasses both legal and distributive justice, and is also concerned with the various social, economic, political, and legal structures through which the other forms of justice are carried out.

In addition to the other duties we have with regard to justice, we have a particular moral obligation to help persons who are poor and disadvantaged, and, wherever possible, to alleviate human misery. Richer nations have a duty to help underdeveloped countries and to not take advantage of them—for example, by selling them dangerous products that are banned at home, exploiting their desperate workers, or depleting their natural resources in exchange for food to prevent starvation.

For discussion

1. *What kinds of things most often incense you as being unfair? Why?*
2. *In what ways do you think you're most often unfair to others? Explain.*
3. *Why do you think God didn't see that luck and talents were distributed equally among us all?*
4. *How does having to depend on one another benefit us all? Why is being able to help others a privilege?*
5. *Give an example of each type of justice in practice and, in each case, an example of a failure to practice justice.*

Scripture insights
Read Jesus' parable of the talents, Matthew 25:14–30. What does Jesus say we're to do—and not do—with our abilities, even though we are not equally talented?

DO NOT PASS

commutative
transferring, exchanging, or replacing

distributive
how things are divided up or shared

Clarify
1. What is justice?
2. What are the four main types of justice, and what does each concern?
3. What special moral obligation does social justice involve?

"Whoever has two coats must share with anyone who has none; and whoever has food must do likewise."
LUKE 3:11

*... every soul that
rises above itself, raises
up the world.*
QUOTED BY POPE JOHN PAUL II

The social dimension of sin

When you toss a pebble in a puddle, you immediately observe the ripple or domino effect whereby one object causes a chain of effects. The pebble sends out small waves that disturb the whole puddle's tranquillity. Some scientists theorize that, by means of a similar "butterfly effect" principle, the butterfly flapping its wings on your doorstep affects the whole world's **ecosystem**!

In a similar way, Catholic teaching speaks of the **communion of saints** in which each person's goodness affects everyone else. We might also think of a *communion of sin* in which each person's individual sin is also a **social sin** which affects others. In light of the principle of human solidarity discussed in chapter 4, if spirit is the power of all of us pulling together, then social sin is a power that pulls us apart.

When we do something good, we somehow benefit all humanity. When we do something morally wrong, we drag others down with us in some way: "In other words, there is no sin, not even the most intimate and secret one, the most strictly individual one, that exclusively concerns the person committing it. With greater or lesser violence, with greater or lesser harm, every sin has repercussions on the entire [Church] body and the whole human family."[9]

In another sense, social sin refers to the immoral and unjust relationship that may exist between one human community and another. When goodness or evil carries an entire community's clout, its force is powerfully beneficial or damaging.

For discussion

1. *What is the communion of saints? The communion of sin?*

2. *Using one example, describe in practical detail the first five links in a spiritual "ripple" or "butterfly effect" chain by which the morality of one's actions affects more and more people.*

3. *Define social sin and describe its effects and its results.*

4. *Give examples from your personal experience of how individuals who*
   * *rise above their own faults and problems also raise you up*
   * *don't rise above their faults and problems tend to drag you and others down*

5. *Why is every sin a social sin in one sense? Give an example of a seemingly private sin that has social repercussions.*

Homelessness and housing

Having access to a decent place to live isn't a luxury; it's a basic human right. Society is supposed to protect and promote human life and dignity. But societies are failing in their responsibility when millions of people don't have an adequate place to live with dignity. Worldwide, the problem is huge.

The Catholic Church community has always tried to minister to those who are poor, social outcasts, and otherwise in need. Volunteer efforts show what real love can do when it pulls up its sleeves and goes to work. In addition to our participating in works of charity, we must keep insisting that as a nation we develop sensible, effective programs to help eliminate the problems of substandard housing and homelessness in our own society and around the world.[10]

Activity

Find out more about Catholic Charities, Habitat for Humanity, and other social projects in your area that help persons who are hungry and homeless. Organize a group of your friends to participate in one of these projects, and report back to the class on your experience.

> *A house is much more than a roof over one's head. [It is] a place where a person creates and lives out his or her life.*
> **POPE JOHN PAUL II**

Research project (choose one)

1. Write a report on how Catholic charitable and social works have shown a preference for those who are in need and outcast.
2. Write a report about your Church's social and charitable works today.
3. Look into the reasons for homelessness in your community. Write or e-mail your civic officials about your concerns. Give your recommendations regarding this problem.
4. You are mayor of your city. Draw up a plan to eliminate homelessness and substandard housing in your area. Be sure affordable housing for first-time and low-income home buyers is included.
5. Your city has hired you to convince local citizens that it is important to address the city's problems of homelessness, substandard housing, and lack of affordable housing. Develop a media campaign (complete with graphics) to accomplish this.

For discussion

1. Why is it an injustice to deny people adequate housing?
2. What do you think is needed to successfully address the problem of homelessness? What can you do to keep political action focused on the problem?

Landlord

Read the following scenario, which is based on a true situation. Then respond to the questions. When you have finished, your instructor will tell you how one person tackled the same situation with stunning success.

Your rich uncle, after buying an apartment complex, learned he must go overseas on business for a year. To earn money for college, you've accepted his offer to have you manage the complex while he's away. He's told you that the tenants are often low-income and poor. The individuals and families have trouble paying their rent, and the previous owner has allowed the place to run down.

On touring the complex with your uncle, you see that the apartments need many repairs. Drug dealing and illegal drug use are in evidence. The vacancy rate is high.

Your uncle believes that all this can be turned around. He's given you full authority to run the complex as you see fit and will give you a bonus for each apartment you lease while he's gone. His only stipulation is that, if tenants can't pay their rent, they must be evicted. And you must do the evicting.

For discussion

1. What are your main problems? Why are they moral as well as practical problems? What is your primary goal? ➡
2. What do you know about the situation? What further information do you need?
3. What alternatives do you think might solve the problems you've outlined?
4. Who might be harmed or helped by each alternative? Whose needs and rights are involved?
5. What would your plan of action be in running the apartment complex? Be able to explain and justify each of your actions.

. . . seek the things that are above. . . .
COLOSSIANS 3:1

Possessions, profits, power

Consumerism and materialism

Excavations of Egyptian pharaohs' tombs reveal how obviously misplaced were their hopes of taking their possessions with them into the next life. In contrast, for thousands of years, in searching for God, many people have shunned wealth and sought a simple life. They have correctly recognized lasting spiritual values as more important than material possessions.

Up to a point, we must all spend time and energy obtaining enough material goods for a decent life. In fact, we've seen that it is wrong to deprive people of the ability to obtain a decent life. At the **materialistic** extreme, however, are the "I'll never have enough" and "I can never have too much" attitudes. Our consumer-oriented society reinforces these views by creating products designed to wear out and by marketing "must have" improvements.

It's fine to enhance humanity's quality of life. What's wrong is putting material priorities first in life so that one doesn't know when enough is enough. Becoming enslaved to "I've got to have it," "I've got to have a better one," "I've got to have it now" is what's harmful. The endless pursuit of material things leads ultimately to inner emptiness and the unhappy question: "Is that all there is to life?"

Constantly flooded with tempting offers, many people pile up unmanageable credit card debts. Working overtime to have more money (and more bills), they constantly worry they'll never be out of debt! Last year's purchase, still perfectly usable, is often thrown away for the "newer, more exciting" model. Next year that one too will seem outdated and will "need" replacing.

The more one has, the more one seems to need and want, and nothing satisfies for long. Ads, in fact, constantly **tell** us to be dissatisfied with our current brand or model. All this should help us realize that material things will never completely satisfy us and that our main focus should be elsewhere (as Jesus' Beatitudes direct). Instead, many people stay on the endless **consumerism** treadmill: "I want—I need—I must have—I want more—I need more—I must have more. . . ."

In the meantime, blaring commercials silence one's more important hopes and dreams. Spending time with and helping people becomes secondary—"There's never enough time." Rushing to make enough money to accumulate more things consumes one's life. Many people are finally tiring of this "rat race," hating what it does to them, their families, and their lives. They're trying to live more simply, putting first the proper values—not those that product promoters and many celebrities push.

materialistic

having the attitude of esteeming wealth and pleasure above other values and ideals

DEAD END AHEAD

consumerism

the premise that it is good to consume, regardless of need

For the present form of this world is passing away.
1 CORINTHIANS 7:31

Journal entry

1. How have you been guilty of "throw-away" or "waste" behavior this past month?

2. Being honest, in what ways have you been hooked by materialism?

3. In the future, how do you plan to avoid the unhappy consumerism treadmill?

4. What would you like to simplify or re-prioritize about your life now? Briefly state how you can do this.

People of all ages can find themselves trapped by consumerism.

For discussion

1. What is the difference between spiritual and material values? To what extent do you think ours is a materialistic society of consumption and consumerism? Explain.

2. Why are consumerism and materialism morally unacceptable philosophies to live by? What are signs that someone is becoming a slave to possessions and instant gratification?

3. What social influences encourage us to value possessions more than people? To want to "have it all" now? How do these influences affect your and other teenagers' attitudes and behavior?

4. When can blindly pursuing material possessions and advances become a dead-end? How does our desire for "something more" find its ultimate fulfillment?

5. Give examples of products deliberately designed to wear out rather than being made to last. What are the short and long-term moral and other implications of this practice?

> *"For what will it profit them if they gain the whole world but forfeit their life? Or what will they give in return for their life?"*
> **Matthew 16:26**

Pursuing power and profit at any price

Carried to the extreme, individuals' and nations' desire for wealth becomes all-consuming. Along with it comes the craving for power and control over others—no matter what the cost. Being willing to do anything for profit or power gives rise to structures of sin that idolize money, political ideas, social status, or technology[11]

For discussion

1. What evidence do you see of the attitude of power and profit at any price?

2. What evidence do you see of nations pursuing power and profit at any price? How does such modern imperialism interfere with the development of peoples? Why is the unbridled pursuit of power and profit a form of idolatry?

3. How do many sins lead to structures of sin? What steps can be taken to tear down structures of sin?

The fewest and the fittest have the most

More and more, a relatively small percent of individuals and countries control most of the world's power and wealth. Applied to people, a "survival of the fittest" approach treats poorer persons and countries (who are the majority) as expendable: Only the strong and powerful will survive, so why bother with the weak? Those in power may use "tough competition" as an excuse for paying substandard wages, using child and slave labor, and engaging in other illegal and immoral practices. While a "survival of the fittest" theory may account for how the species continue, it's immoral to use it as a guideline for how human beings should treat one another.[12]

For discussion

1. *What is the "survival of the fittest" theory as it pertains to people, power, and wealth? Why is it a morally unacceptable rule of life for the human community?*

2. *What is wrong about so few having so much, while so many have so little? How does this reflect wrongful patterns—of domination and inequality?*

3. *Why is facing tough competition no excuse for immoral economic and business practices?*

4. *Many experts agree that the future threat of global war will most likely result from tension between richer and more economically developed "have" nations and poor, underdeveloped "have not" countries who achieve mass-destruction capability. Do you agree? Explain.*

5. *What measures to help poorer countries should be taken now by governments like ours? By Churches? By individuals like us who live in highly developed nations? Why should we help?*

There may be a relationship between a society's values and who is highly paid.

6. *What relationship do you think there is between our own consumerism and materialism and our government's responses to poorer, underdeveloped nations?*

"Wretched excess"?

Read the following reality-based descriptions, and evaluate each behavior by responding to the questions.

- *A teenage girl drives around her town in a new convertible whose license plate holder reads: "Poverty? What's that?"*
- *A noted business publication estimates that the combined one-year income of the four hundred richest persons in this country could wipe out a deficit of billions of dollars.*
- *A television evangelist who lives extravagantly tearfully implores faithful viewers (many of whom are elderly and poor) to keep sending him their regular donations for his work in "God's ministry." He bases his appeal on the Bible, assuring viewers that God will richly reward their generosity.*

- *Teenagers preparing for school proms feel they "must" rent an expensive limousine for the special evening. They say using the family car just isn't considered good enough by the other kids, and that they don't want to look "cheap."*
- *Concert, movie, and major sporting-event tickets are becoming an expensive luxury that most teenagers can't afford. Meantime, the stars of these events live very well and command salaries in the millions—which, of course, means even higher ticket prices at the box office.*

For discussion

1. *What moral or immoral attitudes do you see in these situations? Why are they moral or immoral?*
2. *What dimensions of social justice and/or social sin do you find in each situation?*

Do you think any of the behavior described amounts to "wretched excess" or putting things before people? Explain.

3. *Which attitudes and behaviors do you think need to be changed? Explain why and how.*
4. *If you were a friend of the girl with the license plate holder and were bothered by its message, what would you say to try to get her to replace the plate?*
5. *Why do you think many athletes, musicians, and film celebrities are paid so much? Under what circumstances would you as a fan join in "striking" for lower ticket prices or better quality for your money? Explain.*
6. *How can we play a role in seeing that wealth is distributed more fairly? Explain.*
7. *Is there any pressure among students at your school to own expensive items? Explain.*

Business ethics

People have a duty and a right to work, as well as a right to receive just wages that will support them and their families. Everybody should have equal access to employment. Discrimination in the hiring, treatment, or firing of workers is wrong.

Catholic social teaching encourages businesses to adopt truly participative and cooperative decision-making approaches. Doing this actually helps businesses avoid failure and it strengthens sound businesses. Labor and management should be partners in the business enterprise, with each having the freedom and ability to affect the decision-making process.[13]

Unions are often important in representing workers' legitimate concerns. Union leaders, however, mustn't jeopardize workers' welfare just to make a point or maintain their own power. Employees need to be vigilant that their representatives truly have the workers' best interests at heart. Strikes are justified if they are directly related to working conditions, are not opposed to the common good, and do not result in violence.

On management's part, it is wrong to treat workers like pawns to be used, abused, and laid off at will. Economic weapons and immoral strategies can cause another type of mass destruction. "Corporate downsizing" sounds beneficial at stockholders' meetings, but it really often means that thousands of wage earners are laid off, family homes are lost, and children lose their hope of attending college.

Granted, business is competitive. But maybe it's time to urge corporate disarmament and insist that companies find ways to compete that don't depend on mistreating people. In the most enduringly successful companies, owners and managers view their employees as partners and motivate them fairly. In reality, many large corporations have publicly admitted using management-by-fear—keeping workers productive by making them constantly afraid of losing their job.

Just before the Christmas holidays, for example, each manager in one major company was called into the boss' office. Regardless of work quality or loyal years with the company, all were led to fear that they might lose their jobs. They didn't know whether they were about to be fired, retained, or promoted. Were those who weren't laid off then supposed to grovel gratefully just because they weren't let go?

Have you ever called to order a product and been informed your call "may be monitored so that we can serve you better"? Personnel training is legitimate. Sometimes, however, salespersons are pressured by unreasonable quotas and call-monitoring to complete the sale and get you off the phone fast so that the company won't have to hire more workers.

> *There are three rules of dealing with those who come to us:*
> *(1) Kindness,*
> *(2) Kindness,*
> *(3) Kindness.*
> **FULTON J. SHEEN**

These are no ways to treat human beings—and they eventually backfire. Employee surveys indicate that when workers feel exploited and stressed out, they begin rationalizing their own unethical conduct. They may then cut corners on product quality, mistreat customers, steal office supplies, or abuse their sick-day allowance. Also, when employees experience no company loyalty, job turnover is high—and so are companies' costs for training replacement personnel.

Unethical business practices add to the "everybody does it" climate that diminishes people's understanding of human dignity and also affects us in practical ways. When business ethics no longer seem to matter, we become the ripped-off purchasers unwittingly sold a stolen car with set-back mileage. We're the mistreated, lied-to customers who pay higher prices for poorer quality products. How management and employees relate with each other affects us individually and as a society.

That's why we have a responsibility to make our objections heard when we become aware of unethical business practices. As consumers and/or investors, we are in a better position to do that than are the employees, who may fear losing their jobs. And, unless we tell them, owners and managers may be unaware of how an employee is hurting their business by ignoring, being rude to, or intentionally misleading customers.

Again, the principle of solidarity applies: All sides must cooperate—employees, management, and consumers. Goods should be made well and distributed equitably, workers paid and treated fairly, and employers given workers' best efforts.

The principle of solidarity also applies to the Church community. As employers, Churches must exemplify just dealings with employees and be sure that all their members have fair access to their Church's spiritual, educational, and charitable services. This is why congregations in more affluent areas assist financially struggling congregations in poorer neighborhoods.

For discussion

1. *How can outside pressures play a role in improving corporate morality? As an employee or consumer, have you been affected by or have you objected to a business practice that you believed was wrong? Explain.*

2. *What is the role of a union? How should a union relate to its members and to company management? Why is this a moral matter?*

3. *What participative and cooperative approaches to decision making have you experienced at home or school? What approaches would you like to see as an employee? What approaches would you use if you were a company manager?*

4. *What is morally wrong with "managing by fear"? When working for another person, what conditions encourage you to put forth your best efforts? When are you tempted to do less than your best? Explain.*

5. *Would you rather work for a company in which you owned a share or one in which you didn't? As owner, would you offer your employees a share in the company's profits or ownership? Explain.*

6. *How do you respond when you are asked your opinion in a matter that affects you and then not really listened to? What's the difference between participating cooperatively in decisions and insisting that things be decided your way?*

7. *Why must both management and employees have the freedom and power to influence decisions?*

8. *What happens in labor-management negotiations when each party takes a reward-punishment approach? Has a "me first" attitude? Tries to please everybody? Refuses to deviate from existing policies and procedures? Considers how both sides can achieve a positive outcome?*

The pizza problem

Read the following situation and respond to the questions.

You make the pizzas at a local restaurant, which is part of a large pizza chain. Your friends avoid eating at the restaurant because its pizza never has enough cheese and toppings. (That's not a problem with pizzas at the chain's other restaurants in your city.)

Representatives from corporate headquarters have come twice this last year to show you how the company wants its pizza made—the ingredients, toppings, and amounts. To save (and, thus, make) more money, however, your franchise's owner (your boss) has told you to cut some ingredients by almost half. Although business is all right, you believe it would be much better if the ingredients weren't skimped on. You've diplomatically told your boss this, but he tells you to keep making the pizzas the way he tells you.

It also bothers you that your manager insists all pizza delivery orders be rushed. Delivery drivers tell you that they have to speed to do this, even though company policy clearly states drivers shouldn't drive illegally or unsafely. The drivers say they don't mind much, though, because more deliveries mean more tips in their pockets.

What, if anything, should you do about either situation?

For discussion

1. *What is your main problem, and why is it a moral one? What is your goal?* ➡

2. *What information do you have about the situation? Do you need any more information? Explain.* ▪

3. *What are your alternatives for addressing the problem?* ▪

4. *Who might be harmed or helped by each alternative? Whose needs and rights are involved, and whose are primary?* 👥

5. *How do you think you should handle the situation? Why?*

racism

unfounded claim of racial superiority; discrimination based on race or ethnic background

ethnic bias

unfounded, usually unfavorable opinion about members of a group which has a common cultural background

prejudice

unfounded, preconceived opinion which is usually unfavorable; bias

Reflection

1. In what ways are you prejudiced against others?
2. How have you been affected by the prejudices of others?

Every form of social or cultural discrimination in fundamental personal rights on the grounds of sex, race, color, social conditions, language, or religion must be curbed and eradicated as incompatible with God's design.
"THE CHURCH IN THE MODERN WORLD," 29:2.

I am not what you call me, but what I answer to.
AFRICAN PROVERB

Prejudice and discrimination

Doesn't it strike you as strange that people can empathize with green-skinned movie space aliens, yet close their minds and hearts to wonderful, real humans just because of their skin color? **Racism** and **ethnic bias** are among the most divisive—and stupid—of human wrongs. Like all sin, biases against others begin in the human mind and heart.

It's impossible to grow up in a society where **prejudices** are common without our perceptions being affected. If we're honest, we should admit how biases affect our attitudes and our understanding—or lack of it. Where racial, ethnic, gender, sexual identity, religious, social, or other prejudice against persons negatively affects our attitudes, we are called to change. Eliminating discrimination has got to start where prejudice itself begins—in our hearts. Just passing laws won't change minds, but our words and example can.

Journal entry

1. List in one column your racial, ethnic, gender, sexual identity, religious, social, or other prejudices against persons.
2. Next to each item, list something positive you can do to change your prejudicial attitude to a more fair one.

We've got to object clearly to prejudicial stereotypes, jokes, and insults. We need to increase our sensitivity to the value of each person and our awareness of the many positive, essential ways each unique group contributes to our society. We must face honestly how unjust economic, educational, and social structures result in disadvantages for individuals, preventing their development. And we must devise better remedies that are fair to everyone.

Hateful and hurtful prejudicial behavior has increased in our society—burning crosses on lawns of Black families, painting swastikas on walls of synagogues, making fun of how devout Hindus or Muslims dress, cracking snide remarks about women, homosexual persons, or those of a particular ethnic background. Racial division in schools is worse today than when the law first banned enforced racial segregation in education. Students have increasingly isolated themselves and one another according to race and ethnic background.

We may not have been privileged to march with those who, led by Anglican Archbishop Desmond Tutu, defiantly "walked in God's water" along their country's "Whites only" beaches in order to end South Africa's official policy of racial separation. But we can combat the derogatory words, stereotypes, divisive attitudes, and hateful behavior that keep us from celebrating our unique gifts and our common humanity.

Recently, over twenty high school students shaved their heads in solidarity with a classmate whose cancer treatment has caused his hair to fall out. They've sent him a picture of all his newly-bald and smiling friends to let him know they care for him, admire his courage, and stand by him in his suffering and his triumphs. Can't we begin responding with similar courage and understanding to the moral diseases of prejudice and discrimination?

For discussion

1. Why are racism and ethnic bias among the most stupid and divisive of wrongs?

2. Which groups most often seem to be the victims of prejudice and discrimination in our society? In your school? Explain, giving examples.

3. How have you or your friends been discriminated against by others or suffered from prejudice? How has this made you and/or them feel?

4. How do you think prejudices originate? Can you identify where your own prejudices have come from? Explain.

5. Why is a change of mind and heart necessary to eliminate discrimination? What helps you most to overcome a prejudice against someone?

6. How do you imagine society would change if prejudice and discrimination were eliminated? How do you imagine your school would change?

7. What are your suggestions for helping to eliminate prejudicial attitudes at your school? In our society?

> *Everybody thinks of changing humanity, but nobody thinks of changing themselves.*
> **LEO TOLSTOY, ADAPTED**

> *Never judge others until you've walked nine moons in their moccasins.*
> **NATIVE AMERICAN SAYING**

The remark

A common—and uncomfortable—opportunity to make a positive difference occurs when someone makes a disparaging ethnic, racial, sexual, or religious remark. Yet many people say that, although they know the remark is offensive, they just don't know how to respond. Indicate your response to each of the following remarks by answering the questions. When you have finished, your instructor will tell you how others have answered.[14]

Remark 1: You are a Black Muslim student. You have shaved your head as a religious gesture. Another student comes up to you in the hall and says to you, "Hey, boy, where did you get that name and that haircut?"

Remark 2: Someone cracks a joke that stereotypes persons of your race or ethnic background. It bothers you, although no harm seems intended.

Remark 3: Someone makes a negative remark about your religious faith, seemingly to "bait" you and make you uncomfortable or angry.

Remark 4: Someone in your Internet chat group makes a snide remark about persons of a race, religion, sexual orientation, or ethnic background other than yours.

Remark 5: A friend tells you she hates being pigeonholed into one category, even though she identifies with more than one race and ethnic heritage in her background.

Remark 6: Somebody in the group you're talking with asks, "Did you ever notice that the news mentions a criminal's race only when he or she isn't Caucasian?"

Remark 7: A student starts a committee meeting you're attending with an "insensitive slur."

Remark 8: Someone starts telling you a demeaning joke about women.

Remark 9: Trying to add a little humor, you make an out-of-place remark which offends another student.

Remark 10: When your teacher is out of the room, someone in class makes an insulting wisecrack about persons with a homosexual orientation.

For discussion

1. How do you find people most often respond to offensive remarks? How do you usually respond? Why?

2. What is your problem and what should be your goal in determining how best to respond in each situation above? ➡

3. Why do people often have trouble responding to offensive remarks that bother them and that they know are wrong?

4. Brainstorm appropriate responses to each remark. ▪

5. What bias, if any, does each remark reflect? How is each remark hurtful? How does such bias affect personal attitudes and judgments? Limit openness? Close one's heart? 👫

6. How can we value each person more? How can we value all groups for their contributions to society? What changes does this require of us?

7. What is the best way—without being preachy, self-righteous, or too judgmental—to help people realize the harm caused by prejudicial attitudes and remarks? What is the best way to respond to each remark? Explain.

Person-centered Morality

1. People come first.

- Morality goes beyond obeying laws and is centered in persons; Christian morality is first of all centered in Jesus.

- The third moral decision-making step involves considering how choices and principles affect people.

- People must come first, always before things and profits, and must never be a means to an end.

- Loving as Jesus did involves desiring others' welfare and doing the most loving thing.

- People who are suffering, vulnerable, helpless, powerless, poor, and most in need of help should receive priority.

- Injustice to anyone affects all of us in the human family.

2. Failing to love

- Personal sin is inner rejection of God's command to love, usually expressed by wrongdoing or the omission of a necessary good.

- Doing right is seeking people's welfare; sin is failing to love God and others as we should.

- Sin intentionally harms, or unnecessarily risks harming, someone or something. Intending wrong is never right.

- Sin is deliberate, hurts us, and distances us from God and others; honest mistakes aren't sinful.

- The risk or harm an act causes must not significantly outweigh the intended or desired good.

- Some acts are always wrong, but personal sin is more in intention and motive than acts.

3. Evil extremes

- The two extremes of moral evil against persons are deliberate inhuman cruelty and indifference.

- Hateful means may never be used to achieve good ends; terrorism and torture are never justifiable.

- The worst moral attitude, according to Jesus, seems to be indifference, not bothering, not caring.

- In our decision making, we must care for the well-being of others and for our own well-being.

- Jesus called us to put others' well-being before our own, loving them as he has loved us.

4. Social justice and social sin

- Justice is the sense of what rightfully belongs to and is owed to people, and includes commutative justice, legal justice, distributive justice, and social justice.

- As God's children, we're equal in value and dignity. However, because we don't have the same abilities and opportunities, we need to help one another and we need to alleviate human misery.

- Each person's goodness and each one's sin affect everyone.

- We must work to eliminate social sins: homelessness, lack of access to decent housing, consumerism and materialism, excessively craving of profit or power, domination, unjust distribution of wealth, selective survival as a human guideline, unethical business practices, and all forms of prejudice, bigotry, and discrimination.

Key concepts

agape

business ethics

communion of saints

communion of sin

consumerism

discrimination

ecosystem

ethnic bias

euthanasia

justice—commutative, legal, distributive, social

materialism

moral indifference

participative and cooperative decision making

person-centered morality

personal sin

prejudice

racism

sin

sins of commission and omission

social justice

social sin

terrorism

torture

*He has told you, O mortal, what is good;
and what does the LORD require of you
but to do justice, and to love kindness,
and to walk humbly with your God?*
Micah 6:8

Chapter 8

Christian Principles

Overview questions

1. What are principles? Why are they important?

2. How does one apply one's principles and make principled choices?

3. What are some of the main Christian moral principles?

4. Which principles should come first?

moral principle

a fundamental ideal, value, or standard of goodness and truth on which to base human laws and conduct; rule of right conduct based on such an ideal, value, or standard

Clarify

1. What are moral principles?
2. Why are moral principles so important?

Reflection

1. In what ways do you most often succeed in living up to your principles?
2. In what ways do you most often fail to live up to your principles?

What are principles?

What does it mean to "live up to your principles" or to say that something is "a matter of principle"? Just what are principles, and how important are they? Are Christian principles the same as other principles?

We said in chapter 3 that **principles are ideal values which are good in themselves.** As with morality itself, we can view principles either objectively or subjectively. Objectively, moral principles are the basic ideals on which we all should base our conduct. Subjectively, our moral principles are our individual perceptions of what those basic ideals are. Our personal principles are sound only if our perceptions of the ideals are correct.

Your **moral principles**, then, are your beliefs about goodness and truth as you understand them in your particular situation. Your principles are the basis for your standards for judging what is important, good, and morally right, and thus your foundation for moral decisions. Christian principles are based on the natural law, the Ten Commandments, and the teaching of Jesus. Most people believe these principles are important, although people of different faiths and societies understand and emphasize them differently. Later in this chapter we will discuss some of the principles Jesus emphasized and the new dimensions he gave to living them.

The principles of physics explain how our **physical** universe operates. For example, due to gravity, you must use more energy to begin moving a friend's stuck car than to keep pushing it once it's in motion. That's a law of physics, a principle of physics. Moral principles, on the other hand, deal with how **people** should or ought to behave. Principles of nuclear physics show scientists how to construct bombs. Moral principles guide our leaders in deciding whether it's moral to explode them. Your moral principles, then, are your beliefs about what is good, what is right.

Activity

1. List as many morally good principles as you can. Briefly explain
   • what each one means to you
   • why you consider it an ideal
   • the kind of person you would become by following the principle
2. List ways of violating each of these principles, and briefly describe the kind of person you'd become by constantly violating each principle.

Journal entry

Write one thing you are willing to do to better live up to your ideal principles.

For discussion

1. *What does it mean to you to say that something is "a matter of principle"?*
2. *What are Christian principles? Are they the same as other principles? Explain.*
3. *Describe the most principled person you've ever met. Tell why you admire the person.*
4. *What are the main moral principles by which you try to live? Why? How do you try to live these principles?*

Step 3B: What principles apply?

In making moral decisions, after seeing how the possible choices would affect **people**, you need to determine what **principles** are involved. (Situations often involve more than one principle.) Your toughest decisions in life will involve following your principles in situations where principles seem to conflict. For example, should I be honest or should I be loyal? Should I tell someone the truth, or avoid hurting the person's feelings? Is there a **conflict** of principles here, or is the problem really in how you apply your principles? There really should not be a conflict between two principles, if they are both good. In the last chapter, we'll discuss how to make decisions that reflect your principles, especially in those difficult situations where you're torn between what may seem to be conflicting principles.

It's enough at this point in the decision making process to simply answer this question:

Which principles are at stake that involve people's dignity or well-being?

If you don't really think about what's at stake, you'll probably make unwise choices, choices that may needlessly harm you and other people. So be clear about what your principles are. When faced with moral decisions, think very carefully about these principles—about what you believe to be right and what you believe to be wrong.

> **Activity**
> Of the situations described in one day's news reports, briefly list those that have a moral dimension. Note the principles which are supported and/or violated in each instance.

For discussion

1. *What role should your principles play in making moral decisions? Why?*
2. *What happens when people make moral decisions without following their principles?*
3. *List three moral decisions that face teenagers.*
   - *Which principles are at stake in each instance?*
   - *In each case, how do these principles involve people's dignity and well-being?*
   - *For each situation, list two alternatives that would uphold the principles involved and two alternatives that would violate those principles.*

Making principled choices

Your moral principles are the standards by which you judge whether certain decisions or actions are morally good or bad. For example, the moral principle of honesty would be important in determining whether you should tell the truth. To the extent that you value the **principle** of honesty, you will try to **be** honest.

Your moral principles reflect and influence what's most important to you in life. The principles you live by represent you and what you stand for; they determine the kind of person you are and will become. When you violate your principles, you violate yourself. Acting as if your principles are worth nothing is acting as if you are of no value. Acting according to your principles shows you believe in yourself. Acting according to your principles says: Loved by God, I am a valuable and worthwhile person, whose dignity and rights should be respected and who should be treated justly, equally, and honestly by others just as I try to treat them.

Applying your principles

In reality, how do you apply your principles when making moral decisions—especially when the right answer isn't clear at first? When you just don't know what the right thing to do is, your principles can help guide you to the correct choice. After completing the initial decision-making steps and identifying the people and principles involved, answer these questions:

- **How do the principles involved apply to my available alternatives?**
- **Does each choice uphold or violate my principles?**
- **Will each choice protect or unjustifiably harm people?**

Answering these questions will help you determine which choices to make in order to uphold the principles which protect the well-being of the people concerned. You will decide against actions that violate the people and the principles involved. You will decide in favor of actions that are in accord with your principles, in accord with your well-being and the well-being of others.

> ### Activity
> List the five major areas of life in which you think principles are most important (business dealings, personal relationships, sexuality, politics, and so on). For each area, explain which principles you think are most important, and why.

Your basic moral principles underlie your code of ethics. If your principles are sound, they will be valuable in every situation and decision. Like a ship's rudder, they'll guide you through some of life's difficulties and treacherous storms. In fact, when you feel yourself floundering and without direction in life, turn to your principles. Live according to them. You will rediscover your sense of direction and your courage.

So select your principles carefully, for they're the foundation for your decisions and your life. Stand by your principles and follow them faithfully.

It is not what you have, nor even what you do, which directly expresses your worth, but what you are.
HENRI FREDERIC AMIEL, ADAPTED.

Activity

1. Write an essay on "The Principles I Live By." Talk about the most important principles in your life. Explain why these principles are important to you and what they mean in terms of how you live your life.

2. Write a paper on "What I Would Be Willing to Die For." Talk about those things in which you believe in so strongly that you hope you'd have the courage to die for them if necessary. Explain what principles these beliefs are based on and why these beliefs and principles are so important to you.

3. Write an essay about five principles others have given their lives for, and explain why they have done so.

4. Ask a politician or another authority figure to name the principles he or she tries to live by and to explain why. Write a paper on your findings and your reactions.

Do your best to present yourself to God as one approved by him, a worker who has no need to be ashamed, rightly explaining the word of truth.
2 TIMOTHY 2:15

For discussion

1. How are your principles related to your actions? Give examples of what you mean.

2. How do your principles represent what you stand for and believe you're worth?

3. For each of the three moral decisions facing teenagers that you discussed in the preceding section (page 189), answer these questions:

- *How do the principles involved apply to the available alternatives?*
- *Would the alternatives uphold the principles that protect and support people? Explain, considering each alternative.*
- *Would the alternatives unjustifiably harm people by violating these principles? Explain, considering each alternative.*

4. What difference do you think it makes if a person does not live by good principles? Why?

Christian moral principles

Jesus didn't give his followers specific rules and regulations about religious practices and moral concerns. Rather, he taught us basic principles to guide us in making specific decisions. He told us which principles are most important and will bring us true and lasting happiness. Jesus taught us how to use these principles in making decisions about which course of action is right, but he didn't make our decisions for us.

The principles Jesus taught are so basic, universal, and important that they've become ideals throughout the world. Although individuals and societies sometimes fail to act according to them, Judeo-Christian principles today serve as model guidelines of human conduct. In fact they're deemed so fundamental to human existence, harmony, and happiness that they're incorporated into constitutions and laws. In determining the main principles by which you want to live, seriously consider these principles and the meaning Jesus gave them, as well as Jesus' example in living them.

Judeo-Christian
based on Jewish and Christian religious beliefs and traditions

hierarchy

structure or ranking in the order of importance, power, or authority

> *"Make purses for yourselves that do not wear out, an unfailing treasure in heaven, where no thief comes near and no moth destroys."*
> **LUKE 12:33**

> *"No one can serve two masters; for a slave will either hate the one and love the other, or be devoted to the one and despise the other. You cannot serve God and wealth."*
> **MATTHEW 6:24**

Spiritual values come first

There is a proper **hierarchy** of values in which spiritual values are in themselves more important than material ones. Sometimes, however, we live as though the most important things in life involve material success—money, fame, looks, power, possessions, athleticism, and so forth. Jesus cautioned us not to base our lives on such secondary, transitory things as wealth, prestige, dominance, or material goods. By example and words, Jesus taught us that spiritual principles, such as loving concern for people, are far more important and fulfilling.

Spiritual values, Jesus pointed out, are the source of peace and happiness. Spiritual "treasure" is the only lasting reality. One of the most regretted, misery-causing mistakes people make in life is putting things before people—like money, getting ahead career-wise, owning an expensive car, buying an expensive home. We must not put things ahead of spending time with and caring about people. As Jesus reminded us, we can't put **both** material and spiritual values first. We must choose.

So when you're feeling down on yourself and your life because you lack material success, or when you're tempted to put material things above more important values, remember this principle:

You are more precious for what you are than for what you have.[1]

For discussion

1. *Describe which kinds of things should come first in your values hierarchy.*
2. *Which spiritual values do you think teenagers emphasize most? Which material values do you think your peers emphasize most? Give examples.*
3. *Which kind of values do you think our society emphasizes most? Explain and give examples.*
4. *Why does putting the wrong kinds of values first so often bring regret and unhappiness? Why do you think many people choose these values anyway?*
5. *What types of behavior reflect whether spiritual, or material, values are placed first in a person's life?*

Reflection

Would you say your time, thoughts, and energies are mostly focused on people and spiritual values, or on material values?

Spiritual values are the source of peace and happiness.

Love—the "people principle"

The most important spiritual principle on which to base choices, according to Jesus, is love: love of God and love of others. In fact, Jesus said we love God especially by loving others as we love ourselves—and with an unselfish concern for their well-being. Love is the most important principle of Christian moral conduct:

"By this everyone will know that you are my disciples, if you have love for one another."

John 13:35

Jesus didn't specifically tell us what to decide or do, but how to tell whether our choices or actions are morally good. They are good if they "bear good fruit," if they're intended to unselfishly promote the well-being of others as well as our own.

"A good tree cannot bear bad fruit, nor can a bad tree bear good fruit. . . . Thus you will know them by their fruits."

Matthew 7:18 and 20

In addition to *agape,* unselfish concern for someone's welfare, Jesus also acknowledged the importance of special love relationships like marriage and friendship. All things being equal, some relationships in our lives should take priority, and certain individuals' welfare should come first. But Jesus also emphatically called our attention to those who are poor and suffering, to strangers and those who are outcast, and to those considered enemies. He showed his love for them in his actions. He lived his love, just as he said we should:

"In the same way, let your light shine before others, so that they may see your good works and give glory to your Father in heaven."

Matthew 5:16

Thus, Jesus' "people principle" tells us this: Put people first in your decision making—above structures, institutions, rules, laws, material success, possessions, schedules, or time. Use material things responsibly in the service of people.

"For where your treasure is, there your heart will be also." **LUKE 12:34**

For discussion

1. *Why do you think Jesus taught moral principles rather than giving specific rules and regulations about moral conduct? Do you think it would have been easier for us if he had been more precise? Explain.*

2. *Do most people seem to you to base their lives more on spiritual or on material principles? Explain, giving examples.*

3. *Why does living according to spiritual rather than material values make one happier? Why do so many people seek happiness through material things?*

4. *What does Jesus' "people principle" mean to you?*

5. *How did Jesus say we could tell whether our choices or actions are morally good? What did he mean by this?*

6. *What role do you think material things should play in our lives? Explain.*

Activity

Find examples in the media of placing material values before spiritual ones, and examples of giving spiritual values priority. Discuss how you think media portrayal of material values and of spiritual values influences us.

Respect for human dignity

See what love the Father has given us, that we should be called children of God; and that is what we are.

1 John 3:1

> *To understand the bitter cry of the anguished soul, we must . . . at the very least have felt with those who have suffered.*
> **Leo Baeck**

Flowing from Jesus' "people principle" is the principle of respect for each person's dignity and basic rights. Jesus told us God cares about each of us and that God's love makes every person infinitely valuable.

"Are not five sparrows sold for two pennies? Yet not one of them is forgotten in God's sight. But even the hairs of your head are all counted. Do not be afraid; you are of more value than many sparrows."

Luke 12:6–7

Jesus taught us not to look down on anyone. We can—and sometimes should—disagree with what others think, say, or do. But we should never think that someone's well-being isn't worth caring about. Each person has a basic dignity that comes from being created and loved by God.

It's wrong to violate a person's dignity. Cruelty, torture, and depriving people of life's essentials (food, clothing, shelter, love, work) are totally unacceptable. Likewise, if someone dislikes or hurts us, we shouldn't let our negative feelings prevent us from caring about that person's well-being. Jesus said we're to love and try to understand and help everyone—friends, acquaintances, strangers, even enemies. No one should be beyond our loving concern.

Let mutual love continue. Do not neglect to show hospitality to strangers, for by doing that some have entertained angels without knowing it. Remember those who are in prison, as though you were in prison with them; those who are being tortured, as though you yourselves were being tortured.

Hebrews 13:1–3

Each of us also has certain God-given rights which flow from our dignity as persons. These human rights are essential to being fully human. They may not be violated except where it's necessary to choose between those whose rights have equal claim, or where someone—a criminal, for instance—forfeits certain rights by infringing on those of others. All democracies guarantee certain human rights in order to protect life, liberty, and the pursuit of happiness. We've spoken in previous chapters about these rights in general, but Catholic teaching also identifies certain specific human rights as universal.

These basic human rights belong to everyone regardless of age, race, creed, color, gender, sexual orientation, or economic situation. We must all do our part to protect human rights. The real threat to human rights generally isn't governments, but our everyday attitude and behavior that chip away at human rights and dignity one person and one incident at a time. When added up, these individual responses become the social injustice that jeopardizes basic rights for all of us.

Clarify

1. In general, what is meant by human dignity and basic human rights? Where do these come from?

2. How does Jesus' teaching safeguard and promote human dignity?

3. Why is it wrong to deliberately violate anyone's basic rights?

4. Is it ever morally permissible to limit or suspend someone's basic rights? Explain.

The rights everybody has

1. *The right to life and the means necessary and suitable for the proper development of life—the right to*
   - *food, clothing, shelter*
   - *rest, medical care, and necessary social services*
   - *security in cases of sickness or inability to work, of old age, or of unemployment through no fault of their own*
2. *The right to moral and cultural values—the right to*
   - *respect for one's person and one's good reputation*
   - *freedom in searching for truth*
   - *be informed truthfully about public events*

   - *basic education or professional training according to the local culture, and higher education on the basis of merit*
3. *The right to freedom of religion and conscience—the right to*
   - *honor God according to conscience*
   - *profess one's religion privately and publicly*
   - *choose freely one's state in life*
4. *Economic rights—the right to*
   - *free initiative in the market-place*
   - *work, and earn a just wage*

   - *have just and humane working conditions*
   - *private property within the limits of social responsibility*
5. *The right to assembly and association*
6. *The right to emigrate and immigrate*
7. *Political rights—the right to*
   - *take an active part in public affairs*
   - *contribute to the common good*
   - *have one's rights protected under the law*

Pacem in Terris, *Pope John XXIII.*

Catholic leaders in the Second Vatican Council pointed out that the best way to protect principles involving human dignity is for each of us to live as Jesus taught us:

By no human law can the personal dignity and liberty of [humanity] be so aptly safeguarded as by the gospel of Christ which has been entrusted to the Church.

For this gospel announces and proclaims the freedom of the [children] of God, and repudiates all the bondage which ultimately results from sin. The gospel has a sacred reverence for the dignity of conscience and its freedom of choice, constantly advises that all human talents be employed in God's service and [people's], and finally, commends all to the charity of all.[2]

WARNING ABSOLUTELY NO TRESPASSING

Where, after all, do universal human rights begin? In small places, close to home— so close and so small that they cannot be seen on any maps of the world. Yet [these places] are the world of individual persons. . . Such are the places where every man, woman and child seeks equal justice, equal opportunity, equal dignity without discrimination. Unless these rights have meaning there, they have little meaning anywhere. Without concerned citizen action to uphold them close to home, we shall look in vain for progress in the larger world.
ELEANOR ROOSEVELT

Activity (choose one)

1. List the basic rights you think we all have just because we're human. Rank them in the order of importance, as you see them. Compare them with the universal human rights Catholic teaching identifies.
2. Look up and list the basic human rights upheld by the United Nations Universal Declaration of Human Rights. Rank these in the order you think them important. Compare them with the universal human rights Catholic teaching identifies.
3. Create suitable icons for an Internet Web-page to represent each of these seven rights. Each icon must symbolize graphically what the right means or represents.

For discussion

1. *In what specific ways do you think our society best upholds and protects each of the seven universal human rights listed in this section? Give examples.*
2. *How do you think these rights are most commonly violated or not protected enough in our society? Elsewhere in the world? Give examples.*
3. *Why do you think the word* love *is used so frequently in Scripture and in Church teaching in relation to human rights?*
4. *How do each of the seven universal rights affect you personally now? Are there any in the list that you question? Are there any you would add? Explain.*

Trade-offs

A terrorist's setting off one nuclear, biological, or chemical weapon could bring humanity to its knees. Crime is costly and scary. As a result of these threats, individual privacy is increasingly being compromised by monitoring devices. Terrorists, lawful authorities, and businesses—from health insurance organizations to credit-card companies—are gaining greater control over our lives and privacy.

Companies record your phone conversations with them. Stores capture you on camera. Many students must pass security checkpoints on entering their school building. The technology even exists to "strip search" you electronically.

What restrictions and monitoring are morally and legally permissible? Which trade-offs of rights and freedoms might be more dangerous than the threats they're designed to stop? Consider these questions:

- Do you favor or oppose being fingerprinted or having your eye patterns traced to obtain a credit card? Being electronically "strip-searched" by airport security?
- Should the government be able to monitor or control certain aspects of the Internet—and, if so, which ones? Should parents and schools do this regarding children's access to the Internet?
- Should school authorities be allowed to search students' possessions or lockers for weapons? For illegal drugs?
- Do parents have the right to spy on their teenager's behavior?
- Is it right for parents to install a computer device on their teenager's car to be sure their son or daughter isn't driving recklessly?
- Is it right for a parent to use a home drug test to see whether or not their children have been using drugs?

For discussion

1. *What is the real moral problem in each instance? What should the goal be in resolving it?* ➡
2. *What facts would you need to know about each situation to make the best decision?*
3. *In each instance, what alternative solutions are there for the underlying problems? Who might be harmed or helped by each one? Whose needs and rights are involved?*
4. *What principles are involved in each case, and which principle is most important? Explain.*
5. *Which of the above trade-offs of personal privacy and freedom are not justifiable? Under what circumstances, if any, would you consider each to be morally justifiable? What limits would you impose? Explain.*

Equality and justice

The principles of equality and justice also flow from concern for human welfare and entitle everyone to fair treatment. The rights given to one of us must be given to all of us in the same situation or circumstances. In practice, treating others as we'd like to be treated means that we must respect and protect others' rights as we'd like our rights to be respected and safeguarded. If we have the opportunity to do or obtain something, then everyone in the same circumstances should have that opportunity. We shouldn't restrict, limit, or penalize others in ways we'd consider unjust if we were in the same situation. Everyone's entitled to just and equal opportunities.

> *My brothers and sisters, do you with your acts of favoritism really believe in our glorious Lord Jesus Christ? For if a person with gold rings and in fine clothes comes into your assembly, and if a poor person in dirty clothes also comes in, and if you take notice of the one wearing the fine clothes and say, "Have a seat here, please," while to the one who is poor you say, "Stand there," or, "Sit at my feet," have you not made distinctions among yourselves, and become judges with evil thoughts? . . .*

> *You do well if you really fulfill the royal law according to the scripture, "You shall love your neighbor as yourself." But if you show partiality, you commit sin and are convicted by the law as transgressors.*

James 2:1–4, 8–9

Justice is the very least we can do if we claim to follow Jesus. Justice and equality are another way of saying, "Treat others as you want them to treat you." Christianity and democracy both maintain that if we're to accept justice and equality as our rights, then we must also see that they're extended to others.

We **are** our sister's and brother's keeper. We have a responsibility to be concerned about others' well-being. We're morally obligated to act justly toward everyone. If we believe we shouldn't be discriminated against because of our race, background, gender, religion, physical characteristics, and so forth, then we shouldn't tolerate discrimination against others. If we expect others to protect us from being dealt with unjustly, then we're obliged to prevent others from becoming victims of injustice or inequality. Jesus had harsh words for those who didn't treat others justly. He called them fools and said:

> *"But woe to you Pharisees! For you . . . neglect justice and the love of God. . . ."*

Luke 11:42

If we believe in the principles of justice and equality, we must also recognize our obligation to uphold and protect these basic rights for others.

> *Profound and rapid changes make it particularly urgent that no one, ignoring the trend of events or drugged by laziness, [be content] with a merely individualistic morality. It grows increasingly true that the obligations of justice and love are fulfilled only if each person, contributing to the common good, according to his [or her] own abilities and the needs of others, also promotes and assists the public and private institutions dedicated to bettering the conditions of human life.[3]*

If you are neutral in situations of injustice, you have chosen the side of the oppressor. If an elephant has his foot on the tail of the mouse—and you say that you are neutral, the mouse will not appreciate your neutrality.
ARCHBISHOP DESMOND TUTU

For discussion

1. *Why do you have the right to be treated justly and fairly? What does that right mean to you?*

2. *Describe a time when you believe you were treated unjustly or unfairly. Explain your feelings then and now.*

3. *What major injustices and inequalities do you think exist in our society and world today? Do you think there are any injustices or inequalities in your school? Explain.*

4. *How do you think teenagers most often fail to live the principles of justice and equality? Explain.*

5. *Why do you think people fail to respect others' right to be treated justly and equally?*

6. *What movements and institutions are you aware of that work for justice and equality? In what ways do **you** stand up for these principles?*

7. *What does "we are our sister's and brother's keeper" mean in a moral sense?*

8. *Why can't we just narrow our concern to how we're affected personally by injustice and unfairness?*

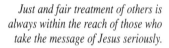

Just and fair treatment of others is always within the reach of those who take the message of Jesus seriously.

Drug testing

Read the following and respond to the questions.

Drugs, including alcohol, are obviously a major societal problem. We wouldn't board a train, plane, or bus if we knew the engineer, pilot, or driver was impaired by a legal or illegal drug. Yet, trains have derailed because engineers were high on marijuana, pilots have flown and crashed planes while impaired by alcohol, and bus drivers' drug use has resulted in fatal accidents. Consequently, in occupations where public safety is at risk, drug testing is now often required. Yet an appalling number of auto injuries and fatalities are due to someone driving under the influence of alcohol and/or drugs.

We wouldn't want to be operated on by a surgeon who is under the influence of bourbon, cocaine, marijuana, or amphetamines. Alcoholism is a particular problem in the medical community. Even so, the nurse responsible for monitoring critically ill patients or the doctor who removes your appendix usually wouldn't be required to be drug tested.

In schools, use of alcohol and other drugs often prevents students from learning and contributes to disruptive or violent student behavior. Illegal drug use among high school athletes is so widespread that many coaches—and athletes who don't use these drugs—complain that some of the drugs give competitors an unfair advantage. Teachers and school principals have been arrested for using and dealing in illegal drugs, and some are among the one in ten adults in our population who are alcoholic. Drug use affects a teacher's classroom effectiveness and ability to properly supervise student safety. Certainly, drug use negatively affects the quality of teaching.

Increasingly, businesses administer drug-screening tests as a condition for employment, even in non-hazardous occupations. Now questions are raised about whether students and teachers should be routinely tested for drugs. Some high schools require all students involved in competition— athletes, debaters, band members, cheerleaders, and even chess players—to undergo periodic random drug screening. Some people propose routine or random drug testing for all high school students and teachers.

Those opposed to drug screening generally object: It invades personal privacy—a right for which countless lives have been given. If we treasure personal freedom, drug testing opponents say, we shouldn't have our bodies and personal lives monitored by authorities unless there is an overriding concern for the public welfare and there are well-established reasons to suspect others may be harmed. In most instances, they believe, drug screening doesn't pass these tests.

For discussion

1. *What are the main problems involved in abusing alcohol and other drugs, especially for teenagers? In deciding whether to test for drug use? What should be the goal in addressing these problems?* ➡

2. *What facts would you need to know to make a sufficiently informed decision about drug testing in a particular situation? Explain.* ▪

3. *What alternatives might best solve the problems caused by drug use in each instance mentioned above?* ▪

4. *Who might be harmed or helped by each alternative? Whose needs and rights are involved?* 🚶🚶

5. *What principles are involved on each side of the drug testing issues? Which principles do you consider most important regarding this issue? Why?* 🚶🚶

6. *Why is personal privacy an important right? How is it related to the Golden Rule?* 🚶🚶

7. *What should Jesus' "people principle," and his teaching about justice and equality specifically, lead us to consider in resolving the drug testing dilemma? Explain.* 🚶🚶

8. *Based on the moral principles involved, what is your stand on drug-testing the following persons? Why?*

   • *Transportation workers, such as airline pilots, train engineers, and bus drivers*

   • *Applicants for driver's licenses or license renewals*

   • *Medical personnel who perform invasive medical procedures, or all nurses and doctors*

   • *Student athletes, all student competitors, or all students*

   • *Teachers and/or school principals*

   • *Law enforcement officers*

   • *Government leaders*

   • *Employees applying for non-hazardous jobs, all prospective employees, or all employees*

   • *Pregnant women, and/or all parents*

   • *All children under age thirteen, and/or all teenagers*

Honesty

Why is truthfulness so important?

We must be able to depend on one another's integrity. The principle of honesty is basic to societal and personal well-being. Trust and truthfulness are necessary for social relationships and human survival. Dishonesty damages trust. Christianity addresses the key reason for esteeming and upholding honesty:

So then, putting away falsehood, let all of us speak the truth to our neighbors, for we are members of one another.

Ephesians 4:25

Because the principle of honesty is so important to the common good, our laws protect it by forbidding dishonest behavior that seriously harms people. When there's a legal obligation to be honest, society prohibits and punishes stealing, cheating, and lying—sometimes severely. For example, laws commonly stipulate that, if your perjury results in a person being executed, you can be sentenced to death.

Nevertheless, people often try to justify their "little" deceits by claiming these deceits "don't really hurt anyone" or that "everybody does it." But the dishonesty of all those who pad their insurance claims, fudge on their taxes, or use bootleg software adds up to a significant cost for the rest of us. Insurance companies estimate that about one-fourth of what we pay for auto insurance is due to fraudulent insurance claims. The high cost of dishonesty also affects the cost of medical and other types of insurance.

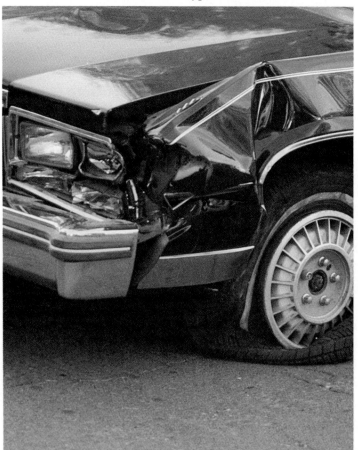

Everything you buy at the store costs you extra because some people shoplift. When you purchase music, movies, or software, you also pay more because others make illegal copies instead of buying the products. Even if you're not defrauded directly, over your lifetime others' dishonesty will probably end up costing you thousands of dollars.

Many individuals have rationalized their own dishonesty so often that they can't seem to tell the difference any more between truth and falsehood. Not only do they fail to consider that what they're doing is dishonest, but they don't recognize when others are being dishonest with them!

Insurance fraud and shoplifting negatively affect everyone. Honesty benefits everyone.

Whenever we violate justice and truth, we have a moral obligation to repair the damage. Just saying we're sorry isn't enough, even if we've been forgiven. We still have a duty in conscience to try to somehow compensate others for the harm we've caused them—even if the only way it's possible to do it is secretly.

What we must do to make amends depends on how much and what kind of harm we've caused. Civil law's rule of thumb is usually to require that the guilty party do whatever will help put the wronged party in the same position as if the damage hadn't been done. This obligation to make restitution prompted one man to send his victim the small amount of money stolen from him over thirty years ago—plus interest.

> **Clarify**
> 1. Why is truthfulness important to each individual and to society as a whole?
> 2. What duty do we have in conscience when we violate the principles of truth and justice? How does civil law also recognize and uphold this obligation?

For discussion

1. *What reasons do you think people most commonly give for their "little" dishonesties? Are these dishonesties really as harmless as some people claim? Explain and give examples.*

2. *In what ways do you pay for others' dishonesty? How do you feel about this? Why?*

3. *What evidence is there in our society that many people don't seem to realize when they're lying or being lied to? Why do you think this happens?*

4. *How widespread do you think disregard for truth is in our society? Among teenagers in particular? Explain and give examples.*

The lover's dilemma

Read the following reality-based account and respond to the questions.

Todd says he loves Erin. He has been pressuring her to have sex with him. She loves Todd, but the possibility of getting pregnant worries Erin. She's heard the usual sex talks in school, but isn't sure how easy it is to get pregnant or when during the month it's most likely. She figures just having sex only once in awhile can't be **too** dangerous, but she's not sure.

Erin has also heard about sexually transmitted diseases, but she thinks her teachers exaggerate to scare kids out of having sex. She doesn't think these diseases are as common or dangerous as they say. Erin doubts **she'd** ever get anything really awful. Besides, some kids she knows make no secret about having had sex—in a few cases, with four or five different people. They've never mentioned getting a disease from it.

Both pregnancy and the possibility of disease are on Erin's mind, although she and Todd have never discussed them. Todd's parents haven't really talked with him about sex, except to caution him to not get a girl in trouble. He isn't really concerned about sexually transmitted diseases, because he's sure neither he nor Erin has ever had sex with anyone else. Nor is he concerned that Erin might get pregnant.

Erin feels she can trust Todd, but in the back of her mind she wonders whether he's told her the truth about not having had sex with his previous girlfriend. She knows Todd thinks she's never had sex before with anyone, and she's never told him—or anyone—that she did once last year with an older guy from college that she met over the summer. She's afraid Todd will break up with her if he finds out, so she has no intention of telling him.

Erin remembers how afraid she was afterward about what could have happened had she gotten pregnant or contracted a disease. She doesn't want to go through that scare again. Erin appreciates the fact that Todd seems to trust her so completely, but sometimes it bothers her that he doesn't appear concerned at all about what could happen.

For discussion

1. What is Erin's moral dilemma here? ➡ What do you think her goal should be, and why?

2. What alternatives does Erin have here?

3. How realistic and well-informed do Erin and Todd seem to be about the possibilities of pregnancy and sexually transmitted diseases? Explain.

4. How realistic do you think most teenagers are about the possibilities of pregnancy and sexually transmitted diseases? Explain.

5. How concerned does Todd seem about Erin's well-being? What do you think their attitudes indicate about their relationship? Why? How is trust a factor?

6. What principles are involved in this situation? How does each principle affect Todd and Erin and apply to their alternatives? Which principle seems most important here?

7. Which alternative do you think would be most in keeping with the most important principle(s) involved here? Why?

8. If Todd and Erin discussed the matter with you as a close friend, how would you advise them? Explain why you would give this advice.

When must you reveal and not reveal the truth?

Of the many offenses against truth and honesty, lying is probably the most common. **Lying is speaking or acting in an untruthful way with the intention of deceiving somebody who has a right to the truth. You don't, however, have to divulge the truth to someone who isn't entitled to know it.**

Loving concern for others' welfare, together with respect for the truth, should determine how we handle others' requests for truthful information. There might be times when you have sufficient reason to not reveal the truth to someone—for example, for the sake of someone's safety or the common welfare, or out of legitimate respect for personal privacy. In such situations, it's best to be candid when possible: "For various reasons, that's something I don't feel free to tell you."

However, if a killer, for example, wants to know in which direction his next victim went, you'd be obligated to carefully word your response so as to throw him off course. He wouldn't have the right to know the truth, and telling him the truth could cause someone grave harm. A priest may never in any way disclose what a penitent reveals in the Sacrament of Reconciliation. Doctors, lawyers, soldiers, public officials, and other professionals and business persons—and their employees—have a duty to keep certain information confidential, except when the only way to prevent very serious harm would be to reveal it. **No one should ever reveal private and prejudicial information about someone except for a proportionately grave reason.**

The media also has an obligation to respect the right to privacy for individuals, fairly balancing this right with the common good. The public's craving to know isn't the same as the public's right to know! Hounding public figures and publicizing intimate details of their private lives is wrong when it intrudes on their personal freedom and privacy just to satisfy people's curiosity.

When we are entitled to the truth, we should have access to it. Lies keep us from knowing what we need to know to make good decisions. If people weren't guaranteed the right to know the truth in certain situations and if that right were not honored, everybody's well-being would be jeopardized.

Rid yourselves, therefore, of all malice, and all guile, insincerity, envy, and all slander.

1 Peter 2:1

Sometimes, for a greater good, telling the truth is necessary even if it means someone will be upset with us or hurt. While people don't always want to hear the truth, we may have an obligation to tell it anyway. Paul confronted head-on the results of telling the unpopular truth:

What has become of the good will you felt? For I testify that, had it been possible, you would have torn out your eyes and given them to me. Have I now become your enemy by telling you the truth?

Galatians 4:15–16

What often makes enemies, however, isn't telling the truth, but telling it in less than the best **way.** There's a big difference between being truthful in a kind way and insensitively blasting someone with candor! Being honest is no excuse for being inconsiderate, imprudent, irresponsible, or unkind.

A truth that's told with bad intent Beats all the lies you can invent.
WILLIAM BLAKE

For discussion

1. *How would you respond to a friend who pressures you to reveal something you believe you shouldn't?*

2. *When would you be justified in revealing private information that is prejudicial to someone? Give two examples.*

3. *How would you feel if a member of the staff in a doctor's office discussed your health problems with your friend without your permission? Why would you feel this way?*

4. *What types of personal information do you think the professionals you deal with (teachers, doctors, and so on) should not reveal about you? Why?*

5. *What types of personal information do you think teenagers most often reveal about each other? When do you think this is wrong? When do you think it's morally permissible or obligatory? Explain and give examples in general.*

6. *Give examples of how you think various media commonly respect individuals' rights and privacy. Of how they violate these.*

7. *How can keeping people from knowing the truth jeopardize everybody's welfare?*

8. *Without revealing the person's identity, describe a situation in which you felt obligated to tell the truth to someone who didn't want to hear it, or who was upset or hurt by it. Explain why you felt obliged to tell the truth.*

9. *Give an example of a time when someone told you a truth you didn't want to hear. How did you feel later about it? Why?*

10. *Why does the way the truth is told often make a difference? Give examples, preferably from your own experience, that illustrate this.*

Pontius' Puddle

The secret

Read the following account and respond to the questions. When you have finished, your instructor will tell you the case's outcome.

Robyn and Sherri had been friends all through elementary and high school. Robyn knew that Sherri had always hoped to pursue a modeling career and encouraged her friend to do so. But when Robyn returned from several weeks' vacation at her grandmother's, she noticed Sherri had lost a lot of weight over the summer. Then, in one of their classes at school in the fall, a teacher talked about **bulimia**, a dangerous eating disorder. Sherri's appetite seemed terrific, but when Robyn heard Sherri vomiting on two occasions shortly after eating, she decided to confront Sherri about it.

At first Sherri denied deliberately trying to lose weight by purging. When Robyn pursued the issue, Sherri finally confided that she was trying to look like the model she hoped to be. She said she was fat (which Robyn thought wasn't

at all true) and still had a lot more weight to lose. And she made Robyn promise not to tell Sherri's mother or anyone else about it.

Meantime Robyn became increasingly concerned about her friend's weight loss—which Sherri tried to cover up by wearing loose-fitting clothes. When Robyn put her arm around Sherri's shoulder one day, she was shocked at how skinny her friend had become. Truly worried about Sherri's health, Robyn kept wondering whether her friend might be bulimic.

Even Robyn's mother and some of the students had asked Robyn if Sherri's health was all right. Robyn wondered why Sherri's mother didn't seem to notice and debated whether or not she should tell her Sherri's secret. Sherri had told Robyn, however, that revealing it to anyone would end their friendship. Robyn was torn between keeping Sherri's secret and genuine concern for her friend.

For discussion

1. What was Robyn's main moral problem? What should her goal have been in resolving it? ➡
2. What facts did Robyn have? What alternatives do you think she had? What further information did she need?
3. Who might have been harmed by each of Robyn's alternatives? Who might have been helped? Whose needs and rights were involved, and how?
4. What principles were involved in Robyn's dilemma and how? Which was most important, and why?
5. Do you think Robyn had a moral obligation to keep Sherri's secret or to reveal it to Sherri's mother? What, if anything, do you think Robyn should have done? Explain.

bulimia
psychological eating disorder involving a low self-image, an exaggerated perception of being overweight, and a compulsion to eat and then purge large quantities of food by vomiting, dieting, or using laxatives or other means, often resulting in serious physical harm or even death

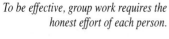

I hope I shall possess firmness and virtue enough to maintain what I consider the most enviable of all titles, the character of an honest person.
GEORGE WASHINGTON

Why are people dishonest?

Some people think it's perfectly all right to lie, cheat, or steal as long as they're not caught. As a result, everybody else is cautioned: "Guard your purse and watch your wallet." "Be careful who you tell personal secrets to." "Consumer, beware." Unfortunately human nature was likewise flawed in the prophet Jeremiah's day:

They all deceive their neighbors,
    and no one speaks the truth;
they have taught their tongues to speak lies;
    they commit iniquity and are too weary to repent.

                                    Jeremiah 9:5

We usually have one of four reasons for being deliberately dishonest:

• We hope to gain or achieve something by our deceit.

• We're ashamed to admit the truth and/or we lack the courage to accept the consequences.

• We feel the need to cover for lies we've already told.

• And/or we want to keep someone from getting hurt.

For discussion

1. How acceptable do you think lying is in general? Among teenagers? Explain why you think this is so.

2. What reason do you think teenagers most often have for lying? Cheating? Stealing?

To be effective, group work requires the honest effort of each person.

The cheats

Consider each of the following and then discuss your answers to the questions which follow.

The cheating politician

A news report says a well-known politician, widely rumored to be thinking of running for president, was once reprimanded for cheating on a college test. Former officials and students from the college have confirmed the report.

For discussion

1. Would you think twice about voting for this politician? Explain.

2. Under what circumstances would this revelation definitely keep you from voting for this person for president? Not keep you from voting for the person?

3. How is the principle of honesty involved here? How would upholding honesty affect your vote? Explain.

Drugs and the Supreme Court nominee

The presidential nominee for Supreme Court justice has admitted to having occasionally smoked marijuana in college, but denies having used illegal drugs since then. The candidate now strongly opposes illegal drug use. Legislators must now decide whether to confirm or deny the candidate as a Supreme Court judge.

For discussion

1. What principles are involved here?

2. Should someone who once habitually broke the law be appointed to uphold laws in the nation's highest court? Why?

3. Would you confirm or deny the candidate's appointment based on the admission of past marijuana use if the candidate were otherwise extremely well-qualified? Explain.

What if teachers cheated?

Consider how you'd respond if this hypothetical report were true:

In a nationwide survey, 75 percent of teachers say they've "cheated" at least once by throwing away a stack of student papers so that they wouldn't have to correct them. They give students excuses like "the janitor accidentally threw the papers out." Their reasons include being too pressured with other work to correct their paper load. They blame students and administrators for expecting too much of them.

The teachers say students' grades aren't affected negatively: "Good students always do well and would end up with the same grades anyway. If anything, perhaps some students get better grades because a failing paper or two gets thrown out."

Surprisingly three of four teachers say that teachers get away with this practice all the time, often recommend it to overworked colleagues, and have no qualms about it. Only one percent of teachers surveyed say they'd report another teacher who routinely throws out student papers. All teachers who "circular-file" student papers agree they do so only when sure they won't get caught.

For discussion

1. What principles does this involve?

2. How would you react if the survey results were true? How much would you be bothered to discover that these actions and attitudes accurately described your teachers' actions and attitudes? Explain.

3. How are the reasoning and behavior of the teachers in this hypothetical instance the same or different from that of students? Explain.

4. How widespread is cheating in your school? What are students' attitudes about it? What do you think would help curb student cheating? What keeps you from cheating?

When one takes an oath, one holds one's own self in one's hands. Like water. And if one opens one's fingers then— one needn't hope to find oneself again.

St. Thomas More in A Man for All Seasons by Robert Bolt, adapted.

What's so wrong about lying?

Lying violates the purpose of speech, which God has given us so that we can communicate the truth to one another. As with other moral wrongs, there are degrees of lies. While people commonly recognize the difference between lies and "white lies" or fibbing, they often underestimate how serious even a "little" lie may be. How serious a lie is depends on the person's intent, the kind of truth at stake, the circumstances involved in the situation, and the amount of harm done.

Thus, what's "only" a fib, a slight bending of the truth, may do great harm if it ruins someone's reputation. Whereas a braggart's whopping tale might only slightly worsen the storyteller's already strained credibility in others' eyes. Untruthfully saying someone looks nice in order to boost the person's self-confidence isn't right, but it also isn't the same as telling a self-serving lie to wriggle out of a jam. A "white lie" meant to spare somebody's feelings surely isn't as seriously wrong as a lie deliberately told to injure someone.

Lying itself, though, is more dangerous and important than the seriousness of the circumstances alone. Perhaps that is because untruthfulness always violates more than the one principle of honesty. Dishonesty not only offends against God who is Truth, but it also is an injustice to those entitled to know the truth and is a breach of love as well. Especially if habitual, but even in one serious instance, dishonesty can destroy the trust between people, trust that is necessary for love and happiness.

Our right to know the truth and our obligation to be honest with others involve matters that greatly affect our personal relationships. Deep down, we all want to be able to trust people. Dishonesty is a barrier rather than a bridge between people.

If someone is dishonest in any situation, it's reasonable to assume they'll sooner or later be dishonest with you. If someone cheats in school, it's more likely that they'll cheat on you. If you can't trust someone in small matters, you surely won't trust them in big ones. Jesus tells why:

"Whoever is faithful in a very little is faithful also in much; and whoever is dishonest in a very little is dishonest also in much."

Luke 16:10

Judges today echo the truth of Jesus' words in their instructions to jurors: "If you think a witness has lied to you about a material fact, then you can disregard everything the witness has told you. One who is willfully false in his or her testimony is to be distrusted in others."[4] People find Jesus' words true also in personal relationships where one betrayal of trust prompts continued suspicion.

Another moral hazard of dishonesty is that it often leads to a chain of dishonest acts designed to cover for the previous ones. Thus, one lie turns into a string of lies and the increasing fear (and likelihood) of being tripped up and losing one's credibility permanently. Owning up to a lie as soon as possible may salvage one's credibility. It's much better—and often far easier—just to tell the truth in the first place!

Being honest may risk bringing to light our embarrassing or wrongful behavior, but dishonesty is much more perilous! We risk losing others' trust and respect, possibly forever. Of all the things we can ever lose, one of the most precious—and one of the hardest to regain—is someone's trust. Without trust, close relationships become impossible—we can't love unless we can trust.

That's why St. Paul says,

We have renounced the shameful things that one hides; we refuse to practice cunning or to falsify God's word; but by the open statement of the truth we commend ourselves to the conscience of everyone in the sight of God.

2 Corinthians 4:2

We can't be truly close to someone we can't trust, and others can't feel close to us if they can't trust us. Likewise, only to the extent that we have integrity and are trustworthy can we trust and therefore love others. Habitual dishonesty makes one afraid and suspicious that others are being dishonest. Thus dishonesty damages not only others' ability to trust us, but our ability to trust others and therefore to experience the deepest bonds of loving relationships.

Love . . . rejoices in the truth.

1 Corinthians 13:6

Out of respect for truth and for ourselves, we also have a duty to be reasonably careful not to be deceived, misled, used, or betrayed by others. This means being wary of swindles and rip-offs, being a vigilant citizen and an alert consumer, and not letting our thoughts and feelings be manipulated by individuals, groups, or the mass media. Whether in personal relationships, business dealings, or other matters, carelessly becoming a gullible target of others' deceit and exploitation is no virtue!

We must no longer be children, tossed to and fro and blown about by . . . people's trickery, by their craftiness in deceitful scheming. But speaking the truth in love, we must grow up in every way into him who is the head, into Christ. . . .

Ephesians 4:14–15

The principle of honesty recognizes that your words and actions represent your inner self. It's important to value yourself highly enough to stand by what you believe and know is true. To lie or deceive is to betray yourself as well as others. So strive to be a person of integrity whom others admire for your honesty, and who can say along with the apostle:

For we cannot do anything against the truth, but only for the truth.

2 Corinthians 13:8

Consider honesty among your most important principles. Don't be afraid of telling or hearing the truth: "Stand therefore, and fasten the belt of truth around your waist . . ." (Ephesians 6:14). For, as Jesus said, "the truth will make you free" (John 8:32). It will free you of the fear that the truth will be discovered, and the burden of having to cover up for and tell more lies. It will free you of shame at lacking integrity. Most importantly, it will keep you close to God, and earn for you the respect, trust, and love of others.

Now that you have purified your souls by your obedience to the truth so that you have genuine mutual love, love one another deeply from the heart.

1 Peter 1:22

Clarify

1. Why does dishonesty put a barrier between people? How and why does it damage trust?
2. Why are lying or deceiving a betrayal of oneself?
3. What are the hazards of lying?
4. Why is it also a moral duty to not let ourselves be deceived, misled, used, or betrayed?

Activity

A movie portrayed a man's struggle over being absolutely truthful for one whole day. Spend a day being absolutely honest (while exercising the proper discretion, of course). Don't lie by word or action in even the smallest way. Record and report to the class on what happens.

For discussion

1. *When someone lies to you, how does that affect your ability to trust the person? Why?*

2. *If someone lied to you in little ways, would you trust the person in a bigger matter? Why is someone who's dishonest in one way likelier to be dishonest in other ways? Explain.*

3. *How would it affect your relationship if you knew your future spouse occasionally lied to others? Lied to you? Cheated? Stole small things? Explain.*

4. *Would you be more likely to confide a secret to someone who thought nothing of cheating at school, or to someone who refuses to cheat because it's wrong? Explain.*

5. *Have you ever gotten caught in a chain of lies—or caught someone else in one? If so, why did you or the other person get caught up in it? How did it end?*

6. *How important do you consider honesty in your life? Why? In your personal relationships? Why?*

7. *Have you ever continued to be suspicious of someone who was once dishonest with you? How difficult is it for someone to regain your trust after they've betrayed it? Explain.*

8. *How do you think truthfulness sets people free? Explain.*

Personal honesty profile: How much of a Pinocchio are you?

Many businesses give prospective employees a rather tricky test to assess their honesty. This questionnaire is straightforward, and merely asks that you be honest with yourself. Your responses will remain known only to you unless you choose to share them.

Would you probably be honest or dishonest in these situations?	**Honest**	**Dishonest**
1. *A friend gets her nose pierced and asks you how it looks. (You think it's extremely unattractive for her.)*	_____	_____
2. *A friend offers you the answers to a homework assignment you didn't do or a test you didn't study for.*	_____	_____
3. *You find a wallet containing five hundred dollars.*	_____	_____
4. *You went to a movie your mom probably wouldn't approve of and she asks you which movie you saw.*	_____	_____
5. *Someone in your group dares you to steal a candy bar from a store.*	_____	_____
6. *A store clerk gives you $5 too much in change.*	_____	_____

Check your answer to each question on the blank provided.

	Yes	No

1. *Do you often lie about why your homework isn't done?*

2. *Do you frequently lie about why you're late for class or for school?*

3. *Have you ever lied about somebody to get even?*

4. *In the past month, have you lied to your parents about where you were, who you were with, or what you did while out?*

5. *Have you ever lied about whether you cheated or copied homework?*

6. *Have you ever lied to cover up other lies?*

7. *Do you have a habit of volunteering personal compliments that aren't true?*

8. *Do you lie to get out of chores at home?*

9. *Do you occasionally lie to your friends?*

10. *Do you lie to make yourself look better in the eyes of others?*

11. *Do you lie to get out of trouble?*

12. *Do you occasionally lie yourself into deeper trouble?*

13. *If someone asks you if an aspect of their appearance looks all right, do you lie so as not to hurt the person's feelings?*

14. *When asked for an honest opinion you think will make someone uncomfortable, do you usually*

   • *fib so as not to make the person uncomfortable*

   • *tell the truth bluntly*

   • *try to be as kind as possible while telling the truth*

15. *Do you ever reveal people's secrets to others?*

16. *Would honesty and trustworthiness be among the **first** characteristics you would use to describe yourself as a person?*

17. *Would honesty and trustworthiness probably be among the **first** characteristics by which others would describe you as a person?*

Compassion, forgiveness, and mercy

The quality of mercy is not strained,
It droppeth as the gentle rain from heaven
Upon the place beneath: it is twice blessed;
It blesseth him that gives and him that takes:
'Tis mightiest in the mightiest it becomes
The throned monarch better than his crown;
His sceptre shows the force of temporal power,

The attribute to awe and majesty,
Wherein doth sit the dread and fear of kings;
But mercy is above this sceptred sway,
It is enthroned in the hearts of kings;
It is an attribute to God himself,
And earthly power doth then show likest God's
When mercy seasons justice.

William Shakespeare, The Merchant of Venice.

As Shakespeare understood so well centuries ago, mercy goes beyond and operates on a higher level than strict justice. People must never be treated as mere robots. The Scriptures record the development of human views of justice—from all-out retaliation, to tit-for-tat vengeance, to viewing justice in relation to our personal covenant with God whose merciful love is generous far beyond what each person deserves. The teaching and example of Jesus, whom Catholic teaching calls the *Justice of God*, likewise emphasizes God's mercy.

"I desire mercy and not sacrifice."
Matthew 12:7

As the life and death of Jesus reveal to us, God's mercy and forgiveness are unlimited and are offered always. But to accept this mercy and forgiveness, we must acknowledge our failings. As St. Augustine said, "God created us without us, but did not will to save us without us."

By reason of justice alone, none of us sinners deserves God's mercy. We should therefore breathe big sighs of relief and gratitude that God doesn't dish out justice harshly, as we sometimes do to one another! Instead, God desires only to help us become better persons—and asks that we have the same attitude toward those who wrong us. So the strictly just choice may not necessarily be the most moral choice where people are involved; and, when it comes to moral choices, people are always involved.

Compassion, forgiveness, and mercy are essential human and Christian principles. If we're compassionate, we'll try to understand and empathize with others in their troubles. If we're forgiving, we'll give others the chance to change and to once again be trusted, respected, and loved. If we're merciful, we'll seek to help rather than harm someone who has done harm, even to us.

"But I say to you, Love your enemies and pray for those who persecute you. . . ."
Matthew 5:44

Compassion and forgiveness occur in our mind and heart. Mercy is really compassion and forgiveness in action. Mercy, for example, never punishes for the sake of punishing, venting anger, or seeking revenge. Whether it involves disciplining young children or penalizing hardened criminals, **punishment should always be in proportion to the seriousness of the offense. The punishment should fit the crime and be in keeping with human dignity.**

The four main legitimate purposes of punishment are

1. To remedy, where possible, the harm caused

2. To seek pardon for the offense done

3. To preserve the necessary order and safety

4. To help reform the offender

Mercy, wherever the greater good allows it, doesn't harm the offender at all. When others must be punished for the sake of a greater good (either the offender's own or that of others), mercy confines punishment only to that which is necessary to prevent further harm and accomplish the most positive good.

Do not repay anyone evil for evil, but take thought for what is noble in the sight of all. . . . Beloved, never avenge yourselves. . . . No, "if your enemies are hungry, feed them; if they are thirsty, give them something to drink. . . ." Do not be overcome by evil, but overcome evil with good.

Romans 12:17, 19–21

Belief in mercy is behind the law that no punishment may be cruel or unusual. Mercy also underlies efforts to improve our legal and penal system to rehabilitate rather than just punish criminals.

So speak and so act as those who are to be judged by the law of liberty. For judgment will be without mercy to anyone who has shown no mercy; mercy triumphs over judgment.

James 2:12–13

To believe in compassion, forgiveness, and mercy is to believe in basic human goodness and one's ability, with the help of God and others, to change and replace evil tendencies with good. It's to believe that we're all worthy of understanding, care, pardon, and help despite our guilt and shamefulness. In this regard, we must remember what Jesus told us:

"Be merciful, just as your Father is merciful.
Do not judge, and you will not be judged;
do not condemn, and you will not be condemned.
Forgive, and you will be forgiven;
give, and it will be given to you.
A good measure, pressed down, shaken together, running over, will be put
*   into your lap;*
for the measure you give will be the measure you get back."

Luke 6:36–38

For discussion

1. *What is the difference between justice and mercy, and why is this important to understand in moral decision making?*

2. *What is the difference between being compassionate and merciful, and being too easy on wrongdoers?*

3. *Which do you think is the greater human tendency—to be merciful, to seek strict justice without mercy, or to seek revenge? Explain.*

4. *What do Jesus' teaching and example tell us about mercy?*

To Sam "Golden Rule" Jones: What I know about your earthly career convinces me that . . . you really earned your [nickname]. I know that once, while Mayor of Toledo, Ohio, you presided on the police-court bench and heard the case of a man who had stolen food for his family. You fined him $10 because he was guilty and you were not one of those sentimentalists who don't believe in the Majesty of the Law. Then you handed to the bailiff that big sombrero of yours and ordered him to pass it among the people in the courtroom, fining each of them 50 cents for living in a city where a man had to steal in order to feed his children. The hat came back very full; you gave its contents to the defendant and remitted his fine. That justice and mercy can coexist in one person, if he's big enough to contain them both, is a truth of which we can't be reminded too often, and the only effective reminders of it are people like you.

Teen court

In teen courts of many cities, teenagers hear testimony, act as prosecuting and defense attorneys, render judgment as the jury, and determine punishments for youthful offenders. Read the following based on cases brought before teen courts. Decide what sentence you would impose.

Case 1: Mark

Mark comes before you for his sentencing hearing. He's admitted having kept over $300 stolen from a school field-trip fund. He still insists he was keeping the envelope containing the money only as a favor for a friend and that he didn't know the money inside was stolen. He says, when he found out there was money in the envelope and realized it must have been stolen, he meant to turn it in but was afraid he'd be accused of having stolen it. So instead he kept the checks and split the cash among a few friends. Although Mark says his behavior at home is good, he's frequently been in trouble for fighting at school.

Case 2: Candi

Candi, fifteen, while buying Christmas gifts for her family, was caught shoplifting over $50 worth of jewelry from a department store. The jewelry she shoplifted, however, was for herself. She tells you it's the first time she's ever done anything like this. She says she had seen her older sister shoplift, and presumed it was all right because her sister had never gotten caught. Candi's parents yelled at her for it when they found out, but "that's pretty much it," she says.

Case 3: Juan

You already found seventeen-year-old Juan guilty of "tagging" the side of the school building with graffiti. After hearing your verdict, and before you deliberate on his punishment, Juan laughs and jokes with one of the other gang members and his older brother, who have come to court with him. When shown a photo of his graffiti, Juan seemed more proud than sorry.

Juan's parents are divorced, and his father is in prison for auto theft. Juan's mother says she doesn't know how to control her son anymore. She says strict punishments at home don't work—that Juan just disobeys her orders. She's afraid he's becoming a bad influence on his younger brothers. Juan often skips school and is barely passing. The only class he says he likes is art, where he's making a B this semester. The letters Juan's teachers have written to the court indicate Juan "is bright but doesn't apply himself" and "appears to have an attitude problem."

Case 4: Melissa

Melissa was seen and has admitted to setting off a false fire alarm at school during exam week. She says she did it mainly because she was afraid a poor math test score would ruin her chances of getting into the college she wants to attend. An A student, Melissa says she just needed more time to study for the test. As a result of the false alarm, exams given during the period were postponed, teachers had to formulate and give new tests, and the other students had to go through another exam session. Melissa's main concern now seems to be that she surely won't get into the college because she was caught.

Case 5: Vic and Alison

A police officer caught Vic and Alison smoking marijuana in Vic's car after a high school football game. The officer testifies that Vic became somewhat belligerent when asked to get out of the car. The officer thinks Vic was trying to impress his friends who were watching. Neither Vic nor Alison think what they did is a "big deal." They claim they were just minding their own business and shouldn't have been bothered. Vic's father seems to feel the same way about the matter.

Alison's parents, however, are quite upset. They say their daughter's attitude and behavior have changed for the worse, and that her grades have dropped at school, ever since she started dating Vic. They've tried unsuccessfully, they say, to keep Alison from seeing Vic, but she goes behind their backs. They claim Vic has a reputation for heavy drug and alcohol use and fear their daughter is headed down the same path. They ask the court's help in keeping her away from Vic, who's been arrested twice before—for possession of marijuana and for stealing a sports car to go joyriding with friends. Both times, after promising not to get in trouble again, Vic was let off with just an admonition from the judge.

For discussion

1. *In each case, what is your main moral problem and your goal in the sentence? Explain.* ➡

2. *What facts do you know about each situation? What further information would you try to find? Why?*

3. *What alternatives for punishment do you think you should consider in each instance?*

4. *How might each punishment be harmful? Helpful? Whose needs and rights are involved?* 🙌

5. *In each case, what principles were involved in the wrongdoing? Which principle is most important now in imposing a sentence? Why?* 🙌

6. *In each case, what sentence would you impose? Explain why.*

Catholic teaching on capital punishment

Kurt Bloodsworth was on death row when he was cleared by DNA evidence. Every year, several thousand persons are convicted of crimes of which they are later found innocent. The American Bar Association contends that innocent people have been executed by the state each year for the past thirty years. In one of the early American colonies, it was mandatory to execute children who cursed or hit their parents. In some places in our society, teenagers and even children may be sentenced to die for certain crimes.

Imposing the death penalty for crimes has long been highly controversial and raises profoundly troubling moral questions. Crime causes such harm and fear that many people are understandably tempted to overreact. But while there are no simple solutions to the evil many people do, putting people to death doesn't solve the real problems.

It's with these things in mind, that a majority of Catholic bishops in the United States voiced their opposition to the death penalty. While they acknowledged that capital punishment isn't necessarily opposed to Christian tradition, they've asked that we form our views on this tough issue carefully, prayerfully, and with respect for everyone's rights. For it deals with some of the most important values involving the sacredness of human life and protecting human life through law and order. In recent years, opposition to the death penalty in all but the rarest of situations has been voiced by Pope John Paul II and in the *Catechism of the Catholic Church*. The reasons why the bishops oppose capital punishment are detailed in the following paragraphs.[5]

Reasons for opposing the death penalty

The death penalty doesn't rehabilitate. Capital punishment takes away every chance for the criminal to be rehabilitated. It's certainly not necessary to threaten someone with imminent execution in order for God to touch and change the person's heart so that the criminal repents. In addition, there's always the chance an innocent person might be executed. The legal safeguards that lessen this possibility also delay executions, making them even less effective deterrents. And they make it more costly to execute criminals than to imprison them for life.

The death penalty doesn't deter crime. Execution prevents the person from committing further criminal acts, but research hasn't shown conclusively that it deters others—especially from violent crimes of passion where no thought is given to the threat of punishment. In addition, so few murderers are executed that lethal punishment is too remote a threat to be an effective deterrent. It's important to protect everyone from others' violence. But because there are other ways to do so, capital punishment can't be considered a legitimate form of societal "self-defense" or justified as a deterrent.

Revenge is unchristian. Crimes certainly justify punishment, but killing the criminal isn't necessary or justifiable to restore justice. Justice and revenge aren't synonymous. In fact, poverty and racism appear to make it likelier that a murderer will be sentenced to die, thus violating justice even further. We shouldn't punish the guilty by injuring them. Instead, Jesus urges confronting evil with restraint and self-control, and forgiving injuries. We must follow the example of Jesus, who forgave the unjust and gave up his life for all sinners.

It's brutal and cruel to return an eye for an eye by torturing the torturer or maiming one who maims. Killing the criminal to satisfy the desire for revenge is inhumane and unchristian. Besides, no amount of punishment can ever right the wrongful taking of human life. Punishment should never be enacted for its own sake, but to accomplish a positive good—in this case, protecting society and trying to reform the criminal. In our society, capital punishment isn't necessary or justifiable to achieve these rightful purposes.

There are better ways to combat violence. Doing violence doesn't stop violence. We must look for intelligent, compassionate ways to reduce violent crime. Rather than resorting to vengeful violence, we must use no more force against criminals than necessary. To eliminate violence, we must reject using it unjustifiably ourselves. The long, agonizing wait for execution, and the execution itself, cause great anguish for others as well as for the criminal. The publicity surrounding executions often arouses unhealthy, unchristian reactions in many people.

Scripture activity/insights

Read Matthew 5:38–42 and 18:21–35, and Mark 10:45.
1. What was Jesus saying or showing here about confronting evil and forgiving injuries?
2. How does what he said apply to using the death penalty today?

Clarify

1. Why is it especially important to respect the lives of those guilty of capital crimes? What would abolishing capital punishment make clear about respect for human life?
2. As Christians, why should we extend forgiveness even to the worst sinners?
3. What serious problems do the bishops point out regarding the death penalty?
4. What are their positive suggestions regarding violent crime and its effects?

We must always respect human life. Each person's value and dignity is sacred and unique. It's especially important to recognize this in persons who, crushed by suffering or twisted by hatred themselves, have violated others' rights. No one's life is worthless or disposable, not even that of a murderer. We must seek instead to help those who are despised, rejected, and often mentally as well as morally ill. We can't truly uphold the sanctity of human life in one area—war, poverty, or abortion, for instance—without upholding it in all areas. Our views about life and death matters must be morally consistent.

We should recognize how much suffering violent crime causes and provide compassionate and practical support for crime victims and their families. We should seek just punishment for crimes and make it harder for criminals to obtain violent weapons. We need to change our correctional system to protect society better by truly rehabilitating criminals into law-abiding, productive citizens, and we need to guarantee the safety of those in penal institutions who guard the criminally dangerous. We must object to glamorizing violence in our society and encourage greater respect for human life and dignity. We must also consider what it does to us as a society when we become the killers—sometimes of innocent people who are executed. If we don't stop the killing by the courts, how will we ever hope to stop it in the streets?

Clarify

1. Why is capital punishment a moral as well as a legal and political issue?
2. How do the bishops say Christians should form our views on the "difficult matter" of capital punishment?
3. Why do the bishops say that capital punishment does not rehabilitate the criminal or deter violent crime?
4. Why is revenge unchristian? Why do the bishops say it is a wrong reason to support capital punishment?
5. On what do the bishops say we should we base the punishment of criminals?
6. Why do the bishops say capital punishment is not necessary or justifiable in order to punish criminals? What do they recommend as an alternative to the death penalty?
7. What does it mean to be morally consistent in our respect for human life? How ought we to do that?

We need God's help "to discern the often narrow path between the cowardice which gives in to evil, and the violence which under the illusion of fighting evil only makes it worse." **Pope John Paul II, Centesimus Annus (546), 25.**

For discussion

1. What values are at stake on both sides of the capital punishment debate?
2. Why shouldn't we expect simple solutions to the problem of violent crime?
3. What other suggestions would you offer to address the causes and effects of violent crime?
4. What is your response to each of the reasons for opposing capital punishment? Why?
5. Do you agree that "it's better to let 100 guilty people go free than convict one innocent person"? Do you find it acceptable to continue imposing capital punishment, knowing that sometimes innocent persons are executed? Explain.
6. What is your response to Catholic teaching, which says bloodless means should be used wherever they are enough to protect the common good? How does this apply to capital punishment? Explain.

Hostage!

One of the most challenging ethical dilemmas world leaders confront is how to respond to terrorist threats when human lives are at stake. Follow your instructor's directives; you'll be asked to respond to a terrorism scenario. Afterward you will be told what a panel of former government leaders recommended in the same hypothetical situation. You can then compare and critique their decision-making process and your own.

To help you arrive at your recommendations, respond to these questions.

For discussion

1. What is the main moral problem facing the president, and what do you think the president's goal should be? Why? ➡
2. What facts does the president have about the situation? What further information should be obtained if possible?
3. What alternatives does the president have for resolving the problem?
4. Who might be harmed or helped by each alternative? Whose needs and rights are involved?
5. What principles are involved, and how? Which one is most important here? Why?
6. As the president facing this crisis, what would you pray in asking God to help you resolve it?
7. Considering Catholic teaching on terrorism and capital punishment, the available data, and your assessment of the predicament thus far, what decision do you think the president should make? Why?

Is the death penalty the best alternative?

Read about the following cases, and respond to the questions.

The Oklahoma City bombing

Timothy McVeigh decided eight law enforcement officials had to die so he could make a political point about the government. When he parked the truck carrying the bomb that would destroy them at the Oklahoma City Federal Building, he also saw innocent, vulnerable little children there. He knew they and many others would die, too, but he believed their probable deaths were acceptable and important to making his political point.

Killed in the bombing were 168 innocent people, including nineteen children under the age of five. In creating an explosive weapon of mass destruction to use in an act of political vengeance, McVeigh "knowingly, premeditatedly, and willfully" murdered. He said he did so because he felt that federal officials had overstepped their authority in a previous incident which resulted in the deaths of many, including innocent children.

McVeigh viewed his role in the Oklahoma bombing as a patriotic duty designed to inspire others to counteract the abuse of authority by the government. After finding McVeigh guilty, the jury contemplating his sentence had to consider whether executing McVeigh would make him a martyred hero among those who shared his extremist views and perhaps lead to even greater violence, or whether life imprisonment would be a too-light punishment for a cold-blooded killer.

For discussion

1. If you had been on the jury in this case, what sentence would you probably have felt like giving McVeigh? Why?

2. If McVeigh had shown genuine remorse about what he had done, do you think your feelings about what punishment he deserved might have changed?

3. If McVeigh had been a teenager, would that have made any difference in how you felt about the sentence he should be given? Explain.

4. What is the difference between viewing it as a patriotic duty to execute McVeigh and McVeigh's view that he did a patriotic act?

5. Perhaps most of the world's terrorists view themselves as patriots for a cause, and many believe being killed for that cause gains them eternal paradise. Do you think executing convicted terrorists is more, or less, likely to deter future terrorism? Explain.

The execution of Pedro Medina

Pedro Medina's last words before being executed for murdering his teacher were, "I'm still innocent." The victim's daughter and the pope had pleaded that Medina's life be spared. But as the switch was pulled to send 2,000 electrical volts through his body in the electric chair, five- to six-inch flames shot out of the mask covering Medina's face as witnesses gasped in horror. Some of them said Medina was gruesomely "burned alive."

The prison's medical director said that afterward he found only "routine electrical burns" on Medina's body. But during the Holy Week that commemorates Jesus' execution as a criminal, the Vatican condemned Medina's execution as tragic and barbaric and urged justice officials to abolish the death penalty.

For discussion

1. Do you think Medina's execution constituted "cruel and unusual punishment"? Explain.

2. Should jurors be required to view the execution of the person they sentence to die? If you had known how Medina would die, could you have pulled the switch to electrocute him?

3. What do you think executing criminals does to us as a society? Explain.

4. Some people on both sides of the death penalty debate have said executions should be televised. Most people disagree. What is your opinion? Why?

Ted Bundy—serial killer

Referred to as one of history's worst serial killers, Ted Bundy had a sociopathic personality and used his looks, charm, and wit to lure victims. A few days before being executed, he finally confessed to over twenty murders, starting with that of an eight-year-old girl when he was only fourteen. As a youth, Bundy had belonged to the Boy Scouts and had been an A student. He later attended law school; some felt he had a promising political career. While on a crime prevention committee he even wrote a booklet telling women how to avoid being raped! Ted Bundy appeared the ideal date, citizen, and neighbor.

On the eve of his execution, a tearful Bundy blamed exposure to sexually violent pornography as decisive in his becoming a serial killer. He said continued exposure to sexual violence whets the appetite for more powerful, explicit material "until you reach a jumping off point where you wonder if maybe actually doing it would give you what's beyond reading or looking at it." Many psychologists agreed that pornography had gradually desensitized Bundy to the wrongness of sexually violent acts and had led to his compulsion to brutally kill women. He may have come to enjoy dodging the electric chair as the ultimately thrilling risk.

Many considered Bundy an evil "monster," and they lit sparklers, cheered, and waved signs reading "BURN, BUNDY, BURN" and "ROAST IN PEACE" to celebrate his execution. Officials even authorized a license plate that read "FRY TED." Had Bundy lived, he may have confessed to many other murders that are unsolved and still haunt the victims' loved ones. His death has cost us a chance to learn how to identify and treat others like him before they kill. Many experts had hoped Bundy's life would be spared so that they could learn from him how to apprehend and treat similar criminals in the future.

Bundy evidently displayed sociopathic tendencies early in life and manic-depressive illness at the end. His grandfather, with whom he had lived when very young, was said to have been an "extremely violent, frightening" person who craved pornography. That influence may have radically and permanently distorted a highly impressionable young Bundy.

Medical experts suspect that behavior-altering brain dysfunctions may indeed make serial killers "crazy." Perhaps the criminals people most love to hate and kill are actually not fully responsible for their heinous crimes. In the past, people were stoned or burned to death as "possessed by devils" or as "witches" for exhibiting behavior now recognized as seizures. "Vampires'" craving of blood is a medically-diagnosable physical disorder. The autopsy on a man killed after fatally shooting several others from atop a tower revealed that a brain tumor likely caused his unprovoked, uncontrollable violence. Further discoveries may show we've been compounding tragedies by executing people who may actually be physically ill.

For discussion

1. How can pornography negatively influence individuals—particularly young persons—without their even realizing it? Why does pornography—in its exploitation of people as sex objects, especially in a sexually violent way—have such a negative effect on those continually exposed to it?

2. How do you think Bundy would probably have been different if he had not been exposed to so much violence when young? Explain.

3. Where do you think the line should be drawn on the types of pornography allowed in a free society? What do you think is the best way to oppose pornography? Explain.

4. What in the Ted Bundy case argues in favor of capital punishment? Against it? Explain.

5. What is your assessment of the morality of people's reactions to Bundy's execution? What moral responsibility do you think news media have in covering stories like this? Explain.

6. If it is found true that the most hateful criminals are among the least responsible for their crimes, how might future generations view us when replaying news coverage about the Ted Bundy execution? Explain.

7. How can negative background influences affect one's behavior in the future? How do they affect your behavior now?

8. How do you think growing up with the kind of background Bundy had probably would have affected you as a teenager? As an adult? Explain.

9. How might lack of remorse indicate that a killer is fully responsible for murder? That the killer couldn't be morally responsible for murder?

10. How do you think Jesus would have instructed the McVeigh and Bundy juries before they deliberated on the sentence? How do you think he'd have responded to Medina's execution? Explain.

11. To be in line with Catholic teaching about capital punishment, what sentence do you think McVeigh and Bundy should have received?

Chapter 8 summary
Christian principles

1. What are principles?

- Principles are ideal values which are good in themselves and the foundation for moral decisions.
- Christian principles are based on natural law, the Ten Commandments, and the teaching of Jesus.
- The next decision-making step is to determine what principles apply that involve people's dignity or well-being.

2. Making principled choices

- Moral principles are the criteria for judging moral goodness or evil.
- Moral principles reflect and influence one's values and goals in life.
- Acting according to your principles shows you believe in yourself.
- To apply your principles, determine how they pertain to the available alternatives and decide whether each alternative upholds or violates them
- Principles are important guides in providing moral direction and courage.

3. Christian moral principles

- Jesus taught us basic principles as moral guides, rather than giving us specific solutions to moral dilemmas.
- He told us to give priority to spiritual rather than material values.
- Loving others unselfishly is the basic, overriding guiding principle of Christian moral conduct.
- Human dignity and human rights are based on God's love for each person, and violating these is generally wrong.
- All persons have certain universal human rights.
- Honesty is essential for human survival and relationships, and requires not deceiving those who are entitled to the truth.
- Mercy means being compassionate and forgiving as God forgives and is merciful to us.
- Punishment should fit the seriousness of the offense, be in keeping with human dignity, and accomplish a legitimate positive purpose.
- The Catholic Church tends toward viewing capital punishment as not necessary, vengeful, ineffective, and not morally consistent with respect for all human life.

Key concepts

applying principles

basic human rights

capital punishment

Christian principles

compassion

equality

forgiveness

hierarchy of values

honesty

human dignity

Judeo-Christian principles

justice

material values

mercy

the people principle

principles

reasons for dishonesty

revealing the truth

spiritual values

unselfish love *(agape)*

*I do not understand my own actions.
For I do not do what I want, but I do the very
thing I hate.
. . . when I want to do what is good, evil lies
close at hand.
. . . the Spirit helps us in our weakness. . . .
And God, who searches the heart, knows
what is the mind of the Spirit. . . .*
Romans 7:15, 21; 8:26, 27

Chapter 9

Being Morally Responsible

Overview questions

1. What does it mean to be a morally responsible person?
2. How should you identify and weigh the consequences in a moral situation?
3. What determines the extent of moral responsibility?
4. What is your responsibility for accidents, acts of negligence, deliberate actions, and for others' wrongful acts?
5. What does accepting responsibility for your actions involve?

Responsible morality

> *Do nothing without deliberation,
> but when you have acted, do not regret it.*
> SIRACH 32:19

Please don't view moral responsibility negatively, as being burdened by all sorts of *do's* and *don'ts*. Rather, understand it positively, as responding compassionately and intelligently to people and situations. As many people have suggested, perhaps responsibility should be two words: **response ability.** Being a responsible person includes how you respond to a situation—your ability to:

1. **Be aware** of how your moral principles apply to people and to their needs, circumstances, and well-being.

2. **Assess the consequences—the risks and benefits** of your actions beforehand.

3. **Make a decision and act** for the right reasons.

4. **Accept the consequences** of your decisions and actions.

Clarify

1. What does it mean to be a morally responsible person?
2. Why should this be viewed positively rather than negatively?

Being aware

The human spirit is the lamp of the LORD, searching every inmost part.

PROVERBS 20:27

Considering the circumstances and being aware of what's needed in a situation can help you respond more intelligently and helpfully. If you're unaware that a friend has a problem and needs to talk, you won't be able to help. While a friend remains miserable and lonely, you'll wonder about the reason for the moodiness and whether you've done something wrong. If you encourage your friend to talk, however, you'll probably both feel better.

Suppose you don't think about the possible results of revealing a friend's secret which should be kept private. You'll regret telling someone else when the secret gets around and back to your friend. Perceptiveness and careful thought in the beginning can help you make wise judgments that keep you from hurting others and yourself.

Step 4: Considering the consequences

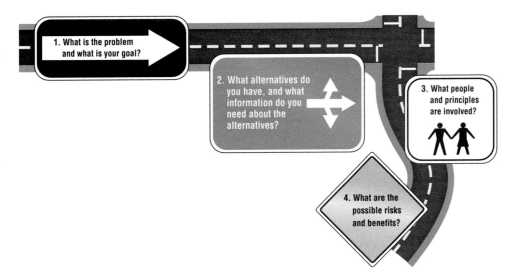

We've said that listening to your conscience is using your head—to determine what is the best, most loving thing to do in a situation, while doing something that might result in harm only if it is justifiable and necessary. To determine what's best, however, you must first properly assess both the risks and the benefits of each available alternative.

If you don't consider in advance the possible outcomes of each alternative, you're likely to make a decision you'll later regret. Think through the consequences of available choices before you make your decision. Consider exactly whether and how a choice might harm the **people** involved (including you) and whether it would violate your **principles.**

Also consider how each available alternative might be **beneficial:** How might a particular choice help you and others? How might it reflect and support your principles? Then you can make a choice that accomplishes the maximum good for the people involved. When people don't think through their alternatives beforehand, they often don't make the most beneficial decision. To avoid disappointing, unhappy consequences, learn to consider carefully exactly what the risks and benefits are, and how they might affect you and others.

. . . they shall bear their shame, and the consequences of the abominations that they have committed.
EZEKIEL **44:13**

Step 4A: Identifying the risks and benefits

Whenever you choose a course of action, you are also choosing its consequences. If you know what could happen and you select that path, you're choosing the action's consequences, be they beneficial or harmful, pleasant or unpleasant. Not considering the consequences beforehand is irresponsible. In a moral situation, such irresponsibility carries its own guilt.

Civil law too holds people responsible for doing harmful things, even if they failed to foresee the harm that might result from their actions. In fact, legally, people are responsible for the harm they reasonably **should** have foreseen. Moral responsibility means trying **your best** to make the best decision and to follow through on it. **Legal** responsibility determines what is "best" according to what the "reasonable person" in the same circumstances would do. Christianity goes further than legal responsibility and proposes not only following the "reasonable person" standard, but also acting with Jesus' loving, forgiving, and reconciling heart and mind.

To be more morally responsible, work first on being more aware of how your behavior affects people, positively and negatively. Think in advance about an action's effects—possible risks and benefits. Then pray and act with reason and compassion.

For discussion

1. *What does moral responsibility mean to you?*
2. *Do you agree that when you choose an alternative, you choose its natural consequences, even if the consequences are unpleasant? Explain.*
3. *Do you usually think carefully about the consequences of your alternatives? Do you think about what's needed in a situation before you say or do something that might hurt you or others? Explain.*
4. *Describe an instance when you didn't think carefully enough about the consequences of an action and made a decision you regretted.*
5. *How do morality and the law compare in terms of responsibility for the harm that results from decisions people make?*
6. *How does civil law's reasonable person standard compare with Christianity's standard for being a responsible person? Give two examples for each standard.*

What could happen now?

Have you ever raced to answer the phone because you didn't want to miss an important call, only to trip and almost break your neck on the way? If you had broken your leg, or far worse, would racing to the phone have been worth it? A certain choice might accomplish good in the future; nevertheless, one must consider the harmful effects the choice might cause in the meantime. Before you act, you must consider both the **immediate** and the **long-range consequences** of your decisions.

If a parent takes a second job working evenings and weekends to save for his or her children's college education, this decision might negatively affect the family now in ways that aren't worth it. If you worked so many hours now to save for college tuition that you didn't have time to study for the grades you need to even get into college, you'd defeat your purpose! By being too focused on career goals, some young adults let friendships and family relationships suffer and die. You can't go back later and remake some choices.

So consider from the start how the short-term results of your actions will affect people. Consider whether the results are compatible with your principles. Don't let your attraction for a future good blind you to the consequences you're risking **now.**

No harm happens to the righteous, but the wicked are filled with trouble.
PROVERBS 12:21

SPEED KILLS

What could happen later?

People go bankrupt every day. Perhaps a family wanted that new car or house so much that they weren't realistic about how they were going to pay for it. When people want something too much or too soon, they often lose sight of what their choice could cost them later. The negative consequences which may occur **later** (perhaps not much later!) can far outweigh the benefits sought **now.**

Not to consider now what can happen later is often to regret it later! Every year, over a million unwed teenage women become pregnant; they didn't base their sexual choices **now** on what might happen **later.** A couple in love and sexually aroused are tempted to have sex now. It's only after the romantic date, the loving words, and the immediate physical pleasure that they face the long-term consequences. One thoughtless choice now completely changes many lives forever.

Consider the inner, personal consequences

We must also evaluate our choices according to how their consequences reach into our hearts and souls. Our moral choices can and do have profound effects on us as persons. Moral choices influence further moral choices, which eventually can bring a person to the point of making a life-decision for or against God. Our decisions can also affect the direction of other people's lives.

So in addition to thinking about immediate and long-term "external" consequences of your action, think about how the action will affect you as a person and how it will affect your relationship with God and others. Think about the eternal implications of your choice. Consider these things especially in every moral decision. Paul wrote about this need to consider present, future, and eternal consequences of our choices and to do so in the context of loving our neighbor as ourselves.

> *For you were called to freedom, brothers and sisters; only do not use your freedom as an opportunity for self-indulgence, but through love become slaves to one another. For the whole law is summed up in a single commandment, "You shall love your neighbor as yourself." If, however, you bite and devour one another, take care that you are not consumed by one another.*
>
> *Live by the Spirit, I say, and do not gratify the desires of the flesh. . . . But if you are led by the Spirit, you are not subject to the law. Now the works of the flesh are obvious: fornication, impurity, licentiousness, idolatry, sorcery, enmities, strife, jealousy, anger, quarrels, dissensions, factions, envy, drunkenness, carousing, and things like these. I am warning you, as I warned you before: those who do such things will not inherit the kingdom of God.*
>
> *By contrast, the fruit of the Spirit is love, joy, peace, patience, kindness, generosity, faithfulness, gentleness, and self-control. There is no law against such things. . . . If we live by the Spirit, let us also be guided by the Spirit.*
>
> *Galatians 5:13–16, 18–23, 25*

EXERCISE CAUTION

Do not be deceived; God is not mocked, for you reap whatever you sow. If you sow to your own flesh, you will reap corruption from the flesh; but if you sow to the Spirit, you will reap eternal life from the Spirit. So let us not grow weary in doing what is right, for we will reap at harvest-time, if we do not give up. So then, whenever we have an opportunity, let us work for the good of all, and especially for those of the family of faith.
GALATIANS 6:7–10

By rejecting conscience, certain persons have suffered shipwreck in the faith. . . .
1 TIMOTHY 1:19

Clarify

1. What is the best way to identify and weigh the consequences of your actions beforehand?
2. What does Paul say to the Galatians about considering the consequences of our choices?

For discussion

1. *When making a decision, which are you less likely to consider adequately—the short-term "external" consequences, the long-term "external" consequences, or the "inner" moral consequences of your alternatives? Explain.*
2. *Which type of consequences do you think teenagers are least likely to consider? Explain.*
3. *What consequences are teenagers most responsible about considering? Least responsible about considering? Give examples.*

The pledge and the wedgie

Read the following reality-based account and respond to the questions as if you were a juror in the case. Your instructor will then explain the actual case's outcome.

Marcus, a college student, is being tried for the misdemeanor of hazing after a young pledge in his fraternity lost a testicle due to one or more of the hazing activities in which they both voluntarily participated.

Hazing is defined by the law here as substantially risking loss of life or substantial bodily or psychological harm by recklessly endangering a student or prospective member's mental or physical health or safety. Among other actions, hazing includes beating, tattooing, prolonged or extreme exposure to heat or cold, or forcing the person to eat, drink, or consume alcohol, another drug, or any other substance.

During the hazing, Marcus "wedgied" the victim by lifting him off his feet by his underwear waistband. He also held the victim's belt while making him do sit-ups. Due to the injuries these actions caused, doctors had to remove one of the victim's testicles.

Marcus doesn't deny that the specified activities occurred, but he contends they didn't constitute hazing, since they weren't really dangerous. Others, his lawyer points out, participated in the same activities without being harmed. In addition, the victim also willingly participated in the activities and so assumed any risks involved.

If guilty, Marcus may be sentenced to up to a year in jail and fined $4,000. The fraternity, which is charged with organizational hazing, can also be fined—$10,000 or more.

For discussion

1. Keeping in mind the four main legitimate purposes of punishment discussed in chapter 8, what is your problem and your goal as a juror in this case? ➡
2. What are the case's important facts as you know them? Which are most important?
3. Do you think Marcus' actions meet the definition of the misdemeanor hazing? Explain.
4. What are your alternatives here?
5. What people, principles, and harm are involved in this case? Explain.

6. Did the victim assume the risks by participating in the activities? Would that excuse Marcus from also being responsible? Explain. ◆
7. Should a reasonable college student have considered beforehand that the wedgie and sit-up activities might constitute illegal hazing? Might be injurious and dangerous? ◆
8. How do you think Marcus and the victim should have answered the weigh-your-alternatives questions before participating in the hazing activities? ◆
9. To what extent are each of the following morally and/or legally responsible for the victim's injury— ◆
   • Marcus
   • the victim
   • the other fraternity members who participated
   • the university, for not taking stronger action against hazing practices sooner
10. Do you find Marcus guilty in this case? If so, what sentence do you impose? Explain.
11. What fine or sanctions, if any, would you impose on the fraternity and other participants? Explain.

Step 4B: Weighing the risks and benefits

In this fourth step in moral decision making, you need to consider not only **who** or **what** is involved in the situation, but also **how** and **how much** they'll be affected now and in the future. To do this, answer these questions:

1. **What risks and benefits are involved in each alternative solution?**

2. **How important is each risk or benefit and how likely is it to happen?**

How important are the possible risks and benefits?

To begin putting your available alternatives in proper perspective:

1. Rule out any obviously morally wrong alternatives—things you wouldn't consider doing no matter what.

2. Determine each remaining alternative's possible positive and negative consequences.

3. Decide whether the risks of harm and possible benefits are great or small.

4. Weigh the relative importance of the risks and benefits.

For example, an alternative's benefit might be so great that its relatively minor risk is worth taking. Or the benefit, however appealing now, might be minor compared with the great harm you'd be risking in terms of the future.

BRIDGE AHEAD

NO VEHICLES OVER 2,000 POUNDS

Weigh your alternatives

Even after ruling out obviously immoral choices, weighing everything else can be confusing—especially in complex dilemmas! To sort things out, answer these questions:

1. Is there a law, rule, or special obligation I must or should consider here? If so, should I obey it, or is there enough reason to set it aside in this situation?

2. How many people would this affect now and in the future—one, a few, many?

3. How—and how much—would this affect me and others positively? Negatively?

4. Are there any people who should get priority because I owe them a special duty, maybe because they're suffering or can't help themselves?

5. Would the possible harm or benefit to one or a few persons be much greater or less than that for many people? How much greater or less?

6. Which principle is most important here—that affecting the individual or that affecting many? Why?

Clarify

1. How can we foresee the possible risks and benefits of a course of action?

2. How can we determine the importance of each?

Answering these questions intelligently and objectively can help you wade through tangled issues, especially in complicated or emotion-laden situations. Otherwise, you may get so frustrated or confused that you make an unwise and harmful decision. So take care to assess the risks and possible benefits and their importance sufficiently before you make your decision.

What chance is there that the risks and benefits will happen?

In addition to considering the importance of an alternative's risks and benefits, you must also evaluate the probability, the likelihood, of their occurring. There could be enormous risk of harm, but so what—if its chance of happening is ninety billion to one? Knowing the odds can sure be helpful! Likewise, knowing that a harmful consequence is likely or probable may sway your decision to avoid it.

Determine the degree of probability

To judge how likely it is that a risk or benefit will occur, consider the degrees of probability: Is the chance that this consequence will result

- certain
- remotely possible
- probable
- impossible
- fairly possible

Keep in mind that any major decision or action usually involves some risk. That's why making big decisions can be so hard. But you can minimize poor decisions and harmful consequences by considering in advance each alternative's probability factors. After assessing how likely it is that a certain action will help you reach your goal, you'll know better if the risk is worth taking.

Assessing your alternatives

Read these situations and respond to the questions.

1. *A few weeks before high school graduation, you go with your class to a water-slide park. About thirty of the class want to go down the big slide together to set a new school and city record for the number of kids going down at once. You've heard about how last year's class tried to break the record. Posted signs warn against more than one person at a time going down the slide. As your group begins climbing to the platform on top of the slide, the lifeguard warns that only one person at a time is to go down the slide.*

2. *While you are riding around with friends late one night after a party, someone suggests stealing a few traffic signs for souvenirs—beginning with the stop sign at the nearby intersection.*

For discussion

1. *What is your problem in each case, and what do you think your goal should be?* →
2. *What are your alternatives in each situation?*
3. *What information do you have and need to know in each instance?*
4. *What people and principles are involved in each? Explain.*
5. *What possible risks and benefits are involved with each of your alternatives?*
6. *Answer the weigh-your-alternatives and probability questions regarding each situation's alternatives.*
7. *What do you think you should do in each situation? What do you think you'd do?*
8. *Did carefully weighing the consequences change your decision from what it probably would have been? Is it good that you changed your mind? Explain.*

Luke's choice

Read the following story and respond to the questions.

Luke knows that his girlfriend Carrie wants to make love with him. Whenever she and Luke are alone and he starts kissing her, he feels like she's instantly all over him. The way it turns Luke on, it's getting increasingly hard for him to resist going all the way. Carrie's also confided to one of Luke's friends that she'd really like for Luke to make love to her.

So far Luke hasn't had sex with Carrie because, frankly, he's not sure he wants to get that involved with her—or at least not involved in that way right now. Luke's dad once told him that if a guy has sex with a young woman, she immediately hears wedding bells. His dad said some women will try to trap a guy by having sex with him. A young woman may carelessly or intentionally let herself get pregnant because she wants a baby or so the guy feels he has to marry her. She might even claim she's using "protection" when she isn't.

Luke has plans for college and doesn't want anything to disrupt those plans. He knows he's not ready for marriage, much less to be a father. If things continue to go well in his relationship with Carrie, Luke thinks marriage might be in their future—someday, but not now. Luke gets the feeling, though, that the way he and Carrie feel about each other physically and emotionally, it will be only a matter of time before they give in to their feelings.

Luke's mother keeps telling him not to have sex until he marries. She says that, besides being the morally right thing to do, abstinence is the only way to make sure he won't get a sexually transmitted disease or get a young woman pregnant. She reminds him that if he did father a child, he would have to pay child support for the next eighteen years, even if he didn't marry his girlfriend.

Luke's best friend tells him that, if Luke wore a condom, there'd be no danger of pregnancy or disease. But Luke's mom gave him an article about how using the wrong kind of condom doesn't protect against diseases. It also said that if a condom breaks, which sometimes happens, his girlfriend could get pregnant. Carrie hinted to Luke's friend that she's "prepared—just in case." But even if it's true, the article also said that birth control pills aren't always 100 percent effective.

Another friend of Luke's says that if he is "prepared" ahead of time, Carrie will think he's had sex before. She will be hurt and mistrust Luke and might even break off their relationship. Luke also thinks he'd be too embarrassed to buy condoms or to insist that Carrie use some protection.

Luke doesn't want to lose Carrie and wonders if she'll believe he really loves her if he doesn't ask her to have sex. He thinks maybe he should just let things happen, rather than deciding about it in advance. On the other hand, he doesn't want to make a mistake that will "mess up" the rest of his life. That fear and the unspoken pressure he feels from Carrie to have sex with her sometimes make Luke wonder whether he should just break off their relationship. . . .

For discussion

1. What is Luke's problem? What should his goal be? Why? ➡
2. What facts should Luke consider in making up his mind whether to have sex with Carrie? In deciding when to decide about it? Explain. ■
3. What alternatives does Luke have? Which ones do you think Luke should rule out immediately as morally unacceptable? Explain. ■
4. Who might be helped or harmed by what Luke decides? 👫
5. What principles are involved? Which ones could be violated by what Luke decides? Which principles are most important here? 👫
6. How great would the benefits and/or risk of harm be for each of Luke's alternatives? ◆
7. Answer the weigh-your-alternatives and probability questions regarding Luke's alternatives.
8. Given your assessment of the risks, what and when should Luke decide? Explain.
9. What is your response to Luke's thoughts and feelings? To what his parents and friends have told him? To the information in the article Luke read? Explain.
10. If the situation were reversed, and Carrie was the one feeling pressured by Luke to have sex, would your responses to any of the above questions be different? Explain.
11. In a relationship, do you think it's usually the guy or his girlfriend who feels pressured to have sex? Explain.

The stop sign prank

Read the following reality-based account as if you were a juror in this case. Then render your verdict by responding to the questions.

A stop sign had been uprooted at a busy intersection. As a result, three teenagers died. A semi-trailer truck came through the intersection and slammed into their car. Three other teenagers, Nissa, Tom, and Chris, are now on trial, a year and a half later, for grand theft of the stop sign and three counts of manslaughter.

Police officers testify that the teens who were killed "probably never knew what hit them," and that the stop sign post had been lying face down by the intersection when the fatality occurred. A defense expert testifies that the truck might have knocked the sign down, while a prosecution expert says it was pulled out of the ground. A prosecution witness testifies that Chris told him that the day before the accident the trio had stolen a bunch of street signs, including at least one other stop sign. Chris told the witness that he helped his friends dispose of those signs in a river, but later got scared he'd be charged with a crime.

The trio on trial deny removing the stop sign at the intersection where the accident occurred. A sheriff's department investigator testifies that when charged with the crime, Tom remarked that he guessed the other two "rolled over on him." Tom denies having said that. The trio does admit stealing nineteen other traffic signs along other roads a week or two before the accident. They stole street signs, railroad crossing signs, and other signs, as Chris said, "for a rush" because "it was fun."

The trio had told police investigators that they put the stolen signs in their pickup truck, or, if a car was coming, just left it lying there—intending to come back for it later. They say that when they heard about the accident, they panicked and threw the stolen signs in a river so nobody would think they'd also taken down the crash site stop sign. The uprooted stop sign now at issue was in the same area as the other signs the trio stole, but no fingerprints, eyewitnesses, or other physical evidence ties the trio to the crime.

The father of one teenager who was killed says the trio, no matter what their punishment, can never know how he felt when he learned his son was dead. He says that by uprooting the stop sign at that intersection, these three young people killed his son. If found guilty, they could each be sentenced to up to forty-six years in prison.

For discussion

1. As a juror in this case, what is your main problem? Your primary goal? What are your alternatives? ➡ ▮

2. What are the relevant facts? Which are most important? Why? ▮

3. Which people and principles are involved in the various aspects of this case? How are they involved? 👫

4. What risks and possible consequences should Nissa, Tom, and Chris have considered before they uprooted traffic signs? How should they have answered the weigh-your-alternatives and probability questions about their alternatives? ◆

5. What are the risks and possible benefits of your available decisions as a juror in this case? How would you answer the weigh-your-alternatives questions? Explain. ◆

6. Based on what you know, what is your verdict? Why?

7. Review in chapter 8 the four main legitimate purposes of punishment. If the trio were found guilty, what punishment would you suggest? Why?

The extent of responsibility

. . . what the law requires is written on their hearts, to which their own conscience also bears witness. . . .

ROMANS 2:15

Common sense tells us that some things are much worse than others. It's obviously far worse to kill someone than to pick the person's pocket. Morality and the law both acknowledge what our own experience confirms: **There are degrees of wrong doing and degrees of responsibility for it.**

We can compare the degrees of wrongdoing and their effects to the troubles in a relationship. If you exchange angry, unfair, and unkind words with someone who hurt your feelings, the problems that causes between you won't necessarily sever your relationship. If one of you deliberately betrays the other's trust, however, that may distance you enough to break up the relationship. Then a complete change of heart and behavior, a willingness to forgive, and a sincere effort to make amends might be needed to patch things up. It's the same with moral wrongdoing.

We can somewhat damage our love for God and others and offend God without destroying our relationship with God and others (venial sin). It's possible to kill all the love in our hearts and turn entirely away from God by freely choosing to do something that we know is seriously wrong (mortal sin). Although we need not believe that any humans have ever done so, we do need to realize that we have the power and freedom to choose to exclude ourselves forever from God's love and from eternal happiness. Like all genuine love, God's love is never forced on us. We can accept it or reject it.

> *. . . in its very nature, the exercise of religion consists before all else in those internal, voluntary, and free acts whereby [one] sets the course of [one's] life directly toward God.*
> **"DECLARATION ON RELIGIOUS FREEDOM," NUMBER 3.**

Moral wrongs activity—Part 1

1. Draw a line down the middle of a piece of paper. Then draw another line down the middle of the second column.
2. In the first column, list ten examples of different types of moral wrongs you find in one day's news. Don't list more than one example of the same type of moral wrong—such as murder.
3. Next to each example, in the second column, list whether the wrong is gravely serious or less serious.
4. Leave the third column blank for now and save your list.

> *It's not love's going hurts my days,*
> *But that it went in little ways.*
> **EDNA ST. VINCENT MILLAY**

As with other damaged or broken relationships, to make things right again requires repentance and conversion. This means being truly sorry for what we've done wrong and changing our heart around to accept God's merciful love and forgiveness—which is always lovingly offered to us. For Catholics, this is normally celebrated in the Sacrament of Reconciliation.

It's not the great big offense out of the blue, though, that most often destroys a personal relationship, but the dozens of small things that eventually lead to the major blow-up or act of infidelity.

rationalizing

trying to explain or excuse one's thoughts or behavior by giving superficial rather than the real reasons

The habit of doing little wrongs one isn't sorry for usually leads to doing more serious wrong. Even small wrongs show that we prefer the wrong thing over our own welfare and that of others. Small wrongs weaken our ability to love God and others and to do what is good.

It's by repeating small wrongs that our consciences eventually become foggy so that, even though we still sense what's right and wrong, we no longer see clearly enough to make good judgments in particular situations. That's when we begin **rationalizing** that wrong is right and trying to reinforce and explain away our wrongs instead of admitting them. Constantly doing what's right and good, even in small things, works the same way. The more we do right, the more truly free and inclined toward goodness we become, and the clearer and more sound are our moral judgments.

"The good person out of the good treasure of the heart produces good, and the evil person out of evil treasure produces evil. . . ."
LUKE 6:45

Reflection

1. Which small wrongs do you easily excuse in yourself? Which of these are a habit with you?
2. How do you suppose your habitual small wrongs negatively affect your relationships with God and others?

Clarify

1. In your own words, compare the degrees of moral responsibility to having problems in a relationship.
2. Explain the basic difference between gravely serious and lesser wrongs.
3. Why must religion and morality involve free, voluntary choices?
4. Why and how can small wrongs become greatly damaging, and small right choices become greatly beneficial?

Journal entry

Describe the treasure that is in your heart.

The good we do influences the moral attitudes and behavior of others. So does the wrong we do. We mustn't cause others—especially children—to stumble morally because of our bad example:

"If any of you put a stumbling block before one of these little ones who believe in me, it would be better for you if a great millstone were fastened around your neck and you were drowned in the depth of the sea.

"Woe to the world because of stumbling blocks! Occasions for stumbling are bound to come, but woe to the one by whom the stumbling block comes!"

Matthew 18:7

> *Those who are kind reward themselves, but the cruel do themselves harm.*
> **PROVERBS 11:17**

French scientists use the example of lilies on a pond to illustrate how rapidly many small things can multiply to become the overriding reality: On day one, there's a single lily in the pond. On day two, there are two lilies. Each day the lilies on the pond keep doubling, until on the twenty-ninth day the pond is half full of lilies. On the 30th day, the pond is completely filled and the lilies have taken over.

If we associate with others who are always in trouble, we increase the likelihood that we'll join them in doing wrong. By the same token, seeing somebody do what's kind and loving inspires us to do the same. That's how evil spreads evil and good generates more good—for oneself, as well as for others.

For discussion

1. What kinds of wrongs tend to damage your relationships with others? Which kinds would cause or have caused you to end a relationship? Explain.

2. To what extent do you think teenagers consider how their choices affect their relationship with God? To what extent do you? Explain.

3. Which habitual little wrongs do you notice that others (mention no names) don't seem sorry for? How does that affect their relationship with you and others? Explain.

4. In what ways do you think society's moral sense is foggy? What most often seems to cloud teenagers' consciences so that they don't see clearly enough to make good judgments? Explain.

5. What's the difference between a rationalized excuse and a solid reason?

6. Which small wrongs do you tend most to rationalize in yourself? Why do you think you do this?

7. How do the good things your friends do influence you to do good? How do the wrongs other teenagers do influence you to do wrong? Give examples.

8. How does your kindness to others reward you? How does your unkindness to others harm you?

Wrongful death

Read the following reality-based account, and then respond to the questions as if you were a juror deciding this case.

Carl is seventeen years old. His parents agreed he could have a party at his home one Friday night. Carl asked them to not hang around to supervise it. They told Carl they were afraid his friend Ron would bring beer, as he often has to other parties. Carl responded that "nobody would come" if no alcohol were allowed. Or else, he said, kids would just drink before they came or would drink outside in their cars.

Carl said drinking at parties is "no big deal—everybody does it." He assured his parents he wouldn't let things get out of hand. Considering their son a responsible young man, Carl's parents said they'd trust him to keep everything under control.

Everyone seemed to have a great time at the party. Ron brought a keg of beer, but, to Carl's relief, nobody got too rowdy or obnoxious. Ron left the party early with a few friends. Carl didn't find out until the next day what happened to them afterward.

Ron, with a history of moving-vehicle offenses, was driving at more than twice the speed limit when the car smashed into a parked trailer. He survived, but the two passengers were killed in the crash. One passenger was Ron's cousin Joe. Ron's blood alcohol shortly after the accident tested above the legally drunk level.

Joe's teenage sister and his parents have filed a wrongful death suit for $5 million against Ron, *Ron's parents, and Carl's parents. The lawsuit says the teenagers' deaths were "extremely tragic and brutal." It charges Carl's parents with letting their son and other minors have an unsupervised party at their home, a party at which alcoholic drinks were served, and at which Ron and some of the other young people got drunk. Ron's parents are charged with "supplying alcohol to minors" at the party.*

Co-defendants in the lawsuit are the girl whose car Ron was driving, the city, the county, the state, the construction company at whose site the trailer was parked, and the trailer's owner.

For discussion

1. What was the initial problem for Carl? For his parents? What goals did they choose, and how did these goals turn out to have been wrong? ➡

2. As a juror in this case, what would your main problem be? Your goal? Your alternatives? ➡ ◼

3. What are the most important facts in this case? Why? ◼

4. Which people and principles are involved in the case? Which principles were violated? How? Which principles should Carl and his parents have considered at the outset? 👫

5. Which risks should reasonably have been foreseen by ◆
   • Carl and Carl's parents
   • Ron and Ron's parents
   • Ron's friends who stayed at the party
   • Ron's friends who left with him
   • the girl whose car Ron was driving

6. How should Carl, his parents, and Ron have answered beforehand the weigh-your-alternatives and probability questions? ◆

7. Given the facts you know, to what extent would you find each of the parties who are being sued legally and/or morally responsible for the deaths? Of these parties, who do you consider most and least responsible? Explain.

8. To what extent do you think the boys who were killed in the accident were also responsible

Party time problems and perils

Read the following situations teenagers sometimes find themselves in; then respond to the questions.

A. You are at a party. Someone has been drinking and starts to leave to drive home. You don't really know the person, but you realize she shouldn't be driving.

B. A friend of yours has also been drinking at the party. He starts to leave the party to drive home. You tell your friend he shouldn't be driving, but he insists he's fine.

C. One Saturday night while your parents are out, a group of your friends show up at your house with booze. You know your parents wouldn't allow drinking by teenagers in their house.

D. It's common knowledge that one of the teenagers you sometimes hang around with has an alcohol and drug problem.

E. You are out with your friends; they encourage you to join them in smoking marijuana.

F. One of your friends urges you to try cocaine and heroin, telling you what a great rush they are and that you haven't really lived until you've experienced them.

G. The person you're romantically involved with keeps wanting the two of you to use a new "romance-enhancing" drug together so that you can feel even closer to each other.

H. Your friends urge you to drink with them in order to "have a good time."

I. Your ride home from a party has been drinking, but insists it's no problem.

For discussion

1. Why do some teenagers and adults feel they have to drink or use drugs to have a good time? What's your response to this attitude? Do you think it's more prevalent among girls or guys? Explain.

2. Which of the A to I situations have you been in? How did you or others respond? Explain.

3. What would your main problem be in deciding how best to respond to each situation? What should your main goal be in each instance? Why? ➡

4. What alternatives do you have in each situation? Which would be obviously morally unacceptable to you? Why? ▪

5. What information do you already have about the factors involved in each situation? Would you need to find out anything else before deciding how best to respond? Explain. ▪

6. Who could be harmed or helped by the available alternatives in each situation? Which principles would each alternative support or violate? 👥

7. How would you assess the short- and long-term risks involved in each situation? How would you assess their importance and probability? ◆

8. How would you answer the weigh-your-alternatives questions about each situation and its alternatives? ◆

9. What would your responsibilities and best alternative be in response to each situation? Explain.

10. What do you think is the best way to discourage teenagers from drinking? From drinking and driving? From using illegal drugs?

11. How does the French (lily pond) example apply to these situations?

One is too many and a thousand is never enough.
COMMON WISDOM AMONG RECOVERING ALCOHOLICS

The degrees of responsibility

Both morality and civil and criminal law recognize how people can be responsible and blameworthy to varying degrees in a situation. If two of you do the same thing, one of you can be held more morally and/or legally responsible for it than the other. Exactly how responsible one is for something depends on several things. To the extent that we choose our decisions and actions freely, they are voluntary and we are responsible for them. **We are fully responsible for whatever we freely and directly will.**

Whether you've acted reasonably and been morally responsible in a situation depends to some extent on your prior awareness of the possible consequences. The degree of moral and criminal responsibility also depends on your motive or intention in performing the action, something we will discuss in a later chapter.

> *". . . there is nothing outside a person that by going in can defile, but the things that come out are what defile."*
> **MARK 7:15**

How morally guilty one is in doing wrong (and often how legally guilty as well) depends on two factors:

- How serious the matter is
- Whether one acts with full knowledge and complete consent

Who is wronged may be an important factor in how serious the matter is. Abuse of a child or parent, for instance, is more serious than harming a perfect stranger because we have a special obligation toward our family and those who are helpless and innocent. For an act or intention to be gravely wrong, morally speaking, one must know fully that the action or intention is seriously wrong, and one must completely, deliberately, freely, and personally consent to it.

Less serious moral wrongs *(venial sins)* involve a matter that is less serious, or in which full knowledge or consent is lacking. Several circumstances may prevent someone from realizing how serious a matter is or consenting to it with full freedom:

Circumstances which diminish moral responsibility and guilt:

1. Being unintentionally ignorant
2. Being unaware
3. Being afraid
4. Doing something out of habit
5. Being too attached to something or feeling so strongly about it that one's reasoning and/or free will are impaired
6. Being pressured from without or within, or having a psychological disorder that affects one's judgment or ability to act

Let's suppose, for example, that a child of five "just playing" and an adult committing a robbery each deliberately point a loaded gun at another person and pull the trigger. The extent of moral and legal responsibility for the deaths that occur will differ. A child at that age normally wouldn't be expected to understand the consequences, whereas the adult would. The moral and criminal law would charge the robber, but not the child, with murder.

If the same adult, while on a hunting trip. fired the gun as a "joke," not realizing it was loaded, he'd still be held responsible for the death. But he wouldn't be morally or legally responsible for murder, as he would be if he had acted with malicious intent to kill. **Thus guilt is judged on the basis of the act, the motive, and the circumstances.**

Circumstances may increase or decrease the moral rightness or wrongness of an action or one's responsibility for it. Morality and the law, in fact, are in accord regarding the main categories of responsibility and guilt—accidents, negligence, and deliberate intent, as we will discuss in the next sections. But circumstances alone can't make a morally wrong action right.

When the man violated a county's "No U-Turn" sign and told the judge he had really made two legal left turns instead—the first exiting one county and the second entering another county, the letter of the law required that the judge let him off the hook. (The law was later clarified to exclude that legal loophole.) One can't, however, weasel out of moral responsibility in the same way.

Morally speaking, what's wrong is wrong and what's right is right. Fancy rationalizing doesn't change that. In fact, **pretending to not know or deliberately ignoring the fact that something is wrongful makes a wrong action even more wrong.**

> **TWO WRONG TURNS DON'T MAKE A RIGHT!**

> ## Clarify
>
> 1. Why can two people who do the same act not be equally responsible for it?
> 2. On what does one's degree of moral or criminal responsibility for an act depend?
> 3. What determines how wrong a person is when doing something wrong?
> 4. What is required for something to be gravely wrong in terms of morality? To be less seriously wrong?
> 5. Which circumstances can diminish moral responsibility and guilt? Why?
> 6. Why does pretended or deliberate ignorance that something is wrong make it even more wrong?

For discussion

1. Describe a situation where two or more of you did the same thing, but were punished differently because you weren't considered equally responsible. Do you understand now why the degrees of responsibility differed for the same action? Did you see that then? Explain.

2. List and explain five situations that illustrate why who is wronged makes a difference in how serious a wrongful act is.

3. List five common gravely serious wrongs, explaining why each is so wrong. List five common less serious wrongs, explaining why they are less wrong.

4. Give two examples each of how the six circumstances listed in your text can diminish a teenager's moral responsibility and guilt for a wrongful action.

5. Why can't circumstances alone make a morally wrong action right?

6. What does this saying mean: "Two wrongs don't make a right"? Give two examples from your experience or other teenagers' experiences that illustrate why this is true.

Accidents

Have you ever claimed when you injured somebody that it was "only an accident"—that you "didn't mean to"?

A true accident will meet either one of these criteria:

- *You weren't **capable** of knowing that the injury might result from your action. (When you asked Doug to pose for a picture in a certain spot, how could you possibly know the falling meteor would hit him?)*
- *You weren't **reasonably expected** to know what might happen. (You wouldn't reasonably be expected to know that Tame, your gentle-breed dog who's never been vicious, would bite the mail carrier who's been on friendly terms with Tame for ten years.)*

Both criminal law and the moral law generally agree that, if you've done your reasonable best in a situation, you're not and won't be held liable for injurious mistakes. **You're not morally (and usually not legally) responsible or guilty for harmful consequences you didn't intend, couldn't avoid, and couldn't reasonably foresee.**

Negligence

In addition to being responsible for our directly voluntary acts, we're also responsible for those which are negligent or indirectly voluntary. People often claim something was only an "accident" when actually it was due to their negligence. If we **could and should have known what might happen** as a result of our action or decision not to act, then we bear the responsibility for having been negligent.

If someone causes a traffic "accident" because she doesn't notice the perfectly visible stop sign, she is morally responsible and will probably be held legally liable as well. In fact, it may be an act of negligence (manslaughter) rather than a true accident, because she **could and should** have seen the sign and stopped. Had she done so, the collision would have been avoided.

People are negligent when they should know better than to do something, but they do it anyway. The law generally holds a person responsible for the harm caused and determines the punishment or damages owed according to the degree or extent of negligence.

Moral and legal responsibility for negligence fall into these same categories:

- *Gross negligence (reckless disregard) occurs where someone exercises no amount of care and has no concern for the consequences of his or her action. The person, in other words, just doesn't seem to "give a damn" (for example, going twice the speed limit in a school zone while children are present).*
- *Careless negligence exists when someone doesn't exercise a reasonable amount of care (for example, taking a sharp curve at the posted speed limit even though the road is slippery and safety requires slowing down).*

According to both the law and morality, we're responsible for our negligent actions—and, to the extent that we failed to respond as we reasonably should have, we're wrong or guilty.

Deliberate intention

> **The greatest moral and legal responsibility occurs when someone deliberately intends the harmful consequences—either directly or indirectly:**
>
> • *Deliberate direct intent is present when one plans and calculates for the harm to happen.*

First the woman tried killing her husband with arsenic, then with a tarantula's venomous poison, then by shooting air bubbles into his veins. When all these methods failed, she finally clubbed him to death! Assuming she was rational at the time, she couldn't get much more deliberate than that!

In trying and sentencing people for murder, the judge instructs jurors according to the law to determine whether the defendant's actions were premeditated and involved malice aforethought: Was there a deliberate choice to do the gravely serious wrong and was it done maliciously—with evil intent? This criterion describes the very worst moral wrongs.

> • *Deliberate indirect intent occurs where one knows the harm that can result, but doesn't intend the harm, yet does the action anyway.*

Such a person is still responsible for the harm, even though it wasn't wanted or intended, because the person knew it might result and could have prevented it. (The boy who killed his girlfriend when she told him she was breaking up with him knew he was pulling the trigger and shooting her, but at the same time "didn't really mean to kill her.")

Spontaneous heat-of-passion acts done out of extreme jealousy or anger aren't as deliberately malicious as premeditated ones. Thus, the extent of moral responsibility (ability to respond) is lessened, as is the criminal punishment.

We're expected to respond in a reasonable manner. According to the law and morality, we owe the minimum standard of good behavior to one another; this is a starting point for human moral conduct. When we're able to act responsibly but choose not to, we're blameworthy and guilty—and must expect to be held accountable.

That view presents morality in a rather negative manner, however. The moral thing to do will often go beyond what the law dictates—as you've already discussed, the law itself sometimes isn't moral! It's interesting, though, how much our laws are intended to correspond to moral responsibility. The law even uses criteria that help us understand the degrees of moral guilt and wrong.

Finally, even though we can determine that what a person **does** is gravely wrong, God alone can judge the person's heart. Even though people are accountable to society for their actions, **we must not pass judgment on anyone as a person.** We should pray for and entrust all sinners—ourselves included—to God's justice and loving mercy. Because of the **grace** of God, which enables us to share in God's life, we are all worth infinitely more than the worst wrongs we do.

Clarify

1. What are the criteria for determining whether something is
   • a true accident
   • due to negligence
   • partially, indirectly deliberate
   • fully and directly deliberate
2. What types of negligence are there?
3. Into which category would spontaneous, heat-of-passion acts fall? Why?
4. What minimum standard does the law hold us to regarding the behavior we owe one another? How does morality—especially Christian morality—often go beyond this?
5. What is the difference between judging others' actions and judging others as persons? Why must we not pass judgment on anyone as a person?

grace
the unmerited gift God gives us of God's own life (sanctifying grace); God's help to us in fulfilling our ultimate vocation as God's adopted children (actual grace)

Moral wrongs activity—Part 2

In the third column of your Moral wrongs list, write the category of extent of responsibility that you think most applies for each item:

• **accident**

• **reckless or careless negligence**

• **deliberate intent.**

Be able to explain your reasons.

For discussion

1. *From your experience or that of other teenagers, give two examples each of actions that are*

   • *a true accident*
   • *partially, indirectly deliberate*
   • *due to negligence*
   • *fully and directly deliberate*

2. *A man cut the front legs of a prize horse the night before a race to keep it from winning. Judge the responsibility of the man if the horse died from the injury. Would it make any difference if the man meant to disable rather than to kill the horse? Explain.*

3. *How do you think teenagers most commonly violate their response abilities in (1) accidental, (2) careless, (3) reckless, (4) intentional but not fully deliberate, and (5) fully deliberate ways in these areas:*

   • *friendship*
   • *family relationships*
   • *sex*
   • *school-related obligations*
   • *romantic love*

Death at the prom

Read this reality-based account based on news reports and respond to the questions.

Shortly after her high school prom began, 18-year-old Tanya went into the restroom with a friend. When her friend went back to the prom, Tanya stayed behind and, inside one of the stalls, gave birth to a full-term, six-pound, six-ounce baby boy. By the time her friend came back, about a half-hour later, to check on her, Tanya had given birth, cleaned up, wrapped the baby in a trashcan liner bag, and dumped him in the restroom trashcan. Thus she temporarily concealed the birth.

Tanya returned to the dance. Other students say she appeared to have a fun time during the evening, laughing and dancing as if nothing out of the ordinary had happened.

Later, several prom-goers reported seeing blood on the floor of one of the stalls. A maintenance worker opened the stall and saw that blood was spattered all over inside. When told by other students that Tanya had been seen in the restroom before that, teachers questioned her, but she denied knowing anything about it.

The worker subsequently discovered the dead infant in the restroom trashcan. Chaperones and emergency personnel tried to revive the baby, but he was pronounced dead two hours later at a local hospital. When the teachers again asked Tanya about it, she finally admitted she had given birth. Tanya was then taken to the hospital to have the placenta removed. She was then released into her parents' custody.

Officials had to decide whether to charge Tanya with killing her baby. Medical examiners determined that the baby had been born alive. They then had to determine whether he could have lived independently of his mother and whether he died of natural causes, of drowning in the toilet water, of neglect after being abandoned in the trashcan, or due to the efforts made to revive him. Evidently no one, not even Tanya's prom date—who acknowledged he probably was the father—knew she had been pregnant. In her loose-fitting prom dress, it was hard to tell.

With a tight stomach and baggy clothing, some girls are able to conceal their pregnancy from friends and family members.

Students later described Tanya as a nice, sweet girl. No one could believe what she had done. Some of the students said they supported Tanya as a person, but not her actions. Others wore arm bands to school in memory of the dead infant. Many students said they couldn't believe anybody could just discard their baby like that—especially after recent publicity surrounding two other teenagers who faced murder charges and a possible death sentence for discarding their newborn baby.

Medical experts have said it's possible, though unusual, for a young woman to give birth so quickly. They said that if the mother's denial that she's pregnant and her fear, emotional upset, confusion, and lack of ability to face reality are extreme enough, she may so disassociate from her body that she doesn't experience pain while giving birth or realize that the baby has died.

For discussion

1. What is the main problem in considering how responsible Tanya was for her baby's death? What should the main goal be in determining this? Explain. ➡

2. In what other ways might Tanya have dealt with her pregnancy? Based on what you know about the situation, why do you think she didn't choose another alternative? ▪

3. What people and principles were involved here? Who was harmed? How were principles violated? Supported? How might people and principles both have been supported better? 👫

4. What risks and benefits do you think pregnant Tanya should have considered about the alternatives available? How should she have answered the weigh-your-alternatives and probability questions about her situation? Explain. ◆

5. What issues do you think teenagers most commonly deny? About which issues do they often refuse to face facts? Explain.

6. Do you think Tanya's actions may have been influenced by society's tendency to rationalize excuses for such behavior? Might she have been influenced by the widespread practice of abortion that many claim makes human life "so disposable that birth seems reduced to the level of a bowel movement"? Explain.

7. Might any of the circumstances involved here have diminished Tanya's responsibility or guilt? Explain.

8. If Tanya was responsible for the death of her baby, explain for what charges she should be arrested:
   • fully responsible morally and legally
   • grossly negligent
   • carelessly negligent
   • only slightly responsible or not at all responsible

9. What punishment, if any, would you impose on Tanya for each of the following degrees of responsibility? Explain your reasoning.
   • fully responsible morally and legally
   • grossly negligent
   • carelessly negligent
   • only slightly responsible or not at all responsible

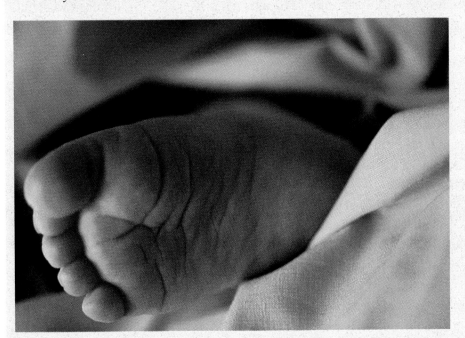

Accepting responsibility

Take action

Being responsible next involves making the correct decision and pursuing the right course of action. After you've weighed the risks and benefits of your available alternatives and figured out which decision is best, you must act on your best judgment. This might mean trusting in and following someone else's judgment in the situation, or deliberately disregarding what others advise. Ultimately, you're going to have to trust your own judgment because **you're responsible for your decisions.**

Seriously think the matter over. Figure out what will accomplish the most good and do the least harm. Then make **your** decision. Just make sure it's your decision and not somebody or everybody else's!

Assume responsibility

Another part of being responsible is accepting the consequences of your choices. If you choose to not go to class, you are also choosing the consequences of breaking school rules—detention, a call home from the office, and possibly a lower grade or being grounded. It's not fair to blame the principal, your teacher, your mom, or the tooth fairy for the natural, normal consequences of **your** choices!

People do try to blame others for the results of their actions. Yet a major part of being a morally responsible person involves taking responsibility for our decisions and actions—and accepting their consequences. Instead of trying to wiggle out of it, we need to own up to what we've done wrong. **If you made the decision, accept the consequences.** Rather than blaming and whining, be prepared to deal with the results of your choice. When things go wrong, just learn from your mistakes and you'll make wiser choices in the future. Also remember this:

> *. . . it is better to suffer for doing good . . . than to suffer for doing evil.*
>
> *1 Peter 3:17*

Accepting responsibility also involves being honest with and not fooling ourselves. People often try to convince **themselves**, as well as others, that their wrongful behavior really wasn't so bad. Hoping to win sympathy without admitting guilt, they give an empty apology, saying in effect, "I didn't do anything wrong, but I won't do it again." Or they try to explain away their wrongs with rationalizations.

When a young man tried to excuse the fact that he sold drugs by saying he was upset over his grandmother's death, the judge didn't buy it. The young man's actions were obviously deliberate, and he should have accepted responsibility for them. When a teenager did over $20,000 worth of damage to his family's home after being cut from the basketball team, he blamed the coach. But, the truth is, only he was responsible.

When a young woman gets pregnant and blames it on her boyfriend or the young man blames it on her, both are refusing to accept responsibility for their lives and decisions. So are politicians who use the "deflect and target" strategy that little children try with their parents—deflecting blame from themselves by targeting it toward others: "So and so did the same thing—or worse!" Well, the other party might be guilty, too—maybe even more so, but that doesn't excuse one's own poor choices and behavior!

There is . . . only a single categorical imperative, and it is this: Act only on that principle which you could wish to become a universal law.
IMMANUEL KANT

Don't spit at me and tell me it's raining.

Assuming the risk is agreeing to accept the consequences. Don't complain about the consequences if you intentionally put yourself in harm's way. It's not fair to blame the innocent mistake of somebody else who was playing within the rules. The judge made that clear to a homeowner who blamed his broken window on a golfer: A golfer has no duty to hit the ball straight, and someone who buys a home on the golf course assumes that known risk. In fact, the judge admitted he doesn't always hit the ball straight either!

ROAD WASHED OUT! PROCEED AT YOUR OWN RISK!

Clarify

1. Morally speaking, what does taking action involve?
2. What does accepting responsibility for your actions involve?
3. What does rationalizing one's wrongs mean?
4. What does assuming the risk mean?

For discussion

1. *Do you find it easy to trust your own judgment, or do you usually need a friend's confirmation before you decide or act? Explain.*

2. *Why is choosing an action also choosing its consequences? Why don't many people want to admit that, not even to themselves?*

3. *Why do you think people often blame someone or something else for the consequences of their actions?*

4. *When you're questioned about something you did wrong, do you usually own up to it immediately, try to deflect the blame somewhere else, or feign innocence until you're proven guilty? Explain.*

5. *What does rationalizing one's behavior mean? What types of decisions do you think teenagers commonly try to rationalize?*

6. *What excuses do teenagers commonly give for*
   - *failing to do their homework*
   - *being late for class or for work*
   - *not getting a better grade in a class for which they've neglected to study*
   - *talking disruptively in class*
   - *not coming home on time*

7. *When one freely and knowingly assumed the risk of a certain action, why then is it wrong to blame other people for the consequences of that action?*

Reflection

1. In what ways do you usually assume responsibility for your actions and their consequences?
2. In what ways do you sometimes fail to do this, placing the blame elsewhere?

Journal entry

Complete this sentence: I will work to become a more responsible person by. . . .

Any risk brings with it a corresponding responsibility.

There are two kinds of injustice: the first is found in those who do an injury, the second in those who fail to protect another from injury when they can.
CICERO

corporate responsibility
responsibility of a group for the members of the group

Corporate responsibility

The panther, rather than the panthers, as a school or team mascot emphasizes the role and efforts of the whole group. An individual member might contribute grace and agility, speed, strength, or stamina, and so on. But every member must work together as a unit to achieve a common goal. Paul talked about something similar when he said:

For as in one body we have many members,
  and not all the members have the same function,
so we, who are many, are one body in Christ,
  and individually we are members one of another.
We have gifts that differ according to the grace given to us. . . .

Romans 12:4–6

According to the principle of **corporate responsibility**, as Paul sees it, each person in the group bears a responsibility for the welfare of the group as a whole. While personal sin is an individual act, it definitely has a social dimension. Criminal law isn't always clear regarding our responsibility for the actions of others, but our moral responsibility is clear: **If we can help stop people from harming themselves or others but fail to do so, we become accomplices in the harm done.**

Activity

Give examples of how people share moral responsibility for others' wrongs by cooperating in those wrongs in each of the ways mentioned here.

We share moral responsibility for others' wrongs when we somehow cooperate in them by
• *taking part in them freely and directly*
• *directing, supporting, or approving of them*
• *not revealing or trying to prevent or stop them when we have a duty to do so*
• *protecting those who commit the wrongs*[2]

"Come to me, all you that are weary and are carrying heavy burdens, and I will give you rest."
MATTHEW 11:28

People aren't responsible just for social wrongs they cause directly, but also for those they support or exploit. Responsibility for social evils belongs to us as individuals as well as to the group. **Social sins don't excuse personal wrongs!** In fact, social sins are the product of many personal sins that have piled up. If we can help limit or get rid of social wrongs, but don't because we're too lazy or indifferent to get involved, to that extent we're responsible for letting the social wrongs continue.

When we consider all the things that are wrong in our society and world, it's no wonder we feel overwhelmed. But saying "it's impossible to change the world" is a flimsy excuse for not doing what we can to bring about positive change. It's true we can't change others—we can change only ourselves. But we can and do influence others, and our society and world.[3]

Some individuals are quite irresponsible—often breaking promises, commitments, and obligations. Others tend to carry the weight of the world on their shoulders, feeling they're responsible for **everything.** If you're one of these overly conscientious people, it's especially important to realize that *corporate responsibility,* being one body in Christ, includes others doing their part, too.

Business managers often find it difficult to delegate responsibility; they tend to do everything themselves. At times in life you will feel—and perhaps be—over-loaded with responsibilities. Instead of collapsing under the weight, learn how and when to rely on others. When you must juggle many responsibilities, establish your moral priorities and do one thing at a time. Put your burdens and worries in God's hands. While you do the legwork, let God carry the load.

For discussion

1. *How does your school mascot reflect the concept of corporate responsibility—or does it?*

2. *In what ways do you wish your school's student body would have a better sense of corporate responsibility? Explain, giving examples.*

3. *Give two examples of how teenagers typically become accomplices in one another's wrongdoing.*

4. *Why is it an injustice to fail to protect another from injury when we can?*

5. *What segments or people in our society do you think exploit social wrongs? Try to rationalize them? Try to excuse personal wrongs by blaming social wrongs? Explain and give examples.*

6. *Do you ever feel as if the world's problems are so great that you can't possibly influence any change for the better? What inspires you to feel you can make a positive difference?*

Clarify

1. What is meant in a moral sense by corporate responsibility?

2. Do social sins excuse personal wrongs?

3. When do we become moral accomplices in the harm caused by others?

4. When do we share moral responsibility for others' wrongs? For society's wrongs?

5. What moral responsibility do we have for influencing others and society?

A team responsibility?

Read the following fact-based account, then answer the questions.

A medical association has proposed that immediately after the competition all athletes on winning teams, especially in championship games, be required to submit urine samples for drug testing. The samples from individual team members would be pooled, and a single sample from the combined specimens tested for drugs.

That way, no athlete would be singled out. But one athlete's use of prohibited drugs would cause positive team test results. If the team's results were positive, its win would automatically be forfeited to its opponents. All individual records and statistics from the game, however, would stand.

For discussion

1. *What should the goal and purpose be in responding to the problem of athletes' use of illegal drugs?* ➡

2. *What alternatives are there for addressing this problem? How are people and principles involved?* 👫

3. *How would you answer the weigh-your-alternatives and probability questions regarding the alternatives here?* ◆

4. *Do you think pooling a team's sample specimens would be a fair way to handle drug testing? The best alternative? Would it reflect or distort corporate responsibility as explained in Scripture? Explain.* ◆

5. *Who is harmed by the illegal drug trade?*

6. *Experts say the illegal drug trade is supported mainly not by addicts, but by those who use illegal drugs only occasionally for social or other reasons. What share in moral responsibility does the casual or once-only drug user have for the tragic deaths related to illegal drugs? Explain.*

Fatal fun—the water slide incident

Read the following reality-based account, and respond to the questions as if you were a juror in this case.

As the soon-to-be graduates' high school class trip was ending, there was time for only one more ride on the huge water slide. In an effort to outdo other schools and previous classes, over thirty of the students climbed the ladder and piled on the platform to go down the slide together.

Trying to set a new record for the number of people going down the slide at once, they ignored posted signs and the lifeguard's warning that only one person at a time could go down the slide. As the group piled on, many holding hands to form a chain, the slide cracked and gave way.

Thirty-three students fell several stories to the ground. Thirty-two students were injured—some critically, many others were traumatized, and a seventeen-year-old girl was killed. Her parents filed a lawsuit accusing the water park of negligence in their daughter's death. The water park's manager says there was no way the lifeguard could have prevented the large group of students from pushing past him to get on the slide.

Evidently students in graduating classes had been going down the slide in groups for years without incident. Water park officials point out that over 100 million people have gone down water slides in the past few years, but no water park slide in the country has ever before structurally failed like this.

For discussion

1. What is the main problem here in determining who's at fault for this tragedy? What should your goal be as a juror in this case? ➡

2. What alternatives did the students who piled on the slide have? What alternative did they choose? Why do you think they ignored the signs and the lifeguard's warnings? ◼

3. What are your alternatives as a juror? Who might have been somewhat responsible for the tragic incident? (Note: The city owns the property and collects a small percentage of the water park's income.) ◼

4. What information do you have about the case? Which facts are most important in assessing responsibility for the tragedy? Which additional information would you like to have? ◼

5. What people and principles were involved here? Which were violated? Explain. 👬

6. What risks should the students have considered before trying to go down the slide together? How great did these risks seem, objectively speaking? To the students? ◆

7. How do you think the students should have answered beforehand the weigh-your-alternatives and probability questions? ◆

8. Were the students responsible for ignoring the warnings? Did they thereby assume responsibility for the consequences? Explain. ◆

9. A fourteen-year-old boy was recently found to be fully responsible for murder; he was sentenced to life in prison. Should the water sliders, who were much older than this boy, be held responsible for their own behavior? Explain.

10. Which of the parties involved do you think bear responsibility—and to what extent—for the water slide tragedy? Whom do you consider most responsible, and why?

11. What verdict would you render in this case? Why? How does your decision here compare with how you responded to the situation in the "Assessing your alternatives" activity found earlier in this chapter?

Responsibility and the media

The TV talk show featured a twelve-year-old girl who had had sex with twenty-five guys. At first the audience hooted and hollered. Then they turned on the young girl and humiliated her—after she and the other young girls on the show were pressured to reveal the specifics of their promiscuous behavior.

The audience jeered at another teenager for having had sex with over fifteen boys. She cried and said her mother's boyfriend had sexually abused her—whereupon the show's moderator prodded to know how far he had gotten in abusing her. Dressed and made up to look seductive, these young "guests" were sexually exploited to satisfy the curiosity of the viewing audience, many of whom are children and very young teenagers themselves.

Preoccupied with sex and violence, some TV talk shows routinely feature topics like "I got twenty girls pregnant" or "I slept with over two hundred men in one day." They urge viewers to call in "if your teenager wants to have sex with everybody you know," or about other tantalizing and highly personal topics. The more bizarre, sensational, and confrontational, the better.

The free-for-all atmosphere arouses audience excitement and participation. Talk-show hosts themselves have admitted publicly: "There's a lot of money" (from the shows' sponsors) in hate. "We will take whatever is hot and juicy and exploit it for ratings." "All they care about is ratings, no matter who gets hurt." Because it's what sells, many talk shows try to out-sensationalize the others in order to draw audiences, boost ratings, and attract lucrative sponsors.

So guests spill their guts and confess their most personal sins to a nation-wide audience—all for a free trip to a big city and a few nights in a fancy hotel. People who are willing to bare their personal lives in this way on national TV are often emotionally unstable. After publicly exploiting the troubled guest for the hour, some hosts may offer the person a few free counseling sessions in a token gesture to appease critics—or maybe their own consciences.

Only when they return home do the guests perhaps realize how they were made fools of, exploited, and humiliated. Yet it's estimated that over 50,000 people have appeared on talk shows in the last several years. Psychologically vulnerable and/or morally weak viewers (and a great many are) may transfer to their lives what they see and hear on talk shows, thereby messing up their relationships and ruining lives. Because of the heavy critical backlash, some talk shows have changed to a more positive format. But with the growing number of channels competing for audiences, it's likely that some talk shows will continue to exploit people.

Pontius' Puddle

For discussion

1. *Which shows do you consider irresponsible or trashy? Why? Why do you think people watch them?*

2. *The sensationalistic, exploitive TV talk shows have been called "sick, loathsome freak shows" and watching them compared with spending an hour in a dirty, smelly restroom. How would you describe these shows? Why?*

3. *Who do you think is responsible for the obnoxious behavior on such shows? Explain.*

4. *Martin Luther King Jr. said that "that which uplifts human personality is just, and that which degrades human personality is unjust."*

   • *Why is the proper use of talk shows a matter of justice? How does it involve corporate responsibility?*

   • *Which TV shows do you think uplift human personality? Degrade it? Explain.*

5. *What responsibility for keeping exploitive and sensationalistic shows on the air do the shows' sponsors have? Does the viewing audience have? Do the rest of us have?*

6. *Without violating the principles essential for a free society, what do you think is the best way to stop the media from demeaning and exploiting people? Be specific.*

Is there a relationship between our society's real values and those portrayed on TV?

The talk show murder

Lawyers now claim "the media provoked me to do it" in defense of certain crimes. In one instance, a national talk show's deceptive, exploitive tactics did lead to murder. The question for the jury: Who was responsible?

Read the following reality-based account, and then respond to the questions as if you were a juror in the case. When you've finished, your instructor will tell you the outcome of the case on which this one is based.

Jonathan's mother testifies that her son was "really getting his life together" when he was invited to appear on a national TV talk show to meet a "secret admirer." She supported his appearing on the show, telling him it might be his chance to meet the "girl of his dreams." The show's real topic for the day, however, turned out to be "Same-Sex Secret Crushes." Jonathan's secret admirer was Scott, another young man, who described on the show his crush on and fantasies about Jonathan.

Three days after the show was taped, Jonathan shot and killed Scott at Scott's home. Now he is being tried for first-degree murder—a crime requiring deliberate, malicious intent to kill. Jonathan's lawyers and his parents contend Jonathan was deliberately misled and embarrassed by the talk-show staff. They claim his emotional and mental stress after being ambushed by the show's surprising revelation—combined with his depression, alcoholism, and other physical and mental problems—pushed Jonathan over the edge.

As a result, they maintain Jonathan couldn't form the intent and premeditation necessary for first-degree murder. If anything, they say, the talk-show staff who humiliated him is responsible for the murder—a humiliation underlined by an anonymous note left at Jonathan's apartment after the show was taped.

Donna, a friend of Scott's and Jonathan's, testifies that she called the show to suggest that the two young men appear after seeing its ad for guests with same-sex crushes. She admits she lied by telling Jonathan that neither she nor Scott was going to appear on the show. On the taped segment, which never aired due to the murder, you see the audience howling at the surprising revelation. Jonathan laughs embarrassingly, but doesn't appear angry.

The talk show's producer testifies that she told Jonathan beforehand his secret admirer could be either male or female. She says she didn't see a difference between telling Jonathan the show's topic was "secret admirers" or "same-sex crushes." She says Jonathan chose to appear as a guest, and she denies having lied to him.

The talk show's host testifies that she doesn't know whether Jonathan had been lied to by the show's staff. She denies the show was an example of "ambush television," and says it was a "light-hearted show" about surprises. She admits that the staff had Jonathan sign a form beforehand which didn't mention the show's real topic: same-sex crushes.

For discussion

1. What is your problem and goal as a juror in this case? ➡

2. What are the important facts of the case, and what are your alternatives? ▬

3. What people, principles, and rights were and are involved in the situation? Which were violated? Explain. 👫

4. Did the show seem to have weighed the risks and benefits of having Jonathan appear as a guest? How should its staff have answered beforehand the weigh-your-alternatives and probability questions? ◆

5. As a juror, how would you weigh your alternatives and assess their probability? ◆

6. Based on what you know about this case, what is your verdict? Why?

7. To what extent, if at all, do you think the following individuals or groups also share moral responsibility for what happened? Why?

   • Jonathan's mother for supporting her son's decision to appear on the show
   • the show's host
   • the show's producer
   • Donna
   • Scott
   • the show's corporate sponsors
   • the show's studio audience
   • the show's viewers
   • whoever wrote Jonathan the anonymous note after the show was taped

8. Do you think any of the above should be held in any way legally responsible for Scott's death? Explain.

Chapter 9 summary
Being Morally Responsible

1. Responsible morality

- Responsible morality means responding to people and situations compassionately and intelligently.

- Responsible morality depends on awareness of people, needs, and circumstances; on assessing and accepting consequences; and on deciding and acting for the right reasons.

- Responsible morality involves identifying and weighing the foreseeable risks and benefits.

- Responsible morality means trying your best to make the best decision.

2. The extent of responsibility

- There are degrees of wrongdoing and responsibility for it.

- Fully intentional, deliberate, grave wrongdoing can turn us entirely away from God, while lesser wrongs somewhat damage and offend our love for God and others.

- Making things right requires repentance, conversion, and accepting God's mercy and forgiveness.

- Wrongful habits lead to greater wrong, while habitually doing right leads to sounder moral judgments.

- The good and wrong we do influences others' moral attitudes and behavior.

- Moral guilt depends on the act's seriousness and on one's degree of knowledge and consent.

- Certain circumstances may diminish moral responsibility and guilt, but they don't change the act's moral nature.

- One's extent of responsibility increases with greater intent—from accidents to negligence to deliberate intent.

- We must not pass judgment on anyone as a person, but must pray for and entrust all sinners to God.

3. Accepting responsibility

- Being responsible involves deciding and acting rightly and accepting the consequences of our choices.

- It also involves being honest with ourselves and others, rather than rationalizing, excusing ourselves, or blaming others.

- By the principle of corporate responsibility, each person in the group bears a responsibility for the group's welfare.

- We share in others' wrongdoing when we actively cooperate in it or could help stop it but don't.

- We must do what we can to fulfill our moral responsibilities, while also entrusting the burden to God.

Key concepts

degrees of wrongdoing

deliberate indirect intent

accidents

Christian moral standard

circumstances

consequences, short-term and long-term

corporate responsibility

degrees of responsibility

deliberate direct intent

extent of responsibility

grave wrongdoing (mortal sin)

less serious wrongdoing (venial sin)

media responsibility

negligence, carelessness, gross negligence

personal sin

rationalizing

reasonable-person standard

responsible morality

risks and benefits

social sin

spiritual consequences

. . . let us love, not in word or speech,
but in truth and action.
And by this we will know that we are from the truth
and will reassure our hearts before him whenever
our hearts condemn us;
for God is greater than our hearts,
and he knows everything.

1 John 3:18–20

Chapter 10

Developing Character

Overview questions

1. Why is moral character important? How can you deepen your moral character and be a force for good?

2. What powers (virtues) has God given us to help us meet life's moral dilemmas and challenges?

3. How important is motive in moral decision making? Which motives should we have?

4. How important is forgiveness in our lives?

5. Why do Catholics celebrate the Sacrament of Reconciliation?

6. What is the role of guilt, and sorrow (repentance), in our lives? What is the role of compassion?

Character

character

moral strength; a person's moral views, qualities, and behavior patterns

Discuss

1. What character traits do you admire most? Why?
2. Which character traits do you think people in general most need to improve?

Character is what you are when nobody's looking.

". . . consider whether the light in you is not darkness."

LUKE 11:35

When you apply for a job (or for college), you are asked for references. These are usually written statements from people who can vouch for your qualifications and your **character**. If your moral character seems sterling but your skills need work, you might be offered the job—and given additional training. But if your moral character seems to be a problem, your application might be rejected, even though your skills are excellent.

The reason is simple: Employers want to hire people they can trust. Nobody wants to hire someone who might steal, treat customers or other employees shabbily, or consistently fail to do a quality job or a fair day's work. Thus your moral character may be as important to your future career as are your job qualifications.

When reference letters don't mention character traits, prospective employers may wonder why. Why aren't the applicant's good character traits mentioned? Some businesses even give job applicants written tests designed to measure moral character!

Lawyers who violate professional ethics can be disbarred. Doctors who violate professional ethics can lose their medical license. One's moral character counts—not just for one's religious and personal life, but for one's business career as well. Recognizing this, many colleges offer or even require courses in business ethics.

The principle of honesty is a key element of character. It's very hard to have any kind of business or personal relationship with someone you don't trust. This chapter will discuss how strengthening other virtues is also important for your life.

How much do you think character counts?

During a recent U.S. presidential election, voters exiting the polls were asked which they considered more important in a president—the candidate's character or the candidate's understanding of the issues.

1. *Have you been asked for character references when applying for a job or for college? In a character reference, what would you want the person to say about you? Why?*

2. *If you were an employer, what positive traits would you look for in the employees you hired? Which character traits would keep you from hiring someone? Explain.*

3. *Which character traits do you think are essential in a student-government leader? In a candidate for president of the country? Explain.*

4. *If you had to choose, which would you probably vote for as president—a highly experienced political leader who seems to lack integrity or a trustworthy candidate who is not so experienced? Explain.*

Virtue

. . . be temperate, serious, prudent, and sound in faith, in love, and in endurance.

TITUS 2:2

As human beings, we all inherit certain character weaknesses. None of us matches up to our ideal of the person we'd like to be. But we can all become better by harnessing the power of **virtue.**

The root of the word *virtue* refers to being strong, good, and brave. Virtues are powers—the powers of moral goodness in action. With God's help, practicing virtue forges character in us, making it easier for us to do what is right and good. **Virtue, then, is a force for goodness.**

There are two kinds of virtues—**divine virtues** and **human virtues.**

And now faith, hope, and love abide, these three; and the greatest of these is love.

1 Corinthians 13:13

The most important virtues of all are **faith, hope,** and **love**—the three *theological virtues* that direct us toward God. With **faith** we believe in God and the truths God has revealed. It's your religious faith that will get you through life's worst difficulties. When you feel alone and discouraged, **hope** will open your heart to new possibilities. It will also comfort you with the ultimate promise of everlasting life and happiness. **Unselfish love** (charity) is the greatest virtue. It is the gift of God's self (grace) to you, for "God **is** love" (1 John 4:8). If you unselfishly do what's best for you and others, your relationships will be more fulfilling and your life more satisfying and complete.

Clarify

Name and describe the theological virtues and how a person can live each one.

Being a force for good

Your human virtues are your firm convictions, stable personality traits, and habits that help you do what is right. By helping you keep your moral balance, the human virtues assist your conscience in understanding and choosing what is right.

When people respect someone's character, they're usually admiring that person's virtues. How do you acquire admirable virtues? Just as physical skills improve and become easier and more enjoyable with practice, so do virtues.

That is why the *Catechism of the Catholic Church* calls human virtues the "fruit and seed of morally good acts" (#1804). We develop these moral virtues as we repeatedly do what is right. These virtues then make it easier and more satisfying for us to do what is right in the future. Most important, they enable all of our human powers to be in touch with our loving God, whose grace purifies and elevates these virtues. Thus, "practice makes perfect" concerning virtue, just as it does in learning how to drive or to play basketball!

The measure of your real character is what you would do if you knew no one would ever find out.
THOMAS MACAULAY, ADAPTED.

virtue
moral goodness, power, or effectiveness; moral righteousness, often expressed in action

divine virtues
the theological virtues: faith, hope, and love

human virtues
firm convictions, stable personality traits, and habits that help one do what is right

Activity
Write a poem or song about what faith, hope, and/or unselfish love mean to you.

Key human powers

Among the qualities people most admire in others are the **four main (or cardinal) human virtues: prudence, justice, temperance, and fortitude.** These moral virtues relate directly to doing good and rejecting that which is wrong. But what do these virtues mean in practice?

Being prudent

> **The simple believe everything,**
>   **but the clever consider their steps.**
> **The wise are cautious and turn away from evil,**
>   **but the fool throws off restraint and is careless.**
>   PROVERBS 14:15–16

. . . I want you to be wise in what is good. . . .
ROMANS 16:19

prudence
good judgment

When words are many, transgression is not lacking, but the prudent are restrained in speech. . . . Fools show their anger at once, but the prudent ignore an insult.
PROVERBS 10:19 AND 12:16

Prudence guides our reasoning to understand what's truly good in a situation and what is the right way to achieve it. Prudence helps us make sound judgments by considering the circumstances, the reasons for and against a choice, and the good that's at stake. Being prudent doesn't mean being timid, fearful, or deceitful. Prudence helps us avoid being gullible, careless, and manipulated. It helps us overcome doubts and apply moral principles correctly.

To be prudent—Approach moral problems with the appropriate care, caution, and consideration. Don't jump to conclusions or make careless, thoughtless decisions. Don't believe everything you hear—especially if it's gossip, a rumor, or a deal that sounds too good to be true! Don't base decisions mainly on feelings. Verify information with reliable sources before acting on it. Weigh all the important factors and put each factor in its proper perspective.

Be honest and tactful. Remember that speaking the truth kindly is far more effective—and Christian—than just spouting a careless opinion. Keep confidences, rather than gossiping about others' personal and private concerns. In potentially volatile situations, avoid a spontaneous reaction. Reason things through to the best response before you speak or act.

To make a prudent moral decision:

• Ask God's help to make the best decision.
• Think things over and seek wise advice. For Catholics, this should include consulting, understanding, and applying Jesus' message and pertinent Church teachings.
• Based on the available evidence, form a morally correct judgment.
• Act according to your conscience's best judgment.

Being just

Justice is the steady, determined desire to give God (virtue of religion) and other persons (virtue of justice) what is due them. Love is founded on justice, and loving unselfishly fulfills justice. You have already discussed some of the other aspects of justice.

To be a just person—Recognize and respect everyone's dignity and rights. Be fair with people. Look out for each person's welfare. Especially care for those who are helpless, innocent, or oppressed. At the same time, keep in mind the common good. Work toward unity and harmony rather than dissension. Above all, practice the Golden Rule—always treating others as you would want to be treated. If you think and act rightly and fairly, you will be a just person.

Being temperate

"As for what fell among the thorns, these are the ones who hear; but as they go on their way, they are choked by the cares and riches and pleasures of life, and their fruit does not mature."

LUKE 8:14

Temperance is the moral virtue that moderates and properly balances our desire for material things and physical pleasures. The desire for these things isn't bad, as some people seem to think. God gives us such desires to help us enjoy and care for ourselves, one another, and our world. However, when the desire for material things or physical pleasures becomes our main focus in life, such desires drag us away from loving God and others. The desire for the wrong things then demeans rather than uplifts the human spirit. Maybe that's why the ancient Greek writer Euripides called moderation "the noblest gift of Heaven."

Enjoying legitimate pleasures in an appropriate way is a wonderful part of life. However, we are sometimes tempted to let our desire for material things and pleasures steer or control us. There is a high price to pay for giving in to such temptation. Risking death and addictive misery just to see what a drug high is like, for example, obviously jeopardizes happiness. Such a poor choice indicates a moral vision that is clearly out of focus. Temperance helps us keep a proper focus and balance in life.

To keep your life in balance—Love wisely; let your head inform your heart. Don't overdo things so that you hurt yourself or others. Don't take senseless risks. Be suitably discreet; don't pry into things that are none of your business. Rather than choosing a rigid either-or approach to life and decision making, look for the in-between areas and the less-than-extreme responses. But don't rationalize or be a pushover.

Dress and act with reverence for your body and God's gift of sexuality. Respect the mystery of yourself and others as persons. Control your desires for food, drink, sex, and other pleasures, rather than letting those desires control you. Self-control is a characteristic of maturity that will help you enjoy life without regrets.

Fools think their own way is right, but the wise listen to advice.
PROVERBS 12:15

You shall not render an unjust judgment; you shall not . . . defer to the great: with justice you shall judge your neighbor.
LEVITICUS 19:15

temperance
moderation and balance regarding the desire for physical goods and pleasures

fortitude

moral courage, determination, and perseverance; the virtue of being firm of spirit or having a steady will in doing good despite difficulties and temptations

Activity

Write an essay about a time when you or someone you know made a decision that required moral courage.

Clarify

Name and describe the main (cardinal) human virtues.

For this reason I remind you to rekindle the gift of God that is within you . . . for God did not give us a spirit of cowardice, but rather a spirit of power and of love and of self-discipline.
2 TIMOTHY 1:6–7

Being determined and courageous

Fortitude is the virtue of moral strength that keeps us on the right track amid life's difficult decisions and circumstances. Fortitude, which ensures that we firmly and steadily seek what is good, helps us resist temptations and overcome obstacles. Fortitude is the courage to conquer fears and the persistence to keep doing one's best despite the odds.

To be a courageous person—Determine to do the right thing no matter what. Become a strong person who can handle pressure. Be strong enough to seek advice, help, and support when you need it. Make deliberate decisions, thus avoiding solely emotional reactions. Honor your legitimate commitments and promises. Make the hard choices and accept responsibility for them. Don't dodge responsibility for your mistakes or wrong choices. Instead, accept the consequences and learn from your experience so that you're better prepared and more determined to do the right thing.

Reflection

1. What character traits and virtues do you think others most admire in you?
2. Which character traits do you think you need to improve?
3. Which character traits would others probably say you need most to improve?

For discussion

1. *This section dealt with four key virtues. What does each virtue mean to you?*
2. *In your opinion, how are teenagers usually good at—and/or usually not good at*
   - *being prudent*
   - *being temperate*
   - *practicing justice*
   - *having determination and true courage (fortitude)*
3. *How could practicing each of these moral powers help teenagers cope better and succeed more often? Explain.*
4. *What virtues do you admire in people? In your mind, why are these virtues attractive and admirable?*
5. *What virtues seem to be lacking in individuals you find hard to like or get along with? Explain, but don't name names.*
6. *Have you ever been in trouble for not being prudent, fair, temperate, or courageous? Have you ever been complimented for displaying one or more of these virtues? Explain.*
7. *How have you been hurt when someone failed to practice one or more of these virtues?*
8. *In your experience, which virtue do you think teenagers should practice more? Why? Which virtue do you think they practice most? How?*

Meeting life's challenges

In addition to the virtues, God has given us other helps to support our moral life. **The seven *gifts* of the Holy Spirit,** which complete and perfect the other virtues, are *wisdom, understanding, counsel, fortitude, knowledge, piety,* and *reverence for God.* The **twelve *fruits* of the Spirit** are *charity, joy, peace, patience, kindness, goodness, generosity, gentleness, faithfulness, modesty, self-control,* and *chastity* (see Galatians 5:22–23). The more we practice virtue and do what's right, the more all these gifts from God become part of who we are.

Because you've grown in experience and wisdom, decisions you found challenging when you were younger probably seem rather trivial now. For the same reason, decisions you find tough now will seem much simpler when you look back on them years from now. Throughout your life, you will be challenged to exercise your moral powers. As you work to make your positive character traits into stronger habits, you'll find that it does become easier to live these positive traits.

To maintain your moral balance, follow your conscience—love what is good and avoid what is wrong. Frequent participation in the sacraments is also a key way Catholics grow in moral strength. Continue to pray for God's Spirit to enlighten and help you to become morally stronger.

Discuss
1. Which kinds of decisions and dilemmas that you found challenging when you were younger seem more manageable now? What accounts for this?
2. What do you think is a good way to keep your moral balance and grow in moral strength?

Handling hardships

It's easy to be strong when everything is going our way. The real challenge to character is how we get through—and help others through—the hard times. Jesus showed a very special love for and desire to help those whose lives were touched by suffering. Catholic teaching reminds us of the moral responsibilities we have toward those affected by suffering and illness:

- **God does not send us suffering!** God doesn't test or punish us. God doesn't try to make us squirm like guinea pigs to see how much we can tolerate. **Illness and pain are due to natural and/or humanly caused processes.** God helps us bear suffering, grow personally and spiritually through suffering, and ultimately triumph over suffering.

- It's important that we stand by those who suffer. We all need each other and will all experience suffering. We will all eventually face death.

- We must comfort and support those who are directly affected by serious illness— the one who is ill, the family, and the friends.

- With understanding, we should help persons with life-threatening illness work through their anger and alienation. Gently, respectfully, and sensitively, we can help them experience God's strength, comfort, and peace.

- We should become informed enough to overcome prejudices and unwarranted fears about illnesses. We should welcome those who cope with illness and help them remain as involved in society as they are able.

- We should support persons and institutions who responsibly and compassionately care for those who are sick and dying.

- We should support interfaith efforts to minister to the spiritual, psychological, and practical needs of persons who are sick and their families.[1]

Research
Select a physical condition about which some people have prejudices and unwarranted fears (for example, AIDS, cancer, Alzheimer's disease and other debilities of elderly persons, multiple sclerosis, epilepsy, diabetes, asthma, emotional or mental illness, mental retardation, physical disabilities or disfigurement, or other marked physical differences). Do research and write a paper on the harm common misunderstandings cause. Recommend ways of educating people to respond better.

Clarify
Tell why you would consider each of the seven gifts of the Holy Spirit and each of the twelve fruits of the Spirit to be a welcome characteristic in yourself.

Then . . . wisdom will come into your heart, and knowledge will be pleasant to your soul; prudence will watch over you; and understanding will guard you. . . . Therefore walk in the way of the good. . . .
PROVERBS 2:9–11, 20

Clarify
1. Explain in your words Catholics' moral responsibilities toward those who suffer from or are directly affected by serious illness.
2. What obligations do we have because of justice? Which obligations reach beyond justice to love?
3. It has been said that "our first duty toward those who suffer is to weep with them." What do you think this statement means?

For discussion

1. What common major illnesses or diseases do you fear catching from someone else? What do you know about how these diseases are transmitted? Explain.

2. What ignorant, unjust, and unchristian reactions do people sometimes have toward persons who are ill? Why do you think some "God-fearing Christians" occasionally react that way?

3. If someone you knew contracted AIDS, cancer, or another life-threatening or debilitating disease, what practical things could you do to stand by and help the person?

4. Have you ever had to cope with a serious illness or disability or care for someone with a serious illness or disability? What did you learn from the experience that deepened your character? If you have yet to have this experience, what do you hope to learn when the time comes?

Turning your life around

Do you feel you've gotten on the wrong track in life? Would you like to get rid of a negative habit, attitude, image, or character trait? How do you turn things around?

1. Seek the appropriate advice and help **soon.**

2. Try behavior modification techniques.

3. Address the underlying reasons for your attitudes and behavior. (This will be discussed in the next section.)

Teenagers often hide a serious problem (such as trouble at school, pregnancy, or alcohol or other drug addiction). They try to handle it themselves because they don't want to seem weak, upset their family, or be told what to do. Or they dump the problem on a trusted friend who hasn't the expertise or resources to help. Meanwhile the problem worsens, harming and upsetting everybody far more. A calm, serious talk with a parent or counselor about the problem can bring new hope. So when you have a major problem, don't hesitate! Seek the right kind of help you need from those you trust and love.

By studying Scripture and listening to the advice of behavioral experts, we learn an effective way to change behavior patterns: Deliberately and consistently do and think the opposite of the negative traits you want to change. For example, if others say you are arrogant or conceited, focus more on the good qualities of other people. If greed, envy, or jealousy often get the best of you, try being more generous and appreciating the good fortune of others. If your temper carries you away, find an acceptable way to let off steam; respond to conflicts with reasoned self-control.

Making such changes may seem difficult at first. Just remember that the more you do the right and virtuous thing, the easier it becomes to do what's right. Others will notice and admire the positive change in you. More importantly, doing what's right is its own reward.

In addition to practicing the key virtues, you can enhance your positive character traits in dozens of other ways. An excellent way to learn what having real character means is to observe people you admire: How have they practiced virtue? How have they truly lived what they believe? Study how and why Jesus' virtues made him the most admired person in history and the most powerful single force for good. Becoming a more Christ-like person is the best way to develop character and grow morally.

For discussion

1. *Have you ever felt like you needed to "turn your life around," or have you had a friend who felt like this? Explain.*

2. *Which serious problems do you think teenagers most try to hide or handle by themselves? Why?*

3. *Why do you think teenagers don't always seek proper help in dealing with these problems? What further problems can result from failing to seek help?*

4. *What do you think the role of a good friend should—and should not—be in helping someone deal with a serious personal problem? Explain.*

5. *What most helps you to change a negative behavior pattern in yourself? Have you ever tried to deliberately do the opposite of the negative behavior? Explain.*

6. *What is your advice for enhancing one's positive character traits? How do you try to enhance your own?*

> *. . . you must make every effort to support your faith with goodness, and goodness with knowledge, and knowledge with self-control, and self-control with endurance, and endurance with godliness, and godliness with mutual affection, and mutual affection with love.*
> **2 PETER 1:5–7**

Journal

What negative behavior pattern would you most like to change in yourself? Write down five practical ways you could begin changing this behavior pattern for the better.

The party

Read the following, and respond to the questions.

Jean is trying to decide whether to attend a party. She knows liquor probably will be served and some college students who are legally old enough to drink will be there.

Knowing liquor will be served, Don is going to attend the party.

While Julio is at the party, some of the beer-drinkers become obnoxious and rowdy.

Someone Christie has been wanting to date offers her a ride

home from the party. She knows he's been drinking beer most of the evening.

Tran sees that one of his friends, who's obviously drunk too much beer, is about to leave the party and drive home.

At the party, Linda sees that someone she doesn't know is somewhat drunk and about to leave and drive home.

For discussion

1. *What moral decision confronts each of the above individuals?*

2. *What virtue is each person being called upon to practice? Explain how.*

3. *What do you think most teenagers would probably do in each of these situations? Why?*

4. *What harm might result if each person fails to practice the virtue needed in the situation?*

5. *What do you think is the best way each of these individuals can exercise the virtue called for? How would you handle each situation? Why?*

CLIFF AHEAD

THE END DOESN'T JUSTIFY THE MEANS

Examining your motives

. . . the Lord weighs the heart.

PROVERBS 21:2

We shouldn't base moral decisions on feelings alone. But we do make most choices in the context of our relationships with living, breathing, feeling humans. Religious and moral responses don't involve just our behavior. They always also involve our attitudes, thoughts, feelings, and relationships. So making moral decisions must include evaluating our motive: What are our **reasons** for deciding and acting?

Being united with God and others is morality's whole point and focus. How right we are with God and others is determined by what is in our mind and heart. **So, morally speaking, our motive or intention is at least as important as the results of our decision. To deliberately intend serious harm is immoral.** It's still wrong even if, by accident, the intended harm never happens.

Civil and criminal laws also recognize the great importance of motive and intent. People are convicted of attempted murder, intending and trying to kill someone, even though they didn't succeed. One who deliberately and maliciously kills another person is charged with murder. But if the intent is less evil—say, voluntary but not malicious or premeditated—the charges and penalty are adjusted downward.

Intent and motivation make a big difference in how someone is charged with a crime. They are also at the heart of the moral life. It's not just what we do that counts, but also **why** we do it.

A good end doesn't justify using wrong means to obtain it, and a good intention can't make bad behavior good or right. Good intent may, however, diminish a person's moral guilt for the act. But doing something for wrongful reasons is always morally wrong, even if good results. From a moral standpoint, it's the wrong our minds and hearts intend that harms us most, because that's what truly distances us from God and others.

Clarify

1. What role should—and shouldn't—feelings play in moral decision making? Why?

2. How important is motive (intention) in moral decision making? Why? How does our legal system recognize this importance?

3. Can a good end justify using wrong means to obtain it? Explain.

4. What role does intent play in one's moral guilt for an action?

Hidden motives

It's frustrating (sometimes infuriating) to ask individuals why they did wrong, only to get "I don't know" in response! Acting or reacting in a hurtful way without thinking is a major problem in society and in personal relationships. Often the individuals themselves don't realize the underlying reasons for their behavior. Those reasons may be rooted in disturbing past experiences which the person has never addressed properly. Sometimes the most troublesome motives are concealed even from oneself.

The majority of convicted spouse and child batterers, for instance, were themselves abused in their youth. That doesn't excuse their abusing others! It does provide an explanation that can lead to effective treatment and prevent further abuse. Teenagers who've been abused swear they'll never abuse their own children. Yet statistics tell us that many of them will do just that. Many already engage in self-destructive or harmful behavior.

Overreacting, unreasonable defensiveness and destructive behavior can signal unresolved past issues that still generate strong internal responses. Facing these issues can help persons overcome negative character traits.

Have you ever come home from school frustrated and then gotten upset about doing a simple routine chore? Have you argued at home in the morning and then become incensed at the slightest correction in class? Have you done poorly on a test at school and then later been rude to a friend? Did you ever snap back when someone merely asked a reasonable question? If so, it's likely that your real reason for responding as you did was that an old problem still troubled you.

Most such problems are minor and quickly blow over. However, some people have a major chip on their shoulder that affects every aspect of their life and relationships. They treat others gruffly, unfairly, or violently because of an experience they're still bitter about even though they no longer consciously admit that it is a problem. St. James spells out the problems that festering attitudes and motives cause:

> . . . if you have bitter envy and selfish ambition in your hearts, do not be boastful and false to the truth.
> Such wisdom does not come down from above, but is earthly, unspiritual, devilish.
> For where there is envy and selfish ambition, there will also be disorder and wickedness of every kind.

> *James 3:14–16*

So if you feel at odds with life and loved ones and want to turn things around, examine the underlying reasons for your attitudes and behavior. See if an unresolved guilt, resentment, or other issue still negatively affects your attitudes, behavior, and relationships. Facing and resolving serious underlying issues can take courage and may require professional help. But resolving past issues can make an enormous positive difference in your life.

"For it is from within, from the human heart, that evil intentions come. . . ."
MARK 7:21

Reflection

1. What types of things usually prompt you to overreact or become defensive? Do you ever engage in destructive behavior?
2. Why do you think you act or react in these ways?
3. How might these actions or reactions on your part relate to troublesome past experiences?
4. Have you been told that you have a bad attitude or a chip on your shoulder?
5. Does your tendency to overreact or your defensiveness cause problems in your life or relationships right now?
6. Do you feel at odds with others or with life right now?
7. What troublesome past experiences still bother you? Do you think you might benefit from help in dealing with these?

For discussion

1. *When someone does something that hurts you, how important to you is the reason why the person did it? Explain.*
2. *What is your reaction to "I don't know" when you ask someone why he or she did something that hurt you? Explain.*
3. *How can hidden motives (including those concealed from oneself) be troublesome? Give examples.*
4. *What do overreacting, defensiveness, and destructive behavior signal about past issues? Why is it important to recognize these tendencies in yourself as well as in others?*
5. *Without mentioning names, do you know anyone who generally seems to have a bad attitude or a chip on their shoulder? Who routinely treats others gruffly, unfairly, or violently?*
6. *What do you think is the best way to respond to such persons' reactions?*
7. *Describe a time when a festering attitude temporarily affected your behavior or relationships? What helped you improve the attitude?*
8. *When do you think someone should seek professional help in resolving serious underlying issues? Where would you go to receive such help?*
9. *Have you ever felt like you wanted to turn your life around? How did you, or how would you try to do this? Explain.*

For discussion

1. *What is the difference between motive and emotional bias? Why is it important to not confuse these?*
2. *Describe one of your biases, the reasons for it, and how it affects your relationships and decisions.*
3. *What do you think is the best way you can keep your personal biases from negatively affecting your better judgment? Explain.*

Confronting bias

It's also important not to confuse motive with emotional bias. For example, we might lean toward a particular alternative out of affection **for** someone, or because we feel sorry for the person. But those might not be the best motives for making our decision in this situation. Or a motive might be based on emotional prejudice **against** someone.

Biased motives can keep us from being reasonable, fair, and objective. We should admit our biases and examine the reasons behind them. Understanding our real motives can shed light on a situation and reveal important neglected factors. Recognizing and rejecting biases can help you make more intelligent decisions.

So gain insight from your feelings, but don't let them become motives overruling your better judgment. The Letter of James describes the signs and results of having good motives:

Who is wise and understanding among you?
Show by your good life that your works are done with gentleness born of wisdom. . . .
But the wisdom from above is first pure, then peaceable, gentle, willing to yield, full of mercy and good fruits, without a trace of partiality or hypocrisy.

James 3:13 and 17

Having the right motives

Do not be conformed to this world,
but be transformed by the renewing of your minds,
so that you may discern what is the will of God—
what is good and acceptable and perfect.

ROMANS 12:2

Morality doesn't involve just doing the right thing. It also involves doing it for the right reason. Having the proper motive is perhaps most important in being a person of good moral character. What's in our hearts brings us close to or alienates us from God and others. Making decisions for the wrong reasons can easily result in unnecessary harmful consequences.

As long as we've tried our best to make the wisest choice, we're not morally guilty for our honest mistakes, even if those mistakes are stupid and hurtful. But doing the correct thing with an immoral motive (the right thing for the wrong reason) is morally wrong. So we must consider our **real**, perhaps underlying, motives before we act. And decisions should be based on solid reasoning rather than on emotional bias. Evaluating and having the proper motives is part of the fifth step in wise moral decision making.

> *We were made for action, and for right action—for thought, and for true thought.*
> **JOHN HENRY NEWMAN**

Step 5A: What should your motive be?

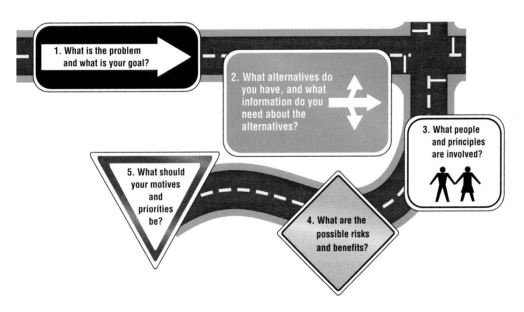

What are the right kinds of motives or reasons for our decisions and actions? To answer this, we need to understand the difference between external and internalized motives.

Let all that you do be done in love.
1 Corinthians 16:14

As a very young child, you based your decisions on **external motives** and self-interest. You obeyed the rules to please your parents or avoid punishment. Outside motivations introduced you to proper behavior and helped train you to choose what's right and good. In later childhood and as you entered your teens, peer pressure also became a powerfully motivating external influence. One hopes that going along with peers has mainly helped you do what's right. But occasionally it's probably led you down the wrong path straight into trouble!

Throughout life, outside motivations play a positive role in decision making. Rules, laws, and other people's good examples can remind, encourage, and guide us to do the right thing. Rebelling against rules, regulations, and authority simply for the sake of rebellion indicates a regression to childish self-interest. Often the only way to reach self-centered individuals is to appeal to their self-centered motives. For instance, the only curb to a young woman's recklessness on the road may be threatening to revoke her driver's license if she's caught speeding again.

Even now as a teenager, you can begin moving beyond making moral decisions on the basis of primarily external influences and motives. As you mature morally, the good principles and values you've been taught must become your own. To grow morally, you've got to learn how to base your decisions on **internalized motives** rather than on blind obedience, self-interest, or peer pressure. Otherwise your moral growth will remain stuck at a childish level.

As Catholic teaching points out, human dignity demands that we "act according to a knowing and free choice. Such a choice is personally motivated and prompted from within. It does not result from blind internal impulse nor from mere external pressure."[2]

Interiorizing your reasons for doing what's right and good changes you. Your faith and moral principles truly become yours. You do good not just because you're supposed to, but because of who you are. Christians' motives should be internally rooted in Jesus' teaching. We should put aside selfish interests to make loving decisions based on Christian principles.

Once you've identified what seems to be the best choice, and before making your final decision, **ask these questions about your motives:**

- **Why** do I favor this option over the others?
- Are my motives for leaning toward this choice selfish or unselfish?
- What might be my underlying reasons for making this decision?
- Are my reasons in line with my principles and my original goal of the good I want to accomplish?
- What motive would Jesus and others I admire have for making this decision?

Paul speaks of the motives that should underlie our decisions:

As God's chosen ones, holy and beloved, clothe yourselves with compassion, kindness, humility, meekness, and patience. . . .
Above all, clothe yourselves with love, which binds everything together in perfect harmony.
And let the peace of Christ rule in your hearts, to which indeed you were called in the one body.
And be thankful.

Colossians 3:12, 14–15

Remember that people with the highest moral motives seek to apply the Golden Rule. This means trying to treat everyone equally and fairly as persons loved by God; it means setting aside self-interests for the greater good of others. If you can do these things, then no matter what the outcome, you will know that you did the morally right thing and that you did it for the right reasons. Finally, as Jesus taught, our real motives reflect in the good that results from our customary choices and actions:

"But as for that in the good soil, these are the ones who, when they hear the word, hold it fast in an honest and good heart, and bear fruit with patient endurance."

Luke 8:15

"You will know them by their fruits . . . every good tree bears good fruit. . . ."

Matthew 7:16–17

> *Every act leaves the world with a deeper or fainter impress of God.*
> **ALFRED NORTH WHITEHEAD**

For discussion

1. Why is it important to consider your real, perhaps underlying, motives before you act? What results from making decisions for the wrong reasons? Give examples.

2. What are external motivations? What do they accomplish with children? How do they play a positive role in decision making throughout life?

3. Which external motivations do teenagers sometimes rebel against? Most often go along with? Give some examples of external motivations that effectively influence you.

4. What are internalized motives? Why should moral decisions be based primarily on these interiorized motives?

5. How does your religious faith influence your motives? How do you think it should influence them?

6. In general, what do you think are the best motives to have for making moral decisions? Why? What motives should Christians have?

7. How can you determine what your real motives are? What does Jesus say about this?

Murderous intent

The following dilemma is often presented to law students. Read it and then discuss the questions.

Someone jumps from a building intending to commit suicide. As he passes the fourth floor on his way down, someone shoots and kills him before he reaches the ground.

For discussion

1. Of what crime, if any, is the shooter legally guilty? Explain.

2. Of what wrong, if any, is the shooter morally guilty?

3. Suppose, instead of the above scenario, the man survives. With what crime, if any, would the shooter be charged? Of what moral wrong, if any, would the shooter be guilty? Explain.

4. If the shooter's bullet completely missed the falling man, is the shooter legally guilty of a crime? Guilty of a moral wrong? Explain.

5. How important is the shooter's intent, morally and legally? Why?

To lie or not to lie

The following describes one man's "mini-moral dilemma" in the sticky kind of situation we all face from time to time. As with most of our moral dilemmas, this one isn't a matter of life and death. Yet, it can sometimes seems just as hard to arrive at the right solution. In addition, the measure of our character is largely determined by how we respond to everyday moral situations.

Read the account and then discuss the questions. Your instructor will then tell you what the man decided and how he later felt about his decision.

My wife and I stopped for breakfast at a small coffee shop....

It became immediately apparent that the place was run by just one young man. He did everything. He took the orders, cooked the food, poured the coffee, brought the plates to the table, and worked the cash register. Despite the fact that there were only a few people in the place, he was running around at a furious pace, a harried look on his face and his hair hanging down over his eyes.

We ordered sausage and eggs over easy. When our order arrived, the sausage was greasy, the eggs were overcooked, and the hash browns and toast were cold. It was a terrible breakfast.

When I came to the cash register to pay the bill, however, the overworked young man looked at me hopefully and asked "Was everything okay?"—and I realized I was in the middle of a mini-moral dilemma.

If I said "Yes," nothing would ever change at that little coffee shop. The breakfasts would remain lousy. And I would be lying.

On the other hand, if I said "No," and told him the breakfast was awful, it was still probable that nothing would change, since the young man was already doing everything a human could possibly do. I'd just be laying a guilt trip on top of his other problems. But I'd be telling the truth.

I looked at him for a moment. Then. . . [3]

For discussion

1. *What is the man's moral dilemma? Which goal (consider long-range goals) do you think he should have in making his decision? Explain.* ➡

2. *List three reasonable alternatives the man should consider in resolving his dilemma.* ◼

3. *What information does the man already have? Does he need any more information before making his decision? What guidance from Scripture or Catholic teaching might help him make a wise decision? Explain.* ◼

4. *Who will likely be affected by the man's decision? How? Which principles are involved in the man's choice? Whose needs and which principle(s) do you think merit priority here? Why?* 👥

5. *What kind of moral attitude does the man demonstrate in the things he considers? If he had an attitude that was contrary to Christian principles, how might he respond? Explain.* 👥

6. *What immediate risks or consequences are there in the man's alternatives? What future risks might be involved? What are the short-term and long-term benefits of each alternative—for both men?* ◆

7. *Are any of the alternatives intrinsically immoral? Is there a pertinent law that must or ought to be considered?* ▽

8. *How many people might be affected positively and negatively by each alternative solution? How seriously would they be affected?* ▽

9. *Which person(s) and principles do you think should have priority? Why?* ▽

10. *Which risks and benefits are greatest?* ▽

11. *What should the man's motive be for whatever he decides? Explain.* ▽

12. *What do you think you would probably decide to do if you were faced with this man's dilemma? If you were running the coffee shop, what would you want the man to do? Explain.*

13. *Which alternative do you think the man should choose in this situation? Why?*

Forgiving others

Why is it important to forgive?

Is there anyone who's never done something deliberately wrong? Has anyone never hurt someone by a careless mistake? We've all made a selfish decision we later regretted. We've all done wrong at some time. We might not always realize how careless or selfish we were until we have to deal with the consequences. Then we're really sorry. We feel terrible. We promise we'll never do it again. We ask for—sometimes plead for—forgiveness.

Although we may try to do the right thing, we're not perfect. Occasionally we fail—not always innocently or accidentally, but sometimes deliberately. There are times we really should have known better, and there are times when we knew better but did something hurtful anyway. Maybe we should have kept quiet—or spoken up—but didn't. Our main human fault is choosing wrong knowingly and hurting deliberately—sinning. One of our most positive human qualities is being sorry, seeking forgiveness, and forgiving.

Without forgiveness, we probably wouldn't have a friend left! Forgiving is one of the most beautiful and important gifts we can receive or give one another. It is the glue that keeps re-sticking us humans together. We all know how it feels to carry a burden of guilt for something we've done wrong. But what a relief when forgiveness lifts it from our shoulders and we're reassured that everything's all right! Those who don't receive forgiveness or extend it to others are often depressed and seriously troubled as a result.

As Catholic teaching points out, we must help make the world more loving and human. One way we do this is by promoting forgiveness and mercy in our society and relationships. Without forgiveness, people can't be reunited with God or with one another.

The souls of the wicked desire evil; their neighbors find no mercy in their eyes.
PROVERBS 21:10

Forgiveness demonstrates the presence in the world of the love which is more powerful than sin.
JOHN PAUL II

Jesus' message of God's forgiveness

When they came to the place that is called The Skull, they crucified Jesus there with the criminals, one on his right and one on his left. Then Jesus said, "Father, forgive them; for they do not know what they are doing."

Luke 23:33–34

When we study Jesus' life and death, we can see how forgiving God, is. Jesus' told us that sincere repentance with the desire to make amends and change is all God asks of us. Unfortunately, many people today believe something much different about God, as did many of Jesus' contemporaries. They view God as a bloodthirsty tyrant who tests us sinners and then, when we fail, seeks revenge.

In ancient times, some peoples sacrificed guilty or even innocent persons to appease God's "wrath." Jesus, however, tells us that our relationship with God should not be based on fear. He said God is our Father who is always loving and forgiving. God does not send wars, famines, diseases, disasters, death, or personal misfortunes to punish us for sin! Moral wrongdoing produces its own terrible consequences.

As Jesus' forgiving words from the cross exemplified, no matter how bad the evil we may do, God still loves and wants to forgive us. God's grace precedes, prepares, and calls for our free response, and so helps us perfect our human freedom. Jesus deliberately associated with sinners in order to help them: *"Those who are well have no need of a physician, but those who are sick; I have come to call not the righteous but sinners."* (Mark 2:17)

"Just so, I tell you, there will be more joy in heaven over one sinner who repents than over ninety-nine righteous persons who need no repentance."

Luke 15:7

According to Jesus, there's only one sin that can't be forgiven: *"Therefore I tell you, people will be forgiven for every sin. . . , but blasphemy against the Spirit will not be forgiven."* (Matthew 12:31)

People often misunderstand what Jesus meant by that. We merit God's forgiveness only because God has loved us first. God's mercy is without limit, but it is never forced on us. We must be sorry for our wrongs and freely accept God's forgiveness. The only "unforgivable" sin, then, is to forever refuse to accept God's loving, merciful forgiveness.

Thus, "unforgivable" doesn't refer to an unwillingness on God's part to forgive. Rather, it acknowledges the reality of human freedom—a person might forever choose to not accept God's forgiveness. (It does not say anyone has ever done so.) No matter what our sin or how hard our heart, God is always willing to forgive us.

For discussion

1. *Describe how you felt when you really needed forgiveness. How did you feel when forgiven? How would you have felt if the person hadn't forgiven you?*

2. *For what types of things have you apologized this last week? Give two examples.*

3. *How is forgiveness the glue that keeps re-sticking us humans together?*

4. *What did Jesus' life and death emphasize about God's forgiveness—and ours? How was this view different from how people had viewed forgiveness before?*

5. *What is meant by the "unforgivable" sin mentioned in Scripture?*

The runaway

Read the following story and respond to the questions.

A wealthy man had two teenage sons. The elder son never caused problems. But the younger son was stubborn and rebellious, and his middle name was trouble. Twice he'd been at fault in reckless driving accidents. A few years ago, he'd been picked up for shoplifting. Recently, he'd been put on juvenile probation for minor acts of vandalism. After constantly cutting classes and almost failing out anyway, he was finally kicked out of school shortly before graduation. His girlfriend had become pregnant (by him, she insisted, although he denied it), and he had become increasingly dependent on drugs.

Refusing to obey any of his father's orders, this younger son did entirely as he pleased. He kept talking about leaving home, but didn't have the money to make it on his own. Finally, he said to his father, "Dad, you know the money you've always said you've set aside for us in case something happens to you—well, I want my share right now."

The boy's father decided he could do nothing else to help this son. Not wanting him to steal or sell drugs to support himself (as his son threatened he'd otherwise do), the father gave him the money. A few days later, the son packed his things, bought a plane ticket, and headed off. Within a few years, all his money had been thrown away on drinking, gambling, and women he picked up here and there.

The son then tried to find a job, but an economic recession made jobs scarce. Finally, he couldn't afford the rent for his one-room dump and had to beg for food. Desperate, the young man at last got a job feeding pigs on a farm. He thought about how he would give anything just to eat the corn he was feeding the pigs. He was still living on practically nothing and hungry half the time.

Seeing no future, the young man began to realize how good he'd had it back home. He started thinking, "The servants who work for my dad have more than they want to eat, and here I am practically starving! I'll go back home and tell him, 'Dad, I know now how wrong I've been and how very much I must have hurt you. I know I don't deserve to even be called your son after the way I treated you. But, please, just hire me to work for you as one of your servants.'" So he got passage home on a freighter by helping the ship's cook and wrote his dad saying when he was coming.

The boy's father went to meet the ship. When he spotted his pale, weary son, he felt sorry for him. He ran up to his son, put his arms around him and kissed him. On the way home, the son kept saying, "Dad, I know I've been foolish and hurt you so much. I can understand it if you completely disown me." But when they got home, his father told the servants, "Buy my son a new wardrobe. Call all his old friends and plan the biggest party we've ever had! We're going to celebrate—my boy was as good as dead, and now he's come back. We'd lost him, and now he's found!" And so they celebrated the son's return.

As the older brother was driving up to the house on returning from a business trip, he heard music and laughter. The servant at the door told him the good news, "Your father's having a party for your brother who's come home." Furious, the older brother refused to go in. His father tried to reason with him, begging him to greet his brother. But he said, "Look, Dad, I've worked hard for you all this time and never disobeyed you—and you've never had a party for **me**. My brother, that so-called son of yours, comes home after carousing and throwing away your money and you throw a party! **I don't get it—it just isn't fair!**"

His father replied, "Look, I know you've been a good son, and what I have will one day be yours. But it's only right to celebrate your brother's return. We worried he might be dead, and now we know he's alive. We'd lost him, and now we've found him again—and he's found us!"

For discussion

1. What do you think of the younger son's attitude toward his father? Explain.

2. If you were the father, how would you feel if your son treated you that way? Why?

3. Do you think the father should have taken his son back and forgiven him after the son said that he was sorry? Why?

4. Should the father have completely forgiven and taken back his son? Should he have imposed further consequences? Explain.

5. What do you think about the older son's reaction? Why?

6. If you were the eldest and something similar happened with a younger sibling, how would you feel if your parents reacted as this father did? Why?

7. How do you think the younger son felt when his father completely forgave him? How would you have felt? Explain.

8. Have you ever wronged a loved one and been completely forgiven? How did you feel? Why?

9. This story was based, of course, on Jesus' parable. But similar scenarios occur every day when runaway youth return home to loving parents. Is it realistic to expect parents today to forgive their kids as this father forgave his son? Explain and give examples.

Why can it be so hard to forgive?

Beloved, never avenge yourselves. . . . No, "if your enemies are hungry, feed them; if they are thirsty, give them something to drink. . . ." Do not be overcome by evil, but overcome evil with good.

ROMANS 12:19–21

It can be difficult to forgive someone who's hurt or wronged us. Perhaps we had good reason for trusting someone who failed us. Or maybe it was poor judgment to trust the person. No matter—whenever someone has betrayed us, it's hard to trust that the person won't do so again. Notice, though, that it's easier for **us** to promise we'll never repeat a wrong than it is to accept that promise from somebody **else!**

Have you ever failed to get home when you said you would or gone where you promised you wouldn't? Although you may have disobeyed orders or broken your word the last time, you might feel it is unreasonable not to trust you next time. You promise you won't do the same thing again. You want to be believed and trusted. Why, you wonder, is it so hard for someone else to trust you with another chance?

When you're on the other side and someone has wronged **you,** isn't it a different story? Don't you find it hard to trust someone who's lied to you, betrayed your secret, or otherwise turned on you? In addition to not trusting, you may find it hard to even forgive. It's easy to understand why **we** should be forgiven and trusted again. Why is it so hard to extend to others the same forgiveness and trust?

Forgiving can be hard when it threatens our pride—when it's not so much that someone has **wronged** us, but has wronged **us!** After all, they did do wrong. They're guilty. It serves them right; they deserve what's coming. The temptation is to want to get back at others, to give them a taste of their own medicine. So we sit in judgment instead of recalling the times we were in their shoes and needed forgiveness.

It may be difficult to get beyond our anger and hurt pride, but we must try. It helps, as Jesus taught us, to remember that we, too, have faults: "'Let anyone among you who is without sin be the first to throw a stone. . . . ,'" he said, challenging those threatening to stone an adulterous woman to death. "When they heard it, they went away, one by one. . ." (John 8:7, 9).

Lest we think we're beyond being wrong or making mistakes, Jesus cautioned us to remember those times we've needed forgiveness:

"Why do you see the speck in your neighbor's eye, but do not notice the log in your own eye? Or how can you say to your neighbor, 'Friend, let me take out the speck in your eye,' when you yourself do not see the log in your own eye? You hypocrite, first take the log out of your own eye, and then you will see clearly to take the speck out of your neighbor's eye."

Luke 6:41–42

We easily understand what tempts us to do wrong or make mistakes. Why is it so hard to understand why others could be tempted to do the same? Instead of self-righteously snubbing and scorning others who've done wrong, we should recall our own wrongdoing—including the wrongdoing no one else knows about.

So who, then, are you to judge your neighbor?
JAMES 4:12

Saints and Sinners

When some fellow yields to temptation,
And breaks a conventional law,
We look for no good in his makeup,
But, God, how we look for a flaw.
No one will ask, "How was he tempted,"
Nor allow for the battles he's fought;
His name becomes food for the jackals;
For us who have never been caught.
"He has sinned!" we shout from the housetops.
We forget the good he has done.
We center on ONE lost battle
And forget the ones he has won.
"Come. Gaze on the sinner," we thunder.
"And by his example be taught
That his footsteps lead to destruction,"
Cry we who have never been caught.
I'm a sinner, O Lord, and I know it.
I'm weak, I blunder, I fall.
I'm willing to trust in [your] mercy;
To keep the commandments [you've] taught.
But deliver me, Lord, from the judgment
Of saints who have never been caught.[4]

When we do wrong, we hope for forgiveness. Another chance. An opportunity to prove ourselves and improve, to change and make things different. Why then, when others are at fault, should we think first of punishment—of how they should hurt for what they did? Scripture tells us we shouldn't respond with vengeance, but with understanding:

Do not repay evil for evil or abuse for abuse; but, on the contrary, repay with a blessing. It is for this that you were called—that you might inherit a blessing.

1 Peter 3:9

Jesus' teaching takes issue head-on with vengeance. So whenever you hear someone misquote the Bible as promoting "eye for an eye" revenge, remind them that Jesus strongly and clearly taught the opposite:

"But I say to you, Love your enemies and pray for those who persecute you. . . ."

Matthew 5:44

Though extremely difficult to do at times, forgiving is possible. Pray that God will help you have a forgiving heart, not a vengeful one.

Clarify

1. What in the difference between seeking "eye for an eye" revenge and seeking justice?
2. What did Jesus say about dishing out vengeance instead of extending our forgiveness?
3. How do anger and hurt pride affect one's ability to forgive someone? Should they?
4. What advice of Jesus can help when we find it hard to forgive someone?

Scripture activity

Read the full context of this Scripture passage in Matthew 5:38–48.

1. How does Jesus respond here to the "eye for an eye" mentality?
2. What examples of the "eye for an eye" mentality have you heard?
3. What kinds of persons do you think could benefit most from following these words today? Explain.

Project (choose one)

1. Rewrite Jesus' story of the runaway son from a first-person point of view—as if you were either the younger son, the elder son, or the parent.
2. Write an essay about a personal experience in which you had to seek someone's forgiveness or had difficulty forgiving someone.

In your story or essay, present your insights about what forgiving means and how hard it can be to seek forgiveness or to be forgiven.

For discussion

1. What wrongs against you do you find easiest to forgive? Hardest to forgive? Explain.
2. What wrong actions on your part have you found others most willing to forgive? Most reluctant to forgive? Explain why you think they were willing or reluctant to forgive you.
3. Why do people find it hard to forgive others? Give examples.
4. Why is being able to trust someone again sometimes even harder than forgiving the person?
5. What does someone who has betrayed your trust need to do to regain it? Why? Do you ever find it upsetting that you're forgiven, but not immediately trusted again? Explain.
6. Why should we try to help rather than get even with someone who wrongs us?
7. Why do you think it's easier to understand why we should be forgiven than to see why we should forgive someone else?
8. How do you overcome your reluctance to forgive someone—especially when you feel like being vengeful?

It is fitting for a great God to forgive great sinners. TALMUD

Trust and the ability to forgive are two essential elements in all human relationships.

The victim

Read the following account. Then respond to the questions.

Laura had been wanting to date Paul, a college student she had met a few months before at a party. She'd met him only once, but he'd asked her for her phone number. Finally, he called and asked her out. They went to a movie, and both seemed to have a good time—until the ride home.

Paul said he wanted to show Laura how beautiful the view is from a hill overlooking the city lights. They parked on the deserted knoll under some trees and admired the view—for about two minutes. Then suddenly Paul's hands were all over Laura. She protested—mildly at first, not wanting to upset Paul. When she saw that he had no intention of stopping his sexual advances, she firmly told him "No" and tried to push him away.

Laura tried to get out of the car, but Paul was considerably stronger than she was. He pinned her down, and she couldn't get away. Paul kept telling Laura that he knew she "wanted it" as much as he did. Within a few minutes of struggle, he had raped her. When Paul finally let go of her, Laura tried again to get out of the car. But Paul grabbed and held onto her arm so tightly that it hurt. Then he drove Laura home.

Before he dropped her off in front of her house, Paul told Laura, "If you tell anyone, nobody will believe you. It will just be your word against mine."

Laura's mother was sleeping, and Laura didn't want to wake and upset her. Shaken and frightened, Laura called her best friend, Jamie, for advice about what to do. Inwardly, Laura felt like it was her fault that she'd been raped because she'd gone out with someone she hadn't known well. She also felt stupid about falling for the line about seeing the view, and that made her feel even guiltier.

For discussion

1. What moral wrongs were committed by Paul?
2. Had Laura done anything morally wrong? Had she acted unwisely? Should she feel guilty and partly at fault for what happened to her? Explain.
3. What is the moral dilemma now facing Laura's friend Jamie? ➡
4. What do you think Jamie's main goal should be in resolving her dilemma? Why? ➡
5. What are the three best alternatives Jamie might recommend to Laura? Is further information needed? What guidance from Scripture or Catholic teaching might help her give Laura wise advice? Explain. ◼
6. Are any of the alternatives intrinsically immoral? Is there a pertinent law that Jamie must or should consider? ◼
7. Who will be affected by what Jamie decides to recommend? Which principles are involved in her choice? 👫

8. How many people might be affected positively and negatively by each alternative solution? How seriously would they be affected? ◆
9. What risks or consequences are involved in each alternative Jamie might recommend? ◆
10. Which risks and benefits are greatest? ◆
11. What should Jamie's motive be for whatever she decides? Explain. ▽
12. Whose needs and which principle(s) do you think should take priority here? Why?
13. Faced with Jamie's dilemma, what do you think you would advise Laura? If you were Laura, what do you think you would do? Explain.
14. Which alternative do you think Jamie should recommend to her friend Laura? Why?

Broken trust

Although told in the present tense, the following is a true account. Read it and respond to the questions. Your instructor will then tell you the actual decision and outcome.

Sal is a twelfth-grade teenager. Sal's mother is called out of town suddenly to help care for her seriously ill mother. She leaves Sal's sister, Maria, who is home for the summer after her first year at college, in charge.

Their mother says she is trusting them to behave and gives strict orders that Sal and Maria are to each have no more than two friends over at a time. There are to be no parties in the house while she is gone! Maria and Sal promise to obey. They are told to notify their mother if there are any problems—or violations of the main rules.

The second night, Sal decides to invite two of his buddies over to watch TV. Unfortunately, they show up with a whole bunch of other kids, who have brought beer. When the friends want to come in, Sal doesn't feel he can say no.

When Maria, who had been talking on the phone in her room upstairs, comes down and sees the group, she tells Sal they will have to go. Sal argues with her that everything will be all right. Maria insists that the friends leave or she will notify her mother. Sal assures Maria that he won't let the crowd get rowdy and won't let anything bad happen.

When Maria threatens again to call their mother, Sal begs her not to. He's already been grounded for a whole month recently for getting into trouble at school. He says he doesn't want to go through that again, but he still stubbornly refuses to tell his friends to leave.

Maria is upset and doesn't know what to do. She's scared that the party will get out of hand, since quite a few of the kids are drinking and already getting pretty loud. She is also afraid the neighbors will call the police. Maria wants to do the right thing, but doesn't know what to do.

For discussion

1. What is Maria's moral dilemma? What do you think her main goal should be in resolving it? Why? ➡

2. What are Maria's three best alternatives? Does she need more information? What guidance, if any, should she seek? Explain. ◼

3. Who will be affected by what Maria decides to do? Which principles are involved in her choice? 👫

4. What risks or consequences are involved in each of Maria's alternatives? Are any of them intrinsically immoral? Is there a pertinent law she must or should considered? ◆

5. How many people might be affected positively and negatively by each of Maria's alternatives? How seriously would they be affected? ◆

6. What should Maria's motive be—and not be—for whatever she decides? Explain. ▽

7. Whose needs and which principle(s) do you think merit priority? Why?

8. Which risks and benefits are greatest?

9. What do you think you would probably do if you were in Maria's situation? Why?

10. What do you think Maria should choose to do? Why?

Consequences and change

Our reluctance to trust someone who's wronged us is reasonable. This reluctance cautions us to be careful, to protect ourselves and others from further harm. Forgiving doesn't mean there aren't consequences. It doesn't mean asking for additional trouble or letting offenders off the hook so they continue to harm. People must become truly convinced they've done wrong and firmly resolved not to do it again. While we are obliged by love to forgive those who wrong us, we are also obliged by love to encourage and help them change for the better.

People sometimes take advantage of others' forgiving hearts. Public figures violate ethical standards and then expect to win back our support by their tearful apology or mention of turning to God and religion. Abusers cry and plead that they're sorry they've bruised and battered the one they claim to love. They promise never to do it again and are forgiven—only to continue their abusive pattern.

A heartfelt "I'm sorry" for the damage caused and a firm resolve to change should merit our forgiveness. But an apology and a promise to change don't excuse wrongful behavior or take away the consequences. Nor do they mean that the offender should automatically be reinstated in a position of trust.

It's prudent, for example, to distance oneself from an abusive relationship until the abuser gets the professional help needed. Society must separate violent criminals from our midst as long as they remain a threat. We must hold public figures accountable and require them to pay a price for their misconduct. Otherwise we encourage further abuse, violence, and irresponsibility.

If you were brutally mugged, you wouldn't want the mugger set free just because he cried in front of the judge. People must learn enough self-control and the discipline to think before they act so that they don't continue harming themselves and others. Imposing consequences is one way to help individuals realize how wrong they were. It may be the only way to motivate some people to not repeat their wrongs.

So forgiving someone doesn't necessarily mean forgetting about the offense as if it never happened. Forgiveness requires even more of us. It may mean standing up to the person, letting the offender know that the wrongful behavior won't be tolerated. It might mean removing people from circumstances that would tempt them to repeat the offense. It may require protecting oneself and others from again being victimized. It might mean benching a star athlete, impeaching an official, or refusing to buy the musician's recordings or see the actor's films.

True forgiveness always involves trying to help the person realize the seriousness of the wrongs and trying to help the person change for the better. The kind of help required depends on the wrongdoer and the nature of the wrong done. For minor wrongs, accepting someone's apology and then forgetting about the whole incident often suffices. Sometimes stricter measures are needed to help people truly get the message and change.

Clarify

1. What does true forgiveness involve?

2. What should be the purpose of imposing consequences?

Clarify

How can you try to help someone not repeat personal wrongs toward you in the future?

Clarify

1. What is mercy? What is the difference between mercy and forgiveness? Between justice and mercy?

2. Why is mercy indispensable in relationships? Why is mercy needed in addition to justice?

All consequences imposed should have a positive purpose. They should protect and rehabilitate rather than just punish. The goal should be to help reconcile individuals with one another and with the community.

Be at peace among yourselves. And we urge you, beloved, to admonish the idlers, encourage the faint hearted, help the weak, be patient with all of them. See that none of you repays evil for evil, but always seek to do good to one another and to all.

1 Thessalonians 5:13–15

For insights on how to help others not repeat wrongs, consider these things:

- **Why** did they do what they did? (What might you have done under similar circumstances?)

- What would **help** them not **want** to do this type of thing again?

God gives us all the help (grace) we need to reach our eternal destiny, for whatever God asks of us, God's help always makes it possible for us to achieve. In responding to someone who wrongs us, Jesus' words are our best guide: "Treat others as you would want to be treated" (see Luke 6:31). Help. Forgive.

Jesus said we'll be forgiven as we're able to forgive others. Forgiving mustn't be an empty formality. Jesus said it must be "from your heart" (see Matthew 18:35). In his parables of the prodigal son, the lost coin, and the lost sheep, Jesus exemplified what such forgiveness means. While justice deals with externals, love and mercy involve bringing people's hearts together. Even justice must be kept on the right track by a patient, kind, and merciful love that is gracious, tender, sensitive, and forgiving.

"Go and learn what this means, 'I desire mercy, not sacrifice.' For I have come to call not the righteous but sinners."

Matthew 9:13

For discussion

1. When seeking forgiveness, why is just saying "I'm sorry" not always enough? Give examples.

2. When do you think being reluctant to trust someone who's wronged us is prudent? When do you think it's not?

3. How do you think people take advantage of others' forgiving nature? Do you ever feel that others take advantage of your forgiving nature? Explain and give examples.

4. When do you think consequences should be imposed for behavior that harms someone? When do you think it's not necessary to impose consequences?

5. Describe a manner of forgiving someone that doesn't seem heartfelt or that feels demeaning. Describe a gracious way to sincerely forgive someone.

6. How is merciful love demonstrated between parents and children? Between friends? Between husbands and wives? Give examples.

A snap reaction?

Read the following account and respond to the questions.

During round three of the heavyweight boxing title fight between Mike Tyson and Evander Holyfield, a shocking incident occurred. Tyson, who appeared to be losing at that point, spit out his mouthpiece and bit off a chunk of Holyfield's right ear. Over six billion television viewers around the world were horrified and sickened.

The referee warned Tyson, but let the fight continue. Ignoring the warning, Tyson then bit off a chunk of Holyfield's left ear. Tyson was immediately disqualified and temporarily suspending from fighting in the state of Nevada. Even as the loser, Tyson was to have collected a $30 million purse for the fight. At the time of the fight, Tyson was an admitted wife beater and was still on parole after serving a prison term for rape.

Holyfield later said that he had forgiven Tyson, but felt there should be consequences. He also commented that doing the easy and quickest thing to get out of the fight by fouling shows that one has no courage.

At a news conference, Tyson said he was sorry and "saddened that the fight didn't go on further so that the boxing fans of the world might have seen for themselves who would come out on top." Tyson explained his outrageous conduct in remarks directed toward Holyfield: "When you butted me in the first round, accidentally or not, I snapped in reaction. . . ."

Tyson apologized to the world for "snapping in the ring" and said he'd never do it again. He said he didn't know exactly why he did what he did and reiterated that when he thought he might lose because of the cut above his eye from the head-butt, he "just snapped and reacted and did what many athletes have done."

Tyson remarked further: "You have seen it in basketball with fistfights on the floor, in baseball with riots on the field, and even spitting in the face of an official. For an athlete in the heat of battle to suddenly lose it, it's not new, but it's not right. . . . I was wrong. And I expect to pay the price like a man. . . . I only ask that it's not a penalty for life for this mistake. . . . I am willing to accept [the penalty] I have coming to me."

Tyson said he'd made mistakes thus far in his life because he had grown up on the streets without others' support and "had no other way." He said, "I will learn from this horrible mistake, too." He said that he was reaching out to God to help him, and to the medical profession to help tell him why he did what he did. Tyson said he would train his mind so that it wouldn't happen again. Finally, he asked that everyone forgive him "as you have forgiven other athletes of this profession in sports and so that I can be given a chance to redeem myself. . . ."

One news correspondent called Tyson's statement "a pure act of repentance" and also "obviously,

damage control." Another commented that the biting was "one instance in which he snapped" and that "we all go a little berserk occasionally—isn't that open to forgiveness?" Yet another said Tyson would "just fight elsewhere" if not allowed to fight [in Nevada], and that everybody should just "move on," rather than punishing him for life.

Other sport commentators called Tyson's actions repulsive, intentional, and malicious. They called him "an animal that belongs in a cage," someone who "should be in therapy" rather than the boxing ring. Since Tyson was already losing the fight, they suspected that he deliberately sought to be disqualified in order to steal Holyfield's claim to victory. These sport commentators didn't buy Tyson's excuse of "snapping" in retaliation for the head-butt. They also said fighters don't head-butt intentionally, because they would risk injuring themselves as much as their opponent.

The state athletic commission was to meet within the next two weeks to decide what further sanctions, if any, they should impose on Tyson. Formerly, a national poll had ranked Tyson among the top ten persons most admired by youth in the United States. Tyson's actions, if committed outside the boxing ring, Tyson's actions clearly would have violated his parole, and he would have been returned to prison.

For discussion

1. Which virtue(s) helped Tyson succeed thus far in his life? Which virtue(s) could have prevented his conduct in this case? Explain.

2. Presume that you are to recommend which sanctions, if any, should be imposed on Tyson. What would your moral dilemma be? What should be your main goal? ➡

3. What information do you have about this case? What other information or guidance should you seek? Explain. ▪

4. What is your opinion of Tyson's "apology"? Of commentators' reactions to his statement and what he did? Explain.

5. How would you respond to the same type of explanation and apology from

   • a police officer who brutalized a subdued suspect who had resisted arrest earlier

   • a frazzled, harassed school-bus driver who intentionally caused an accident that maimed several students after they had dumped a soda on her head

   • your opponent in a sports competition who intentionally maimed you after you had accidentally caused the opponent a minor but temporarily disabling leg injury

6. What would be your three best alternatives for sanctions in the Tyson case? ▪

7. Whom would your decision affect? Which principles are involved in your choice? 👫

8. What risks or consequences does each alternative involve? Are any of these alternatives intrinsically immoral? Which laws must or should you consider? ◆

9. How many people might each alternative benefit or harm (and how much)? ◆

10. Whose needs and which principle(s) merit priority? Why? ▽

11. Which risks and benefits are greatest for each alternative? ▽

12. What should your motive for your decision be—and not be? Explain. ▽

13. What further sanctions, if any, would you recommend be imposed on Tyson? Should he be criminally charged or returned to prison for the incident?

14. How should the public respond to Tyson's ear-biting incident in view of his appeal for forgiveness, prior record, and responsibility to youth and society?

15. For what type of violent behavior during competition would you hold athletes civilly or criminally liable? Ban them permanently from the sport? Explain and give examples.

16. Many suggest banning the sport of boxing because the only objective is to injure the opponent? Do you agree? Explain.

17. Should persons who, because of their jobs, are trained and disciplined to cope with violence be held more accountable than are other people for "snap reactions" like Tyson's? Explain.

18. What influences encourage excessive violence in athletics? How might fans discourage this? Explain, giving examples.

Forgiving yourself

Have you ever kept reliving something you did wrong or a mistake you made, although others had already forgiven you? People know they should forgive others, but they often forget to leave room in their hearts to forgive themselves.

Good and responsible parents may blame themselves for failing, when it's actually the son's or daughter's choice to get into trouble. Parents have an even harder time forgiving themselves when they know they've made mistakes or failed. Teenagers who lose a cherished relationship also find it hard to forgive themselves, when it's too late to undo their thoughtlessness.

If you've been through this, did you find it hard to accept that you'd done wrong or hadn't done better? You probably know how bitter it is to swallow the consequences and how difficult it can be to forgive yourself.

Along with forgiving others, we've got to forgive ourselves. We must stop reliving old mistakes. We must humbly and patiently learn to accept that we're not perfect. While being remorseful and trying to improve, we need to learn to forgive and heal ourselves.

Jesus told us how willingly God forgives us. No matter how bad the wrong or how terrible its consequences, God's love still enfolds you and invites you to come back home. Just as God forgives you, so you must be willing to forgive yourself.

For discussion

1. *Why do you think it's often so hard to forgive yourself for hurtful mistakes or deliberate wrongs?*
2. *Have you ever kept "kicking yourself" inside for some wrong you did? Explain.*
3. *Why is forgiving yourself so important? How is it different from just letting yourself off the hook?*
4. *How should God's forgiveness help us to forgive ourselves?*
5. *What kinds of things do you find hardest to forgive in yourself? Why?*

Guilt, sorrow, compassion

At a physicians' meeting, the doctors discussed how they feel when a patient dies. Most said that, despite all their efforts to save the patient's life, they feel extremely guilty, as if they're responsible. They said coping with their feelings about this is so hard that they often shield themselves from feeling anything. (Carrying this heavy "guilt" burden is thought to be a reason why doctors have a high suicide rate.) After much discussion, the doctors began to realize that they'd never distinguished between feeling guilty and feeling sorrow, regret, or compassion.

Centuries ago, Paul distinguished the benefits of being genuinely sorry from the negative results of excessive sorrow.

This punishment by the majority is enough for such a person; so now instead you should forgive and console him, so that he may not be overwhelmed by excessive sorrow. So I urge you to reaffirm your love for him. . . .

Now I rejoice, not because you were grieved, but because your grief led to repentance. . . , so that you were not harmed in any way by us. For godly grief produces a repentance that leads to salvation and brings no regret, but worldly grief produces death.

2 Corinthians 2:6–8; 7:9–10

There's a difference between feeling **guilty** for something and feeling sorry that it happened or compassionate toward those who've been hurt. Like the doctors, many people carry heavy guilt burdens because they haven't made this distinction. Sometimes people **feel** guilty even though they've done their best and are **not** guilty. Others don't feel guilty when they **should**, such as when they have deliberately hurt someone.

"I will never leave you or forsake you."
Hebrews 13:5b

Scripture activity/insights

When Peter asked Jesus how often one should forgive, Jesus replied with an interesting story. Read Matthew 18:23–35.

1. What was Jesus saying here about God's forgiveness and compassion?

2. What was he saying about the compassion we are to show toward others?

Project (choose one)

1. Collect several examples of advertisements designed to make people feel guilty about something. Write a paper analyzing the type of guilt each ad represents and the human weakness to which the ad appeals. State your reactions and conclusions.

2. Collect several examples of things parents and children (including teenagers) or friends say or do that make each other feel guilty without due cause. Write a paper explaining how and why each remark or behavior unfairly "lays a guilt trip" on the other person.

Being guilty refers to knowingly doing wrong and thereby hurting someone or risking harm. **Feeling** guilty about having intentionally done wrong is a good thing. It's a sign that our conscience is working properly. It is frightening, however, that an increasing number of violent youthful offenders seem unable to feel disgust, remorse, sorrow, or shame for what they've done. They feel no guilt. Unless they can learn to experience those things, it's unlikely that their behavior will change.

Guilt prompts us to assume responsibility for what we've done wrong. It helps us face up to what is good and what is evil. It reminds us that we need forgiveness and that there's hope, with God's help, that we can turn things around. It tells us we've got to try harder and do better to get it right in the future.

People often **feel** guilty, however, when their best efforts simply haven't been good enough or when they've made an honest mistake. Being sorry that something happened doesn't mean one is morally guilty of causing it to happen. Rather, it indicates compassion for those who've been hurt. It is our compassion—the ability to care and to feel with another—that makes us fully human.

The Gospels tell us of many times when Jesus "felt sorry" for or showed compassion toward an individual or a group of people. Jesus told many stories about persons who "felt sorry" or "took pity on" or were "moved with compassion" for someone. Indeed, Scripture tells us of God's own compassion.

Ideally, our emotions—what we **feel** is right or feel good about having done—should reflect our conscience—what we **think** is right. Likewise, what we **feel** guilty about should also coincide with our conscience—what we **know** is wrong. We shouldn't **feel** guilty if we have done nothing for which to be guilty. On the other hand, we **should** feel guilty if we've done something morally wrong. Even if we haven't caused the hurt, we should feel compassion for those who experience misfortunes.

The media often reinforce people's confusion about what we should feel guilty for. Ads, for instance, aim to make us feel **guilty** if we don't use a certain product. Thus they relate moral guilt to matters which really aren't moral concerns. No wonder people's emotions often don't echo their consciences! Distinguishing between what you should and shouldn't feel guilty about will be an important factor in how well you cope in life.

One teenager found it very hard to cope with the guilt he felt because of injuries his best friend suffered. The teenager had been driving on a rainy day, with his friend as a passenger in the front seat. When he swerved to avoid another car that recklessly cut him off, his own car slid into a tree. His friend was seriously injured and hospitalized for many weeks in considerable pain. Every time he visited his friend, the teenager felt terribly guilty and responsible.

This teenager hadn't been careless. He had done the best he could and what he thought was right at the time. Under the circumstances, that was all he or anybody could have done. He needed to realize that he was not responsible for what happened to his friend, and should not feel guilty. But it was understandable that he still feel bad about what his friend had to suffer. This is what compassion is all about.

Many times in life you will have to assume responsibility for and suffer the consequences of your actions. Sometimes this will be for things you knew were wrong but did anyway. In those instances, you should feel guilty about the hurt you've caused, recognize your action was wrong, and realize you shouldn't do again. At other times your actions, though done with a clear conscience, may harm someone. You should indeed feel sorry about the results of your actions and regret the harm. You should feel compassion for those who suffer because of your actions. But you shouldn't **feel** guilty, because you **are not** guilty.

For discussion

1. Why is it so important to distinguish between guilt—and sorrow, regret, or compassion?

2. What are the benefits of feeling guilty or being genuinely sorry? What are the negative results of bearing needless guilt or excessive sorrow?

3. When should you feel guilty about something you've done? When shouldn't you feel guilty—and how should you feel instead?

4. Describe a time you felt guilty over something for which you weren't morally responsible. Why did you feel guilty about it? How should you have felt instead?

5. As a doctor, how would you hope to react if your patient died despite your best efforts? Explain.

6. How do you think the teenager whose friend was hurt in the car accident should have felt? How do you think you would have felt in the same situation? Explain.

7. If that teenage driver had been a friend asking advice in coping with his feelings, how would you have tried to help him? If you had been the driver, how would you have tried to deal with your feelings of responsibility and guilt? Explain.

Panic at the bridge

Read this reality-based account and respond to the questions.

Cheryl was driving a group of her teenage friends home one summer night after a day of playing softball in the hills. Unsure of the directions, she was trying to follow the car of friends in front of her.

The other driver, who was speeding, lost control on a sharp curve. Horrified, Cheryl saw the car careen off of a bridge. She instantly tried to swerve out of harm's way by slamming on her brakes. In her panic, however, Cheryl accidentally stepped on the gas pedal. Consequently, her car veered off the road, through some

bushes, and into a tree. All of the teenagers in the first car were killed. The passengers in Cheryl's car were injured seriously. Cheryl escaped with only minor injuries.

None of the teenagers had been drinking or using drugs.

For discussion

1. What were Cheryl's and the other driver's responsibilities to their passengers?

2. Did either driver appear to violate their responsibilities in any way? Explain.

3. Cheryl now feels terribly guilty, believing that the other

teenagers' deaths and injuries were somehow her fault.

• Were any of the deaths or injuries Cheryl's fault? Explain.

• Should Cheryl feel guilty about what happened? Why?

• How do you think Cheryl should feel about the incident? As a friend of hers, how would you help Cheryl cope with her reactions? Explain.

4. What do you think Cheryl and the other surviving teenagers should learn from this experience?

Aftershock

Read the following account, and respond to the questions.

During an earthquake, the upper deck of a two-tiered highway collapsed, immediately killing most of the motorists on the lower deck. Rescue workers searched the rubble for survivors who might be trapped in the tiny space between the pancaked tiers of highway. Finally, they found a little boy—still alive, but pinned beneath his dead mother's body.

A surgeon carefully crawled through the precarious debris to check the boy's vital signs. The boy was conscious. But the surgeon determined that they had about twenty minutes to rescue him or he would die. There wasn't time to remove the wreckage from on top of the boy. Such efforts could also cause other parts of the freeway to collapse, killing both rescuers and the boy. There was only one way to free the trapped boy. The surgeon must cut through portions of the mother's body and amputate one of the boy's legs.

Within the precious minutes remaining, lying flat in the tight space with barely room to maneuver, the surgeon completed the grisly task. The boy was pulled to safety and survived.

Afterward, the tearful surgeon was badly shaken. A nurse at the hospital tried to console him as they talked and prayed together. The surgeon told her that, because the boy had been in shock, he most likely wouldn't remember how he had been rescued. But the doctor said he would never forget; he found it extremely difficult to cope with the gruesome rescue "surgery" he had performed.

For discussion

1. Did the surgeon do the right thing? Should he feel guilty about what he did? Explain.

2. Why do you think the doctor found it so hard to cope with what he had done? How should he feel about it—should it bother him at all? Explain.

3. What would you think if the surgeon lacked any feeling about what had happened? Explain.

4. If you were the nurse talking with the anguished surgeon afterward, what would you say to him? If he asked that you pray with him, what would you pray? Explain.

5. Some fear that one day someone will show the boy a news article describing how he was rescued.

• Suppose that several years later another student slips into the boy's locker an article detailing his rescue. If intended only as a "joke," would that be morally wrong? Explain.

• When, if ever, should the boy be told how he was rescued? Explain.

6. If you knew the rescue's details and the boy, when a teenager, asks you to tell him exactly what happened, would you? If so, what and how would you tell him?

7. Suppose, while researching a high-school assignment several years later, the boy finds out how he was rescued. As a close friend, how would you try to help him cope with the shocking discovery? Explain.

Reconciling

Why forgiving is sacred

Bear with one another and, if anyone has a complaint against another, forgive each other; just as the Lord has forgiven you, so you also must forgive.

COLOSSIANS 3:13

Jesus told us we have a sacred responsibility to forgive others. We're to forgive, as God willingly forgives us: "Whenever you stand praying, forgive, if you have anything against anyone; so that your Father in heaven may also forgive you your trespasses" (Mark 11:25). Jesus said our worship of God is empty and unacceptable if we're not willing to forgive others: "So when you are offering your gift at the altar, if you remember that your brother or sister has something against you, leave your gift there before the altar and go; first be reconciled to your brother or sister, and then come and offer your gift" (Matthew 5:23–24).

Jesus even said we can't be forgiven unless we're willing to forgive others: "For if you forgive others their trespasses, your heavenly Father will also forgive you; but if you do not forgive others, neither will your Father forgive your trespasses" (Matthew 6:14–15).

Jesus also said we must "turn the other cheek" (see Luke 6:27–35) and give another chance to one who's **sincerely** repentant. That ". . . you must rebuke the offender, and if there is repentance, you must forgive. And if the same person sins against you seven times a day, and turns back to you seven times and says, 'I repent,' you must forgive" (Luke 17:3–4).

As you've discussed, this doesn't mean irresponsibly or naively letting yourself or others be hurt over and over. Notice that Jesus said "**if** there is repentance." Feeling sorry isn't enough without repentance—the resolve and effort to change so as to not repeat the wrongs in the future.

Jesus said we should willingly forgive as many times as we'd like to be forgiven. Even more, Jesus said that our forgiveness mustn't be just a formality, but that we must each forgive one another **from our heart** (see Matthew 18:35). We especially shouldn't withhold forgiveness from someone as a way to get even or make the person feel even worse.

> *A love of reconciliation . . . demands courage, nobility, generosity, sometimes heroism, an overcoming of oneself rather than of one's adversary. . . it is the patient, wise art of peace, of loving, of living with one's fellows, after the example of Christ, with a strength of heart and mind modelled on his.*
> **POPE PAUL VI**

Scripture insights

Read Luke 6:27–36. What was Jesus saying here about forgiveness?

We know we're not perfect, but we shouldn't forget that other people aren't perfect either! Sometimes they too do wrong things, **are** sincerely repentant for them, but then end up doing them again. We've all been sorry for something, failed to learn a lesson from it, and later stupidly done the same wrongful thing again. Being "only human" doesn't make it right or excuse us from consequences. But it does explain why all of us at times give in to the same temptations.

Forgiving means being willing to give, to help someone. On our part, it can mean being able to heal an injured relationship and to risk trusting and loving again. So forgiving someone can help us as much as it can the person we forgive. As Jesus showed us, we should willingly extend others our forgiveness whether or not they're sorry. But to **experience** forgiveness, one must be truly repentant for the wrong done and sincerely desire to not do it again.

This repentance is far different from just feeling sorry one was caught and has to suffer the consequences, or feeling awful that somebody got hurt. It also requires a real intention to not do the wrong again. God freely offers forgiveness to us. To fully reconcile with God, to accept and experience God's forgiveness fully, our repentance is also needed.

As he was being executed, Jesus forgave those who were nailing him to the cross, saying, "Father, forgive them; for they do not know what they are doing" (Luke 23:34). He realized that the soldiers just thought they were punishing a common criminal. Even those who plotted his death did not realize the magnitude of their act, because they did not recognize who he truly was. On our part, we should certainly understand that when mistakes and accidents happen, it is often pointless to blame someone. Following Jesus' example, we should never hold a grudge against others for mistakes they've made in good faith.

Finally, we must realize how devastating a refusal to forgive can be. We must never withhold from one who asks the words, gestures, and healing peace of forgiveness.

Clarify

What did Jesus say about forgiving others? About repentance?

How did he exemplify in his own life what forgiving others means?

For discussion

1. *How can you tell whether somebody is sincerely sorry? Explain.*
2. *What do you find most challenging about Jesus' message regarding forgiveness? What do you find most reassuring or comforting about it? Explain.*
3. *Might a person ever be justified in refusing to forgive another? Explain.*
4. *The old proverb says, "Forgive and forget." Which do you think is harder—to forgive or to forget? Why?*
5. *Why do you think some people find it harder to forgive than others do? In which group are you?*
6. *It is sometimes said that women forgive but don't forget, whereas men find it harder to forgive but much easier to forget. Do you agree or disagree? Explain.*

Why reconciling is a sacrament

My friends, if anyone is detected in a transgression,
you who have received the Spirit should restore such a one in a spirit of gentleness.
Take care that you yourselves are not tempted.
Bear one another's burdens, and in this way you will fulfill the law of Christ.

GALATIANS 6:1–2

Forgiveness is so sacred that Catholics celebrate it as a sacrament. Jesus' risen life began with giving his apostles the power and authority to bring God's forgiveness of sins to people. The Sacrament of Reconciliation continues Jesus' own forgiving and reconciling mission and celebrates God's initiative of mercy in reaching out to us.

In celebrating Reconciliation, Catholics individually and privately unload our burden of guilt by confessing our sins to the priest celebrant with sincere sorrow and a firm resolve to not do them again. Thus, in the essential sign of this sacrament, the priest speaks God's forgiving words on behalf of the entire Church while making the sign of the cross over the penitent. Through the priest's words and gesture, God absolves us. We receive the assurance that God has forgiven us and that we are reconciled with the Church community.

The penance the priest then gives us to do reinforces our change of heart and resolve to change our behavior. It helps us fulfill our obligation to repair what we can of the damage our sins have caused. Catholics must participate in sacramental reconciliation whenever we've knowingly and freely done something gravely wrong, but we're encouraged to do so occasionally anyway. Realistically, we understand that we're sinners who throughout our life will need God's healing, pardon, and peace.

Sinful attitudes and actions don't exist isolated from others. It's appropriate that sacramental forgiveness and reconciliation occur in the presence of a community representative. Celebrating the Sacrament of Reconciliation as a community emphasizes that we've hurt others and need to reconcile with them as well as with God.

While sacramental forgiveness has been celebrated in different ways over the centuries, the substance has remained the same: Through the sacrament's minister, God forgives us individually. But the sacramental reconciliation we celebrate must carry through in our everyday lives.

The personal gift of forgiveness we're able to give others is an incredible power and a tremendous responsibility. Sometimes we alone will be able to lift the weighty guilt from another's shoulders. Christians exercise the priesthood of our baptism by reassuring others that they're worthwhile persons, able to be forgiven and healed. We also do so by bringing people together rather than tearing them apart.

Clarify

1. Why do Catholics celebrate the Sacrament of Reconciliation? What does this sacrament mean to Catholics?

2. As part of the Sacrament of Reconciliation, what purpose does doing penance serve?

3. What are the essential elements of the Sacrament of Reconciliation? Explain each one in your own words.

4. Although God forgives persons individually, why is it most appropriate to celebrate Reconciliation in a communal context?

5. What is the priest's role in the celebration of this sacrament? Why?

6. How often must Catholics participate in this sacrament?

7. What part is this sacrament to play in everyday life?

8. Has this sacrament always been celebrated in the same manner? What has remained unchanged?

9. How is forgiving others related, for Christians, to the priesthood of the faithful?

Activity

Develop and celebrate together a prayer service on the theme of forgiveness.

For discussion

1. *What seems most meaningful to you about the Sacrament of Reconciliation? What would make its celebration more meaningful for you? Explain.*

2. *How do forgiveness and mercy benefit the one who gives as well as the one who receives them?*

3. *What power and responsibility do you have in forgiving others?*

4. *Has anyone ever refused to forgive you even when you were sincerely repentant for what you had done wrong? How did you feel when that happened, or how would you feel if it did happen?*

"God's punishment"?

Read the case below and respond to the questions:

Allen is a young, homosexual man who was raised Catholic but stopped attending church after admitting to himself that he was gay. He knew Catholic teaching views as morally wrong the homosexual conduct he engaged in. For a few years, Allen led a promiscuous life.

Recently, Allen began experiencing physical symptoms he knew might be related to the dreaded AIDS virus. Scared to death, he was tested and found to be HIV positive; Allen has AIDS.

Allen is now being treated for the life-threatening disease, but is reluctant to tell his parents and brother that he's gay and has AIDS. His parents are devout Catholics and believe homosexual sexual conduct is wrong. Allen is most afraid, though, of how his brother might react. Allen has heard his brother express loathing toward homosexual persons and say, "AIDS is God's way of punishing gays for their sexual lifestyle."

In anguish and terror, Allen wonders: What if AIDS is God's punishment for being gay? Is it a sign God's angry with him? Allen's considered suicide, recalling his brother's words that "Homosexuals would be better off dead." In his heart, Allen wonders: Is his brother right?

Allen doesn't intend to resume an actively sexual lifestyle that would risk infecting others with AIDS. When he tries to pray, he ends up feeling God probably doesn't want to listen to the likes of him. Twice he's gotten as far as his parish church's door, intending to participate in Mass. Once he almost got the courage to participate in the Sacrament of Reconciliation. But as he stepped inside the church building, he felt he wouldn't be welcomed and didn't belong.

Allen has already isolated himself from friends. Now, at this darkest time of his life, he especially feels the pain of being estranged from those whose love and understanding he needs most—his family, Church community, and God.

For discussion

1. Why do you think Allen feels as he does? How do you imagine you would feel if you were he?

2. What does Allen's brother not understand about his responsibility as a brother and his moral responsibility as a Catholic? Explain.

3. What just plain human and moral responsibilities does Allen's family have toward him as he faces this crisis? Explain.

4. How would you probably feel initially if your brother, sister, or close friend told you he or she had AIDS? How would you respond? Why?

5. If you were the priest in whom Allen confided, what would you tell Allen?

6. How would you respond to those who view AIDS as God's punishment for homosexuals? What is your view of God? Of AIDS? Of people with a homosexual orientation?

7. What would you tell Allen about the Sacrament of Reconciliation?

8. If Allen asked you, a close family friend, to help him tell his family he has AIDS, how would you help them understand and accept the situation? Explain.

9. How do you think Jesus would respond to Allen and his questions, feelings, and fears? What does this tell us about how we should respond?

Catholic teaching regarding homosexuality views genital sexual activity between same-sex partners as immoral and encourages gays to lead a chaste life. But it clearly distinguishes between such sexual conduct and homosexual orientation:

Generally, homosexual oreintation is experienced as a given, not as something freely chosen. By itself, therefore, a homosexual orientation cannot be considered sinful, for morality presumes the freedom to choose.

All in all, it is essential to recall one basic truth: God loves every person as a unique individual. Sexual identity helps to define the unique person we are. God does not love someone any less simply because he or she is homosexual.

From *Always Our Children*, pastoral letter of the United States Bishops.

Deepening your character

Pursue peace with everyone, and the holiness without which no one will see the Lord.

HEBREWS 12:14

Religious faith and moral growth are inseparable. Like all relationships, religious faith calls for our response. If we really believe in God, then the ongoing personal ways we encounter God will keep improving our motives, actions, and behavior. So how we respond to God in faith is what helps us grow in character. And how we respond to others morally is the evidence of how we respond to God in faith.

To nourish and support our religious faith and inner growth, we need other people. Our inner character develops and is expressed in community. Our moral character is strengthened by having the proper internalized motives and people who support us in acting according to those motives.

This is why teenagers often find that being actively involved in their parish youth group is such a supportive experience. They can link up with others who share their moral values and beliefs about life. This helps them further internalize their moral principles and make the things they truly value a greater part of their life.

Parish **youth ministries** should help meet teenagers' needs through prayer, instruction in God's word, meaningful worship, opportunities for community service, and programs that guide and enable teenagers to strengthen their moral character. So especially if you feel lost or adrift in life right now, look into the supportive programs that your religious community provides for you. They can be a great help in turning your life around or in keeping it steered in the right direction.

Clarify
1. Why are religious faith and moral growth inseparable?
2. How does inner character develop?
3. What is the role of the faith community in moral growth?
4. What role can youth ministries play in helping teenagers strengthen their moral character?

For discussion
1. *How has your faith community helped you grow as a moral person?*
2. *How does your local faith community involve young people?*
   - *What opportunities does it offer for you?*
   - *What more do you think it could and should offer teenagers?*
   - *What more could you do to benefit from the opportunities that are offered?*
3. *How much would you say your moral character has grown since you were a child? How much do you expect that it will grow in your early adult years? Explain.*
4. *What influences most help strengthen your moral character? What influences most weaken it? Explain why.*
5. *What advice does the Scripture quote from Sirach offer for maintaining your character and moral integrity? Do you think it's good advice? Explain.*

Let mutual love continue.
HEBREWS 13:1

youth ministries
religious programs designed to meet the spiritual needs of young persons

But associate with a godly person whom you know to be a keeper of the commandments, who is like-minded with yourself, and who will grieve with you if you fail. And heed the counsel of your own heart, for no one is more faithful to you than it is. . . . But above all pray to the Most High that he may direct your way in truth.
SIRACH 37:12–13, 15

Activity
List the youth programs available to you in your faith community and answer these questions about them:
1. In which ones would you be most interested in participating?
2. Which programs (not now available) would you find helpful? Are there any that you might help initiate?

Developing Character

1. Character

- Moral character is important in life and is strengthened by practicing virtues, which are powers for goodness.
- The divine (theological) virtues of faith, hope, and unselfish love direct us toward God.
- Key human powers, or virtues, are prudence (exercising due care), justice (giving God and others what is due them), temperance (moderation), and fortitude (courage and persistence in doing right).
- God's seven gifts and twelve fruits of the Spirit also help us live rightly.
- Habitually doing right, and, for Catholics, frequently participating in the sacraments, make us morally stronger.
- God does not send us suffering but strengthens us with virtues to help us bear and grow from it.
- To overcome negative character traits, modify behavior and address the underlying reasons, motives, and biases that affect attitudes and behavior.
- Morally, our motive or intention is at least as important as the results of our decisions; it is immoral to intend harm.
- A good end doesn't justify using wrong means to obtain it; a good intention can't make wrong behavior right.
- Outside motivation can support moral growth; but the morally mature person bases decisions on internalized motives that reflect the Golden Rule and Christian principles.

2. Forgiving others

- Forgiveness is essential in order to reunite people with God and one another.
- Jesus' word and example taught us that God is always loving and forgiving and that we are to forgive without limit.
- We need to accept and extend to others God's loving, merciful forgiveness.
- We should encourage and help wrongdoers to change and to accept the consequences of their actions, but all punishment should have a positive purpose.
- Jesus told us that we will be forgiven as we forgive others.

3. Forgiving yourself

- It is important to forgive yourself, as God forgives you.
- Guilt results from doing something that is morally wrong.
- Our conscience should prompt us to feel guilty when we've intentionally done wrong.
- Compassion is the ability to care, to feel with another which, as Jesus showed us, makes us fully human.
- We must assume responsibility for our actions and their consequences, and regret the hurt we cause, but need not feel guilty when we are not morally guilty.
- Ideally, our emotions should reflect how our conscience judges the morality of our behavior.

4. Reconciling

- Jesus said we have a sacred responsibility to forgive others as God willingly forgives us.

- To be forgiven by God, we must be willing to forgive, reconcile with, and help those who are repentant.

- To experience forgiveness, one must truly repent of the wrong done and sincerely resolve to make amends and not do the wrong again.

- Sacramental Reconciliation continues Jesus' forgiving and reconciling mission, and celebrates forgiveness and God's initiative of mercy in reaching out to us.

- Sacramental Reconciliation involves expressing sorrow for sin, confessing one's sins, receiving absolution, and performing an act of penance.

- Communal celebrations of Reconciliation emphasize the social nature of wrongdoing and reconciliation.

- God forgives us individually through the priest's ministry on behalf of the Church community; Christians exercise our baptismal priesthood by being forgiving and reconciling persons.

5. Deepening your character

- Moral growth affects and is supported by our faith response to God.

- Our inner character develops and is expressed in community.

- Involvement in a supportive community, such as parish youth ministries may provide, can help strengthen one's moral character.

Key concepts

absolution	fortitude	prudence
behavior modification	fruits of the Spirit	repentance
cardinal or human virtues	gifts of the Holy Spirit	Sacrament of Reconciliation
character	God's forgiveness	sorrow
compassion	guilt	temperance
consequences	justice	theological virtues
confession	mercy	virtue
contrition	motives	youth ministries
forgiving	penance	

*And this is my prayer,
that your love may overflow more and
more with knowledge and full insight to
help you to determine what is best. . . .*
Philippians 1:9–10

Chapter 11

Making Tough Decisions

Overview questions

1. Why is it not possible to avoid making decisions? What happens when we try to avoid making decisions?

2. What does being reasonably open-minded have to do with making good decisions?

3. What does it really mean to stand by your principles?

4. How do you establish the proper moral priorities—especially where principles conflict?

5. What guidelines has Jesus given us and what is the role of prayer in moral decision making?

6. How can you make the best decision—especially among less-than-ideal alternatives?

7. What is the value of discussing hypothetical moral dilemmas?

NO TURNS
PROCEED STRAIGHT AHEAD

The dilemma of deciding

Telling lies to the young is wrong.
Proving to them that lies are true is wrong.
Telling them that God's in . . . heaven and all's well with the world is wrong.
The young know what you mean. The young are people.
*Tell them the difficulties can't be counted, and let them see not only what will
be but see with clarity these present times.*
Say obstacles exist they must encounter, sorrow happens, hardship happens.
The hell with it. Who never knew the price of happiness will not be happy. . . .[1]
                                        "Lies," by Yevtushenko.

It would be nice to tell you that life's problems and decisions will always be easy for you. Unfortunately, that's not the case. All isn't always "well with the world." Most people do face major decisions in life, decisions that require making difficult choices. Fortunately, most of us don't have to deal with critical moral dilemmas as often as some must: medical personnel, national leaders, soldiers in combat. . . .

In deciding what's right, you might expect by now always to have to think until your head hurts! If you feel confused at this point about things you previously thought you had the answers to, don't be surprised or dismayed. It would be alarming if you did arrive easily at quick, simple solutions to complex problems. You should find, though, that you're growing in the habit of considering carefully the factors involved in making moral decisions. That's an excellent beginning—but something many people fail to do.

As Yevtushenko's poem points out, things won't always be easy. You will no doubt face some painfully difficult moral dilemmas. Despite that, the more you strive to do good and what you sincerely believe is right, the greater will be your inner peace and happiness.

Not deciding is deciding

First the Nazis went after the Jews,
but I wasn't a Jew, so I didn't react.
Then they went after the Catholics,
but I wasn't a Catholic, so I didn't object.
Then they went after the worker,
but I wasn't a worker, so I didn't stand up.
Then they went after the Protestant clergy,
and by then it was too late for anybody to stand up.
                        Pastor Martin Niemoeller

Some people seem unable to decide. When asked for their decision, these individuals may respond, "I don't know—what do **you** think?" Their indecisiveness results from being afraid to make a choice. Because of their fear of the consequences, of what others will think, or of making a mistake, they avoid making decisions. That's far different from remaining unsure of the best course of action after carefully studying a complex matter.

Reluctant to take responsibility for their own decisions, some indecisive people let others make even moral decisions for them. It's easier to blame someone else when something goes wrong or someone criticizes or rejects the decision: "But he **made** me." "It was all **her** idea!"

When torn between two choices, some people freeze and decide nothing. Thus they leave the decision to chance or to somebody else. But deciding to let something or someone else decide really **is** a decision. Not to decide or act when the situation calls for decisive action isn't merely choosing to do nothing. It is to decide in favor of whatever happens. It is to choose the course of action that will occur if you **don't** decide or act!

Some people avoid making decisions on the pretext of being open-minded. There's a big difference, however, between weighing all reasonable options, and "being so open-minded your brains fall out"! Indecisive individuals who go along with the crowd and let others decide for them don't make good leaders—or intelligent followers.

So make up your own mind, rather than letting others make your decisions for you—especially in moral matters. Never abandon your conscience or your common sense!

When a stance is called for, especially in moral matters, you can't remain neutral and indecisive. Indecision amounts to refusing one's moral responsibility to choose rightly. Such inaction can have serious consequences.

Suppose you see someone about to step into the path of an oncoming car. A warning from you will save the person from being run over. If you warn the person, you've made a decision to save a life. If you do nothing, you've just as truly decided—decided that the person should be hit by the car.

In failing to make a necessary choice between two principles, we may violate both principles. For example, by doing nothing when a friend falsely accuses another person of some wrongdoing, we may end up being both dishonest with the accused person and disloyal to a friend who should be challenged to do what is right. So as difficult as it can be in such a situation, you must make a decision.

It's not right to leave serious matters up to chance. If we do, we dodge our moral responsibility. It's also not fair to dump onto others our moral responsibility for deciding. **The ideal isn't always possible.** In order to prevent a greater harm from occurring, sometimes we must choose the "least lousy" option. For example, a political candidate may not be the ideal choice, but he or she may also not be as bad as the alternatives!

This is how one man expressed his experience with having to choose from less-than-ideal alternatives: "When growing up, we all learn how to choose between right and wrong. We get good at choosing between good and better—like which model of car do I want to buy? But how do you choose between bad and worse? That's what I got stuck with at my job."

When an ideal choice isn't possible, at least rethink and try to improve your alternatives. But even in the dreaded "damned-if-you-do-and-damned-if-you-don't" dilemma, you're still responsible for making a decision. If it is truly not possible to take a completely different approach, you may have to choose the "lesser of evils."

"Whoever is not with me is against me. . . ."
Matthew 12:30

Like the turtle, you'll make progress only when you're willing to stick your neck out!

> *If you're not part of the solution, you're part of the problem.*

Voters are familiar with that type of situation! Some discouraged people don't bother to vote if they don't like either candidate. Nor do they try to generate a grass-roots third-party solution. Again, their non-action **is** a decision—to let those who **do** vote determine who's elected. By not deciding, we **do** decide.

For discussion

1. *Why do you think some people have trouble making decisions? Do you? Explain.*
2. *What is the difference between being reasonably open-minded and being too open-minded?*
3. *In what areas do you think teenagers tend to follow the crowd rather than make their own decisions and stick with them? What can be done to overcome this tendency and be one's own person?*
4. *Why is not deciding actually a decision? Give examples.*
5. *In a moral situation, when shouldn't a person remain neutral because of indecisiveness? Explain and give examples.*
6. *Have you ever been in the dreaded "damned if you do, and damned if you don't" situation? How did you, or how would you, make the tough choice between poor alternatives?*

Serious decisions must not be left to chance, nor can others make our decisions for us.

Bill's decision

Read the following account and respond to the questions. Then your instructor will tell you the case's actual outcome.

At sixteen, Bill was diagnosed with cancer. Such a diagnosis is often followed by a period of anger and denial. In the beginning, Bill said he'd rather have no treatment. Eventually he agreed to several months of the chemotherapy and radiation regimen. Doctors then told Bill that the cancer was gone from all but one area of his body. But they said he'd need four more months of treatments to effect a cure and keep the cancer from returning.

Bill didn't complain a lot about his treatments, which can cause hair loss and which left him nauseous, tired, and depressed. But as is common even when the treatments work, with each one Bill felt worse. He decided he'd had enough. Bill then sold some of his things, packed up his duffel bag and skateboard, and ran away from home. A friend drove him to the subway station.

Bill left his parents a note saying this wasn't a last-minute decision. He said he loves his parents and is sorry, but can't stand going to the hospital each week and feels the treatments are killing instead of curing him. He says he's given his life to God and believes that God will cure him.

Bill's parents say they hadn't realized how strongly their son opposes his treatments. His doctor says it's tough enough being a teenager without also having cancer. Medical experts say there is an 60 to 80 percent chance that, if treated fully, Bill can be cured.

Having no success in finding Bill, his parents appeared on national television to beg him to come home. They want Bill to talk to some cancer survivors and to look over the new information on alternative therapies.

Many people (including former cancer patients) think Bill should continue the treatment, if only for the sake of his parents and others who love him. Others think Bill's parents should call off the nationwide search for Bill, because he'll just run away again. Some parents of teenagers cured by the type of treatments Bill has had say they probably would have honored their teenager's wish to stop treatment because they realized how painful it was and how uncertain they had been at the time that the treatment would work.

For discussion

1. What is Bill's moral dilemma? What do you think his goal should be in resolving it? ➡

2. Why would not making any decision about his treatment be a decision on Bill's part? How might delaying his decision also be a decision?

3. What three main alternatives do you think Bill should consider? ◼

4. What information does Bill have? What further information and guidance should he seek? ◼

5. Whom would Bill's decision affect? How? What principles are involved here? 👫

6. What are the probable risks and benefits of each alternative? How likely is it that each one will occur? Are any morally unacceptable? ◆

7. What should Bill's motive be in making his decision about his treatment? ▽

8. Which people and principles do you think should have priority in Bill's decision? Why?

9. What decision do you think Bill should make about continuing his treatments? What would you probably decide in the same situation? Explain.

10. Would your decision be different if the odds of being cured were 50–50? If the odds of being cured were only 20 percent?

11. Do you think Bill's friend should have helped him run away by driving him to the subway station? Explain.

12. What do you think your basic criteria should be for any medical treatment you consent to?

Activity

Imagine that you could take Bill on a "journey of life" to show him the reasons for living and having the treatment. Describe what you would tell and show him.

Assignment

A friend of yours, diagnosed with a life-threatening illness, wants to run away and asks your help. Use the six steps of moral decision making to describe how you would make your decision. Explain under what circumstances you would decide to help, and not to help, your friend.

Choosing well

You cannot insist on the right to choose without also insisting on the duty to choose well.

POPE JOHN PAUL II

Opposite indecisive individuals are the know-it-alls who immediately think they have all the right solutions. Although at first they may seem wise, in time people begin seeing through their easy answers and phony wisdom. Eventually the know-it-all is perceived as a pain in the neck rather than a font of wisdom. Determining what's best involves far more than what instant-answer people think it does!

These attitudes turn people off: "I've made up my mind; don't confuse me with the facts" and "Don't question my opinion; I have all the answers." Yet it's tempting to respond to difficult problems with ready answers. With such stubborn, one-sided approaches, however, we fail to thoughtfully test and weigh alternatives or consequences. We don't uncover the complicated truth or generate sound solutions to problems. Know-it-all attitudes merely produce **bigoted** viewpoints and big mistakes.

bigoted
extremely biased; unwilling to consider other ideas or viewpoints

The proverb "Act in haste; repent at leisure" makes the point that hastily made decisions are often mistakes. So when faced with tough choices, the wise person pauses to ask more questions and seek more information before deciding. The wise person considers all pertinent sides of the situation, weighs everything carefully, and prays for guidance. This is especially necessary where time is limited and the stakes are high. As the surgeon said during a critical operation, "We must proceed carefully because we have no time to lose."

People often defensively argue or debate matters, considering only **their** side rather than searching for the truth. They staunchly defend their position, unwilling to admit there's something they don't know. Some television interview shows and some talk shows encourage arguments between extremely biased individuals because the sensationalism captures viewers' attention. The complex, many-sided truth often gets lost in the controversy.

A closed mind learns nothing because it doesn't **want** to learn. If your teachers, parents, or friends occasionally tell you they don't know an answer, consider yourself lucky. That takes honesty—and a lot more wisdom than does being one-sided or pretending to know everything.

*Fools think their own way is right,
    but the wise listen to advice.*
            Proverbs 12:15

Learn to admit when you're truly baffled. Don't be afraid to say "I don't know." Ask intelligent questions. Seek sound advice. Students often won't ask questions because they're afraid others will think they are dumb. Meanwhile, others usually wonder the same things but are also afraid to ask! Some students even risk lower grades rather than ask for help. Remember: If you don't question, you'll never really learn.

*The one who first states a case seems right,
    until the other comes and cross-examines.*
            Proverbs 18:17

Adopting an open-minded attitude can at times seem frustrating. Have you begun a class discussion knowing where you stand, only to find, after listening to others, that you're not so sure? Perhaps you've ended up more confused about what is the best solution. A few thousand years ago, a proverbist confronted the same frustration:

Sometimes there is a way that seems to be right,
but in the end it is the way to death.

Proverbs 16:25

Temporary indecision is perfectly okay, as long as an immediate decision isn't required of you. Maybe your hesitation is telling you that you need to gather more information. Perhaps your conscience is prodding your better judgment to avoid a harmful snap decision. Also recognize that you'll never be able to answer all your questions accurately. But you're never alone in searching for the right and good response to any dilemma. Others can often help; God always can.

And when you turn to the right or when you turn to the left,
your ears shall hear a word behind you, saying, "This is the way; walk in it."

Isaiah 30:21

Reflection
1. Are you more of a closed- or open-minded person?
2. Do you think others see you as being more closed- or open-minded?

Journal entry
Write down one way you could become a more reasonably open-minded person.

Project

Write a letter to the editor of your local newspaper presenting another side of a current issue. Give reasons for your stand which show that you also understand the other viewpoints.

For discussion

1. *Why does the right to choose involve the duty to choose well?*

2. *What is your perception of and reaction to know-it-all attitudes? When do you think teenagers most often act like know-it-alls?*

3. *About what things do you (be honest) act like a know-it-all? Why do people sometimes feel they must appear to be experts?*

4. *Are closed-minded individuals usually aware that they are that way? About what things do you tend to be closed-minded? Explain.*

5. *Do you think the truth and intelligent decisions are better discovered through arguments or through discussions? Explain.*

6. *How do students usually react when a teacher or parent admits not knowing an answer? Why do you think they react this way?*

7. *Why are some students afraid to ask questions during or after class? Should they be? Explain.*

8. *How hard is it for you to admit it when you're confused or unsure? Explain.*

9. *Have you been somewhat disappointed that not all your questions about moral issues were answered in this course? Explain.*

You desire truth in the inward being;
therefore teach me wisdom in my secret heart.
PSALMS 51:6

Why did the princess die?

Read the following true account and respond to the questions.

Princess Diana of Great Britain and her date Dodi Al Fayed were killed in a tragic accident while traveling through a narrow tunnel in Paris, France. Mr. Fayed and the car's driver were pronounced dead at the scene. Diana survived for a time after rescuers removed her from the car. She and Fayed had been riding in the back seat and had not been wearing seat belts. The bodyguard in the front seat, who was protected by an air bag and wearing a seat belt, was the only survivor.

Tests later confirmed that the driver's blood alcohol level was over double the U.S. legal limit. It was three times the limit in France, a serious-crime for a driver there. Witnesses and accident reconstruction experts agreed that the car had been traveling at an extremely high speed, well over the speed limit, when the accident occurred. Tests showed that the driver had also taken two mood-altering prescription drugs which, in combination with alcohol, can impair one's judgment and ability to drive. One of the drugs can cause double vision and diminish reflexes and coordination.

The driver had been called to duty at the last minute so that the car the couple was supposed to have ridden in could be used as a decoy for eluding photographers. Although trained to drive fast to elude kidnappers and terrorists, the driver evidently did not have the required chauffeur's license and was in no condition to handle the high speed chase. One toxicologist said that, given the driver's alcohol level and the car's high

speed, such a tragic accident was almost inevitable.

The hotel, which had employed the driver and was owned by Fayed Sr., released a videotape showing the driver walking and conversing "normally" just before getting in the car to drive the couple. When the accident happened, several photographers ("papparazzi") on motorcycles were chasing the car, trying to photograph Diana and Dodi. The driver was probably speeding in an attempt to elude the pursuing photographers. Some have speculated that a flashbulb may have temporarily blinded the driver, causing him to lose control of the car, or that a motorcycle or another car had cut ahead and caused the accident.

France's good Samaritan assistance law makes it unlawful for bystanders to not offer aid to victims at the scene of an accident. But witnesses said that, instead of trying to aid the accident victims, some photographers took pictures of the dead and injured victims. Some eyewitnesses said the photographers surrounded the car "like vultures." They said that photographers, wanting to get a better shot, shouted for others— even the doctor ministering to the prin-cess—to get away from the car. Some photographers left the scene and later offered to sell their close-up pictures of the victims for over $2 million. Within a few weeks of the accident, a few tabloids had purchased and published some of the photos.

Several photographers were taken directly into police custody and investigated for voluntary manslaughter, a charge that could merit a five-year prison term. They

denied any responsibility for the accident, or that they had refused to help. One photographer said he merely opened one of the car doors to see if the occupants were still alive and to see if he could help. He said it wasn't a time to take photos but that, when there was nothing helpful he could do, he stepped back and "resumed his work as a journalist" by taking wide-angle shots of the car. When he was taken into custody, however, he tried to shield his own identity from the camera by covering his face.

Pressured by public anger, the tabloids later tried to distance themselves from the celebrity-hounding photographers whose pictures they normally buy. The tabloids called these photographers a "new and unusually aggressive breed" who sometimes create an incident in order to capture a public figure's reaction to it. But bowing to public pressure, many supermarket chains pulled the tabloids from their check-out counters. Public figures themselves say they don't think the average tabloid reader realizes the unethical behavior—the distortion of truth and the constant invasion of celebrities' privacy—that goes into publishing the tabloids.

Some say that Princess Diana and Mr. Fayed should have seen that the driver had been drinking, but like many people in love, perhaps they paid more attention to each other than to common-sense and safety concerns. Some wondered if Mr. Fayed exercised poor judgment in the attempted escape from the photographers.

Many lawsuits were filed against the various parties who might have contributed to the accident. Paris police set out to investigate the possibility of criminal conduct by photographers and others. Under French civil law a corporation, such as the hotel that employed the driver, can also be held criminally liable under certain circumstances.

For discussion

1. List everyone you think bears some responsibility for the accident that caused Princess Diana's death. If you were a juror in a lawsuit against all of these parties, what percentage of the blame for the accident would you assign to each party? Why? In arriving at your verdict, follow the five decision-making steps discussed thus far.

2. React to this comment: "The photographers weren't at fault; they were only doing their job. After all, they have families to support."

3. Do you know how much alcohol it takes to impair judgment?

4. Which of the people involved in this tragic incident would you say failed to exercise good judgment? Which principles did their attitudes or behavior violate? Explain how and why you think they failed to choose well.

5. Do you think any of the parties involved in this incident should have been charged with a crime? Explain.

6. Should photographers and journalists be allowed to invade public figures' privacy and convey information about their private lives to the general public? What important principles seem to conflict in this issue? Explain and give examples.

Making tough choices

For, of its very nature, the exercise of religion consists before all else in those internal, voluntary, and free acts whereby a [person] sets the course of [his or her] life directly toward God.

"DECLARATION ON RELIGIOUS FREEDOM," NUMBER 2.

Standing by your principles

What kind of person do you want to be? On what ideals will you build your life and base your decisions? You must decide what you will stand for in life. You do that by determining your fundamental principles. If you don't do that, other people and influences will shape your life for you, and the result will be painfully unhappy. **You have the freedom, the right, and the duty to direct your own life on the right course.**

Jesus commanded that we love others as he has loved us (see John 13:34). Thus, **the most important principle must always be unselfish loving concern for people's welfare.** How do you apply this principle in specific situations? Begin by asking yourself these two questions:

• What is the most unselfishly loving thing to do?

• What will accomplish the greatest good, while causing the least harm?

This does not always mean that the right decision is what benefits the most people! It doesn't mean that the majority must get priority. In fact, Jesus told us it's sometimes necessary to put the individual's welfare first:

"Which one of you, having a hundred sheep and losing one of them, does not leave the ninety-nine in the wilderness and go after the one that is lost until he finds it?"

Luke 15:4

disproportionately

not in proper balance in relation to the number or importance of the factors involved

I am the inferior of anyone whose rights I trample under foot.
ROBERT G. INGERSOLL

The greatest good might be what greatly benefits only one person. Making way for an ambulance or fire truck causes a slightly delay in traffic and inconveniences people. But one person's urgent need here takes priority over other people's convenience. Sometimes we must reject a choice that would greatly benefit many people, because it would severely and **disproportionately** harm a few people. We may need to vote against raising the sales tax to finance a new stadium if the tax would unduly burden people with lower incomes.

How can you figure out whose needs you should put first? It helps to apply the Golden Rule: How would you want other drivers to respond to the emergency vehicle if **you** were the one being rushed to the hospital or if **your** house were on fire? Isn't it worth putting up with occasional traffic delays in order to insure prompt emergency aid? How adversely would increasing the sales tax affect you if **your** income were in the lower bracket? Would it be an unfair hardship for you then?

Jesus says we should respond as we'd want others to respond to us in the same situation. Always remember, circumstances can change. One day **you** might be in the other person's situation!

An individual's rights should be upheld as long as they don't conflict with other persons' equal or greater rights. Rights should never be taken away or surrendered without a valid reason. Some of the rights of an individual may be taken away to prevent other persons' rights from being jeopardized or violated.

For example, a criminal may lose the right to freedom in order to protect others' right to be reasonably safe from harm. Even prisoners, however, retain certain basic human rights and must be treated justly and humanely. They are still persons created in God's image and loved by God. Allowing prisoners to be mistreated renders us as a society morally guilty.

When we willfully do wrong, we are choosing to bear the reasonable consequences. Suppose you were told, "If you come home late once more, you'll be grounded for a week!" By continuing to stay out late, you'd be choosing the reasonable consequences. In abusing your freedom, you would be choosing to endure the (forewarned) temporary loss of freedom. Grounding you would be confirming your choice. Like it or not, you would have only yourself to blame.

Upholding one person's rights protects everybody's rights. People are understandably upset when a judge must free a guilty party because the offender's rights were violated in order to make the arrest. There's certainly a risk that the offender will further harm society. As history attests, however, making way for a ruthless police state is far worse! If a suspect could be unlawfully searched or roughed up, so could you. So in giving priority to one offender's right to be treated justly, the judge is protecting our right to fair and lawful treatment.

Why can't an exception be made and principles set aside just once? To keep a criminal locked up, why can't the law overlook the unlawful arrest this time? One answer is illustrated by the physical principle of momentum: A slight push starts a car rolling down a steep hill. Propelled by its weight and gravity, the car picks up such speed that it can't be stopped from careening down the hill. The same principle applies if you didn't drive slowly enough to stop safely on a rain-slick highway. Your car's momentum could easily lead to a chain of deadly accidents.

A similar momentum principle, the "slippery slope," applies to morality: **If principles are set aside once, they will likely be set aside again and again.** "Just once" becomes "once more" and "just once more" and then "but it's been done several times before, why not this time?" (Did you ever try using that type of logic on your parent?) Finally, the principle itself is abandoned.

Going to the opposite extreme, some people view every decision as a possible "slippery slope." They leave no room for being appropriately flexible. In fact, their stubborn rigidity violates the important Christian principles discussed earlier: People's welfare comes before rules and laws. Rules and laws sometimes must be adapted to individual needs and to circumstances. We may break a rule or law—only if necessary—to support more important principles. We may not break a rule or law if doing so jeopardizes or violates more important principles.

Today there are many negative influences at work to undermine your principles. That's why you must nourish your principles with positive influences—the teaching of Jesus, the Church's guidance, a loving family, good friends. Your principles represent what you stand for as a person. So reflect long and prayerfully on what your guiding principles are and what they mean. Don't let anyone or anything persuade you to violate your principles. Your principles are at the heart of your conscience and human integrity. Do your utmost to reinforce and live up to your principles.

We know that all things work together for good for those who love God.
ROMANS 8:28

Clarify

1. In every case, what is the most important principle? Why? How can you apply this principle in specific situations?
2. Is the right decision always what benefits the most people? Explain and give examples.
3. How can you figure out whose needs to put first in a situation? Give an example based on your experience.
4. If one person's rights conflict with the rights of many others, when should the individual's rights be upheld? When should priority instead be given to upholding the rights of the many? Give an example.
5. Why does making a choice imply choosing its consequences?
6. How does upholding one person's rights protect everyone's rights? Give an example.
7. What's wrong with making an exception and setting a principle aside just once?

For discussion

1. *Do you think most teenagers base their moral decisions on their principles? Are most teenagers clear about what their principles are? Do most teenagers realize how important their principles are? Explain.*
2. *Why do you think people try to blame others rather than assume responsibility for their own choices? When do teenagers most often do this?*
3. *When do teenagers most commonly use "slippery slope" reasoning? When have you tried using it? Explain and give examples.*
4. *What strong pressures influence teenagers to act against their principles? What pressures most influence you? What helps you resist them? Explain.*

A test of principle

Read the following reality-based account and respond to the questions. When you have finished, your instructor will tell you what the teenager in this case decided.

A month before graduation, Matt and a busload of other students in his class went on a school-sponsored weekend retreat. It was held about an hour away from the school at a retreat center in the hills.

On the ride there, Matt learned that some of his classmates had brought beer and wine along and planned to party late at night after the chaperones were asleep. Evidently the students had smuggled the alcohol onto the bus in soda and shampoo bottles.

Chaperones had warned the students that anyone found with alcohol or illegal drugs on the trip wouldn't be allowed to attend their graduation ceremony or party. Anyone caught using alcohol or drugs would be suspended and possibly expelled.

The students who had brought the alcohol along were bragging about it, and Matt feared that one of the chaperones would get suspicious. One of Matt's friends told him she was afraid the rebellious students would get caught, but said there wasn't anything she and Matt could do about it.

Nobody wanted the trip—or graduation—to be ruined. Matt didn't want to see anyone suspended or expelled. And what if perfectly innocent students also ended up being blamed and punished? Matt inwardly agonized about what, if anything, he could and should do.

For discussion

1. What is Matt's moral problem? What should his goal be in resolving it? ➡

2. What would be Matt's three best alternatives for solving the problem? ▪

3. What does Matt know about the situation? What further information or guidance should he seek? Explain. ▪

4. Whom would Matt's decision affect? How? What conflicting principles are involved for him? 👫

5. What risks and benefits did each of Matt's alternatives involve? How important is each one and how likely to occur? Are any morally unacceptable? ◆

6. What should Matt's motive be in making his decision? ▽

7. To which people and principles do you think he should give priority in his decision? Explain.

8. What do you think Matt should decide? What do you think you would do in his situation? Explain.

Step 5B: Establishing your priorities

You've already determined and weighed your morally acceptable alternatives and motives. Before making your decision, you must establish the proper priorities. What and whom should you put first? Which principles apply and are most important in **this** situation?

Torn between principles

Moral decision making is sometimes harder than just sticking with your principles. Some decisions require choosing wisely and courageously **between** principles. Your hardest decisions will involve situations where important principles are in conflict with each other—or seem to be.

Are we to put above all else the principle of survival? Not always, says Jesus, by word and example: "No one has greater love than this, to lay down one's life for one's friends" (John 15:13). Millions of people have nobly sacrificed their lives for others and for principles other than survival—principles such as justice, freedom, and equality.

Which do you choose when honesty conflicts with loyalty? Teenagers are commonly torn between being loyal to friends and honest with a parent or teacher, or between being loyal to one friend and honest with another friend. The tension between these two principles can be lessened if you recognize that often true loyalty to one person may require honesty with another. For example, loyalty usually is best observed by also looking out for a friend's long-term interests. When you take this approach, you are acting honorably.

How important should the principle of honor be to you? In some countries today, some students view failing a school entrance exam as "losing face," as dishonoring themselves and their families. They believe suicide is the only honorable way to respond to the "disgrace" they feel they've caused.

While such an understanding of honor is not common in Western societies, being respected or standing up for someone's **honor** is often a "matter of principle." What does respect mean in the life of a teenager? Is defending the principle of honor worth risking or causing injury or death to oneself? When should a person let a disrespectful insult slide, even if other persons would respond differently? Questions related to honor and respect in the decisions we make are more common than most people realize.

honor
praise-worthiness, esteem, good reputation

 **Pontius' Puddle**

How do you know **which** principle to give priority to when important principles seemingly conflict? First determine which principles are most important and which are not at stake or as important in this situation. Some principles should almost always get priority.

The right to life, for instance, is usually the higher principle, but it is not an absolute principle. Because God is the author of life, each person's right to life is sacred and to be protected from beginning to end. While preserving human life ordinarily should be among our highest priorities, we may sacrifice our own life on behalf of an equal principle or a greater good in a particular situation.

Thus you may choose to give your life for another's or in defense of your country. Under certain circumstances, you may sacrifice your life to protect basic human freedoms. You may become a paramedic or a firefighter and risk your life for others.

So how **do** you determine which principle has priority? You must do so in a way that affirms rather than violates your principles. Carefully proceed through the first four decision-making steps. That will often clarify which principle should assume a higher importance in the situation. If you're still perplexed, the following questions and guidelines can help you wade through the confusion:

Questions to ask when you're still perplexed about a decision

- Which choice will most likely bring the greatest benefit and least amount of harm? (Don't lose sight of the long-term results.)
- Which choices support the correct motives?
- Which principle best supports the overriding principle of unselfish love?
- What should my priorities be in light of my principles and my relationship with God?

Guidelines to follow when you must choose between principles

- Never do so selfishly or lightly.
- Put spiritual and moral values and principles before material and physical ones.
- Place people's welfare uppermost as God asks of us.
- Where interests conflict, consider the principles involved on both or all sides.
- Pause to reflect on and pray over your decision.

How Jesus handled conflicts between principles

How did Jesus' choose between principles? He lovingly put people's welfare first. What did Jesus do when he experienced the pain of conflicting values and principles? Jesus sought time alone and prayed. Consider, for example, his actions and words just before he was arrested and put to death:

Then he said to them, "I am deeply grieved, even to death. . . ." And going a little farther, he threw himself on the ground and prayed, "My Father, if it is possible, let this cup pass from me; yet not what I want but what you want."

Matthew 26:38–39

Clarify

1. Is the right to life always the highest principle? Explain what priority it should have.
2. How should you determine which principle has priority in a particular situation?

Projects (choose one)

1. Poll five teenage boys and five teenage girls about what they would do if they knew a friend habitually shoplifted. Write a paper describing the conflicts of principles their responses reveal. Also explain what you would do and which principle you would give priority to in this situation.
2. Find a news item about a situation in which principles conflict. Explain what principles are in conflict and how you would determine which one should get priority.

Prayer helped Jesus face his death with peace and courage. Prayerful reflection can also help us make the best decision, one in line with the principles God teaches us through our conscience and the Church and in the Scriptures. The Spirit Jesus sent us after his resurrection gives us wisdom and strength when we're troubled and confused.

Throughout life, keep your integrity by treasuring your principles. Always keep your priorities straight. Remember Jesus' caution: "What does it profit them if they gain the whole world, but lose or forfeit themselves?" (Luke 9:25). Jesus is asking you to properly prioritize your principles without compromising them.

In weighing the relative importance of principles in a situation, much will depend on the circumstances. When you're confused about what to decide, reflect on this: Given Jesus' loving concern for everyone's welfare, what would **he** probably decide in this situation? What would Jesus counsel **me** to do here? The popular motto, WWJD, "What would Jesus do?" reminds us of this method for arriving at the important priority. The answer to the question may reveal the depths of your own conscience—and the right decision.

I can do all things through him who strengthens me.
PHILIPPIANS 4:13

For discussion

1. *One professor tells students to imagine how they'd view their proposed decision if it made news headlines tomorrow. Explain the pros and cons of his advice.*
2. *When faced with a tough decision, have you ever considered how Jesus or someone else you admire would decide? Did that help you make your decision? Explain.*
3. *Which of the guidelines discussed in this section would you find most helpful when making a tough decision between principles? Explain.*
4. *Describe a situation in which you faced an apparent conflict between principles. What decision did you make? How did you decide which was the more important principle?*
5. *What would be the hardest principles for you to choose between? Why?*

Activity
Read Mark 2:23–28 and 3:1–5.
1. What dilemmas did these Pharisees present to Jesus?
2. Which principles seemed to conflict in each situation?
3. How did Jesus resolve each dilemma? How did he explain his response?

The drinking problem

Read the following dilemma one teenager faced recently, and respond to the questions.

Your close friend Adam is struggling with a drinking problem. He's afraid his parents will make him leave home if they find out.

A school counselor suspects that your friend has a problem with alcohol and seeks information from you about it. You believe that being honest with the counselor could lead to the help your friend needs. You also fear your friend might get kicked out of the house if the counselor contacts his parents.

For discussion

1. *What is your moral dilemma here? What would your goal be in resolving it?* ➡
2. *List three reasonable alternatives for resolving your problem.* ■
3. *What information do you have? What further information and guidance should you seek?* ■
4. *Whom would your decision affect? How?* 👫
5. *What principles are involved here? How do these seem to conflict?* 👫
6. *What risks and benefits are involved in each alternative solution? How important is each one, and how likely to occur? Are any of the risks morally unacceptable?* ◆
7. *What should your motive be in making your decision?* ▽
8. *What do you think your priorities should be in making your decision? Must you choose between honesty and loyalty here? If so, which principle should you favor? Explain.* ▽
9. *What do you decide to do in this situation? Why?*

What are human life and safety worth?

People used to think no cost was too great to save a human life. After all, isn't human life priceless? Aren't we more important than money? In reality, it's a different matter. Government agencies often do a cost-benefit analysis to determine whether a proposal is worth enacting. Read the following reality-based situation and respond to the questions.

Consumer advocates favor implementing all of the recommended airline safety changes— from child-safety seats to greater anti-terrorist security. They say it wouldn't cost much more per plane ticket than a meal at a fast-food restaurant. But every time airline ticket prices go up 1 percent, vacation travel decreases about 2 percent.

If safety measures become too costly because of decreased vacation travel, ticket prices will become too high for the ordinary traveler. Therefore the costs of safety in dollars and lives have to be weighed against the benefits of the proposed safety measures.

In this example, then, a human life is assigned a certain monetary value. This value is then multiplied by the number of lives a proposed safety change is projected to save. If that total is less than what it will cost to implement the safety measures, the changes are presumed too costly and usually aren't required.

Suppose, for example, that a life is valued at $5, and a proposed safety measure is projected to save 100 lives, while costing airlines $2 million. Multiplying $5 by 100 totals $500, which would be the projected monetary value of the lives that would be saved. But because it would cost far more to implement the safety measure ($2 million) than the value of the lives it would save ($500), the safety measure probably wouldn't be required. (Needless to say, a human life is presumed to be worth far more than $500!)

If a major airline crash takes more than the projected number of lives, the government agency recalculates the cost of enacting the safety measure that would have prevented the crash. So safety measures that could have prevented a tragic accident are often taken only after the accident occurs.

That's why a city often won't put up a stop light at a busy intersection until after a certain number of accidents and even deaths occur there! That's also why some say it's outrageous to base safety measures on this type of cost-benefit calculation.

As part of a federal aviation advisory committee, you must decide whether to require airlines to install smoke detectors and fire extinguishers in their airline cargo compartments. You must calculate whether the benefits of this added safety measure would be worth the $300 to $400 million it would cost the airlines and their passengers. To determine this using the customary cost-benefit analysis, you must first assign a monetary value to a human life.

For discussion

1. *What monetary value, if any, would you assign to a human life? Why?*
2. *In determining whether to enact the proposed airline safety measures, what is your moral problem? What is your goal?* ➡
3. *Explain three reasonable alternative ways in which you could solve the problem?* ◼
4. *What information do you have about the proposal? What additional information or guidance do you need?* ◼
5. *Whom would your decision affect? How? What principles are involved here?* 🚶🚶
6. *What are the risks and benefits involved? Are any of the risks morally unacceptable? How important is each risk and benefit, and how likely is it to occur?* ◆
7. *What should your motive be in making your decision?* ▽
8. *Which people and principles do you think should be given priority in your decision?* ▽
9. *Would you vote to require the proposed safety measures or not? Explain.*
10. *What is your reaction to the customary cost-benefit method of making decisions that affect public health and safety? Can you think of a better way to make these decisions? Explain.*

Human life and abortion—the moral conflict

Abortion remains one of the most divisive social and moral issues because important principles are in conflict here. Unfortunately, discussions about abortion are usually more heated and emotional than sound and enlightening. Whether people favor or oppose allowing abortion, its moral implications trouble them. Most people admit that abortion is an evil, not a good.

Those who favor legal abortion generally view it as a "necessary evil," a last-resort alternative in a no-win situation. Most people know Catholic teaching opposes abortion, but many don't understand why. Catholics sometimes don't know how to respond to the arguments given in favor of abortion.

This section will discuss Catholic responses to some of the arguments for abortion. It begins with the Judeo-Christian belief in human dignity. Intelligently and compassionately try to understand how Catholic teaching addresses the conflicting principles involved. This will help you refine your own ethical judgments about this complex moral problem.

. . . whatever is opposed to life itself . . . whatever violates the integrity of the human person . . . whatever insults human dignity . . . all these things and others of their like are infamies indeed. They poison human society, but they do more harm to those who practice them than those who suffer from the injury. Moreover, they are a supreme dishonor to the Creator.[2]

Flowing from that belief in human dignity, Catholic teaching upholds these specific principles:

- We must absolutely respect and protect human life from its beginning at conception.

- Abortion directly violates the human person's basic right to life.

- Experiments that manipulate or exploit the human embryo violate human dignity.

- Children are entitled to special help and protection before and after they're born. So are women while pregnant and for a reasonable time after giving birth.[3]

Clarify

1. *What does Catholic teaching say about upholding human dignity? About the specific principles which flow from that belief?*

2. *Which is the basic principle here regarding human life? How do the other principles listed here flow from it?*

3. *What types of medical procedures do you think would be at odds with these principles? Explain why.*

4. *How does opposing human life, integrity, or dignity poison human society? Dishonor our Creator? Give examples that illustrate what you mean.*

5. *Why are the persons who oppose life more harmed than are the persons whose lives they harm?*

For discussion

1. *Why do you think the abortion issue is so divisive? Why is everybody troubled by it? What troubles you about it?*

2. *Have you found that discussions about abortion often generate more heat than light? Explain.*

3. *Which arguments about abortion have you heard? Which of these seem mainly emotional? Which ones involve reasoning and principles?*

4. *Why do you think it's important to personally study the abortion issue carefully, prayerfully, intelligently, and compassionately?*

The right to life

Legalized abortion implies two false assumptions:

• First, that human life is meaningful before birth only if the mother decides it is.

• Second, that only **after** birth is human life meaningful enough for society to fully support and protect it.

It would clearly be immoral to kill individuals after they're born merely because their lives seem "meaningless" to others. It is equally immoral to take human life before birth just because the mother doesn't want the child.

The United Nations says children are entitled to protection before as well as after birth.[4] Our laws protect the child in the mother's womb and prosecute those who injure the unborn child, such as the pregnant woman who uses harmful illegal drugs. Therefore justice is contradicted when a society permits a doctor to kill the human embryo or fetus at the mother's request.

Does a pregnant woman's right to control her body and reproductive system justify denying the unborn child the right to life? Is a woman's right to control her body greater than her offspring's right to be born? The greater and more basic the human right at stake, the more serious society's reason must be for taking away that right. No human right is more basic than the right to life. To justifiably deprive the unborn of life, there must be an overriding greater right at stake.

Our personal freedom to make decisions that directly involve our health is basic and important. Yet our physical freedom ends where another person's equal or greater right to physical integrity begins. If we need a new kidney in order to live, we can't just steal someone else's! The state has the duty to protect us from unjust intrusions on our persons and privacy, and certainly from threats to our lives.

Is an unwanted fetus merely an "intruder" in the mother's body? Especially if the woman didn't behave irresponsibly in becoming pregnant, why should she have to bear the child? According to law, it is generally wrong to kill a trespasser. Such killing is excused only if one reasonably (even if incorrectly) believes that the intruder poses a serious and imminent threat to someone's life. But this is hardly the case when we are discussing elective abortion and the unborn child poses no threat to the mother's life.

Every relationship involves certain rights and duties. A mother has a universally fundamental duty to protect her child's welfare. This relationship doesn't depend merely on the mother's affection for her child, but on her biological link to the child as "flesh of her flesh." The right of the unborn to life is morally greater than the mother's right to control her body. The principle of protecting human life from its beginning also far outweighs the inconveniences of unwanted pregnancy.

One may kill a human directly only to support a **greater** moral principle. But the mother and the unborn child have **equal** claim to the right to life. No innocent person may be directly killed to save another's life. Thus the unborn child may not be killed directly in order to save the mother's life. However, a seriously ill woman may receive medical treatment to save her life, even if that treatment **indirectly** results in the death of her unborn child. The intent is not to kill the child, but to preserve the mother's life.

Life is a flame that is always burning itself out, but it catches fire again every time a child is born.
GEORGE BERNARD SHAW

Clarify

1. How does favoring abortion imply that life isn't meaningful before birth? Why is that assumption false?
2. What responsibility does the state have to protect personal privacy and freedom?
3. What laws legitimately limit our freedom regarding our bodies and reproductive ability?
4. How does the state's responsibility to protect people extend to the unborn? What laws recognize this?
5. What is "the intruder theory" in favor of abortion? Why does Catholic teaching oppose this theory as wrong?
6. When may one justifiably kill another human directly? When may one do something that indirectly results in the death of another? How do these moral criteria apply to abortion?
7. Why do the principles at stake in protecting the unborn outweigh the inconveniences of unwanted pregnancy?

For discussion

1. *How might the assumption that life isn't fully meaningful before birth become a dangerous "slippery slope" position?*
2. *What inconsistencies do you see in our laws and policies regarding the unborn? Explain and give examples.*
3. *What important principles conflict in considering abortion as a personal dilemma? As a social issue?*
4. *Based on your understanding of Catholic teaching, respond to the following arguments favoring abortion. (Explain your responses fully.)*
   - *"If a pregnant woman doesn't want the child, she shouldn't be forced to have it."*
   - *"A pregnant woman should have the right to control her own body—even if it means having an abortion."*
   - *"An unwanted pregnancy is like an intruder; the woman can get rid of it."*
   - *"Abortion should at least be allowed in cases of rape or incest."*

When does human life begin?

People have varying views of when human life and personhood begin:

- **The moment of conception** (when the male's sperm fertilizes the female's ovum)
- **The moment the fertilized ovum implants in the uterus** (which is necessary for continued growth and development)
- **When individual identity is completely established** (when the single fertilized organism can no longer divide and separate, resulting in identical twins)
- **When the respiratory system has formed** (since the heart and lung are essential)
- **When those parts of the brain essential for human consciousness have formed,** somewhere between two and six weeks after conception (allowing for the later development of reasoning and personal relationships with God and others)
- **At viability,** when the fetus can survive outside the womb and apart from the mother (usually during the third trimester, but this may be sooner with advances in technology)
- **At birth**

Fear not that your life shall come to an end, but rather that it shall never have a beginning.
JOHN HENRY NEWMAN

Catholic teaching holds that human life and personhood begin at conception and thus disagrees with all the other viewpoints. It emphasizes that the embryo and the fetus are not "potential humans," but unborn children with potential. They don't become human just because of genes, implantation, viability, breathing, thinking, or birth. They're human because they've been given a **human** life principle (soul) by God at the moment of conception.

Our value as persons doesn't depend on our abilities, relationships, or achievements. Our lives are worth being protected not because we're independent or wanted, nor because we've developed our potential. **Our lives are valuable because as humans we share in God's life.** Just because an embryo or a fetus is still attached to the mother, or is unwanted, or is not yet fully developed doesn't mean that it isn't human.

Almost one in every four pregnancies ends in a miscarriage; the medical term for this is *spontaneous abortion,* whereby the body naturally expels the embryo or fetus. Is this nature's way of insuring that most seriously abnormal fetuses will not continue to grow and develop? It is true that as a society we don't formally mourn the loss of these fetuses as we do babies who die at or after birth. Yet, especially in the later stages of pregnancy, parents do experience the profound loss of a miscarried child.

Catholic teaching has always denounced abortion as a grave moral wrong. Admittedly, centuries ago some Catholic scholars, such as Thomas Aquinas, did think that the human soul wasn't present until many days after conception—many more days for a girl than for a boy! Today, though, we're far more informed about human embryology and fetal development than Thomas Aquinas was. We also have an increased moral sensitivity to the equality of female persons.

This understanding leads us to better appreciate how all human life is continuous from conception to death. All stages of life are essential, and none can be considered less significant. By the loving power of God, our human life principle (human soul) exists from the moment of conception through death—and beyond into eternity.

For discussion

1. Based on your understanding of Catholic teaching about when human life begins, how would you respond to someone who says to you

- *"When do you think human life begins?"*
- *"A fetus is just a potential person, not yet a real person."*
- *"If there's something wrong with the fetus, a woman should be allowed to abort it. After all, miscarriages are God's way of getting rid of mistakes."*
- *"The Catholic Church hasn't always been opposed to abortion—even saints used to have differing ideas about when the human soul becomes present."*

2. Do you still have any additional questions about when human life begins?

For it was you who formed my inward parts; you knit me together in my mother's womb. I praise you, for I am fearfully and wonderfully made. Wonderful are your works; that I know very well.
PSALM 139:13-14

Clarify

1. In your own words, explain each theory about when human life begins.
2. What is Catholic teaching's view of when human life begins? Why?
3. Has the Catholic Church always opposed abortion?
4. Why does Catholic teaching view life as an unbroken line from conception to death?

Reverance for life comprises the whole ethic of love in its deepest and highest sense.
ALBERT SCHWEITZER

Legislating morality

Some people claim that it is unfair to impose one moral viewpoint on everyone by outlawing abortion. But allowing abortion also imposes a moral viewpoint. Indeed, every law that concerns human welfare reflects some moral view about our human nature and worth. Society legislates moral viewpoints all the time. The only issue is how to do so properly and justly. Society has a right and duty to protect its members—especially those who are innocent and helpless, such as the unborn.

If abortions were outlawed, wouldn't women continue to have them illegally—often under dangerous conditions? If we really enforce laws against abortion, won't our prisons be full of women (especially women who are poor) charged with murder or manslaughter? Would or could society ever fully enforce any law against abortion? Would it be more just not to prosecute the woman who has the abortion, but to prosecute and jail the doctor who performs abortions? Isn't it unjust to pass a law that won't be obeyed or enforced equally against all violators?

When the right to life isn't protected on behalf of **everyone,** civilized society is at stake. Just punishing those who perform illegal abortions, rather than the women who obtain them, would at least tell people abortion is wrong. Not banning abortion misleads many people to view abortion as morally acceptable. Thus the principles and good at stake in protecting unborn children outweigh any harmful consequences that might result from banning abortion.

Another argument for abortion suggests that it is just a private matter between a woman and her doctor. We should, of course, have compassion for women who, faced with this terrible moral dilemma, have chosen to have abortions. Only God can judge a person's conscience—none of us has that right.

Yet abortion isn't just a personal matter. Taking innocent, helpless human life is a social sin that is heavily influenced by society's attitudes toward unwanted pregnancies. We all have a moral responsibility to help prevent the harm and alleviate the suffering that result from unwanted pregnancies. We must address the circumstances that prompt some women to see no alternative to abortion. If we don't support practical, life-serving alternatives, we can be morally guilty.

Concern for the child, even before birth, from the very moment of conception and then throughout the years of infancy and youth, is the primary and fundamental test of the relationship of one human being to another.
POPE JOHN PAUL II

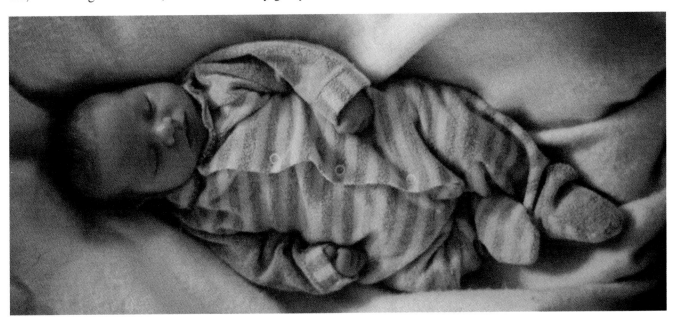

Although women have abortions for serious reasons, most of them dread having an abortion. To eliminate abortion, we must address the pressures on women that compel them to choose abortion. We must support all aspects of life involved in this social and personal tragedy. We must protect the pregnant woman's well-being as well as that of the unborn.

Emotional, financial, and other resources should be readily available to provide life-supporting alternatives for pregnant women. We should educate individuals about sexual reproduction and the moral responsibilities it involves, so that they won't act out of ignorance and then find themselves considering abortion. We must work to eliminate the most tragic causes of unwanted pregnancy—rape and incest. We must also have compassionate understanding for victims of these terrible crimes and offer them practical support.

Circumstances can overwhelm a person's conscience so that the person doesn't see or have the moral strength or freedom to choose correctly. The individual's moral guilt is thereby lessened or may be altogether absent for having made the objectively wrong moral decision. But we shouldn't avoid doing the morally right thing just because its consequences might be difficult or painful. Sometimes there will be suffering no matter which alternative we choose. We can, however, help lessen the burdens that may lead good people to make morally bad choices.

Clarify

1. Why does Catholic teaching call abortion a social sin?
2. What does it mean to truly support life?
3. What must we realize about painful alternatives and their consequences?
4. What social responsibilities do we have regarding the abortion issue? In what practical ways can we fulfill these?

Project

Research and list the resources in your local religious and civic communities that provide pregnant women with spiritual, life-supporting, practical help.

For discussion

1. Based on your understanding of Catholic teaching, how would you respond to someone who says
   - "People shouldn't try to impose their morality on others by banning abortion."
   - "When abortions are outlawed, women get them anyway—but it's a lot more dangerous for them."
   - "Laws banning abortion can cause more harm than good."
   - "We shouldn't pass anti-abortion laws that we can't or won't enforce fairly."
   - "Abortion should just be a private matter between a woman and her doctor. The state has no right to interfere."

2. What attitude should we have toward women who've made the painful decision to have an abortion? Why doesn't the Catholic Church tell us to condemn these women? Can you think of a situation Jesus addressed that would relate to this kind of situation?

3. What do you think individuals and society could do to lessen the problems that lead to abortion? Explain and give examples.

4. What can you and your friends do to encourage a reduction in the number of abortions among teenagers?

Abortion—Your policy statement

As public relations advisor, you are to draft a policy statement on behalf of your local Catholic diocese. Direct it toward Catholic and non-Catholic mothers-to-be who are facing the dilemma of an unwanted pregnancy. Base the statement on your understanding of Catholic teaching about human life and abortion and what you think the Catholic Church community should do to live its teaching fully. Include in the statement:

- *An understanding acknowledgment of these women's situations*
- *The type of support the diocese will provide for these mothers-to-be as an alternative to abortion*
- *The resources the diocese will use in providing this support*
- *Specific programs the diocese will start or encourage in order to help prevent the problem of unwanted pregnancies*

The pregnant teenager's predicament

Each year, over a million teenagers in our society become pregnant. Many of them then face the grave moral dilemma of whether to have the baby or have an abortion. Most of these pregnant teenagers choose to have their babies. Regretfully, many others have abortions.

It's hard to think clearly in any highly upsetting personal predicament—especially amid strong, conflicting emotional reactions. That's why it helps to have a more objective way to think things over and decide. Based on your understanding of Catholic teaching about abortion, sort through the pregnant teenager's dilemma by using the following questions.

For discussion

1. *What is the main moral problem an unmarried pregnant teenager faces in trying to decide whether to have an abortion? What should her goal be in making this decision? Why?* ➡

2. *What alternatives does the teenager have? What facts should she consider, and what guidance should she seek?* ▩

3. *What should the girl's parents, teachers, and friends do to support her?* ▩

4. *Whom would each of the teenager's alternatives affect? How?* 👫

5. *What moral principles are involved in the pregnant teenager's dilemma? Explain.* 👫

6. *What aspects of Catholic teaching about the sacredness of human life should a pregnant teenager consider? Which teachings of Jesus do you think might help her?* 👫

7. *What risks and benefits would be involved in each of the teenager's alternatives? How would you assess the importance and likelihood of these risks and benefits? Explain.* ◆

8. *What motive should the teenager have for her decision? What do you think would be the wrong motives for her choice? Explain.* ▽

9. *What do you think the girl's main priorities should be in this decision? List them in their order of importance and be prepared to explain your reasons and ranking.* ▽

10. *If you were a pregnant teenager or a friend whose advice she seeks, what would you pray about at this point?*

11. *Based on the priorities you've established, what is the best moral decision you think the pregnant teenager can make here? How do you think you would respond if you were in this situation? Why?*

Making your decision

Step 6: What is your decision?

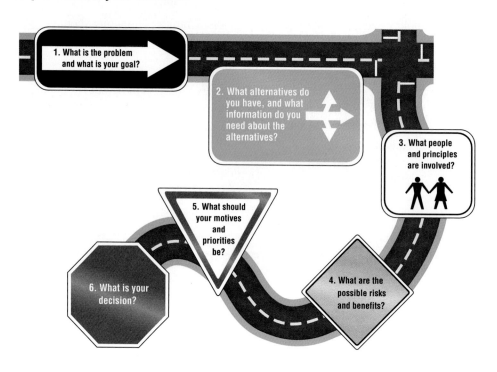

Your final step in solving moral problems is making the decision itself. You established your goal, analyzed the alternatives, assessed the people and principles involved, weighed the risks and benefits, and determined your motives and priorities. Now you're ready to make your decision.

At this point, you still might not be absolutely certain what the best decision is. Other worries may add to your difficulty: Maybe someone will get hurt no matter what you decide to do. Perhaps you'll find out later that you should have chosen differently. At this point people really **recognize** how important prayer is in the decision-making process! So ask God's Spirit to enlighten and guide you. Since God usually speaks to us through our conscience, listen to your best judgment.

We are obliged to follow our conscience in moral matters. As you've probably discovered by now, though, that's often easier said than done. There's still no guarantee that your decision will turn out to have been the best one. God alone knows the wisest choice in advance. You can only try your best to do the right thing.

Sometimes your decision will turn out to have been poor. You'll discover later that you've made a mistake—maybe a terrible or even tragic one. But if you've honestly tried your best to discover and do what's right, you won't have made a **morally** wrong decision. You won't be morally guilty even if, despite your best intent and judgment, your decision resulted in more harm than you anticipated. Remember, you can never do wrong in God's eyes by following your properly formed and informed conscience:

*Conscience frequently errs from **invincible** ignorance without losing its dignity. The same cannot be said of [one] who cares but little for truth and goodness, or of a conscience which by degrees grows practically sightless as a result of habitual sin.[5]*

invincible
unconquerable, cannot be overcome

There comes a time when you **must** make your decision. After you've thoroughly analyzed and unselfishly weighed what's involved and then prayed over your decision, trust your better judgment. Make your decision with confidence that God completely accepts you and understands that you've tried your best.

Never be arrogant about making moral decisions. Always be honestly humble about the harm your decision may unwittingly cause. Admit and learn from your mistakes rather than stubbornly defending them. It shows strength of character to reconsider a poor decision and then correct it. Understand when you've been wrong intellectually but haven't done wrong morally.

If you're sincerely convinced your decision was the best one, don't be afraid to explain it straightforwardly. Stand up for the decisions you're convinced are right. It shows weakness of character to make a good decision and then buckle under pressure and change it. Have the courage to stick by your convictions and your good decisions.

> *Keep your conscience clear, so that, when you are maligned, those who abuse you for your good conduct in Christ may be put to shame.*
>
> *1 Peter 3:16*

God reveals to us in Jesus who we are and how we are to live.
National Catechetical Directory, number 101.

Respect others' right to follow their conscience, but don't be afraid to disagree with their decisions. Also realize that they won't always agree with your decisions. When you make a decision, be willing to assume responsibility for its consequences. If you've properly considered and prayed over the matter and think you know what's best, don't be afraid to make a decision. Whatever its outcome, you'll know you've done what is, for you, the morally right thing.

> *Now who will harm you if you are eager to do what is good? But even if you do suffer for doing what is right, you are blessed. Do not fear what they fear, and do not be intimidated, but in your hearts sanctify Christ as Lord. . . . For it is better to suffer for doing good, if suffering should be God's will, than to suffer for doing evil.*
>
> *1 Peter 3:13–15, 17*

Genuine morality, then, isn't something others impose on us. It's how we accept the possibilities for becoming fully human that Jesus' life, death, and resurrection opened up for us.[6] So deliberately try to make your moral decisions lovingly and unselfishly. Be especially conscious of this if you need to choose some aspect of your welfare over that of others. Finally, never let your decision contradict your religious beliefs or violate your conscience.

Owe no one anything, except to love one another; for the one who loves another has fulfilled the law.
Romans 13:8

Clarify

1. Why is it important to know that one can never do wrong in God's eyes by following one's properly formed and informed conscience?

2. Why is genuine morality not something others impose on us? How would you explain what it is?

For discussion

1. *What most worries you when you're faced with a tough decision?*
2. *When in the decision-making process are you most likely to feel the need to pray for guidance? Explain.*
3. *Describe a time when you made what turned out to have been a poor decision. How did you feel about it afterward? What did you learn from your experience that helped you in making future decisions?*
4. *Have you ever given in to pressure and changed a decision when you shouldn't have? What types of pressures would tempt you most to do that? What would help you most to resist changing your good decision despite the pressures? Explain.*
5. *What does having the courage of your convictions mean to you? Why?*

Quick decision

Occasionally we must make important decisions very quickly. Even then, it's important that we try to do so wisely. In class, your instructor will explain a situation that demands a quick decision from you.

You will then be given several seconds to decide what you would do. After making your decision, you will be asked to explain and try to justify your decision.

So take a few moments now to review the six steps for moral decision making.

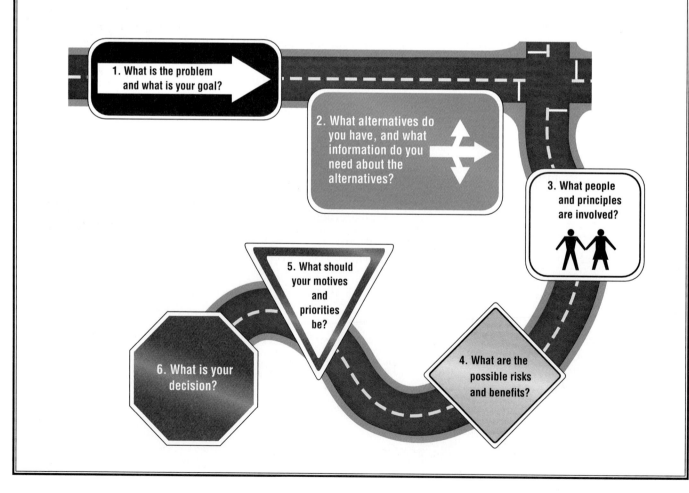

The drug treatment experiments

Read the following. Then follow the directions your instructor gives you.

As biotechnology advances, new drugs are constantly being developed to treat illness and ease human suffering. For each medical problem, researchers relentlessly pursue the "perfect pill."

Sometimes tragedies occur, however, when drugs aren't properly tested before becoming available on the market. Years ago in England the drug thalidomide, when given to pregnant women, caused severe physical deformities in many of their children. Doctors aren't always aware of how potentially harmful a drug's side effects can be. Patients also sometimes fail to follow directions, with harmful or fatal consequences.

Even with strict testing procedures, there may still be problems. Drugs that seem to pose little risk may be approved for clinical trials on relatively healthy individuals. But sometimes drugs that were harmless to laboratory animals cause serious or lethal effects in humans. That's why extremely potent drugs are often tried first only on terminally ill patients who have no better options.

Whenever a new drug is clinically tested, a protocol is established. This protocol specifies how and on whom the drug may be tried. A drug may be an effective treatment for a certain mental or physical disorder, but it also may have troublesome and permanent side effects. One drug, for example, helped certain mentally ill persons live normally. It also caused them to drool constantly and uncontrollably. But patients, doctors, and researchers believed that the mental health benefit was worth risking the undesirable side effect. So the drug was allowed to be marketed for widespread use under medical supervision.

Acetaminophen is a common drug in non-prescription medicines. It too can cause harmful side effects when not used properly or when used for a prolonged period. Yet we can buy it without a prescription because the likelihood of the good it does far outweighs the likelihood that it will cause harm or be abused.

Pharmaceutical companies must follow strict guidelines when conducting drug experiments on humans. Some advocates, however, say clinical trials often violate medical, legal, and moral guidelines. The drug manufacturers claim that a drug's benefits will be shown to far outweigh its risks.

Your instructor will give you examples of drug experiments in which people are currently being invited to participate.

• Read the information about the risks and benefits involved in each of these drug experiments.

(As with most drugs, you will notice that the list of negative side effects is longer than the list of benefits!)

• Next, using the six steps of moral decision making as your guide, decide whether or how each drug should be approved for widespread use. Do this by responding to the following questions. **Remember: You or others will receive the drug's positive benefits only at the risk of suffering its negative side effects.**

For discussion

1. Would you approve of using this drug in clinical experiments on humans? Explain fully.

2. Would you be willing to have this drug administered to you in a clinical trial? Explain.

3. Under what circumstances would you absolutely refuse to let someone be experimentally treated with this drug? Absolutely refuse to be experimentally treated with this drug yourself? Explain.

4. Would you approve this drug for widespread use without further testing? Should it be made available to the public without a prescription? Explain.

5. Which Christian virtue(s) played a role in how you arrived at your decisions about this drug?

Real world decisions

Today the world especially needs believable witnesses. Dear young people, you who love personal authenticity so much and who almost instinctively condemn every type of hypocrisy are able to give a clear and sincere witness to Christ. Therefore testify to your faith through your involvement in the world too. A disciple of Christ is never a passive and indifferent observer of what is taking place. . . [but] feels responsible for transforming social, political, economic and cultural reality.[7]

Pope John Paul II

Certain people must frequently make major ethical decisions involving people's lives—doctors and nurses, government officials, lawyers and judges, and police officers. Yet they're often extremely frustrated and confused because they've had no education in moral decision making. To address this problem, many colleges require students to take an ethics course related to their field of study.

A parent protested to school officials about a class assignment the students at the local public high school had been given. They had been asked to discuss the traditional "lifeboat" dilemma: Survivors marooned at sea on a lifeboat will all sink unless some of them volunteer to jump—or are tossed overboard. Based on information about each person on the lifeboat, the students were to decide who they thought should be allowed to survive and why. The parent thought that high school students shouldn't be asked to make hypothetical life-or-death decisions.

Today a growing number of critical moral dilemmas confront humanity. Recognizing this, many groups and organizations establish ethics committees. Government ethics committees oversee and advise legislators. Hospital ethics boards counsel patients and staff about the moral implications of medical treatment decisions. Most ethics committee members aren't clergy, but lay persons with special training or education in ethics. Perhaps someday you may choose to become an ethics advisor.

At some time you might be called upon to make a life-or-death decision, or someone who must do so may ask your advice. In this course you've dealt with realistic situations, some of which many individuals wrestle with daily. In some sense, many of these dilemmas involve us all.

By our votes and voices, all of us are responsible for establishing public policy. Together, we're the ones who ultimately determine what risks should and shouldn't be allowed and whose lives should or shouldn't be supported. Placing ourselves in hypothetical moral-dilemma situations isn't far-fetched or out of place. Hopefully the practice has reinforced your principles, sharpened your judgment and conscience, and helped you rely more on God and others' wisdom in reaching wise decisions.

I pray that you may have the power to comprehend, with all the saints, what is the breadth and length and height and depth, and to know the love of Christ that surpasses knowledge, so that you may be filled with all the fullness of God.
EPHESIANS 3:18–19

For discussion

1. Which real or hypothetical dilemmas in this course have most helped you reinforce your principles or sharpen your skills of judgment and conscience? Explain.

2. Would you ever consider studying to become an ethics advisor? Who among your classmates do you think might be especially good in that position?

Who shall live?

Due to skyrocketing medical costs, society can't afford to make all of the best medical benefits accessible to everyone who needs them. When we can't give everybody the best health-care treatments, whom do we treat and whom do we not treat? How do we decide who will live and who shall be allowed to die?

Your panel is to decide whether the available public funds will be spent on a life-saving transplant for one person or on prenatal care for many pregnant women. To determine this, consider the following information and then respond to the questions.

Seven-year-old Coby will die within six months unless he gets a bone-marrow transplant. His parents don't have enough money to

pay for it. Treating one burn patient or providing one organ transplant can cost over half a million dollars. Hundreds of children in our society die each year because they need transplants their families can't afford or because not enough suitable donor organs are available.

Your panel might decide that the government won't pay for the transplant Coby needs. In that case, Coby will spend what may be his last months publicly begging for money to save his life. Such fundraising campaigns don't always succeed in time.

Public health-care funding is limited, however. Even if you could shift all funding from bombs and missiles to medical care, you still couldn't provide everyone with the best medical treatment technology offers. The money for a transplant for Coby could provide prenatal care for over a thousand mothers. Without prenatal care, many babies will die or require intensive neonatal care that costs a few thousand dollars a day in public health-care funding.

You are also aware that in Third World countries more than 40,000 children under the age of five die every day. While the news media rallies around one desperate child who needs a life-saving organ, tens of thousands of Third

World children die daily. Many or most of these children could be saved by just five dollars per year for medicines to counteract simple malnourishment and diarrhea.

For discussion

1. *If asked to open your panel's meeting with a prayer for guidance, what would you pray?* ➡

2. *As a member of this panel, what is your moral dilemma? What should your main goal be, and why?* ➡

3. *What are your three or four best alternatives in deciding how health-care funds will be spent here?* ◼

4. *What information do you have on which to base your decision? What further information would you like to have before deciding? Explain.* ◼

5. *Whom would your decision affect? What important principles are involved here?* 👫

6. *What important risks and benefits would each alternative involve? How likely are these to occur?* ◆

7. *What motive should you have for your decision? What would be the wrong motives? Explain.* ▽

8. *What do you think your social health-care priorities should be in making this decision? Rank these in the order you think they are important.* ▽

9. *Given your priorities, how do you choose to spend the available public health-care funds? Explain.* ⬢

Baby Daniel

Every day in neonatal care units across the country, doctors, nurses, and parents confront an anguishing question: What treatment should they provide for a newborn infant with severe medical problems? This is one of the most difficult and painful moral dilemmas medical personnel and parents must face, and they often wish they were better trained to deal with it.

Read the reality-based case presented here, and respond to the questions. Then your instructor will tell you the outcome of the two situations on which this one is based.

While pregnant with Daniel, Shawna, a teenager, drank alcohol and occasionally used marijuana. She paid no attention to nutritional concerns and didn't seek prenatal care until late in her pregnancy. Doctors say that's probably why infant Daniel was born with part of his brain missing. They've told Shawna that her son is permanently blind, won't survive past infancy, and probably will never be able to leave the hospital. Even if he does live longer, Daniel's mental capacity will never progress beyond that of a four-month-old baby.

Daniel is now being kept alive by a respirator and may require surgery to prolong his life. Hospital bills for his care have already exceeded $500,000. The doctor recommends that all treatment—except for comfort measures—be discontinued, and that Daniel be allowed to die naturally.

Shawna keeps daily vigil at her son's crib and says she's not ready to let Daniel die, even though some of her relatives are pressuring her to do so. Shawna's mother strongly supports efforts to keep Daniel alive, but Shawna's sister thinks it amounts to torturing or abusing him. (Privately, most—but not all—of the nurses agree with Shawna's sister.) Shawna tells a nurse that maybe she's being selfish, but she just can't bring herself to let Daniel die because she loves him so much.

Any decision to stop providing life-prolonging medical treatment for Daniel must be made by the doctors with Shawna's consent.

For discussion

1. What is Shawna's moral problem here? What should her goal be in resolving it? ➡

2. What three main alternatives do you think Shawna should consider for dealing with this dilemma? ◼

3. What does Shawna know about Daniel's condition? What further information and guidance should she seek? ◼

4. Whom would Shawna's decision affect? How? What principles are involved here? 👥

5. Who might be harmed by each of Shawna's alternatives? Who might be helped? 👥

6. Whose needs and rights are involved in this situation? What principles are involved? (Be sure to consider both the individual and the broader social concerns.) Explain. 👥

7. How would you assess the risks and benefits of Shawna's alternatives? ◆

8. Whatever Shawna decides, what should her motive be? ▽

9. What should Shawna's priorities be in making her decision? Which principle is most important here? Explain. ▽

10. What do you think Shawna should decide about continuing Daniel's treatment? Why? ⬣

11. Should a parent be allowed to make the decision in this type of situation, or do you think there's a point at which doctors, the hospital, or the courts should decide what treatment to provide on behalf of infants like Daniel? Explain.

A Christian is someone who shares the suffering of God in the world.
DIETRICH BONHOEFFER

In the time of your life

The following reflection sums up many of the things you've studied during this course. While reading it, consider what you've discussed and learned. Then write your own reflection on the type of morally good person you want to be in the time of your life.

In the time of your life, live—

so that in that good time there shall be no ugliness or death for yourself or for any life your life touches.

Seek goodness everywhere, and when it is found, bring it out of its hiding-place and let it be free and unashamed.

Place in matter and in flesh the least of the values,

for these are the things that hold death and must pass away.

Discover in all things that which shines and is beyond corruption.

Encourage virtue in whatever heart it may have been driven into secrecy and sorrow by the shame and terror of the world. . . .

Be the inferior of no one, nor of anyone be the superior. Remember that everyone is a variation of yourself.

No one's guilt is not yours, nor is anyone's innocence a thing apart.

Despise evil and ungodliness, but not persons of ungodliness or evil. These, understand.

Have no shame in being kindly and gentle. . . .

In the time of your life, live—

so that in that wondrous time you shall not add to the misery and sorrow of the world,

but shall smile to the infinite delight and mystery of it.[8]

Final project

Create and name a personal robot. Assume that it's physically much stronger than you are and can't be de-activated. Introduce your imaginary robot to the class, explaining the following about it:

• Which values, virtues, and principles you've given your robot, and how it will behave toward you and other humans

• The kind of "artificial conscience" your robot has that will let you sleep well nights while the robot is fully activated in your house

• How you would have your robot make decisions about what would help or harm

• Which of your robot's "moral traits" are found in God's natural and revealed law, and/or in Jesus' teaching

Chapter 11 summary
Chapter 11 summary
Making Tough Decisions

1. The dilemma of deciding

- Not to decide is to make a decision
- Indecision can violate principles and one's moral responsibility, and cause serious consequences.
- When decisions must be made from poor alternatives, one must choose the "lesser evil."

- The wise person considers all pertinent sides of the situation, weighs things carefully, and prays for guidance.
- Stubborn defensiveness doesn't discover the truth; it is better to admit one's confusion.
- Temporary indecision for good reasons may point out the need to seek more information or guidance.

2. Making tough choices

- The most important principle must always be unselfish loving concern for people's welfare.
- The right decision might benefit one person rather than the majority, while the wrong choice might disproportionately harm only a few persons.
- To determine whose needs to put first, apply the Golden Rule.
- An individual's rights should be upheld if not in conflict with others' equal or greater rights.
- When we willfully do wrong, we are choosing to bear the reasonable consequences.

- Upholding one person's rights protects everybody's rights.
- Setting aside principles once makes it far easier and more likely for one to do it again.
- We must properly nourish and live up to our principles.
- When torn between principles, we must correctly determine which one should get priority.
- When he had to choose between principles, Jesus prayed and lovingly put people's welfare first—as we should do.

3. Making your decision

- It is important to pray for guidance before making moral decisions.
- There is never a guarantee that we will always make the correct decision.
- We can never do wrong in God's eyes by following our properly formed and informed conscience.

- We should pray over our decision, trust our better judgment, and be confident that God accepts that we've tried to do our best.
- We should admit and learn from our mistakes, and stand up for and be able to explain our decisions.
- We should try to make all our decisions lovingly and unselfishly.

Key concepts

bigoted

conflict between principles

disproportionate harm

greatest good

indecisiveness

individual rights

know-it-all attitudes

less-than-ideal alternatives

lesser of evils

priorities

reasonable consequences

"slippery slope"

Endnotes

Chapter 1: Why Be Good?

1. "Not All Rabbits Come Equipped with Lucky Feet," by Pete Dexter, *The Herald* (15 August 1988): 9.
2. Information based on interview by Lynn Sherr, "Amy's Choice," on ABC's *20/20* (6 May 1994), #1418.

Chapter 3: Conscience

1. See the *Catechism of the Catholic Church*, #1789.
2. *Documents of Vatican II*, "Decree on the Instruments of Social Communication," numbers 2 and 4.
3. See the *National Catechetical Directory*, number 103.
4. See the *Documents of Vatican II*, "Declaration on Religious Freedom," number 3.
5. See the *Documents of Vatican II*, "Pastoral Constitution on the Church in the Modern World," number 16, and the *National Catechetical Directory*, number 103.

Chapter 4: Moral Convictions

1. *Documents of Vatican II*, "Pastoral Constitution on the Church in the Modern World," number 27. Pope John Paul II, *On Social Concern* (30 December 1987), numbers 39–40.
2. *What Have You Done to Your Homeless Brother?* Document of the Pontifical Commission *Iustitia et Pax*, 1987, 3.
3. See *Documents of Vatican II*, "Declaration on Religious Freedom," number 14.

Chapter 5: The Path to Love and Freedom

1. See the *Documents of Vatican II*, "Dogmatic Constitution on Divine Revelation," number 5.
2. Adapted from *All I Really Need to Know I Learned in Kindergarten* by Robert L. Fulgham. Copyright © 1986, 1988 by Robert L. Fulgham. Reprinted by permission of Villard Books, a division of Random House, Inc.

Chapter 6: Following Your Conscience

1. See *Documents of Vatican II*, "Declaration on Religious Freedom," numbers 2 and 37.
2. *Documents of Vatican II*, "Declaration on Religious Freedom," number 14.
3. This is stated in the *Documents of Vatican II*, "Dogmatic Constitution on the Church," number 25.
4. This is emphasized in the papal encyclical of Pope Paul VI, *Humanae Vitae*, number 4.
5. Sacred Congregation for the Doctrine of the Faith, *Declaration on Abortion* (18 November 1974).
6. See the *Catechism of the Catholic Church*, #2309 and #2243.
7. Title from and story condensed and slightly adapted from *The uNclear Option* by Edward F. Beutner, as quoted in *Foundations of the Gospel in Life* (Faith and Family, Inc., Vol. 3: 2, Fall, 1987): pages 4 and 9.

Chapter 7: Person-centered Morality

1. Reprinted from *For Mature Adults Only* by Norman C. Habel, copyright © 1969 Fortress Press. Used by permission of Augsburg Fortress.
2. See *Documents of Vatican II*, "The Church in the Modern World," number 35.
3. United States Bishops, *Catholic Social Teaching and the U.S. Economy* (1986), numbers 87 and 88.
4. Canadian Conference of Catholic Bishops, *Ethical Reflections on the Economic Crisis* (January 1983), number 3.
5. See the *National Catechetical Directory*, number 98.
6. See the *Declaration on Euthanasia*, Vatican Congregation for the Doctrine of the Faith (26 June 1980), pages 4–5, and the *Catechism of the Catholic Church*, numbers 2276–2279.
7. See *On Social Concern*, Encyclical of Pope John Paul II (30 December 1987), number 24.
8. U.S. Bishops' *Statement on Capital Punishment*, United States Catholic Conference (November 1980), IV. Conclusions.

9. Pope John Paul II, *Reconciliation and Penance*, Post-synodal Apostolic Exhortation (2 December 1984), number 16.

10. *Homelessness and Housing: A Human Tragedy, A Moral Challenge*, Administrative Board of the United States Catholic Conference (24 March 1988), page 3.

11. *On Social Concern*, Encyclical Letter of John Paul II (30 December 1987), number 37.

12. Canadian Conference of Catholic Bishops, *Ethical Reflections on the Economic Crisis* (January 1983), number 3.

13. United States Catholic Bishops, *Economic Justice for All*, Pastoral Letter on Catholic Social Teaching and the U.S. Economy (18 November 1986), numbers 301–302.

14. Some remarks are based on situations recounted in "It's OK to Let People Know You're Offended by Slurs," by Keith L. Thomas, *The Herald* (1 February 1988): 27 and 28.

Chapter 8: Christian Principles

1. This statement is based on a sentence in *Documents of Vatican II,* "The Church in the Modern World," number 35.

2. *Documents of Vatican II,* "The Church in the Modern World," number 41.

3. *Documents of Vatican II,* "The Church in the Modern World," number 30.

4. See, for instance, the State of California's juror instructions.

5. See the U.S. Bishops' *Statement on Capital Punishment*, United States Catholic Conference (1980).

Chapter 9: Being Morally Responsible

1. Inspired by a prayer of Thomas Merton.

2. See the *Catechism of the Catholic Church*, number 1868.

3. See Pope John Paul II, *Reconciliation and Penance,* Post-synodal Apostolic Exhortation (2 December 1984), number 16.

Chapter 10: Developing Character

1. See, for instance, *The Many Faces of AIDS: A Gospel Response*, Administrative Board of the United States Catholic Conference (November 1987).

2. *Documents of Vatican II,* "The Church in the Modern World," number 17.

3. Ray Orrock, Fremont, CA ARGUS, "Moral Dilemmas," first published in *The Herald* (22 September 1987): 15.

4. Lena Urioste, originally published in the *Rocky Mountain News,* Denver, CO. Present copyright owner unknown.

Chapter 11: Making Tough Decisions

1. "Lies," by Yevtushenko from *Selected Poems: Yevtushenko,* translated by Robin Milner-Gulland and Peter Levi SJ (London: Penguin Books, 1962), 52.

2. *Documents of Vatican II,* "The Church in the Modern World," number 27.

3. See the *Charter on the Rights of the Family*, The Vatican (22 October 1983), Article 4.

4. See the *Declaration of the Rights of the Child.*

5. *Documents of Vatican II,* "The Church in the Modern World," number 16.

6. See the *National Catechetical Directory*, number 102.

7. Message of Pope John Paul II for the VII World Youth Day.

8. Slightly adapted from "The Time of Your Life," by William Saroyan, in *Best Plays of the Modern American Theatre: Second Series.*

Glossary

absolution—
the words of forgiveness spoken by the priest in the Sacrament of Reconciliation

accident—
an unforeseen and unplanned event or circumstance

adultery—
sexual intercourse with someone other than one's spouse, or sexual intercourse with a married person

agape—
a Greek word for unselfish love

amoral—
morally neutral (not good or bad), people who act without reference to moral principles

autonomy—
state of being independent and self-reliant

basic human rights—
those God-given rights due each person by virtue of his or her human dignity

capital punishment—
the death penalty for a major crime committed against an individual or society

cardinal/moral virtues—
prudence, justice, temperance, fortitude

character—
moral strength; a person's moral views, qualities, and behavior patterns

circumstances—
conditions, facts, or events accompanying, conditioning, or determining an outcome

code of ethics—
a system of principles, rules, or values by which to live

communion of saints—
the spiritual unity between good persons who have died and those who are still living

commutative justice—
what one person rightfully owes another

compassion—
"feeling strongly with"; concern for others and sensitivity and understanding toward them in their difficulties

confession—
the vocal admission of one's sins to a priest in the Sacrament of Reconciliation

conformity—
agreement in behavior with that of another person or group

conscience—
the human capacity to weigh and evaluate right and wrong

conscientious—
thorough and careful about doing what is right

conscientious objectors—
those who, for carefully deliberated reasons of conscience, actively and responsibly oppose civil laws they consider unjust

consequences—
the results of one's choices—immediate, long-range, and personal

contrition—
heartfelt sorrow and aversion for sin as an offense against God, with the firm intention of sinning no more

corporate responsibility—
responsibility of a group for the members of the group

covenant—
an agreement of loving support and fidelity, as the one God initiated with humanity through the Jewish people's ancestors

conversion—
a profound change of the whole person by which one begins to conform more with other values, such as those of Christ

Creed—
statements of Christian belief which date back to the early Church and the apostles' teaching

cult—
broadly, a religious group or sect; more narrowly, an extremist or fanatical religious group that seeks to control members' thoughts and behavior

culture—
the ideas, customs, and so on, that a group passes along to subsequent generations

decision—
conclusion arrived at after consideration

desensitized—
made less sensitive or responsive to, or less aware of

disarmament—
the reduction, elimination, or rendering harmless of destructive weapons

disciples—
those who are willing to learn; a follower or convinced adherent

discrimination—
acting in ways unjustly partial toward or biased against certain persons or groups

distributive justice—
what society owes its members in proportion to their needs and contributions

divine virtues—
the theological virtues: faith, hope, and love

doctrine—
official Church teaching

empathize—

feel with another

ethics—

moral conduct; standards of moral judgment and behavior

ethnic bias—

unfounded, usually unfavorable opinion about members of a group which has a common cultural background

euthanasia—

literally, good death—to die with ease and not in severe suffering; mercy killing

evil—

something which is morally wrong or which can be harmful or injurious, unfortunate, or disastrous

external motives—

external reasons for making a choice

extramarital—

outside marriage

feelings, emotions—

internal sensations and responses that are both mental and physical in nature and draw us toward or away from certain ideas, things, or persons perceived as good or bad

forgiveness—

pardon of and reconciliation with a person who has offended or hurt one

fortitude—

moral courage, determination, and perseverance; the virtue of being firm of spirit or having a steady will in doing good despite difficulties and temptations

free will—

the ability to choose without undue restraint, or not to choose

freedom—

the ability to use our abilities of will and reasoning to make moral choices and act on them

genocide—

the attempt to exterminate a people, nation, or ethnic group

goal—

aim, purpose, end

Golden Rule—

Always treat others as you would like them to treat you.

grace—

the unmerited gift God gives us of God's own life (sanctifying grace); God's help to us in fulfilling our ultimate vocation as God's adopted children (actual grace)

guideline—

policy or other indication for proper action

guilt—

a feeling of moral responsibility for wrongdoing

Hebrew Scriptures—

the Bible of the Jewish people; most of the books that comprise the Old Testament of the Christian Bible

Hebrews—

the Jewish people's early ancestors, who later became known as the Israelites

hierarchy—
structure or ranking in the order of importance, power, or authority

honesty—
the quality of being honorable and truthful in words, actions, and relationships

honor—
praise-worthiness, esteem, good reputation

hospice—
a service which provides care and support for terminally ill patients in their homes or in a home-like facility at little or no charge to the patient or family

human dignity—
the respect due each person regardless of circumstances

human moral consciousness—
people's awareness of what is right and wrong

human virtues—
firm convictions, stable personality traits, and habits that help one do what is right

ideal—
standard, ultimate aim

immoral—
that which is bad, how people ought not to act and behave

infallibility—
the dogma of the Catholic Church regarding the ability to believe or teach without error

infallibly—
without error

infidelity—
being unfaithful or untrue, not keeping one's solemn promise or commitment

informed conscience—
decision-making ability which has the proper input; correct conscience

instinct—
inborn tendency to act in certain ways

integrity—
soundness of moral principles; honesty and sincerity

internalized motives—
reasons for acting that are based on one's faith, principles, and/or value system

intrinsic wrong—
an action or attitude that is automatically immoral by its nature

intuition—
a quick perception or understanding, without recourse to reasoning

invincible—
unconquerable, cannot be overcome

Judeo-Christian—
based on Jewish and Christian religious beliefs and traditions

judgment—
decision, discernment

justice—
the principle, ideal, or virtue of just dealing or right action; giving God and others their due

justifiable—

able to be sufficiently explained, supported, and defended as right, reasonable, or correct

law—

binding custom or practice of a group; rule of conduct or action

legal justice—

what citizens in fairness owe their society

legal responsibility—

the obligation to do what is best according to what the "reasonable person" in the same circumstances would do

legitimate—

established according to the proper principles, standards, or procedures

legitimate authority—

the God-given right and responsibility to make rules or regulations which others are expected to obey

legitimate laws—

rules of conduct enacted by a rightful authority to promote and safeguard the common good

liturgy—

worship; a religious rite or ceremony

magisterium—

the Catholic Church's highest teaching authority, the pope and the bishops in union with him

manipulator—

one who directly or indirectly tries to control or take advantage of others

martyrs—

faithful witnesses who die for their religious beliefs

mercy—

compassion to the point of overlooking deserved punishment

monotheists—

those who believe only one God exists

moral—

morality in general, that which is good in particular

moral personality—

the distinctive characteristics of moral goodness or badness a person expresses

moral principle—

a fundamental ideal, value, or standard of goodness and truth on which to base human laws and conduct; rule of right conduct based on such an ideal, value, or standard

moral responsibility—

the obligation to try one's best to make the best decision and to follow through on it

moralists—

those who weigh the good and bad, the right and wrong implications of various possible decisions

morality—

a sense of right and wrong

mortal sin—

a sin which includes three elements: serious matter, full knowledge, and complete consent

motive—

reason for acting

natural moral law—
the God-given ability to distinguish right and wrong

negligence—
failure to exercise prudent care

norm—
standard or principle of right action

oath—
a solemn swearing which calls on God to witness to the truth of what one says

obedience—
submission to the command of another

objective—
purpose, direction, aim

objective moral norms—
basic moral standards which exist apart from whether others perceive them or not

objective morality—
judgment that corresponds to an action or attitude's goodness or badness in itself, without reference to how its moral quality is perceived

objective reality—
that which actually is so or exists, apart from whether or not a person thinks it is or does; that which actually exists as distinct from how people perceive it

obligation—
duty, responsibility, commitment

organized religion—
a generally recognized Church group

palliative—
that which eases or alleviates pain or discomfort, making it easier to bear

parable—
a short, simple story which teaches a moral lesson

penance—
an act performed to show sorrow or repentance for sin

person-centered morality—
right living based on love of others

personal integrity—
the quality of showing moral principles by knowing what is right or wrong and choosing to do the right thing

philosophy—
the principles an individual chooses to live by

polytheists—
those who believe in many gods

prejudice—
unfounded, preconceived opinion which is usually unfavorable; bias

principle—
fundamental law, rule, or code of conduct

prophets—
those who speak divinely inspired revelations

prudence—

good judgment

racism—

unfounded claim of racial superiority; discrimination based on race or ethnic background

rational—

able to reason, form judgments, and reach logical conclusions

rationalize—

positively: to bring into accord with reason; negatively: to provide plausible but untrue reasons for conduct

rationalizing—

trying to explain or excuse one's thoughts or behavior by giving superficial rather than the real reasons

reconciliation—

the act of asking for and granting forgiveness

reparation—

the act of repairing some of the damage caused by our wrongdoing

repentance—

the process of amending one's life

responsibility—

accountability, trustworthiness, reliability

retaliation—

returning like for like, that is, causing the same kind of injury that was inflicted on oneself

revenge—

damaging, injuring, or punishing the offender in return for an injury done to oneself

righteousness—

longing for and working for truth and justice

Sacrament of Reconciliation—

the rite celebrating God's forgiveness through confession of sins, sorrow, absolution, and satisfaction

sacrilegious—

violating or disrespecting persons, places, things, or ideas which are considered sacred

Sermon on the Mount—

Jesus' sayings on right living, collected in the Gospel according to Matthew

sin—

moral wrongdoing

social justice—

broad understanding of justice, especially regarding disadvantaged groups

society—

an organized group working together to achieve a common end

solidarity—

unity with a group, usually based on common interests, objectives, and standards

sorrow—

from a moral standpoint, grief or sadness over something one has caused; remorse with the intent to change

subjective morality—

judgment concerning the perceived goodness or badness of an action or attitude, which may or may not correspond with its actual moral quality

subjective reality—

that which a person perceives to be so; a personal perception influenced by one's feelings or state of mind

subsidiarity—

giving auxiliary support to, or being subordinate or secondary to

superstitious—

believing that merely performing certain acts makes them effective, apart from what God wills and one's own internal state of mind and heart

temperance—

moderation and balance regarding the desire for physical goods and pleasures

temptation—

enticement to sin

Ten Commandments—

a list of ten basic moral laws found in the Hebrew Scriptures of the Bible

testimony—

solemn declaration, sometimes under oath

theocracy—

government ruled by God or by those claiming to rule in God's name and with divine authority

theological virtues—

faith, hope, and love (charity)

touchstone—

the standard, test, or reference point by which to measure or judge something's true nature or quality

value—

that which is considered important and held dear

virtue—

moral goodness, power, or effectiveness; moral righteousness, often expressed in action

will—

the God-given human ability to make rational, free, and intentional choices—especially between right and wrong, good and evil

wisdom—

insight, good judgment

Yahweh—

the Gentile pronunciation of the Hebrew name for God, the sacred tetragram YHWH, which was not to be said

youth ministries—

religious programs designed to meet the spiritual needs of young persons

Index

* defined

O

oath, 112*
obedience, 4*
  blind, 42, 129, 134–136, 148, 154
  of legitimate authority, 103, 118–126, 148
objective, 72*
  in life, 72
objective moral norms, 59*
objective morality, 21*
objective reality, 20*, 21–22
obligation, 89*
  of Christians, 89
On Social Concern (Pope John Paul II), 169
organized religion, 56–57

P

Pacem in Terris (Pope John XXIII), 195
pacifism, 136
pain and suffering, 165–168, 261
palliative, 165*, 166
parable, 77*
  of the good Samaritan, 77–78, 90
parents, honoring one's, 103–104
participative decision making, 179
"Pastoral Constitution on the Church in the Modern World," 122, 129, 140
peace, 83, 105, 139–141, 149, 192
peace making, 71, 105, 140
peer pressure, 43, 268
penance, 289
person–centered morality, 151–185
"personal honesty profile," 210–211
personal integrity, 7*
personal moral wrong doing, 163–164
personal sin, 161*
philosophy, 26*
piety, gift of the Spirit, 260
politics, and morality, 122–125
  and the Church, 122–123
pollution, 85–86
polytheists, 99*
Pope John XXIII, 129, 195
Pope John Paul II, 29, 139, 169, 175, 215, 216, 217, 271, 300, 315, 322
Pope Paul VI, 287
possessions, and morality, 176–181
prayer, 7, 21, 32, 55, 144, 149, 309, 318
pregnancy, teenage, 227, 231, 244, 317
"preferential option for the poor," 158, 173, 184
prejudice, 13, 58, 182*, 183–185
principle, 5*
  moral, 188
  of love, 193, 303
  of priority of labor, 160
principles, 44, 88–90, 153, 305
  applying, 190–191
  determining, 188–189
  moral, 188–221
  of Christianity, 188–221 (see also Jesus' teachings)
  of compassion, forgiveness, and mercy, 212–213
  of equality and justice, 197–198
  of honesty, 200–211, 256
  universal ethical, 44
priorities, 307–308
"priority of labor principle," 160

privacy, 13, 112–113, 196, 199, 203
prophets, 9*
proportionate (punishment), 120*, 212, 220
prudence, 130, 258*
  and decision making, 258
punishment, legitimate purposes of, 213, 215–221
  proportionate, 120, 212, 220

R

racism, 13, 42, 135–136, 161, 182*
  as sin, 182–185
rape, 45, 107, 277
rational (decisions), 30*
rationalization, 26*, 48, 234
reality, objective, 20*
  subjective, 32*
reasons (see motives)
rebellion, 268
reconciliation, 233, 271–280, 287–290
  as a sacrament, 288–289
religion, nature of, 68, 90
religious discrimination, 13, 135, 161, 182–185
religious faith, and morality, 291, 318–320
religious freedom, 56–57, 62, 65, 128–130, 195
reparation, 112*, 201
repentance, 233, 272, 288–289
repression, 23*
respect, for family, 103–104
  for God, 99, 101–102
  for human dignity, 194–199
  for human life, 105–106, 194–199
  for people and relationships, 107–108, 194–199
  for self, 259
  for the human community, 103–115, 194–199
  for the rights of others, 109–111, 194–199
  for the whole Earth (see caring for the world)
  for truth, privacy, and personal freedom, 112–113
responsibility, 21*
  accepting, 244–253
  and decision making, 55, 126, 223–253 (see the case studies)
  and freedom, 30, 126 (see the case studies)
  and moral choices, 164, 223–253, 292
  (see also moral decision making)
  degrees of, 238–243
  diminished, 238
  extent of, 233–237
  media and, 249
responsible morality, 223–253
retaliation, 97*
revealed law, and natural law, 96
revenge, 97*
  as unchristian, 216, 275
reverence for God, gift of the Spirit, 260
rich and poor, 178
right and wrong, 20–22, 32, 94–95
right to life, 166, 195, 311–317, 322–324
right to work, 179, 195
rights, of all people, 195 (see also human rights)
  of all creation (see caring for the world)
righteousness, 71*
risks and benefits of choices, 229–232
rules, and laws, 131–135, 152–153
  of conscience, 39
  to live by, 114

Photo Credits

Nancy Anne Dawe—37, 102
Mimi Forsyth—53, 66, 160, 315, 325
Robert Fried—110, 155, 172, 177, 178, 201, 276, 323
Mary Messenger—12, 31, 40, 80, 85, 200
Gene Plaisted/THE CROSIERS—96, 129, 264
Robert Roethig—2, 92, 122, 127, 222
James L. Shaffer—22, 24, 58, 69, 76, 84, 87, 89, 100, 105, 133, 136, 147, 162, 167, 192, 198, 232, 234, 236, 248, 250, 275, 279, 286, 311
Skjold Photography—34, 205, 271, 298
D. Jeanene Tiner—ix, 116, 138, 150, 186, 243, 254, 294
Jim Whitmer—7, 10, 15, 18, 27, 50, 62, 74, 79, 145, 202, 206, 245, 277, 306

Art

Joey Taylor—page 141